A MATTER OF DESTINY

A Novel by

N. L. Williams

British Library Cataloguing In Publication Data
A Record of this Publication is available
from the British Library

ISBN 978-1-84685-451-4

First Published 2007 by

Exposure Publishing,
an imprint of Diggory Press Ltd,
Three Rivers, Minions, Liskeard, Cornwall, PL14 5LE, UK
and of
Diggory Press, Inc of Goodyear, Arizona, USA

WWW.DIGGORYPRESS.COM

Printed in the USA on acid free paper

[People] occasionally stumble over the truth, but most of them pick themselves up and hurry off as if nothing had happened.

Winston Churchill

Note To Readers

This novel is based on an incident which reportedly occurred on November 22, 1992 at Brookhaven, New York. In this context, I should like to gratefully acknowledge the report made by J. B. Michaels in his non-fiction book, *UFO Encounters*.

The characters, events, institutions, and organizations in this book are wholly fictional or are used fictitiously. Any apparent resemblance to any person alive or dead, and to any actual institution or organization, is entirely coincidental.

Acknowledgements

I would like to thank my publisher, Exposure Publishing and Holly McClure of Sullivan Maxx Agency for their unwavering support and belief in me. Thanks also to Joan Upton Hall for her patience and untiring contributions. A special thanks to Sandy Smyth of the U.S. Forest Service Office in Salida, Colorado (even though I was unable to keep the Colorado fire sequence), and J.B. Michaels, who wrote *UFO Encounters*. Thanks to Frank Findlay of the U.S. Forest Service Office at Massey Branch, NC, and the entire staff of the Cherokee National Forest Service Office in Tellico Plains, TN. Special heartfelt thanks to my husband, Tab, who never failed me. Kudos to Rick and Matt Williams, my sons, who helped as did Rick Bassette, a friend, who was always there with advice and information when I needed it. Finally, a huge thank you to all my amateur radio friends, and especially those whose call signs I have borrowed: N4OZZ, WR4RR, KG4PIR, K2PTQ, and W4DGI.

About The Author

Born in Seattle, Washington, N. L. Williams wrote her first novel, *The Last Saddle*, in sixth grade then burned it two years later. She has been writing ever since. As a child, she was heavily influenced by her father and his love of flying. During World War II, he had served in the Army Air Corps as a B-29 flight instructor at Mather Field, California. Near the end of the war, he transferred into defense work with Boeing Aircraft Company in Seattle. In July, 1955, while on a picnic along the Tolt River, Williams was involved in a five-minute, daylight, low-altitude UFO sighting, as was her family. Her father made everyone promise to keep the sighting a secret, as long as he was alive. It was a secret they kept.

Always near aircraft, Williams joined Civil Air Patrol as a teenager and participated in more than one search and rescue mission for downed aircraft in the Cascade Mountains. In 1960, she entered the Air Force, serving most of her enlistment at McGuire Air Force Base, New Jersey as an Air Passenger Specialist with the Military Air Transport Service, later known as the Military Airlift Command. For a period of time, she also worked with weight and balance of aircraft. She met and married her husband in 1962, a career Air Force man who worked in power production and later with MACE missiles. Between 1963 and 1969, she lived overseas, mostly in Asia. While on Okinawa, Williams worked with military equipment in Civil Service at Camp Smedley D. Butler, as well as with Armed Forces Radio and Television Service, AFRTS.

Back in the United States, she earned a bachelor's degree in Anthropology from the University of Central Florida and her M.S. degree in English from Nova Southeastern University. She taught writing and literature in public education at Orlando, Florida for ten years, and then taught English at Tri-County Community College in Robbinsville, North Carolina. Her husband, though retired, is still involved in defense work with the government. Both she and her husband are avid ham radio enthusiasts, and she holds the highest level amateur radio license issued by the FCC. Williams is currently at work on her second major novel, *The Agenda 21 Conspiracy*. She has published many news stories and several pieces of poetry, including some through the Gwendolyn Brooks Literary Society of Florida, which recognized her as a "poet of merit." A recent poem, *Moving On*, is being published this year by Old Mountain Press. She's a member of MWA, Writer's League of Texas, and board representative for NCWN West.

CHAPTER 1

DESTIN pushed through the throngs of people packed against him and groaned. In these crowds, George Eisenhardt would be impossible to find. He'd already blown fifteen minutes, searching the masses of people jammed on the main convention floor of the Orlando, Florida Hamfest, an amateur radio convention. Had George vanished into thin air? Destin brushed back his thick, brown hair. At twenty-nine he might be a good PR man for Lockheed Martin, but he'd failed in the lost friend department.

He squeezed past men and women, past vendors selling radios, trays of connectors, baseball caps, coaxial cables, DC and antenna wire, and antennas. The air, thick with the aromas of chilidogs and cokes, made his mouth water, but he put his hunger on hold.

At the far end of the convention floor, he found the Icom radio sales booth, their meeting spot, but George wasn't there. He leaned against the table, slipped his portable ham set from his shirt pocket, and tried to call George. No luck.

"Excuse me," a voice said near his side. He wheeled to face a young Puerto Rican radio dealer who stood inside the booth.

"Yes?"

"You Destin Campbell?"

Destin straightened, surprised. "How'd you know?"

The Icom salesman grinned. "Mr. Eisenhardt told me to look for a six foot guy with brown hair and a square jaw. Said you'd come here and to tell you he's in the bathroom. He wants you to meet him there."

"The bathroom? Destin frowned. "Odd place to meet me."

"Yeah." The rep rubbed his ear. "I thought so too."

"Thanks. Where's the restroom?"

"Out those doors." The technician pointed, and then turned to waiting customers.

Destin nodded and made his way to the rear entrance foyer. The empty lobby's silence unnerved him. It was weird that George, a fellow ham, had driven all the way to Orlando from North Carolina for ham radio equipment. Earlier, his secretary said George was upset when he called. Now the bathroom.

Two bored volunteer guards in orange vests stood near the outer doors and checked arrivals. George was not there.

He entered the restroom, tucked down a short hall. Without air conditioning, the room was oppressively humid and redolent with decaying odors. Destin stopped. *Something's not right. Too damn quiet.*

The suffocating heat and smell bothered him, and his pulse thumped in cadence to dripping faucets. Drip, tick, drip, tick – it pounded an eerie beat.

On his right most of the room's four stall doors hung open. Only one was closed near the far wall of the windowless room.

He inched toward the closed stall door at the rear. In the stall before it, through the open door, a man sat hunched on a toilet seat, leaning on the stall wall for support. It was George.

George's vacant eyes stared beyond the stall and the restroom. Splotches of red dripped down his face. Destin leaned close and heard a gurgle well from deep within. George gasped. "Destin, I couldn't — stop them."

The shadow of a man coalesced and sprang from the last stall as he shoved the adjacent stall door forward. Too late Destin straightened. When the door slammed full force into his head, he dropped to his knees in agony. The room spun wildly and through the blur he watched his attacker, a man dressed in black clothes and white sneakers, sprint out the restroom door.

The silent room unnerved him. He pulled himself up and looked back. But George didn't move and didn't see anything anymore.

"Oh God," Destin murmured. "Friend, how'd you get yourself shot?" A bubbling fountain of blood welled up and spread across the entire side of George's head. He sat to one side, his pants unzipped.

Destin leaned forward and touched George's face. He ached to move his friend, to help him, but he stopped himself. If he searched George's pockets, he might send his friend sprawling.

A second cascade of pain hammered his head. He stepped back and grabbed the stall for support as the floor moved and rose. When his vision blurred, his tongue thickened and he couldn't shout. He touched his head and found his hand wet with his own blood. As he slid to the floor, he allowed the pain to help him focus. Helpless rage replaced his shock.

Why? What the hell was going on? He looked back at his friend and spotted a scrap of paper protruding from George's fingers.

Destin inched back into the stall and tugged the paper free. He dragged himself across the room and pulled himself upright at the sinks where the light was better. The paper, now blood soaked from his own hands, had four letters scrawled on it followed by two words: *QGPB, alien tech.* He tried to stuff the paper in his slacks pocket, but the scrap, less than a one-inch square and now limp with blood, fell to the floor.

He bent over and retrieved it in pieces, but a fresh wave of pain and dizziness cascaded over him. The scrap dropped again. He watched in horror as it dissolved in a pool of slowly draining water in the sink while the faucet continued its staccato drip. Nauseated, Destin slipped to the floor and crawled toward the stall.

A hefty, jeans-clad stranger sauntered into the bathroom, studying a radio magazine. When he saw Destin, the man's eyes protruded. He backed toward a stall. "Hey, man." The stranger's voice trailed away into a moan, which reverberated in the dead air. Then he bumped into George's stall door. At the sight of George's body he fled, screaming.

Destin heard sounds of a scuffle as two Orlando police officers in short-sleeved blue uniforms ran into the room, guns drawn.

"Freeze!" The taller officer sidled forward.

Behind him crept his companion, a guy whose head touched his shoulders, a guy with little observable neck.

"Don't move!"

"I didn't..." Destin stood up.

"I said freeze," the taller officer said. "Get your hands up!"

Destin nodded, raised his arms, and the tall officer shoved him toward the nearest sink. Before Destin could protest, they'd frisked him and spun him around. No-neck holstered his gun. He moved to the stall and checked George's pulse. "Do you know this man?" The expression on No-neck's bulldog face was ugly.

"My friend, George." Destin slurred the words. Both officers stiffened. *Wrong thing to say?* The one in the stall drew his gun again.

"Hey, slow down, Burns," the taller one said. "This guy's seriously hurt. Can't you see that? Look at his head."

No-neck holstered his pistol. He said something, but the words reverberated from the walls, as the moans had earlier. And though he tried, Destin could not understand. The voice and his vision rushed away from him at full speed, echoing within a vast and darkening tunnel. He slid into the welcome peace and darkness of unconsciousness.

CHAPTER 2

THE unusually warm October afternoon vanished into the gathering chill of an Arkansas night. Rocky Bradford found the coolness a relief as he drove east. In the distance, the bejeweled lights of Little Rock hung on the horizon. Home.

He could no longer see the patchwork quilt of fields and small farms along the highway, but the smell of cut hay was a fresh smell in the dark, better than soap. He inhaled the fragrance and tapped the steering wheel of his blue, eighteen-wheel Peterbilt rig.

Many times he'd made a turnaround run to Fort Smith, which straddled the Texas-Arkansas border. He always enjoyed the drive because the sun stayed at his back and he could return home the same day. Rocky glanced at a small stuffed lion on his dash, a gift from his girl, Arlene.

No one bothered to question his penchant for the toy lion as not masculine, for one look at the muscle-bound Rocky would make such a question unthinkable. Most people thought he was named after Rocky Gratziano the boxer, though that was not true. His family named him Rocky after his lifelong home, Little Rock.

He turned up the volume on his amateur radio, a Kenwood TS 50 HF and patted the black box. Ham radio was his other love besides Arlene and trucking because radio friends cared not that he was black or a trucker. It was a brotherhood. But tonight he only heard static or white noise on most bands.

He put out a general call on 14.310 since he could not raise his friends Jacob, Milt, or Loco on their prearranged frequency, 14.235. "CQ, CQ, CQ. This is N4OZZ, November Four Oscar Zulu Zulu. CQ twenty. Anyone copy?" White noise. An empty band.

He grimaced and switched off the HF long-distance radio. No time to talk anyway. He turned off I-40 and swung down several back streets to the Fleet Transport warehouses. After he'd parked at the terminal, he sauntered into the dispatch office. The night foreman, a thin, morose man took his manifest.

"How was your trip?" Shep barely glanced up at Rocky.

"Went fine." Rocky thought of his sweet Arlene again, and for a moment he visualized her showing cleavage in a sequined, low-cut evening dress. The thought was mint-chocolate sweet. He sighed.

"Tired?"

Rocky ignored the question. "What have you got for me tomorrow?"

Shep peered around the dispatch office. The room, not large enough to hold more than three desks, filing cabinets, and some dog-eared metal chairs, held no lurking strangers.

Rocky grinned. "Top secret stuff, right Shep?"

Shep scowled. "As a matter of fact, it is. Sit down."

Rocky grabbed a chair and so did Shep. From behind his desk, the dispatcher shoved a sheaf of papers across. "It's a priority load. The Department of Defense needs a bunch of electronic parts delivered ASAP to an outfit in North Carolina. A place called Fontana Labs."

"So what's so secret about a bunch of electronic parts?"

Shep glanced around the office again. "Scuttlebutt says they're components. For some sort of new weapon."

Rocky sat back. His time with Arlene had narrowed to a few hours rather than a day or two. "I was supposed to have tomorrow off, right?"

"Yeah, I know, but this is an urgent delivery. Got a problem with that?"

"Guess not." Rocky knew his voice was sullen.

"Wait," Shep warned. "I shouldn't know this, but my source let it slip that this weapon was developed by the government for global defense against alien invasions."

Rocky doubled up, laughing. He decided that Shep had gone around the bend, which was not a far reach. He'd always felt that if Shep had another brain, it would be lonesome.

Though Shep's face contorted, he sat unmoved.

Rocky ignored him. "Let me use the phone, so I can call Arlene. I have plans for tonight."

"Let me save you the trouble." Shep smirked. "Arlene called here about fifteen minutes ago. Said she'd been assigned to night duty again at Memorial."

Rocky threw up his beefy hands. "Great. Absolutely great. At least I'll get plenty of sleep." He stood up and ducked to avoid one of the lights that hung from the ceiling.

Shep stood. "Aren't you interested in knowing where you have to pick up those parts?"

Rocky swiveled around to study Shep. "I assumed they were right here, ready for me tomorrow."

Shep laughed and hooked his fingers into the belt loops of his worn jeans. "Not hardly. You, my friend, are headed west. Your first stop will be Colorado Springs. From there you'll go on to Edwards Air Force Base in California. After you have your components, you'll stop here again and pick up some more parts being shipped here from Minneapolis. Then you'll take them all to North Carolina."

Rocky straightened. "This makes no sense. They have plenty of trucks out on the west coast that could head east."

Shep shook his head. "Few truckers have the necessary top secret clearance you had while in the Air Force. That's why they want you for the run. Their own trucks are currently involved in the base decommissioning and realignment process, so they can't spare one."

"Damn." Rocky paused. "While in Fort Smith, I bought Arlene a gift for her birthday tomorrow. A camcorder. Guess her birthday will have to wait until I get back. She won't be happy about this."

Shep smirked again, sat down, and folded his hands. "Look, if you don't get through to her at the hospital tonight, I'll be sure to tell her that you'll be back in about a week. Promise."

Rocky ignored him and sauntered out the door. During his drive home, he thought about his new assignment. Would Arlene understand his absence? What had promised to be a night of dancing and fun had become some kind of military emergency. Life was too damn unpredictable. Worst of all, he was alone again. In his turmoil of self-pity, he didn't notice he'd left the camcorder on the truck's passenger seat.

CHAPTER 3

BONNIE stared out the kitchen window of the mobile home at the rain, which sluiced against the pane in a monotonous stream. An early twilight shrouded the gray world. She sighed. The pot roast and oven-baked vegetables were ready, but her dad had not returned.

She turned the oven off and peered through the window again. The Swaying Pines Mobile Home Park in Christmas, Florida did not appeal to her anymore. Nearby mobile homes were formidable silhouettes, veiled by the fog.

She stepped into the living room and opened the door for a better look at the street but it was empty, as though the localized thunderstorm had swept away all life. She frowned. Stan said he was only going to the local Quick Mart for some milk. It had been almost an hour now.

When the phone rang, she jumped. She went back to the kitchen bar and answered it. "Bonnie Rhodes?" the man asked.

"Yes."

"Your father is Stan Rhodes?"

"Yes." She pushed her long hair away from the receiver and sank onto a barstool.

"I'm Officer Bennett with the Orlando Police Department. Your dad's had a heart attack. He's at Orlando Regional."

Bonnie sat breathless for several seconds. "No. This must be a mistake." She shook her head. "Will he be all right?"

"Can't say for sure, ma'am. You might want to call the hospital and check with them for more information."

"Okay, but first, can you at least tell me what happened?"

"Auto accident. He veered off the road and hit a tree. No one else was involved. I was off-duty, but I saw it happen and stopped to help."

"No." Bonnie brushed back several tendrils of black hair.

"Miss Rhodes, try not to worry. He was conscious when I left the scene."

"Thanks," Bonnie said. "I appreciate your help."

After she hung up, she turned off the stove and raced for her car. Her trip to the hospital on Kuhl Street near downtown Orlando, took an eternity.

The rain shower had become a mild drizzle when she entered the emergency entrance at Orlando Regional. She rushed through the double doors and turned the corner at a dead run where she smacked into a gurney pushed by two attendants. "Watch out, ma'am," the one said.

"Where's the ICU?"

"Fourth floor. The elevators are up ahead on your right."

"Thanks." Bonnie trotted off and took the elevator up. At the ICU, a thin nurse with bony hips told her that her dad was being treated and she could wait. Bonnie retreated to the empty waiting room and sick at heart, she wept.

Later, she bought some instant cocoa from a vending machine in the room, though her tremors made it difficult to hold the hot paper cup. She was sipping it when a young, dark haired doctor poked his head in the doorway. "Miss Rhodes?"

"Yes." She rose.

The nametag on his white lab coat identified him as Dr. Roger Stillwell. He was a thin guy who looked like he lived on too much coffee and not enough sleep. "Ma'am, your dad's had a massive heart attack. He's holding his own though."

"What kind of heart attack? I mean, what caused it?"

Dr. Stillwell motioned to a chair. He took one next to her and continued once she was seated. "Atherosclerosis."

Bonnie gripped her chair. "Clogged arteries?"

"Yes."

Bonnie hesitated. "But Dad was never overweight."

"Weight can be very deceptive." Dr. Stillwell shook his head.

"Will he be all right?"

"Can't say for sure," Dr. Stillwell slid a clipboard under his arm. "But the next twenty-four hours are critical."

"You're saying he may not make it?" She clutched at his stooped shoulders.

"I didn't say that. But your father is critically ill. We've scheduled him for emergency bypass surgery. Dr. Ellison, our surgeon, should be here soon."

Bonnie nodded. "Can I see my dad now?"

"Yes. Keep it short. He's in the second bay of the ICU."

Bonnie nodded again and dabbed at her eyes.

The bay was a large alcove formed by curtains and folding walls, all in soft green. A large window on the far wall looked out to the rear of the hospital, but the window was now black.

She tiptoed across the room. A single light over the hospital bed lit her dad's face, and he was awake, alert.

"Dad." Bonnie grabbed his hand, squeezing it. "You look great. I didn't expect you to look so...normal." She flushed. His coloring was better than she had expected and his crew cut made him look younger than sixty.

"I'm fine. These doctors keep saying I've had a heart attack, but that's hooey. He dropped his voice. "It's a breathing problem. I couldn't catch my breath."

"Dad, give them some credit. At least do what they say."

"Hate doctors." Stan squeezed her hand. "Hate hospitals too."

"Well, all the same." Bonnie pulled a metal chair over to the bed and sat down. "You've given me quite a fright tonight." She caressed his wrist.

"These docs can't diagnose a common cold," Stan said. "But I figure it's time we talk about what happens if I don't make it."

"Dad! Please don't−ᵓ"

"No, listen. As you know, I don't have much money left, not since your mom's cancer. Besides the trailer here in Orlando, there's our farm. The one hundred acres should bring a pretty fair price."

"Dad, stop, please."

"Can't, hon. We must talk about what you'll do *if* you're on your own."

Bonnie bit her lip hard enough to taste salty blood.

"Dad, I'm twenty-eight. The mobile home can be easily sold if that becomes necessary, and I can take care of the homestead."

For a moment, every inch of the one hundred acre farm on the southeastern side of Maryville, Tennessee flashed before her eyes. She loved the old red barn, the clapboard white farmhouse on its separate knoll, a beacon surrounded by green stretches of pasture. The thought of losing her father and her home hit her, and for a moment, the tile floor of the hospital room heaved before her eyes. Sick, she leaned back.

Stan's eyes flickered, both with softness and determination. "You can't maintain it on your own, and you know better than anyone else how many hours I spend to keep it patched together. Face it. You'll need to sell the farm." He sought her hand. "The papers are all in my desk. Everything you'll need."

"Dad, I've lived there all my life. I love our home. Besides, I make a good salary. You know that. I can hire folks to help me take care of it."

He sighed. A film of perspiration formed on his upper lip. His eyes glazed.

"Dad?"

His eyes focused and he smiled. "I'm okay. But stop being stubborn." He waited a second. "Now I want to know about Abe. Has he contacted you since your fight last year?"

"No." Bonnie frowned. "When he left, he left for good."

"Too bad. Always liked him."

"I know." Bonnie sighed. "But he wasn't willing to change his career and move from Colorado to Knoxville, and I wasn't willing to change my career either. If I'd married him, I wouldn't be at the university's Center for Gorilla Research now. Instead, I might be helping him fight Rainbow Trout Whirling Disease in the backwoods of Colorado and raising a pile of kids on a shoestring budget. That's what it boiled down to."

"All the same," Stan insisted, "he loved you."

Bonnie bit her lip again and set his hand aside. "Dad, look. It's a moot point now, but I spent years building my career. Women anthropologists, especially linguistic researchers are rare. I wasn't prepared to throw it away, and it was unfair of Abe to expect that. His job was more flexible than mine. There are plenty of marine biologists working in Knoxville, and for that matter, all along the Tennessee River in TVA territory." She licked her sore lip.

"I suppose," Stan said, unconvinced. "Nonetheless, if you keep this up, you'll wake up one day all alone, and it might be too late to reach out and grab the golden ring." He turned his head away.

"Dad — "

Bonnie's cell phone rang. Puzzled, she pulled it out and read the number displayed. "It's Doc Treadway, the financial officer at the university." She frowned and answered it.

"Bonnie," Doc Treadway said, "I wouldn't bother you while you're out on fall break if it wasn't important, but a few minutes ago, I got a call from the Bledsoes."

"What about?" She stood and began to pace in the small, dimly lit room.

"Jake Bledsoe died the night before last."

Bonnie froze. "Jake?" She stopped. "Dead? How'd it happen?"

"A heart attack."

Bonnie's hands shook. A ringing in her ears would not leave her, and she glanced back at the figure on the bed.

"You okay?" Doc's voice was concerned.

"Yeah, I guess. Only Jake was special. He was such a kind, wonderful man," Bonnie said. "I'll miss him. He believed in my work with the gorillas, you know."

"Wait," Doc interrupted. "The Bledsoes wasted no time in notifying us because the Bledsoe grant to the gorilla center is being suspended, pending the final disposition of the will. We need to meet early tomorrow morning about it."

"I can't." Bonnie swiveled away and shielded the mouthpiece. "First, I'm not in Knoxville. I've been in Florida this week, visiting my dad at his winter place. I'd planned on returning tomorrow, but my dad had a heart attack earlier this evening."

"Oh, dear me." Doc mumbled. "I didn't realize...I'm so sorry."

"How about I call you tomorrow, after his bypass surgery."

"That puts all of us in a bad spot." Doc hesitated. "Without the grant, remember, the center is in serious jeopardy. UT can't support that kind of funding alone. You can bet there'll be a board meeting Monday, so we need to meet first and figure out the best way to deal with this."

Stan spoke, and Bonnie turned back to him. "Go to those meetings, hon. I could hear you both. Do what he wants. Return to Tennessee tomorrow. You need to get your grant problem solved."

"No way, Dad," Bonnie argued. "I wouldn't dream of leaving you now. Forget it!"

"I'll be fine. Anyway, they'll be in here in a moment to get me for the bypass. You'll have to leave."

"Dad!"

"Sweetie, having you hang around here is one sure way to cause another heart attack." He managed a tired chuckle. "Can't you let an old guy get some rest?"

"Dad, I can't leave you." Bonnie gave him a kiss on the forehead.

"When will you learn to be less stubborn? I need the rest." Stan looked past her to a spot on the far wall. "Besides, I have a favor to ask."

"What?"

"Please find that police officer, Bennett, who helped me. If he hadn't stopped, I'd be dead. He gave me CPR."

"Of course. I'll do that later."

"No, now!"

Bonnie hesitated, surprised. Her father was rarely forceful. "All right, if you insist. But I'll do it only because you need to rest. The Orlando Police Department isn't that far from here. Then I'll be back." She turned to the door.

Stan met her eyes. "Good. I love you, Pumpkin. See you then."

Bonnie nodded, but the lump in her throat bothered her. When she left the hospital, she barely noticed that the man being escorted by two OPD deputies was the same man she'd seen earlier, the man on the gurney.

CHAPTER 4

DESTIN regained consciousness in an ambulance. Had reality developed a huge hole? Maybe. But an antiseptic smell hung heavy in the air, and the rocking motion of the ambulance made him sick. Real enough.

Lightning cracked nearby, and the light reflected through the back windows. Two attendants dressed in white scrubs sat next to his gurney. At the back of the ambulance, opposite him, No-neck and his tall companion lounged. When he recognized the officers, he recalled the shooting of his friend, George. Dazed, he looked down. His dress shirt had been removed, replaced with a loose sheet. "What happened?" he asked.

No-neck rose, but the two burly, crew-cut ambulance attendants shot him a warning glance.

"Take it easy," the first attendant said. "You've had a pretty nasty bump on your head. We're on our way to the hospital."

Destin started over. "My friend, George, was — "

"I'm Andy," the attendant said, "and that's my cousin, Leo. Don't worry, now. I want you to be quiet. You can get the answers you need later."

No-neck spoke to someone on his walkie-talkie. "Yes," he said. "His name's Destin Campbell. DL is current." He paused, listening. "Then he's clear with the FCIC and the NCIC." He scowled, disappointed.

The ambulance's medical radio blared on the emergency band. Andy answered it and spoke with the hospital's emergency room. He then administered an IV and dabbed at the scalp wound. Satisfied, he applied cold compresses. Destin watched his every move.

"What hospital are you taking me to?" Destin asked.

"Orlando Regional," Andy said.

Destin nodded. Orlando Regional, located slightly south of the downtown district, was one of Orlando's oldest and largest hospitals. He sank back into the gurney.

"We're pulling in now," Andy said. He nodded to his cousin, opened the back doors, and unloaded his gurney.

Andy wheeled him across a concrete loading platform through a set of double doors that pneumatically opened. Moses parting the waters, Destin thought.

Abruptly, a beautiful woman in her twenties with curly, black hair turned the corner and ran into the gurney.

"Watch out, Miss," Andy said.

"Sorry!" Breathing hard, she glanced at Destin, and her brown eyes regarded him briefly. She looked back at Andy, his cousin, and the two officers. "Where's the ICU unit?"

"Fourth floor," Andy said. "Elevators are down the hall and to the right."

No-neck scowled and shook his head as she rushed away.

They rolled Destin into a U-shaped exam cubicle. No-neck and the tall officer crowded in behind the gurney, though neither spoke. A thin, tired doctor strode in and interrupted them.

"Out!" he said.

"We have to stay," No-Neck insisted.

"We'll wait outside the door," his partner said. "He's in no shape to escape." He grabbed No-Neck and propelled him outside. Destin sighed and relaxed.

The doctor examined him thoroughly and asked him a series of perfunctory questions during a check of his blood pressure and vital signs. Then he examined his eyes and ordered several tests. While they waited for results, No-Neck and the other officer guarded him.

Over an hour passed before Dr. Jensen returned. "The swelling is mostly superficial," he said. "You may experience recurring headaches for a while, but if you take it easy, I think you'll be fine."

"I can leave?" Destin tried to sit up.

"Yes, in a moment." Dr. Jensen helped him up. "I'll send an orderly in with your clothes."

Destin nodded.

An orderly arrived and helped him slide into his shirt and pants. Appalled, Destin studied the streaks of drying blood along one arm and in part of the collar. No-Neck finally spoke. "You're bruised, but Doctor Jensen says you'll live. You're coming with us now."

"To OPD?"

"Yes. Let's go."

"My friend George — "

"Yeah, we know." No-neck snorted. "You put a nice slug into him."

Destin slid his hand back to the knot near his ear and winced. "I may be under arrest, but I had nothing to do with it. You see, I found — "

No-neck's voice rasped. "We haven't arrested you, Mr. Campbell. *Not yet.* But we'll be happy to hear what you have to say after we've read you your Miranda rights."

The tall officer shot him a warning glance. "You might want to wait and not say anything until you've seen an attorney."

Destin ignored him. "Didn't you see anybody in a dark jogging suit or wind suit run out of the restroom?"

"Now that's some story." No-neck's voice developed a caustic edge. "No one ran, unless you count half of the people at the hamfest. It was bedlam."

Destin flushed.

"Why aren't I in handcuffs?" He regretted the question when it slipped out.

"Most people aren't in such a hurry," No-neck said, from behind, as he fastened the cuffs.

The tall officer frowned. "You're in big trouble, Mr. Campbell. We need to question you about George's murder."

Destin gaped at him. *George was gone.* Even though he had known the truth at some level, he couldn't bear to hear it. He closed his eyes against the smell of antiseptic and tried to swivel away, but the officers gripped his arms.

They led him out the double doors and into the ambulance parking area, and at the far end, an OPD black and white stood waiting.

The Orlando Police Department was a bulky three story building next to the Orange County Courthouse in downtown Orlando. Deep thunderclouds obscured the night sky. The smell of fresh ozone hung in the air.

They drove into a covered garage area at the rear of the tan building. Chain bars, remotely operated, swung up and then dropped behind their car. Beyond the garage, the two cops led Destin through double doors and propelled him through the crowded holding and booking area on the ground floor, then whisked him upstairs.

They entered a brightly lit hall with several offices and work areas on either side. The officers led him to the fourth office. The name on the glass read, "Steve Howell, Detective."

He knew of Howell, an honest cop with a good record. Howell sat behind his desk, leaning over the blotter when Destin entered. The cops ushered him into the chair opposite the detective while another policeman sat on Howell's left side, near a bookshelf crammed with books.

Howell wore a sour expression. His thick jaw and belt line had lost their sharpness but not his steely eyes. He drummed his thick, yellowed fingernails on the desk when he spoke. "You're Destin? Or is the name Dustin?"

"Destin Campbell."

Howell peered at him. "Unusual name."

"I suppose," Destin said. "My mom said she chose it because my birth was a new destiny for her."

"Hmm." Howell softened his sour expression and cleared his throat. "Now, Mr. Campbell, I understand you went to the police academy about eight years ago but didn't finish. Correct?"

Destin reddened. "I have a trick knee. That's why I had to drop out."

Howell cut him off with a wave of his arm. "Yeah, I know. A moment ago, we got some information on you from Lockheed Martin." Lost in thought, he stopped drumming his nails.

Destin glanced up at the bored, beefy cop by the bookcase. He looked out of shape and his jowls, a mass of excess skin, hung like loose curtains.

"You've a fine reputation, Mr. Campbell." Howell sighed and pushed his limp hair aside. "Now, your verbal statement to Miller and Burns tells me that you discovered the body of a man." He leafed through some papers in front of him. "Mr. Eisenhardt, correct?"

"Yes."

"And you and Mr. Eisenhardt were friends?"

"Yes, and he was *Dr.* Eisenhardt," Destin said.

"Right." Howell set a sheaf of papers aside. "His home is Sylva, North Carolina?"

"Yes. He came a long ways, coming to Florida and all, but — "

Again Howell cut him off. "I don't mean that. I have his residence in Sylva, but you listed it as Fontana Village. Which is it?"

Destin inhaled. "George worked for Western Carolina University in Sylva where he taught and researched magnetic propulsion. But for the past eight or nine months, he and his wife Linda lived in Fontana Village so he could collaborate with some scientists working with magnetism at Fontana Labs. Their own home, however, is in Sylva."

"I see." Howell rubbed his chin. "But I find it curious that Dr. Eisenhardt came all the way to Orlando simply to go shopping with you at the ham — "

"Hamfest. Hamfest, to be exact."

"Yes. The convention. Doesn't that seem odd to you too, Mr. Campbell?" Howell leaned forward. His eyes bore into Destin, and Destin squirmed.

"George was a real amateur radio enthusiast. Most hamfests are small affairs that don't attract the major dealers, but that isn't true with the Orlando Hamfest. Perhaps only the Dayton, Ohio hamfest is bigger."

"So you're not surprised Dr. Eisenhardt made such a long trip?"

"Not at all."

Howell made a note on a pad on the desk. After a pause he added the word Sylva in capital letters and circled it. "No wonder we haven't located Dr. Eisenhardt's wife."

"Yes." Destin choked at the remembrance of George's wife, Linda. Always energetic, Linda radiated life. Unlike many marriages that ended on the rocks, she and George had been married many years. How would she take the news?

He gazed at Howell. "I don't remember his address offhand, but I do remember his phone number."

He wrote the phone number down on a pad for the detective.

Howell slid it into his jacket pocket and looked up. "Mr. Campbell, do you have any idea why someone would want to murder Dr. Eisenhardt?"

"No, I don't, but I damn well wish I did." Destin paused. "Was he robbed?"

Howell hesitated. "No, that doesn't seem to be the motive." His eyes bored into Destin. "You're saying you had nothing to do with what happened? Nothing?"

"I certainly did not. I thought I made that clear."

"Mr. Campbell, this doesn't make sense. You told Miller and Burns that you received a phone call from Eisenhardt this afternoon."

"My secretary did, yes."

"And George Eisenhardt said he wanted to talk to you and asked you to meet him at the Icom booth in the hamfest."

"Yes. When I got to the booth, they told me he was in the restroom, so I went there to find him."

"But you didn't know what he wanted?" Howell resumed tapping his fingers on the desk.

"That's right. I merely assumed he came to Orlando to buy some new radio equipment."

"Okay. Now think, Destin." Howell leaned across the desk again. "Can you think of anything at all that seemed unusual, out of the ordinary in any way, with George – Dr. Eisenhardt?"

"Not offhand." He didn't know why he chose to hide the fact that George had been scared. He knew he had no answers and he could not dismiss the probability that his secretary had mixed fright for excitement about the hamfest. Better to not confuse the issue. Besides, the slip of paper might not mean anything.

Howell interrupted his thoughts. "One more question, Mr. Campbell. I understand you were hit on the head. How is it now?"

"It hurts," Destin said. "The medics think I'll be fine though. Thanks for asking."

Howell ignored his sarcasm. "Can you describe the assailant?"

"No. Never saw him. I only glimpsed a shadow."

"Oh come on, nothing more?" Howell snorted. "My patience is wearing thin."

Destin sighed. "I was almost knocked out, so my memory is a blur. But I think he wore a black wind suit or jogging outfit. And white sneakers."

Howell slouched back. "That's better. Now let's go back to Dr. Eisenhardt's work. You said he was involved with magnetics research. That's unusual. Perhaps he'd discovered something big, something valuable. That might be good reason for someone to kill him, especially if it meant big bucks."

Destin frowned. "That doesn't sound right to me, because George never spoke of anything involved in his research as being cloak-and-dagger stuff."

"Your answer is a bit too glib for me," Howell retorted. His eyes became knives. "Any groundbreaking new science is saleable. And who would be in a better position than you to find a buyer for his work?"

Destin could barely contain a surge of anger. "That's baloney. He was my best friend."

"And folks have been known to kill their own mothers for a few bucks."

"Look, I have never had any information about George's research. I'm sure that Linda, his wife, can verify that."

"We'll do just that. But don't think that will get you off the hook." Howell's voice was as bitingly sharp as his eyes. "For example, where did you hide the gun?"

"Where did I hide the gun?"

"You sound like a parrot, Mr. Campbell. Try answering the question."

"I didn't hide the gun. I never had a gun with me!"

"Do you expect me to believe that?" Howell slammed his fist against the desk. "You own a Glock. You're no doubt proficient with firearms, something one would expect of a person who works for a defense industry and has a background such as yours."

"Was George shot with a Glock?" Destin felt his throat constrict.

"I ask the questions here. Now, let's talk about Mrs. Eisenhardt for a moment. Describe her to me."

Destin started, surprised. "What do you mean?"

"Well, for starters, is she pretty?"

Destin flushed. "I guess so. But I don't see what that has — "

"Perhaps everything, Mr. Campbell. Is she younger than Dr. Eisenhardt?"

Destin felt his resentment swell. "Yes, though I'm not sure how many years younger."

"Aha!" Howell straightened.

"I don't know what you've been smoking," Destin said, "but as long as I've known Linda, she's been devoted to George. Furthermore, George would have confided in me if he'd had problems with Linda. We were close friends. And don't forget, she didn't come to Florida with George."

Howell shook his head. "Look at it this way. She's young and beautiful. She meets some guy who sweeps her off her feet, and the guy takes care of him. You see, most of the time the murderer is someone close to the victim, very close. Like you."

"Surely, you still don't think I had anything to do with his murder!" Destin vaulted out of his chair.

"Sit down, Mr. Campbell, sit down!" The uniformed officer tensed, but the detective waved him aside. Destin didn't like Howell's scowl which seemed to have taken on permanent residence. He sat.

"If you can't keep yourself under control, a short time in one of our holding cells might improve your disposition."

Destin clenched his fists in his lap. "No outbursts, I promise."

"Good." Howell's scowl softened to a frown. "A while ago, you said you could barely describe your assailant. Are you sure you know nothing about him? Come on, Campbell."

Destin met Howell's eyes. "I'll say it again. I didn't recognize him. Besides the black outfit and white sneakers, I remember a hand with some object, a mere flash."

"I see." Howell twirled a pencil around his fingers. He exchanged glances with the jowled officer. "Anything else?"

"Not really." Destin fidgeted. "Can I call an attorney now?"

"You can, but that may not be necessary today."

Destin gripped his seat. "Why not?"

Howell sighed. "Because this investigation has just begun. It could take a long time to sort it all out. For now, you can go."

"Then you're not arresting me?"

"Not at the moment." Howell pushed his chair back.

"Good. I feel — "

"Hold on, Mr. Campbell. Let's get one thing straight right now. The fact that I'm not arresting you tonight doesn't mean I won't be arresting you tomorrow or the next day, or next week. Officially, you're a person of interest. But as far as I'm concerned, you're our man. So if you think you've gotten away with this, guess again. Everywhere you turn, every step you take, I'm going to be there, watching you." Howell stood up.

"Then if I'm free to go for now, I have one question, Detective." Destin rose abruptly. "How am I to get back to my truck?"

"Go downstairs and wait. We'll round up one of the deputies to drive you back to the fairgrounds," Howell said with disdain. "One more thing: don't leave town."

Destin nodded and was ushered out of the office. While he waited for the elevator, he thought about his interrogation. In spite of his growl, there was something about Howell that he liked. Or was he too weary to grope for meaning? Nevertheless, he only saw questions ahead, not answers.

CHAPTER 5

BONNIE walked into the Orlando Police Department's reception area and stopped, amazed. The main floor was a beehive of activity, packed with derelicts, drug addicts, and prostitutes. Watching her father's detective TV shows had not quite prepared her for the scene. She watched a police officer book a man accused of felony assault. A female cop, her hair knotted into a bun, was handling fingerprinting and forms.

She approached a police officer at the main counter. "Is Officer Bennett here?"

Sergeant Miller, his nametag read.

"Let me see," Miller said. He studied a clipboard. "Yeah, he comes on duty any minute. Why do you need him?"

"To thank him," Bonnie said. "He saved my dad's life tonight."

Miller smiled and reached for a phone. "Send Bennett out to my desk when he arrives." He turned back to her. "He'll be about fifteen minutes." He pointed to a row of chairs along the opposite wall. "Have a seat."

Bonnie grabbed a seat and when Miller turned back to his forms, a man sat down next to her. He was handsome. In his late twenties, she guessed. His shirt was splattered with blood near the collar. He seemed vaguely familiar, and then she remembered.

A drunken prostitute staggered past, interrupting her thoughts. "Hi, Handsome," she said to the man at Bonnie's side. Her words, more purr than slur, made Bonnie grin. The description fit him. Bonnie watched as an officer pushed the woman along.

Another man, a Latino bedecked in enough jewelry to glow, lolled against the wall on Bonnie's other side. She glanced at him, and he leered back, causing a scar to ripple along his swarthy cheek. No doubt an old knife cut.

"Sweet thing," he said, "what's your name?"

Bonnie looked at him in disgust and shrunk away.

"Leave the lady alone," her seat companion said.

"You threatening me? Huh?" The Latino grabbed the man's shirt and hoisted him off his seat.

Wild eyed, Bonnie rose to her feet, but he let the stranger go before she could scream. All eyes were riveted on the prostitute who was trying to undress by the booking desk. A pair of officers hustled her away.

The excitement over, Miller looked her way in time to see the Latino sidling closer.

Miller shook his head. "Johnson, Tappitt, get Wheels out of here. He's bothering the lady." They led him away, one on either side.

When they were alone, Bonnie turned to the stranger. "Thanks for helping me. He gave me the creeps."

"Hard to believe he could do that right under their noses." He extended his hand. "I'm Destin."

"And I'm Bonnie."

Destin chuckled. "I could ask you what a nice woman like you is doing in a place like this but — "

"Guess I could ask the same thing of you."

His eyes flickered. "A very close friend of mine died tonight." He looked away, and when he turned back, she could see pain in his eyes. "I found his body."

"That's his blood on your shirt?"

"Mostly mine, I think."

"How did he die?"

"Shot – murdered."

Bonnie searched his face, now etched with grief.

He looked away again. "Why are you here?" he asked.

"My dad had a heart attack tonight. An off-duty policeman gave him CPR and revived him. I promised Dad I'd stop here and thank him." Bonnie swallowed. "By the way, I met you earlier this evening."

Destin stared at her, startled. "Where?"

"The hospital." Her mouth pursed. "Ran into your gurney. Remember?"

Destin's face sobered. "Oh, then you were there because of your father. I'm sorry." He touched her hand.

An officer interrupted. "Looking for me, ma'am?"

Bonnie looked up. Standing over her was a black police officer. His nameplate read "Bennett." She stood and grasped his hand. "You helped my father tonight. Can't thank you enough. He thanks you too."

He took his cap off. "Glad I could help. How's your father doing?"

Bonnie flushed. "He's scheduled for a bypass tonight. So far he's holding his own."

Her cell phone rang and she fumbled for it in her purse. "Excuse me. Hello?"

"Bonnie Rhodes?"

"Yes."

"Dr. Stillwell here. Ms. Rhodes, your father had another heart attack. We did all we could, but he didn't make it."

Bonnie froze. "No, this must be a mistake." Her hand began to shake. "When did this happen? I haven't been gone long."

"A few minutes ago. I'm sorry, Ms. Rhodes."

"I feel—" She couldn't find any words.

"Ms. Rhodes, are you okay? Ms. Rhodes?"

Odd, Bonnie thought. The phone slid from her hand in slow motion, but it was a cannon shot when it clattered onto the tile floor.

CHAPTER 6

ONE of the uniformed officers gave Destin a ride out to the fairgrounds an hour later. Glum, he looked out the window of the cruiser. The town's amber lights seemed muted, and beyond the city limits, the night took over. A scrim of storm clouds, a pressure cooker of black, sat on the horizon. He rested his aching head against the seat cushion, and thought about the night, but his thoughts were reruns of old movies, and they always returned to George's death – and to Bonnie.

When Bonnie nearly fainted, he and Officer Bennett had remained with her. Finally, Bennett had left, but Destin stayed until he was sure she was able to drive on her own.

In those difficult moments that followed her first tears, she talked about her dad and how close she had been to him, especially after her mother's death. Destin listened, and felt only sad emptiness for her – and for himself. His own father, unlike hers, had been a nasty drunkard. Even the thought of his father, Gavin, made him uncomfortable, so when she asked him about his own family, he talked about the days when he was very young, happier days. He told her about George and of their deep and lasting friendship, and how they had shared their love of fishing and ham radio. When he'd finished, she sat silent. Destin knew that a bridge connected them, allowing them to share their grief at losing someone precious.

Now, as he was driven across town, he felt an unbearable sense of loss. He groped in his pocket until he found Bonnie's business card. He couldn't read it in the darkness, but the small card reassured him. Beautiful and charming, she was a professor from the University of Tennessee. He grimaced then. Orlando was not her home. Too bad.

When they pulled into the fairgrounds, he saw his Ford, his abandoned child, sitting alone amongst the tall grass and ruts. They were alike. Both abandoned. Then he remembered George's car. He turned to the deputy. "Has OPD looked for George's car?"

The officer hesitated. "You mean the man that was murdered here today?"

"Yes."

The deputy looked worried. "Yes, and we've impounded his vehicle. Why do you ask?"

"Because the car might contain evidence."

The officer studied him in the darkness. "Why is that important to you?"

Destin bit his lip. "I want my name cleared. The sooner the better. And I want to find George's killer. I owe him that."

The deputy nodded as Destin got out. Then he waved farewell and slid into his truck. Perhaps, after he got home, a few bourbons on the rocks would help his pain, but he quickly dismissed the thought.

He left the fairgrounds and drove home to the east side of town, where he lived alone in a quiet subdivision of three looped drives. His modest rancher of cement block and brick offered security. He pulled into the driveway. Home always meant stability and normalcy to him, something that had been ripped from him as a child. Now, with the loss of his closest friend, home meant even more. The sense of relief at being home was more powerful and soothing than any drink.

He parked the Ford in the garage and slipped through the inside door into his living room. An amber streetlight bathed it and the L-shaped adjoining dining room in gold, although longer, deeper shadows enveloped the rear of the home.

Rather than close the drapes, he lounged in his favorite tan recliner and gazed at the golden glow for some time, while sorting through the night's events. Hungry, he wandered into his kitchen, turned on the bright overhead lighting, and selected a Chef Boyardee ready-to-eat spaghetti bowl from one of the cabinets. He heated it in the microwave and ate it at the bar.

After the meal, he ambled into his bedroom. Though his bed looked inviting, he sat in a chair by the nightstand and dialed Linda's Fontana number. She answered, her voice punctuated by sobs.

"Linda," he said. Silence. "Linda, you know then, about George."

"Yes." Her ragged voice cracked, and she had a hard time controlling her chuffs.

"What have the police told you?"

"They told me that George has been murdered," she managed. "They told me he was killed at the hamfest, and they were questioning you. You! I told them they were crazy, Destin. Told them! It *is* crazy. Nothing makes sense."

"I know."

"Have the police let you go?"

"Yes, for now."

"Good." She paused for air before her sobs rose an octave. "Everyone loved George. He had no enemies. Why, he was a papa to everyone." She blubbered, and he could visualize the sobs wracking her body. —

"Linda, look, I'm as confused as you. I didn't kill George — "

"I know that!"

"The police have a different opinion."

"Then damn the police!"

"Well, thanks for believing in me. Still, I haven't any idea why he wanted to meet me there, unless he wanted a new radio of some sort."

"No, I don't think so," Linda said. "He did need a bunch of connectors and some other small stuff, but you know us. He would've told me if he'd wanted to buy a radio. Not that I would've stopped him. I never could stop him doing what he wanted."

"He wouldn't have traveled all the way from Fontana to Orlando for a few connectors and some small items," he said, pondering her words.

Linda paused. "No, guess not. Which leaves me with no idea why someone would do this terrible thing to George."

"Maybe he came to tell me something, something very important, but he never got the chance."

"I guess that's possible." Linda stifled her sobs.

"Well, whoever did this, he won't get away with it," Destin vowed. "I plan to look into his murder starting tomorrow. I need to clear my name. And most of all, I owe it to George."

"I don't care for that plan," Linda said. "You could put yourself into danger."

"Oh, I'll be careful."

Destin thought of the scrap of paper then. "Linda," he asked, "Do the letters Q-G-P-B and the phrase 'alien tech' mean anything to you?"

He could hear her inhale, and her silence hung between them. "No." She swallowed her sobs. "Can't imagine what that could be. Why do you ask? Is it connected to George?"

"I don't know," he answered, considering, "but George was clutching a piece of paper with those letters written on it. Are you sure you don't know what it means?"

"No. Don't think I've ever heard George mention those letters or words." She cried, and his heart felt as knotted as tangled fishing line.

When she regained her composure, she said, "You know, something might've been going on, though I don't know what."

"What makes you think that?"

"He was uptight these past few days. He wasn't unkind – don't get me wrong – but he was distant, upset."

"Linda, that's a vague supposition. I know you're upset and all, but — "

"That's why I hope you'll come up to North Carolina and help sort it out. After all, you knew him. You could question some of his associates at the college."

"The police will probably question them," Destin said.

"But I need a friend, someone I can depend on."

Destin shut his eyes. "Linda, whoever killed George is here in Orlando. Doesn't it make more sense for me to stay and see what I or the police turn up?"

Linda's voice cracked. "Maybe, but God only knows, I don't think I can handle this alone. Besides, his colleagues might know why he was so upset. Couldn't you talk to some of them at WCU? Maybe one of them knows something."

Destin leaned back against the pillow and considered her words.

"At least come up and stick by me through the service and all. What do you say?" she asked. "Please?"

"You're right. Possibly the only way to get answers to all this is for me to come to Fontana. Let me make arrangements to take off from work tomorrow, and I'll drive on up." He thought then of Howell's warning but dismissed it.

"Okay," Linda said, "but make it Sylva, not Fontana. I want to hold a memorial service for George in Sylva on the Western Carolina University campus, rather than here at Fontana. Most all of our friends are there, and besides, I want to go home."

Destin nodded. He had often visited George and Linda in Sylva, and he knew how George's work revolved around WCU. The ache returned. "I promise to leave first thing in the morning. Don't worry, Linda. I'll do my best to help."

He replaced the receiver and with new resolve, undressed in the dank, stuffy room and slid between the sheets. Despite his throbbing head, he finally drifted into a light sleep.

He wasn't sure how long he had lain there or when he'd heard the noise. The muffled, scratching sound didn't belong to the night. He arose in slow motion so the springs would not give him away.

Barefoot, he crept through the dining room and into the rear kitchen. There were no streetlights that illumined the back, but he could make out the counters and cupboards in the dim light.

He turned the corner and edged into a small, wood-paneled den, the first room in the guest bedroom wing. The carpet muffled his footsteps. He peered at a set of glass sliding doors on his left. Beyond, ragged shafts of moonlight intermittently lit the room, patio, and fenced backyard. Near the doors, Destin spotted the intruder. The man, a black shadow among deeper shadows, was bent over Destin's desk, and his flashlight beam danced across the surface as he searched the drawers.

"What the hell do you think you're doing?" Destin demanded.

The intruder grunted in surprise. He recovered and lunged at Destin with the flashlight while grappling for a handhold of his pajamas with his free hand. Destin twisted, using all his might to wrench free. The flashlight clattered to the rug and rolled toward the sliding door.

The wiry lightweight's fists punched Destin's side. Pain spread through his ribs and stomach, and he whirled toward his opponent, his right connecting with the man's shoulder. His assailant grabbed his arm and twisted him off balance, sending them both to the floor.

They rolled across the carpeted floor until the assailant slammed into Destin's couch. The black figure grappled for a handhold on a couch cushion and found it. He scrambled to his feet. Cursing, Destin tried to get up but his foe kicked at his groin. Though Destin rolled away, the attacker's foot connected with Destin's trick knee. Paralyzed by pain, he doubled over.

The man laughed, but Destin grabbed his right ankle and with all his might, he yanked. The assailant lost his balance and crashed to the floor, hitting his head on an overturned hassock.

Destin could not will his feet to hold him up, but he launched his body onto the intruder's, and his fists found the stranger's face. His left connected with the man's thin, wiry jaw, and the force of his punch caused an audible crunch. The assailant screamed in blind rage, followed by a volley of slurred curses. A dark shadow of blood welled from his mouth. The attacker shoved the overturned hassock toward Destin, but the effort sent him off balance, and he crashed to the floor.

Destin rose to a crouch but lost his balance when the hassock slammed into him. Both of them rolled in agony on the carpet. The foe, finally free of his hold, rose and lashed out with his foot. His kick was weak and off balance, but it found Destin's stomach.

Free now, the man leaped through the open door and raced for the fence gate to the front yard. Destin only saw the white of his sneakers among the shadows. Although he was only minutes behind the fleeing man, the night swallowed his attacker. Now, the large oak trees of the front yard cast ominous, blackened shadows filled with danger.

Shit. Destin limped back to the den and surveyed the round hole cut out of his sliding glass door. More damage to deal with, not to mention his aching body.

"There is a good side," he mumbled to himself. "The man shouldn't be a problem for a while." He stumbled into his bathroom, swallowed three Ibuprofen, and grabbed a washcloth. Back in the kitchen, he used the washcloth to fashion an icepack. When the pain eased, he hobbled back to bed, since no better course of action came to mind. At last he sank into a troubled sleep.

At half past eight the next morning, he arose and found his knee and groin pain had become a tolerable ache. His head, however, left him wondering if life wasn't a poker game – when a player bets on a fine bunch of aces in his hand, forgetting that aces had been called low.

After stopping at a Denny's in town, he headed for North Carolina. Linda, he told himself, needed his support. She'd made that clear. Still, he couldn't help wondering if leaving Florida was a mistake. She'd hinted that George had been troubled, and somehow, it might be work related. If that were so, then going to North Carolina was the right decision.

He made himself a promise to avenge George's murder, however long it took. George had been one of the best parts of his life. He barely noticed the miles of concrete highway threading through pine flats. Instead, he remembered how he and George met.

Several years before, George had been one of his engineering professors at the University of Central Florida. Little wonder they became good friends in record time. George cared, and everything he did proved it.

They shared their love of engineering and fishing, and they even shared similar values, political beliefs, and ham radio. After George had taken the position of Dean of Engineering at WCU and moved away from Orlando, they remained close. Though George had been 45 and Destin sixteen years his junior, there was no sense of age difference. Destin had always teased him, calling him "Pops," but the term also symbolized Destin's longing for the kind of father he'd never known.

He felt into his trousers pocket, and his fingers cradled the familiar shape of a capacitor, a gift from George, a small good luck token to him the day he had passed his Novice license. But George had warned him as well: "Never forget the power of a capacitor. Remember to respect it, and since it's charged, don't ever let it get wet." Destin had accepted George's unique gift and placed it in a small, sealed, plastic freezer bag.

Now, a wave of loneliness swept him. He fingered the capacitor in his pocket again, wondering if George's luck would have held if George had kept the capacitor. The thought sobered him.

The moment passed, and only the musical hum of the tires echoed through the cab. Destin smiled again. George had been music for his soul. Gavin, on the other hand, had been more dedicated to the bottle than he had been to his son. Destin's smile faded. He didn't want to think about the past.

He turned on his dash-mounted mobile ham radio set, but his preset VHF/UHF frequencies were too weak to reach far. Undaunted, he switched to the simplex frequency, 146.520, with its direct, line-of-sight signal. The 520 band was used by travelers and truckers, and worked better than most CB bands. Today, no one was monitoring 520. Too bad. He could have used the company.

He glanced toward his storage box, mounted in the rear bed of the truck. It held a brand new Icom HF ham radio rig, made for long distance communications. He shook his head. "Wish I'd installed it already," he said to himself. The HF rig would have picked up many hams looking for a QSO, a talk. He sighed. That would be a later project.

With no escape from the memories that haunted him, he prayed his trip north might give him answers to the million plus questions that oppressively weighed on his throbbing head, knee, and groin.

CHAPTER 7

WHEN Bonnie returned to her dad's mobile home in Christmas, the phone was ringing. She switched on the light and answered it on the fourth ring.

"My apologies, Bonnie," Doc said, "but I knew I wouldn't get any rest unless I called. Any change in your dad?"

Bonnie shut her eyes. "He died about two hours ago."

"My God." Doc became silent. Bonnie' tears formed silent rivulets down her cheeks and she wiped them with her sleeve. "I'm so sorry," he said. "Forget the meeting. We'll muddle through the grant business without you. Go take care of your dad."

Bonnie grabbed a tissue from her purse and dabbed at her face. "No, I'll be back on Monday as planned. I'd go crazy sitting alone in this mobile home in Florida. All I want to do right now is return home to Tennessee and go back to work."

Doc interrupted her. "What about your dad's place in Florida?"

"The property down here can wait until later."

Doc's voice was disapproving. "What about his funeral? You aren't going to leave him, are you?"

Bonnie's face reddened. "Of course not. Dad wanted to be cremated. I'll arrange for that tomorrow and have his ashes sent to Tennessee. Then I can hold a memorial service for him near home."

"Good." Doc paused. "Then let's talk now, if you feel you're up to it."

Bonnie sat down with a pad and paper. "Go ahead."

Doc inhaled. "Okay. Do you remember how I mentioned that the grant might be suspended?"

"Yes." She tightened. "But isn't it normal that they'd halt the funding for our grant while we wait for disposition of the will?"

"That sounds logical, but there's more to it. Problems with Jake Bledsoe's will. Today's paper ran a story about it. According to them, Jake left the bulk of his estate to his nephew, Mark, rather than to his grandson, Sam. Now, Sam is contesting the will."

"Oh, no."

Doc's voice sounded frailer than usual. "Between you and me, Bonnie, Sam's a real playboy. He's never known how to manage money responsibly. That's why Jake set up a small trust for him. The trust will pay out a certain sum monthly so Sam will be taken care of for the rest of his life. I think Jake underestimated Sam's savvy, though. Sam's hired a renowned attorney and is disputing the will. That will, I understand, is horribly weak in several places."

"Not good at all." Bonnie sputtered.

"Moreover, the grant wasn't written in clear legalese." Doc paused. He let his words sink in. "Due to Sam's charges and legal action, and the difficulties with the will itself, it seems that the grant could tumble down around us before January first, regardless of who wins that dispute."

"Now I definitely don't like what you're saying."

"Bonnie, UT might have to close the center, the CGR." Doc seemed to skirt a land mine. "That's why President Alcorn has scheduled an emergency meeting of the board at three Monday."

Bonnie felt her stomach wrench. "Surely the University can find some kind of funding to keep the gorilla research going for a while, even if it means cutting some of our work-study students."

"Perhaps." Doc hesitated. "But make sure you bring some of your latest progress reports about the CGR and its financial status on Monday, so we can discuss our next steps. All right?"

A roar of disbelief and despair swept her. "Okay. See you then." She hung up.

If only you could be here to help me now, Mom, Dad. What do I do now? The questions burned and grew. *Where do I turn? Has it all been for nothing? Am I to start over at this point in my life?*

She stood still, thinking. The demon, Justice, gnawed at her guts, and she wondered if it was payback time for her mistakes. She looked past the bar into the night, but the blackness and silence held no answers.

CHAPTER 8

THE monotonous miles northbound melted together until Destin reached North Carolina. Slightly east of Murphy, the valley widened and he found himself ringed by the purple Smoky Mountains. In spite of his grief, Destin grudgingly admired the sun-dappled mountains in the afternoon sun. The greens, browns, and yellows were a fall masterpiece.

When he reached the small burg of Andrews at the eastern end of the valley, his cell phone rang.

"Hello. Destin?" a feminine voice asked.

"Yes."

"I'm Karen Kerr, a friend of George's – George Eisenhardt. Sorry to bother you, but George gave me your number before leaving for Florida. He told you were someone I could trust. He promised to call me after seeing you, but he never called. Do you know if George is okay?"

Destin tightened. "Who *are* you? How do you know George?"

"We worked near each other at Fontana Labs. You see, I work in the forensics lab. The research lab for magnetics, where he worked, was in the same wing. We got to know each other, and we'd often take our lunch break or enjoy a coffee break at the same time and talk. That's how we became friends. Anyway, George had big problems, and he said he was seeing you about them. He hasn't called, and I'm worried. Is he okay?"

Destin chewed his lip. She sounded nice, and he knew George would not have given out his cell number had he not trusted her. He decided to trust her as well. "He's dead. Murdered yesterday."

Karen inhaled sharply and then she sobbed. "Can you tell me what happened?"

Destin told her it was he who had found George. He described how he fought George's assailant at the hamfest.

Her voice became hoarse. "Do you know who would do such a terrible thing to George, and why?"

Destin was grim. "I have no idea, but I intend to find out." He explained about his investigative reporting work through Lockheed Martin, and how he planned to help Linda. "In fact," he added, "I'm in Andrews right now, on my way to Sylva. Linda is going to meet me there."

"Wait," she said. "You and I should meet too."

"Yes. It will be nice to get acquainted with you at the memorial service," Destin said. "I'm anxious to learn more about George's problems, his work, and especially about your friendship. I've never known any of the people he was associated with at the labs, until you, now."

"No, you didn't let me finish," Karen said, between chuffs. "You see, I think I may have some information about George's work here at the labs, and it might cast some light on his murder. At least, I think it might. Is there any way you could come and talk with me soon?"

A trickle of sweat slid down the side of Destin's nose, and he tasted salt on his lips. His trick knee ached. "I'll try to make it tomorrow, but first I have to see Linda. She's taking George's death pretty hard."

"All right," Karen said, "though I tried to call her a few minutes ago. She didn't answer at either home. Funny. I wouldn't think she'd be gone, considering."

"She's probably en route to Sylva. She told me earlier she wanted to go to her home there, so I wouldn't worry."

"Of course." She paused. "One more thing: let's keep this conversation between us, okay?"

"Good idea. That doesn't include Linda, does it? I'm sure she'll want to know."

Karen sighed. "Destin, I may be paranoid at this point, but I think that the less people who know, the better. Let's decide that tomorrow, okay?"

"All right. See you then. I'll call you tomorrow morning for directions."

After she had hung up, Destin drove through the rugged Nantahala River gorge, and not quite an hour beyond, he headed to Cullowhee near the Western Carolina University campus. South of the campus, he turned onto a gravel road and drove through an area of gentlemen farms that sprawled between several valleys or "coves," as Carolinians called them.

Looking at the farms reminded him of George's work. In one of the nearby coves, WCU had built a science research facility, George's workplace until his temporary reassignment to Fontana Labs.

Then he spotted George's southwestern style home. Finished with stucco, it sprawled in front of U.S. Forest Service land. Fenced pasture stretched on all sides.

He parked his truck in front of George's garage and followed the stone pathway to the foyer door. The doorbell chime had not stopped when Linda flung the door open. Her red eyes and swollen, freckled face did not go well with her white slacks and blue silk shirt. She had clipped back her sandy red hair but had not managed to control it.

Sobbing, she embraced him, clutching his shirt. He patted her awkwardly on the shoulder. "There, there," he said, "I understand."

Linda choked on her tears, unable to speak for a moment. "I'm glad you're here, because when I got home about an hour ago, I couldn't believe it. Come in and look!" She grabbed his hand, yanking him through the foyer and into the front kitchen.

Destin understood then. The rectangular kitchen, with its breakfast nook beyond and white cupboards, had become ground zero for a land mine. The contents of every cupboard and drawer had been upended and dumped on the black and white tiled floor. He stepped into the living room at the rear of the house. George and Linda's sofa and matching chairs had been slashed, their stuffing pulled out, and all the drawers in the end tables tossed on the floor. Only the veranda beyond was intact.

He wandered through the house. The bedrooms had also been gutted. Linda tiptoed behind, scared. He felt her pain and put his arm about her shoulders to reassure her. Whoever had searched the house had been thorough. Even the paintings had been slashed. He made a silent vow to support Linda however he could.

Since she was in no condition to talk further, he propelled her past the mess and found seating out on the veranda, and they collapsed on the cushions in silence, trying to sort it out

"Why?" Linda bit her lip, her puffy eyes locking onto his. "What could I possibly have that someone would steal for?"

"I don't know. Wish there was something I could say."

"I should call the police then?"

"You haven't? My God, Linda, why not?"

She hesitated, confused. "I took the time to search the stuff myself. Whatever they were after, I'd hoped they hadn't found it, and somehow, someway, I would. Sounds silly, doesn't it?" She threw her arms out in despair.

"Of course not. You found nothing?"

"No. Should I call the police now?"

"Right away," he said. "I'm sure they'll connect this to George's murder. We have. And there might be some fingerprints here, though I wouldn't bet on it. I only hope you didn't ruin any evidence."

"Guess I didn't think clearly about it." Linda hung her head.

"No matter. I think they're professionals. Heck, I'm sure of it, after running into the same guy twice."

"What are you talking about – same guy twice?" Linda asked, puzzled.

"Well, I might be wrong, but the guy that hit me on the head at the hamfest — "

"What? *Who* hit you on the head?" Linda demanded. Her fingers flew to her throat.

"The police didn't tell you?" Destin then recounted most of the events of Saturday night, including a description of his assailant's clothing and white sneakers.

"Oh, my God!" Linda pushed her unruly hair away from her eyes. "This is awful. This person, whoever he is, may try to attack us."

"I don't think he'll attack anyone for quite a while," Destin said, chuckling. "I broke his jaw. However, we're not out of danger. There are obviously more people involved than Mr. Sneakers. I wouldn't be surprised if two or three people trashed your house."

"Why do you think that?"

"Because going through a house this thoroughly takes lots of time, and time means greater risk of getting caught. So whoever trashed your home did it with lots of help," he said. "Whatever George got himself into, I think it's something big."

"Now I *am* scared," Linda said. She didn't wait for an answer, but rose, went to the kitchen, and dialed the police. After a quick conversation on the phone, she rejoined Destin on the veranda. "They said they'd be over in about thirty or forty minutes, especially after I told them that it was my husband, George, who was murdered in Orlando yesterday." She shivered.

"You need a drink," he said.

"I don't know." She looked at him, dazed.

"Some food might do you some good."

She nodded. "I agree."

"Speaking of George, what arrangements do you want me to help you with?" Destin asked.

"Let's talk about that over food."

"No, really, I'm not that hungry."

"Silly – that was my line. Now when did *you* eat last?"

"I did have breakfast on the road." He rose, surveying the living room with its contents strewn about.

"Who knows when we'll get another chance to eat? I'll throw something easy together. Won't take but a second."

"You shouldn't touch anything, remember?"

Linda shrugged. "That's a moot point now, but I'll be careful." She went to the pantry. "Tuna sandwiches. Not much. Kind of make-do."

"Sounds good."

She quickly prepared their plates and they took them outside, but the two police officers knocked on the door before they could eat. Linda ushered them into the foyer and straight through to the living room.

They had hardly begun to question Linda when the doorbell rang again. A man of about 40, well built, with an olive complexion, brown eyes, and a face that had seen too much sun entered the foyer. Deeply trenched lines seamed his cheeks, ending near his thin lips. He was someone at home with authority.

"I'm Detective Lewis Gilbretti." He fished out his wallet with its badge attached. "May I come in?"

"Yes, have a seat, detective." Linda swept her arm toward the living room. "If you can find a decent seat, that is."

He entered and looked at Destin. "Who's that guy?" He scowled, pointing his thumb in Destin's direction.

"I'm Destin Campbell," Destin said. "Close friend of the family. Look Detective, Linda's husband was killed yesterday. And now this."

"We were told about his death last night." Gilbretti eyed Linda. "So very sorry, ma'am." He inclined his head. He swiveled around to glare at Destin, his brown eyes boring into him. "You're the guy involved in George's murder, aren't you?"

"Involved? My only involvement was that I found his body. That was yesterday in Orlando."

"I know that already. You see, before I drove over here, Mr. Campbell, I had a nice chat with Detective Howell of the OPD. The papers have also covered your story," Gilbretti said.

"I see."

Gilbretti's eyes narrowed to slits. "Mr. Campbell, I think 'trouble' is your middle name. The man gets murdered, and you're there. Mrs. Eisenhardt here – her home is ripped apart, and you're here. Sounds a bit too coincidental."

"Look, Detective, OPD cleared me."

Gilbretti shut his eyes. "Oh? Then why are you here? Because Howell tells me you were told not to leave town. Seems you don't do what you're told."

"Linda asked me to come."

Gilbretti scowled. "Howell is very upset that you left Florida. The only reason you're not in jail this moment is because he knows where you are and because, for some unknown reason, he thought well of your reputation and the statements you gave him. I'm not as easily duped. Want to convince me now,

Mr. Campbell?" He found a dining room chair, brought it over so he could face Destin, and then he sat down, waiting.

Destin rubbed his hands together. "Look, as I told Detective Howell, George had called me." He then brought Gilbretti up to date.

"One more question," Gilbretti said, after he'd finished. "Did George tell you anything before he died?"

"George said something about 'no stopping' or 'no stopping them' and he asked for help. That was it."

"How convenient." Gilbretti grimaced, straightening. "I don't buy your story. Howell may not have felt the need to arrest you, but — "

"Now, Detective." Linda's face contorted with grief and resentment. "Destin had nothing to do with this. I know him."

"Calm down, Mrs. Eisenhardt." Gilbretti's voice sounded conciliatory. "I simply want to know what enemies Mr. Eisenhardt had or what possible reason anyone would have for killing him."

Puzzled, Destin eyed Gilbretti. Gilbretti had been ready to arrest him, but now he had backed off.

The detective, meanwhile, turned to Linda, and his presence commanded obedience. "Now, perhaps you can answer that question if Mr. Campbell cannot."

"I don't know, only — "

"Only what, Mrs. Eisenhardt?"

"I think it might have something to do with his work." Linda explained how George had been nervous and preoccupied prior to his death.

Gilbretti said, "OPD told me you've been living at Fontana Village while Dr. Eisenhardt worked with the lab there, correct?"

"Yes. It was a joint research project funded by both WCU and Fontana Labs. George was working on practical applications for magnetism in the field of mass transit."

"Hmm, heavy stuff," Gilbretti said.

Linda managed a wry chuckle. "Oh, it isn't as spooky as you make it sound. Let me explain. Let's say you have a train sitting on tracks. And you've attached some very powerful magnets on the bottom of your train."

"Train?"

"Yes. And you've mounted magnets on the train tracks too. They're set in such a way that as the train approaches the magnets ahead of the train, the magnets on the track and the magnets on the train are attracted to each other. This causes a forward motion of the train as the train is *pulled* toward the magnets. The moment the train passes over them, the magnets work the opposite way – they repel each other. That increases the forward motion by *pushing* the train forward and away."

"I think I understand." Gilbretti scratched his head.

"I'm being simplistic, but I hope it makes sense. It isn't cloak and dagger stuff in any event because research on this project has been well publicized for some time."

"Very interesting, yes. Is magnetism the only project Fontana Labs has researched?" Gilbretti asked.

"Hardly. They have several government-funded projects. Some private ones too, though I really know very little about that."

"Well, thank you," Gilbretti said. "We're going to look through the house and see if we can find any evidence or fingerprints. If you wouldn't mind, leave the house as it is for a while, until we finish." He eyed their sandwiches that had been set on the veranda table and grimaced. "Guess we can forget about the kitchen being untouched."

"Sorry." Linda reddened. She looked at the remnants of her sandwich.

"Enjoy your food." Gilbretti rubbed his fingers again. "Leave the rest alone, okay?"

Gilbretti sent the policemen to different parts of the house, and they sifted through the mess. Meanwhile, Destin ate glumly and Linda picked at her food. He watched the sun slowly dip below the occasional clouds clustered at the western peaks.

"Guess we can call this supper."

"Best one I've had all day," Destin said. Linda nodded and then fell silent.

"Linda, I want to ask you about George's message – the letters QGPB and the words 'alien tech.'"

"I told you yesterday that makes no sense to me."

"I know. Nothing about the message makes sense, except — "

"Except what?"

"Well, when I hear the words 'alien tech' I think 'alien technology.' I think of Roswell, New Mexico, and the stories about flying saucers that people have seen."

Linda snorted. "That's ridiculous. George was researching magnetism, not UFOs."

"I know, but I've heard some scientists talk about UFOs and how their engines could conceivably be run by using magnetic or gravitational drives, and I thought that George might have been involved in something like that."

Linda grinned and set aside her drink.

"I take it you think that's impossible?"

"I know he didn't work on anything like that." She picked up her drink again.

"And you don't believe in UFOs or alien civilizations out there in our galaxy?"

"Not really. Oh, I don't know." She had sobered though.

"Is it so inconceivable that there could be other planets with sentient beings?"

Linda looked at her lap. "No, I suppose not."

Destin leaned forward. "Haven't you ever seen something in the sky that made you wonder about it?"

Linda stared at him, surprised. "Well, I did see lights at night one time, and they moved across the sky faster than I thought most aircraft could go. But I'm sure it was just one of those moments where I allowed my imagination to go wild."

Destin cleared his throat. "I don't have to wonder, any more. I know. You see, I saw a UFO as a child."

Linda straightened. "Really? Tell me about it."

"I had gone to visit my mom's sister, my aunt, in Washington State. While on that visit, she and her family took me to the Tolt River on a picnic. The Tolt

River is near Mt. Rainier. We had finished our picnic near the river and had begun skipping stones across the swift current. Then, as we got bored, my Uncle Joseph leaned back, prepared to loft a larger stone high in the sky rather than skip it. That's when he froze. There, just a bit to the south of us, was a UFO. It was at about ten thousand feet – no higher – and it hovered there for more than five minutes."

"What shape was it?" Linda asked.

"It was a perfect saucer, like two shiny steel dinner plates put together, and there were small windows along the edge of the saucer. Uncle Joe and everyone, including me, knew that we were being observed, and the hackles rose on the backs of our necks."

"Wow." Linda was breathless. "Did the saucer make any noise?"

"None, though of course, we were so close to the river, it could have masked the noise."

"What was the weather like that day?"

Destin paused. "It was a gorgeous day. Blue sky, puffy clouds."

"Maybe what you saw was some sort of weird reflection off the river," Linda pointed out.

"I've considered that dozens of times," Destin said. "But no. It was very clearly material, and very clear. Besides, we watched the saucer leave. When it started to move, it did so slowly, but then it gathered speed and headed due east."

"Unreal. Too bad none of your relatives were engineers or pilots."

"That's where you're wrong," Destin said. "Uncle Joe was a B-29 flight instructor at Mather Field, California during World War II. Near the end of the war the Army Air Corps wanted to transfer him into the Fleet Command, but he decided to work for Boeing Aircraft Company in Seattle, doing defense work. He didn't like the idea of flying planes across the Atlantic without guns on board. "Anyway," he concluded, "that made him well qualified to analyze what we saw. He was the one who estimated its height, and he told us that the UFO, at maximum speed, could be in New York City in twenty minutes."

"Did you tell anyone before now?" Linda's eyes had formed saucers.

"Very few, and not until my Uncle had retired. He warned us to never divulge our secret, because it would cost him his job with Boeing."

"I can well imagine," Linda said. She finished her sandwich in silence.

"Well, it made me a different person," Destin said. "There are many people in this world who are single minded, stubborn. They dig in their heels, say that thus and so are true, and they're unable to see other possibilities. Take the idea of religion. Many people feel that to accept the idea of alien civilizations would threaten their religious beliefs. I don't feel that way. I feel there is room for both. As early as 2000, at least one Vatican official has agreed with that premise in principle.

"I feel the same way about evolution versus several of our current theories of creation. I feel it is possible to accept both as possibilities, that both occurred. And I'm not alone. But enough about that."

After they had finished eating, Linda moved their dishes to the kitchen. When she returned, they sat in silence, listening to the sounds of the evening birds in the woods. Linda finally spoke. "Destin, what do you think about a memorial service this coming Saturday? I'm considering having a service here at the University Chapel, so most of George's friends and teachers from the school might be able to attend."

Destin nodded.

"His body is being shipped up here, but I understand the police department coroner is going to run an autopsy before they'll release the body. I was told Saturday would be the earliest. Also, a weekend will work better for most of the university staff."

"I think that's a great choice." Destin nodded. "I'll be here for you and if you want, I can help you call these friends you wish to invite, and make any other arrangements you need."

"Then you can stay the whole week?"

"Yes, but I may combine it with some work with contractors in the area," Destin said.

"Well, if you don't mind, I'd still like you to talk to some of George's colleagues at WCU. See if you can find out if they know why George was killed. I need to know, Destin. I can't stand it, knowing someone killed him and not knowing why. "

"Sure." Destin thought of Karen, but in time he remembered his promise to keep their conversation secret. He cleared his throat. "What are your plans for tomorrow?"

She looked at the floor. "I've got plenty of arrangements to make, and I have to straighten up this house."

"You shouldn't stay here alone." Destin stood up. "Whoever did this could come right back and take a pot shot at you. Without any answers, we don't know what to expect. You need protection, for God's sake."

Gilbretti cleared his throat. Neither had realized he was in the living room by the bookcase, listening. "Calm down, Mr. Campbell. I think protection is my department, not yours. You're right to worry about Mrs. Eisenhardt. Her husband's been murdered, and whoever trashed this place was looking for something. And since every room has been searched, I don't think they found what they were looking for. We'll assign an officer to her." He let his words sink in. "And as for you, Mr. Campbell, I suggest you leave the investigative work to us." Gilbretti left the room.

Destin eyed Linda in silence and sat down. He sipped at his drink until Linda stood.

"Forgive me, Destin," she said, "I've not thought a second about your arrangements for staying here in Sylva. With my house a total wreck, I don't think I have very inviting accommodations, but you're welcome to stay in the guest bedroom."

"No, that wouldn't be wise." Destin said. "Besides, the mattress is slashed."

"But mine is too." Linda stopped and flushed. "Right. Then I have the perfect solution. My neighbors, Joe and Maybelle Wright, have a motor home. They've always said any time I had guests and needed more bedrooms, they'd be happy to have them use it. Let me call them and make the arrangements."

"Thanks," he said.

The Wrights lived in a white Cape Cod style home immediately to the north of Linda's place. Next to their fence line was a separated garage with its attached high carport, used for their motor home.

Destin went over alone and introduced himself. The Wrights, he discovered, were both in their seventies. Joe was bent and almost incapacitated with arthritis, but his gray eyes were lively and he had a sharp mind. Maybelle, his wife, hung behind him shyly, but her face beamed in welcome. They were most anxious to help Linda in any way they could and he was welcome to stay as long as needed.

Destin soon settled into the Wright's thirty-foot Tioga. Not half bad, he decided. Homey. He grinned when he discovered Joe's CB radio installed on the dash. Later, he decided, he would have to discuss the advantages of amateur radio with Joe. Maybe after the memorial service.

He showered, put on a pair of shorts, and slipped into bed. Propped against the pillow, he thought about Linda's loss and the horror of George's death. Inwardly, his soul screamed with despair. Though he did not understand why the house had been ripped apart, he vowed to catch the vandals and discover their connection to George's murder. His resolve comforted him, and he fell into a deep, healing sleep.

CHAPTER 9

ON MONDAY afternoon, Bonnie arrived at the University of Tennessee for the board meeting. She parked her car in front of the administration building, known as the Tower, and plodded toward it. The fortress-styled structure dominated the campus and overlooked the nearby Tennessee River. A cluster of buildings surrounded it, and as always, her eye was drawn to the unusual horseshoe-shaped Student Services Building at its flank.

The prior day, she recalled, had exhausted her. First, she'd made the necessary arrangements for her dad's cremation, and then she shut off water and power to the mobile home before the eleven-hour drive to Tennessee.

She rode the elevator to the top floor and passed the open door of President Alcorn's office. A blending of orange and beiges, it faced the river, and though a haze now hid the river, she could see Neyland Stadium. Beyond both, Bonnie knew, was the Center for Gorilla Research, the CGR.

She entered the conference room nearby and chose a seat near the door. The room, with its horseshoe-shaped table, was also decorated in the same oranges and creams, the UT colors.

Harriet Newman, Alcorn's secretary, was seated near the head of the table, her back to the windows. She wore little makeup. All business, Bonnie thought.

Next to Harriet sat Vice President Drummond and Dr. Fisher, the Provost. At fifty, Drummond's weathered face and bulging eyes made him formidable. Fisher, a slightly younger man, lounged back in his chair, relaxed. His usual stance. Bonnie thought he had been an ideal choice for Provost.

Dr. Quinley, Vice President of Student Services for UT, sat primly erect. His bowtie accentuated his Adams Apple. He and Fisher barely tolerated each other.

As Doc Treadway entered, he smiled at her and she nodded. The bags under his eyes looked worse than ever. At the last minute, several other board members filtered in and took the remaining seats.

President Alcorn entered last. A man in his fifties and over six feet, he barely cleared the door's frame. His Roman features accentuated his white hair, combed back. A Caesar. Maybe a godfather.

He took his place at the head of the table, and Harriet passed out the agenda. Bonnie noted the entry, "CGR funding," came last. She sat back.

The meeting, though, progressed quickly. President Alcorn finally turned to Doc. "Why don't you bring everyone up to speed on the CGR?" He sat down.

Doc rose, and everyone became quiet. "You may not know," he said, "that Jake Bledsoe has died." Several of those present shifted in their seats. "Jake was our primary supporter of the Center of Gorilla Research. He established the grant for the CGR some time ago, allowing us to operate without too many financial headaches. In fact, he was responsible for the initial construction of the center. We've depended on him for years, and now that's in jeopardy.

"The problem is a bit complex, but first of all, Jake's will was not written properly. The terminology is confusing and vague. Secondly, Jake left most of his estate to his nephew, Mark, but his grandson, Sam, is contesting the will. Sam can demonstrate closer ties to the business and to his grandfather than Mark can, and this further confuses the problem. Worse, Sam has no intention of keeping Jake's grant to the CGR alive."

Doc looked at everyone in the room. "Now if Mark wins the lawsuit, we believe he may continue our funding, but you must remember that the grant itself has problems. It was written so that it would not perpetuate after Jake's death. It contains no perpetuity clause." Doc studied the group. Several of the board members groaned.

"It gets worse. While the lawsuit is pending, the center will not be funded."

Fisher spoke first. "Can't we shift some funding from the other departments on a temporary basis until it's settled?"

Doc answered. "It could take months, even years."

This time everyone's groan was audible. Bonnie shut her eyes and wished the agony would end. President Alcorn used the moment to stand, his heavy-set frame commanding everyone's attention. He pushed back his thick white hair and adjusted his gray trousers on his ample stomach. "The way I see this, we can't come up with a plan for saving the grant until we know exactly what's wrong with the grant itself."

Several board members stirred. He raised his hand and continued. "We also need to know a lot more about Sam Bledsoe's lawsuit and what it involves. Otherwise, there isn't much we can do at this point. Therefore, we'll need to send someone out to meet with Sam and his attorney as well as the attorney, of course, who's handling Bledsoe's estate and Mark's affairs."

All eyes turned to Alcorn, but he was lost in thought. "We should send Doc," Drummond said. "After all, he is our financial officer and best prepared to look into the matter."

Doc removed his glasses and rubbed his eyes. He and Alcorn exchanged glances. "I agree," Doc said. "I'm the best qualified to go, but there's no way I can. I'm scheduled for prostate surgery."

The room buzzed as everyone offered Doc their sympathies. Bonnie then understood why Doc looked so tired and thin. She hunched over, at a loss for words. First there was her dad's death, and then Destin's friend had been murdered. Jake Bledsoe had died next, and now this.

"Who do you think we should send, then?" Drummond cupped his hands, his fingertips meeting.

Everyone looked to President Alcorn. "For now, I want your input," he said. "Go on."

"Then I recommend that we send Dr. Rhodes," Doc said.

"Yes, but Bonnie here," Quinley said, indicating Bonnie with his finger, "is hardly an expert on legal and financial matters. Shouldn't we send your assistant, Doc, or perhaps one of our deans from the College of Business?"

Bonnie bit her tongue. She knew Quinley had a point. She dared not show the panic she felt at the thought the board might send someone else. After all, it was *her* gorilla center at risk. She knew she had to think quickly and marshal her arguments.

Fisher's casual voice filled the room. "No one is closer to the center than Dr. Rhodes. No one. I think she should go, unless, of course, she can't be spared at the moment."

Quinley cleared his throat, staring at Bonnie. "That's an interesting point. Maybe you can't be spared, Dr. Rhodes. After all, you told me recently that you were on the verge of a breakthrough at the CGR. If we lose funding, isn't it possible that your breakthrough could save it?"

"I don't know," Bonnie said, caught off guard.

"Why not fill everyone in on your research right now?" Alcorn said. He sat back, waiting.

Bonnie stood. "Okay. Most of you know that humans seem to learn language in different ways than we learn other things. More than that, language learning seems to happen almost overnight. Most of us," she added, "learn language around the age of two because human beings have a unique talent for languages. When we're young, we can learn two or even three languages as easily as we can learn one."

"Now, primates don't have that unique ability. For that matter, we humans lose that ability when we become adults. Now, what I am getting at is the fact that while we're young, we seem to have an innate something in our brains – call it a language organ if you will, which other species do not possess."

"Can you prove that?" Drummond asked. Several others leaned forward.

"Perhaps I can," Bonnie said. "I'm not the only Anthropologist making this claim. Linguists now call this the Innateness Hypothesis. A way to disprove the hypothesis is to simply demonstrate that other species have the capacity to speak but for some reason have not developed speech."

After a momentary silence, Quinley snorted. "There isn't such a species."

"Yes, there is," Bonnie insisted. "Take Chimpanzees. They share over 98 percent of our human genetic code. They can't speak because nature gave them a set of vocal cords higher in their throats that don't work well. But that doesn't mean they're incapable of language. Our lowland gorillas, Ollie and Dollie, have proven to be as talented as many of the Chimps, and they face the same difficulties with language. Therefore, my research has been aimed at developing a *computer* program that is based entirely on arbitrary sounds, rather than conventional signing. The computer will allow the gorillas to "talk" to each other, using arbitrary sounds for language. The computer program goes beyond arbitrary sounds standing for words though, because grammar comes into play." She took another big breath.

"You're giving them grammar lessons?" Quinley said.

Bonnie fought to control her patience. "Yes and no. You see, our language – our arbitrary symbols – must be used in a strict, unwavering order. For example, we can say, 'I touched the grass,' but we can't move the words around and say 'the touched I grass'."

Dean Fisher nodded. "So your computer program teaches them a whole new language, and it ensures that there is order?"

"Right. It also involves lexemes and morphemes in a way that languages use them."

"Lexemes and morphemes?" Quinley asked.

"Yes. Forget morphemes for now. But lexemes are constituents of words that we might recognize. But if we transpose them, they can mean something quite different. Take, for example, the word 'houseboat'. A houseboat is quite different than a 'boathouse.' See the difference? And it is these differences that must be built into a language on the computer that we teach Ollie and Dollie, in order to prove or disprove the theory of Innateness as being unique in humans," Bonnie said.

"Why not simply teach them English then," Drummond said, "and be done with it. After all, English contains it all."

"Good point, except that English has almost more exceptions than it has rules. We hope, instead, to teach primates an easier language – easier to learn, but still complex in all the nuances of a true language. That has been the thrust of my research."

Several of the board members respectfully nodded. President Alcorn pointed to Doc, who had cleared his throat.

"Let's get back to our problem," Doc said. "I think Bonnie should meet with the two attorneys. She's a good speaker, and if anyone can convince Sam or Mark to continue the grant, it would be Bonnie."

"But does she know enough about grants and funding?" Fisher asked, lounging back in his chair. "And does she have the time to leave her research?"

Bonnie hesitated. It was true, she realized, that she knew little about legal documents, but she had written a few grants in her time. Besides, resourcefulness was one of her assets.

"Wait. I *am* your best choice. I've two assistants and three graduate students who can keep the CGR going while I'm gone. Ollie and Dollie's routines are well established and our five workers are well trained. They can even work on parts of the computer program while I'm gone. Which of you are that free? Besides, I'm familiar enough with grant writing and I can read the Bledsoe will before driving out there." She straightened. "Where can I reach these attorneys?"

Alcorn spoke then. "Old Jake's attorney is Charles Edwards, who now represents both Mark and Jake's interests."

Bonnie started at the mention of Charles Edwards's name, her father's family attorney. She sat back.

"Where do Sam and Mark live?" Quinley asked.

"Sam lives on his grandfather's estate in Morristown," Alcorn said. "I'm not sure about Mark." He studied Doc. "I've heard from the others about who should go, but you haven't spoken."

Doc didn't hesitate. "I think it should be Dr. Rhodes. She's the one person who can best represent the CGR."

Alcorn then stood. "I agree. We'll send Bonnie."

Bonnie sighed, relieved. As the conference broke up, Doc pulled Bonnie aside. "I've already talked with Sam and Mark. You'll meet with everyone in Morristown. Mr. Brooks, Sam's attorney, will attend the meeting, and I believe we can get Mr. Edwards to join the meeting too. Sam wants the meeting to be on his grandfather's estate at Morristown this coming Saturday, which gives us only three days to prepare. Are you still game?" He squeezed her hand.

"Game?" Bonnie echoed. "You bet. Only this is no game. This is my life."

"I understand," Doc said. "I'll call you tonight with more information."

Bonnie nodded and walked out of the Tower. A late afternoon breeze had sprung up. The sun, she noted, offered little warmth. She shivered. Bad luck runs in threes, she thought. Perhaps now, though, tragedy would become a part of the past.

The Tennessee River, which lay spread out below and in the distance, beckoned her. Instead of heading home, she decided on the spur of the moment to eat out. To pick up her spirits.

She drove her Nissan down by the river, to a small restaurant called The Clam Shack, which was perched on a bluff. Although the modest restaurant was a weathered building painted blue and surrounded by a nondescript parking lot along the bluff, it was hardly commonplace inside. She grabbed a window seat, and a waitress came over and took her order.

After eating a delicious basket full of crisp fries and juicy fillets of fish, she watched dozens of ducks and other birds on the water. They're so different, she thought, from her gorillas, Ollie and Dollie, who exhibited a different level of intelligence.

Bonnie paid her bill and wandered along the bluff, which followed the river eastward. Ahead, she could see a large, covered marina.

As she stood there, time seemed to flow back to a time when she was ten years old, a time when her parents had a 26-foot Chris Craft Cruiser, kept at that very marina. A less complicated time, she thought. She remembered the many cruises they had taken. Her shoulders slumped.

Love, she thought, had always been a presence, a thing. It was not examined or analyzed, it simply existed, and she, Bonnie, had existed in it. When her mother had died, Bonnie had leaned on her father. Alone now, she finally understood how fragile the net of love was. She needed to find other ways to nurture and be nurtured. It scared her. Even the thoughts of being alone made her retreat. *Some success I am*, she thought. *My world is in shambles.*

Returning to her car, Bonnie turned the heater on as she drove away from the river and sped toward Maryville, yet nothing she did could chase the chill away.

CHAPTER 10

DESTIN awoke to spears of sunlight pouring through the cracks of the bedroom blinds, setting the light oak of the motor home aglow. So deceptively peaceful, he thought. He peeked through the blinds on the side of the Wright's driveway that looked across a grassy meadow toward Linda's home. A police officer was stationed on her driveway, drinking his morning coffee out of a Styrofoam cup.

He arose and dressed. Outside, he looked back at the Wright's home, but it appeared that they had not yet awakened, so he strolled over to Linda's door, the officer eyeing him between sips of coffee.

Linda answered the doorbell, more composed and less disheveled than the day before. She grinned in welcome. "Morning. Want some coffee?"

"Sure, could use some." He stepped into her kitchen through the foyer.

A quick look beyond the foyer surprised him. Linda had apparently been at work for some time, cleaning up. At least the living room and kitchen looked tidier.

"Grab a seat at the dining room table," Linda said. She carried out two mugs and set them down, along with a plate of fruit and date bars. "I brought them from Fontana," she said, indicating the food.

"Great." Destin realized he was hungry. He bit into a couple of date bars, and then sampled some cut melon on the plate. They ate in a comfortable silence. After their meal, Linda rose and carried the dishes into the kitchen. Her work was quick and purposeful. Destin tagged behind. "So what are you up to this morning?"

"I have to go to the funeral home in Sylva," Linda said. "I have so many things to take care of. There's George's insurance, his autopsy and cremation, and the memorial service." Her shoulders sagged. Her grief touched him again, and he felt the weight of it. He rose to comfort her but she waved him off and dabbed at her eyes with a tissue.

"Yes, I know how difficult it is for you."

"Don't worry," she said. "If I take it one step at a time, it won't overwhelm me."

"Perhaps I could go along."

She hesitated. "No, but thanks. I need some time alone now. But when you have a chance, talk to George's associates at WCU's Science Center as we discussed. Look, I've already called the secretary at the center and she promised to make up a list of his friends and co-workers, the ones he knew best. She should have that ready by later this afternoon. That's a good place to get started. You can also help by telling them I've planned the memorial service for this weekend, okay?"

"All right," Destin said. "But if it's no problem, I'll hold off going to the Science Center until later today or tomorrow. I need to contact my two Lockheed Martin clients in the area and take care of a few other matters. Then I should be free for the rest of the week."

50

"Good." Linda smiled. "I'll leave the front door unlocked for you." She handed him a key. "That's in case you beat me back, okay?"

"Fine," Destin said, and left for the motor home. After straightening it, he stowed his weekender bag in his truck and returned to Linda's. It was quiet, and the door was open. Linda had already left. He used her phone and called Diotech first.

Diotech, a firm in Knoxville, was a contractor that provided Lockheed Martin with azimuth alignment units on a regular basis. After discussing the status on each of their contracts, he agreed to meet with their board in ten days.

His final call was to Ten-Tec. Ten-Tec was a contractor that made communications equipment for government agencies. Most of their communications sets were either short range or long range radios used on frequencies designated by the FCC for governmental use, though the radios were almost identical to amateur ham radio sets. Which was why, he thought, they also made amateur ham sets. He grinned. Their radios had a reputation for high quality.

He spoke to their CEO, reviewed contracts, and agreed to call again and meet with him in a few days. As he hung up, he chuckled. Because he loved ham radio, he had always wanted to tour the Ten-Tec manufacturing plant. Now that would be possible.

He set aside his notes and called Karen. She picked up the phone on the second ring and gave him directions to her home in Fontana Village. After taking down her instructions on a nearby pad, he hung up.

As he tore the sheet off, he noticed someone had scribbled the letters QGPB at the top of the sheet and boxed it. Stunned, he stared at the scribble but dismissed it. Linda must have written it. After all, he'd talked to her about it.

He stuffed the sheet into his pocket, wrote her a short note saying he'd call later, and locked the door behind him. Behind the wheel again, he left Sylva and headed west on the Appalachian Highway.

An hour later, he crested a ridge along the highway and dropped down the slope into Stecoah valley. From the distance, the village below appeared to be dozing. Quilted patchwork fields spread out beyond the cluster of buildings. Most of the crops had been picked, though in many fields, the drying stalks of corn remained. They rustled in a stiffening breeze. A storm was brewing. He studied the mountains. The reds, oranges, and yellows had begun to overtake the greens of summer. The scenery was spectacular, but he could see that a dry summer had taken its toll.

He reached into his shirt pocket for Karen's directions but could not find them. Frowning, he picked up his cell phone and hit the redial, but she did not answer. *Damn.*

Destin slowed the truck. Ahead, he saw a restaurant near the highway. At one end of its gravel parking lot, a sign read Tootie's Café. He parked, got out, and searched the truck but the note with the directions was gone. Frustrated, he sauntered inside.

Tootie's had been renovated at some point, and the owners had enclosed two separate porches, one extending across the front of the building, while the other provided a separate dining area on the north side of the café. The smell of burgers and fries hung in the air.

"Miss," Destin said at the counter, "can you give me directions to Fontana Village?"

"Sure," the waitress said. "Go straight ahead about eleven or twelve miles. And don't turn onto Highway 143 at the gap, or you'll go into Robbinsville." She smiled at him. "Can I get you something to eat?"

Destin hesitated. It was almost lunchtime. "Not a bad idea." He slid into a booth along the front wall. While studying the menu, a man in the next booth turned around. "Who're you looking for out at Fontana?" he asked. "I've lived here long enough to know most folks from these parts."

"I'm looking for Karen Kerr. She works for the labs."

"Oh, I know her." The stranger's face lit up. "A friend of mine. She's a forensics specialist out there." He stood up.

"Have a seat with me," Destin said.

"Thanks." The man nodded, slid into the booth, and set down his iced tea. "I'm Ben Tirshaw. I have a nickname, Red, but Ben will do." He smiled. "I'm a firefighter with the Stecoah Fire Department."

Destin grinned. With flaming red hair and freckles, Red fit, but so did Ben. "Nice to meet you, Ben. I'm Destin."

"You're not from around these parts, are you?"

"Nope. My home is Orlando."

"What brings you up this way?"

Destin shifted in his seat, hesitating.

"Sorry," Ben said. "I wasn't trying to be nosey."

"No problem. It's both business and personal. Karen Kerr and I have a mutual friend who recently died, and she has some information for me about him."

"I see." Ben took a sip of his tea. The waitress appeared and took their orders. After she left, Ben said, "This is a bad time for Karen. She recently broke up with her husband and she's got her hands full, raising their daughter, Tammy."

"I didn't know." Destin looked up as the waitress returned with his coffee. He studied the man before him and his gut told him that Ben was trustworthy. He decided to go with his instincts. "Karen was a friend of Dr. George Eisenhardt, an engineering professor at WCU who had been working with Fontana Labs recently. Did you know him?"

Ben tightened and leaned forward. "Yes, I knew him well. A friend of mine too. Met him through Karen. Is he all right?"

"Why do you ask?"

"Because Karen thought he was in danger."

Destin chewed his lip. "Karen was right. George was murdered the day before yesterday in Orlando. That's why I need to speak to her."

"This is terrible!" Ben shook his head. He shut his eyes for a moment, and then peered at Destin. "You were close to George?"

"Yes. Very close. That's why I drove here yesterday. I think his murder is possibly connected to his work at WCU, but I have no motive yet. Still, it's the only lead I have."

"All right," Ben said. The waitress brought their orders, and he bit into his burger. "I believe Karen can help you figure out the motive. I have a pretty good idea it involved George's work at Fontana Labs, not WCU, but Karen knows better than I." He chewed on some fries before continuing.

"I need to get a hold of Karen myself because yesterday, my fire crew responded to a house fire in a rural development in Tuskeegee, northwest of Stecoah. A place called Sawyers Estates."

"What does that have to do with George?"

Ben smiled. "Let me finish. Anyway, the dryness this time of year and an almost impassible mountain road worked against us. A trash fire got out of control and set the woods on fire. Technically, the forest was on U.S. Forest Service land, but we got there first. We tried to beat it back until the Forest Service crew arrived to help, but one of the garages owned by Vince Foster, a homeowner there, caught fire, so we had our hands full."

"Yes, but — "

"You'll understand if you bear with me for a moment," Ben said. "Anyway, some members of my crew were dispatched to save the Foster place while others attacked the woods until the Forest Service arrived. My partner, Gus, and I tried to save the Foster garage. It was already on fire when we arrived. That's when I noticed a man running toward the side garage door."

"Go on." Destin sipped his coffee.

"I yelled at him to clear out, that the area was closed, but the guy, Vince Foster, yelled back and told me to leave him alone. Said he had to get some papers out of the garage. Next thing I knew, we were in a fight. He was kind of a thin, sickly guy and not in good shape, so I kept him pinned to the ground until Gus helped me out. We had to threaten police action before he gave up and left."

Destin nodded and nibbled on his fries. "What happened then?"

"For a while, Gus took care of the outside of the garage while I went inside. The back half of the garage had an attic floor reached by a vertical ladder. I used it to get to the roof, which was on fire. The attic was empty, I found, except for a cardboard box near the ladder, which I tripped over it in my heavy boots, spilling papers across the floor. I grabbed some of the papers up and stuffed them into the bib of my Nomex suit and went back to work."

"Later, I came outside in order to switch places with Gus, and while I was outside, I waved the papers at Gus. Told him that had to be what the Foster guy was after. Gus took them and was about to go back into the garage when we both saw Vince Foster again.

"It was spooky. The whole development was thick in smoke, and the emaciated creep simply materialized out of the stuff. Could have been a ghost. His eyes were wild and he screamed at us, but his words were lost in the roar of the fire."

Destin finished his burger. "I still don't see what that has to do with George."

"Patience, my man. I have the first two pages of the document hidden away. The top sheet contains an impressive set of black letters in a heavy font.

Its title reads, 'Oak Ridge Laboratories – TOP SECRET.' A subtitle mentions the Department of Energy, and a second logo reads, 'Fontana Labs.'"

Destin inhaled sharply. "Now I'm interested. Anything else?"

Ben smiled coyly. "I only have two pages of the military document. It's obtusely written, but the papers talk about some weapon, developed or managed by the DOE. Seems the weapon was possibly developed between the two labs."

"Unbelievable!"

"And guess what?" Ben's eyes twinkled; he was the cat that caught the mouse.

"What?"

"I did a bit of research and Vince Foster works for Oak Ridge Labs. Word is, they work closely with Fontana."

Later, when Destin pulled out onto the highway, he was still pondering Ben's words. The only thing more intriguing was the information Karen might have. He also wondered what the letters QGPB meant. Engrossed with Ben's words, he didn't recall how he'd felt something was wrong that morning when he left Linda's home. When he cleared Stecoah Gap he remembered. He had not seen the police security man at Linda's when he left.

CHAPTER 11

DAI YU CHIN, the daughter of Chinese immigrants, stepped out of the high-speed elevator on the main floor of Fontana Labs and blinked. Unlike the lower levels, rays of bright sunshine danced across the green stone-tiled foyer. A pair of large, southwestern style ceramic pots framed the entranceway. The room welcomed visitors.

A security guard worked at one of two V-shaped foyer consoles, and Amy, a receptionist for the labs, used the second console. Both operated a high tech array of security cameras and videos, an intercom system, and telephones.

Dai Yu ignored the ambience. She entered the left corridor and headed for her office, conscious that the guard was ogling her. She was used to it. Her short, straight, jet-black hair fit her delicate features and 5'5" frame. She was beautiful and sophisticated enough to turn heads. Even so, she was also aware that there was something in her almond-shaped brown eyes that made most men – and definitely all women – uncomfortable.

Unlike the warmth of the foyer, her small office was Spartan. High windows lit her workspace. Her desk, though expensive, was bare save for absolute necessities. No pictures of family or friends adorned it. Her preference.

She crossed to her desk, sat down, and immersed herself in distance and speed calculations on her computer.

The intercom buzzed, and Dai Yu frowned. Amy boomed through the squawk box. "Phone for you, Dai Yu." The receptionist's voice was perfunctory.

"I don't have time for calls. Take a message."

"It's Vince," Amy said.

Dai Yu scowled. "Okay." She hated the maggot but he was a necessary pain. She picked up the receiver. "Vince, what's up?"

"You mean, what's *not* up," he whined. "If you knew, you'd show more sympathy."

"Stop speaking in riddles and make your point," Dai Yu shot back, her voice rigid.

"It's our vacation home, sweetheart. The garage burned to the ground yesterday. Haven't you been following the news? Sawyers Estates was the site of a bad fire."

She sat up. "What happened?"

"When some people who live above our place on the mountain burned their trash, the fire got out of hand. Didn't you notice any smoke out that way yesterday?"

Dai Yu tightened. "No, but I worked long hours yesterday. Didn't notice any smoke. The wind was probably blowing out of the north." She paused. "How'd you find out about it?"

"I was out there to watch the leaf change and relax. I also hoped you might get some time off."

"The home is okay though?" she asked.

"Yes, only the garage burned."

"That is unfortunate. But why are you bothering me with this while I'm at work?" Dai Yu demanded. "You know better than calling me here."

"It's our getaway." Vince's voice choked. "You always said you loved the home, so I thought you'd want to know. But second-guessing your reaction is playing hopscotch in a mine field."

Fuming, Dai Yu fought to keep the impatience and anger out of her voice. "I know you...*darling*. There's more to this call than you've said so far, isn't there?"

Vince was silent for a moment. "Well, there's one thing that really has me worried. Remember our get-together there over the New Year holiday?"

"Yes. What of it?"

"Remember how we worked out the particulars together on adapting your accelerators to power the quark beam?"

Dai Yu bit her lip, so hard that she could feel blood oozing from the bite. "Vince, this isn't a secure phone. You know better than talking about this now."

"Can't wait," he said.

Dai Yu ignored him. "Are you at work now?"

"Yes."

"I'll call you right back."

She hung up and replaced the call, this time through her secure phone. In a few moments, he was back on the line. "Okay, what were you going to tell me about our notes on the quark beam?"

"I didn't mean to, but the papers we worked with didn't get back to Oak Ridge with me. I stashed them, along with some of my Oak Ridge notes, in a box in the garage attic. When I saw the fire, I remembered the box. I slipped by the roadblock at the bottom of the mountain and tried to get the box out of the attic, but I never got a chance to get into the garage. It was already on fire."

Dai Yu leaned back and forced her voice to be sympathetic and loving. "Then it's all right, dear. I've already perfected the computer linkup to the beam. The beam is Franz Stjernholm's invention, of course, but he's not aware of our agenda for it, even now. In fact, we're due for a test of it in a few days. If those papers have burned, it's the best possible outcome."

Vince was silent, and Dai Yu felt a sour lump form in the pit of her stomach. "What haven't you told me, Vince?"

After a long pause, he said, "I think one of the firefighters found our papers. He was waving a sheaf of them around."

Dai Yu stopped breathing, even though she could feel her pulse jumping in her neck. She pushed some stray hairs behind her ears. "What fire department was involved – do you know?"

"I haven't had time to verify that, but I think it was the Stecoah Fire Department. The letters SFD were on the fire truck."

"Do you, by any chance, know the name of this firefighter?"

"Yes," Vince said. "Knew you'd ask. His name's Gus Vayhinger. I asked one of the other firefighters during the fire."

"Well then," she said, "it isn't too late to fix this mess after all. You'll have to act fast though."

"What do you mean, act fast?"

Dai Yu paused and took a controlled breath. "That should be obvious, dear. Kill him, get those papers back, and then destroy them."

This time, the silence was profound. Then, "You know, you're a demented, sick — "

"Get a grip," she demanded, exasperated. "Where's your backbone? And you have the audacity to call *me* sick and demented? Who got us in this mess, anyway? Who? Only an idiot would carelessly leave those papers in the garage!"

Vince's voice hardened, though a trace of a whine remained. "I don't kill people, Dai Yu. You've no right to expect me to do that. Besides, *you* were the one who was supposed to take the papers, not me, so don't get on *my* case. I stored them in the garage attic because you left without them."

It was only a partial truth and Dai Yu knew it. She left the papers because they had not resolved all their computer linkup problems. Vince had promised to solve those problems after he returned to Oak Ridge.

She fought to control her white-hot anger because he was twisting facts. Yes, she'd left the papers behind, and she was definitely responsible, but he always shifted blame at the least sign of trouble. It was a weakness that made him look strong, and she hated him for that.

She wondered why she had kept their love affair alive, when most of the time, all she felt for him was contempt. At times, even touching his sallow skin made hers crawl. But he was brilliant, and when it came to high tech, matchless. Theirs was a partnership too valuable to discard.

"Whatever you say," she said. "We'll have to act fast."

"I already told you I won't kill him."

"All right." Dai Yu sighed bitterly. "I'll take care of it. Believe me, *I'll* take care of it."

After she hung up she left her office and walked through the foyer into the north wing, the home for the top-echelon DOE and U.S. Air Force administrators.

She thought of Colonel Petrowski and her eyes became languid. His unusual relationship with the other representatives of government who also worked in the labs called for strength and leadership, and he had it.

She stopped to straighten her tight sheath dress. Colonel Petrowski was a true military man. He'd been assigned to Fontana Labs due to the military weaponry that the labs routinely researched and developed. At the moment, she reflected, a majority of their military R and D was devoted to moving warfare into space because the wars of the future would be fought there. Even more amazing, she thought, was the funding for such projects.

During the early 1940s, with WWII looming on the horizon, the Army Air Corps realized the necessity to develop a whole new level of secrecy, for the future of the free world might depend on it. In July 1947, for example, a few key military generals and members of government developed Majestic 12, an alleged secret group of twelve originally designed to look into UFO crashes such as the one at Roswell, New Mexico.

Majestic and several other groups were funded by Congress. They were allowed almost unlimited funding because these organizations had no fiscal accountability – all in order to prevent security leaks. Though the lack of accountability was important during World War II and allowed for such work as the development of the atomic bomb and the Philadelphia Project, nevertheless, it opened a Pandora's box. Secret funding paved the way for the formation of a "black government," a term loosely applied to secret projects funded without accountability.

Some projects were rumored to be the current agenda of a secret, one-world government, which the United States had blindly financed for years through those loopholes. Whether true or not, the lack of accountability allowed the Department of Energy and the branches of the military to secure funding for their most radical and advanced research and development projects.

Colonel Petrowski. He was an enigma, but she was devoted to him. He was arrogant, but he never wavered from his devotion to duty. He had little use for weak people like Harvey Spenser, the head of the DOE on their project. She smiled.

Spenser, a civilian, never thought of life in terms of defensive or offensive posture, or what was good for the security of the United States as Petrowski did. Yet Spenser was, she had to admit, faithful to the mission of the department. Ironic. He too, secured DOE funding through the same loopholes. Currently, though they both worked on the same energy project, the two men barely tolerated each other.

Colonel Petrowski. The name brought chills of joy to the nape of her neck. If only he were mine. He was so commanding a presence. At fifty-three, he was in perfect athletic shape. Few men at thirty could compare. Delicious. Delectable.

Nevertheless, Dai Yu realized her interest in him was based on his single-minded devotion to keeping America superior militarily at all costs. That, in fact, coincided with her interests.

As a first generation Chinese woman born in the U.S., a woman with amazing talents in computer technology, she had been forced to endure barbs throughout her life about her loyalties, especially during the 1960s and 1970s. Those barbs, she reflected, only made her tougher. She felt driven to prove to the world she was a loyal American citizen, a true patriot. Now, she thought, if only she could get him to notice her.

She knocked on his door and entered without waiting. He was bent over a stack of papers on his desk hard at work. Unlike her office, his was spacious, even elegant, with cherry furniture and wallpapered walls. Two high backed wing chairs sat under the front window.

She strode over to his desk.

He looked up, his brown eyes regarding her, though as always, there was no hint of attraction. She noticed that, as usual, not a hair was out of place. A tall man even when seated, he was a formidable figure, especially in his perfectly tailored Air Force uniform. "Hi there, Dai Yu," he said. "How's the project coming?"

"On target, sir," she said, at full attention. "The computer equipment is all hooked up to work with the beam, and there seems to be no reason for the test not to go without a hitch and on schedule."

"Good," he said expansively, and stretched in his chair, his dark eyes studying her. For the first time, she noticed the exquisite balance of his patrician nose. He continued. "Your work beats most military men I know. You should have joined the Air Force."

"Thank you." The praise lit a white-hot glow of appreciation that spread to every corner of her body. Her problem, though, caused the glow to die.

She shifted her weight and cleared her throat. "There is one small problem you should know about, though." She hated the way her voice quavered.

He frowned, his mouth turning down. "Go on."

"It has to do with security, sir. If you'll remember, it was New Years when I worked with Vince Foster on the CCD – the computer controller – for the weapon. He helped me work out the kinks in linking it to the cyclotrons."

"Yes." Petrowski nodded and waited.

"Well, the research documentation – rough notes actually – was accidentally stored in his vacation home." She paused, dreading the next question.

His frown turned to a scowl. "Well obviously, you put the research together with the notes because we have a finished project. So what are you trying to tell me?"

"I had the original rough notes on the laptop," she said. "And we printed out those notes so we could work with them. A copy got left behind along with some of Vince's papers from Oak Ridge."

He stared at her, incredulous. "What? That's a total disregard for security! You know better than that, Dai Yu. I can't believe I'm hearing this pathetic story. Where are the notes now?"

"Wait a minute," she said. "I thought Vince was going to work on some problems with the computer interpreting telemetry data. He was supposed to take the CCD notes back to Oak Ridge. Unfortunately, he left them behind in his garage attic. Yesterday, a fire destroyed his garage at Sawyers Estates, and apparently a firefighter found those CCD notes in the garage. I told Vince to kill the man, but he won't do it."

Dumbfounded, Petrowski gaped at her. He rose from his chair. "Do you know anything about this firefighter?"

"Vince told me the guy's name is Gus Vayhinger." She wrung her hands. "He's with the Stecoah Fire Department, from what Vince could gather." She clenched her fists behind her back, where Petrowski couldn't see them.

Glowering, Petrowski stood. "God damn it! It's always something. You both ought to be locked up for this one."

She winced at his fury as he swore repeatedly. His eyes studied her as if she were a bug under a microscope. Squashable. She quaked inwardly, but she pulled herself erect and met his gaze.

"You know Vince is an incompetent fool," she said. "He felt we had to check our telemetry calculations, so I left the notes. I should have known not to trust him."

Petrowski began to pace his office. "I think we can take care of this before it becomes a major incident and gets leaked to the press or worse. I've got some boys in the CIA, and they owe me a bunch of favors. Guess it's time to call them in." He stopped. "Yes, we can take care of this." He moved to the window.

Dai Yu stood a minute longer, gazing at his back. It was clear she was dismissed.

"Yes sir." She let herself out of his office.

CHAPTER 12

WHEN Bonnie returned to the Maryville farm, it was well past dark and very cold. As she let herself into the dark tomb of a farmhouse, she shivered. The old house was colder than outside. She grabbed an old sweater from the hall closet beneath the stairs and slipped it on. The warmth reassured her. She switched on the heat and wandered from room to room, switching on lights as she went.

In the kitchen at the back of the house, she put on some decaf coffee. While she waited for it to perk, she looked westward out the glass of her dining nook, studying the farmhouse next door. Several lights were on, which meant Betsy Brinhale was home. Later, when the doorbell rang, she set aside her freshly poured cup of coffee. It was Betsy.

Bonnie stopped, tongue-tied, staring at her friend. Betsy, a woman of Norse descent who was pushing sixty, held few pretenses. Physical appearance wasn't important. A colorless blonde, her hair now bristled with curlers, and she wore a mismatched pajama set in neon-bright colors. "Come on in," Bonnie said. "I have some decaf in the pot. Care for a cup?"

"Sure." Betsy followed her back to the kitchen and they sat at the bar. "I knew you'd gone to Florida to visit your dad while you were on fall break, but I thought you'd be back before now."

Tears welled into Bonnie's eyes and she looked down . "Actually, I did get in yesterday, but it was well past midnight. And today I left for work very early. I needed to work with Ollie and Dollie for a while and take care of several reports. Then I had a board meeting at three."

"Oh, I see." Betsy peered at her, alarmed. "What's wrong? You're crying."

Bonnie kept her eyes averted. Part of her soul screamed to be alone, and yet that was precisely what she had always done in times of trouble. With no parents and no support, she knew things must now change. She looked up, but the lump in her throat made it hard to speak. "Okay," she said. "I have lots to tell you."

Much later that night after Betsy had gone, after they had talked out their hearts and souls in ways Bonnie had never done before, she felt better, almost healed. Tomorrow, she would tackle the stack of bills on her dad's desk and begin arrangements for her dad's memorial service. She would also take Betsy up on her invitation to have dessert with her in two days.

Exhausted, she went to bed, but sleep eluded her. Instead, she thought about Betsy for some time. Bonnie's father had originally purchased the farm from Betsy's father. When Mr. Brinhale died, Betsy and her husband kept their father's homestead next door and it became their home. Though widowed now, Betsy kept the place.

Bonnie heaved a sigh in the darkness. Betsy had managed. She, too, should be able to manage. Still, she could not set aside her dad's last words. He had wanted her to sell the farm.

She yanked at the blankets and thought of Destin. She wondered what he would do. Stupid question, she decided. She turned over on her stomach, punched a depression into her pillow and drifted off to sleep, resolved to take it one day at a time.

CHAPTER 13

AFTER he and Ben parted, Destin drove northward. Thick stands of trees and rhododendrons formed tunnels over the road, giving way to unsettled stretches of forest, where he caught distant glimpses of Lake Fontana. Near the Upper Sawyers Creek area, a blanket of smoke drifted along the distant ridge.

He entered Fontana Village about fifteen minutes later. A modest one-storied building sprawled along the eastern side of the valley. In front of it, within a semicircle, an American flag rode the breeze, and below it, a flag in red and gold was emblazoned with the words *Fontana Labs*.

Opposite the labs, the village rose along the western hills, a mixture of duplexes and small, single family homes, most of them rebuilt or remodeled after the labs purchased it from a resort. He turned, heading westward up the slope, and found Karen Kerr's home, a driftwood-gray rancher at the corner of two avenues, nestled in a thick stand of trees.

He parked his truck in the gravel driveway at the rear of her property and followed a pathway of flat stones around to the front of the small home. He stepped onto a railed, southern style porch, which stretched the length of the home. She opened the door on his first knock.

A woman in her mid thirties, Karen wasn't striking, but she had honest hazel eyes. "You must be Destin," she said, her smile welcoming. She looked carefully up and down the street. "Come in, please." She stepped aside.

He entered a living room barely big enough to hold a large tartan plaid sofa and two easy chairs. "Let's go to the kitchen," Karen said. "I've been making some chocolate chip cookies and the final batch is about ready."

Destin inhaled the delicious aroma. He grabbed a seat at the table and watched her as she opened the oven and removed a cookie sheet. Without asking, she pulled two large cookies from another rack of already cooling cookies and placed them before him.

"Tammy, my daughter, loves them," she explained. She set aside her hot pads. "Want a Coke or iced tea or something to go with them?"

"Sounds great. Coke, thanks."

She got herself a plate as well, poured out two glasses of Coke, and sat down facing him. "It's so great to meet you. Any friend of George's is a friend of mine."

"My pleasure. I feel the same." Destin sampled a cookie. The taste of chocolate and pecans blended with the faint taste of baking soda. Miles better than retail cookies. He grinned. Karen's friendliness disarmed him. He liked her casual directness.

"I'm anxious to hear how you knew George." Destin watched her straighten her brown hair. "Well, as I said on the phone, he worked with a few Fontana employees on magnetics research. They had a lab near mine in the research wing."

"Is that the building across from the village?"

"Yes and no." She smiled. "I can see you're puzzled. What you see from the highway is the administrative wing, but most of the research offices and labs are underground near the base of the dam, along with a labyrinth of equipment that extends much farther underground. Corridors connect the administrative building to areas below. You'll understand better after you get a chance to drive out to the dam and take a peek. My forensics lab is located on Level One, as was George's."

"I see. The place must be huge."

She nodded. "The labs have many projects going. Most people, though, don't know about the labs because their projects are top secret."

He smiled.

"But before we get into all that, I must ask you – aren't you a ham?"

Surprised, Destin straightened. "Yep. Did George tell you?"

"He sure did. In fact, that's what cemented our friendship. You see, I'm a ham too."

"Nah," Destin said. "You had no antenna on your car out back, and I saw no antennas on your home."

She chuckled, grabbing his wrist. "Come here. You're going to enjoy this." She led him out of the kitchen and through the archway to the rear of the house. The master bedroom, a room that opened on his right, held a queen-sized bed along an inner wall, flanked by two nightstands. At the rear of the room, opposite it, was a full-length hand made radio table on wheels, and it was filled with a wide variety of HF, VHF, and UHF equipment.

Destin whistled, surprised. "Is this your husband's hobby?"

"Nope." Karen grinned again. "Quite the opposite. My husband and I recently divorced, but he wasn't a ham. In fact, he did his best to make me miserable about my interest in amateur radio."

"Then you put this all together by yourself?" Awed, Destin stood still.

"Not exactly. I can handle most problems, but I have a bit of trouble with electrical stuff. Actually, the people in SMART, our local club, helped me hook up the equipment. George too." She sighed. "That was one of the main reasons we got to be such good friends. We'd also see each other at the monthly SMART meetings."

"What is SMART?" Destin asked.

"Smoky Mountains Amateur Radio Team."

Destin walked over to the radio table. Karen's main radio was a Yaesu FT-897D, an especially good radio for a woman ham because it contained all HF bands, as well as UHF and VHF bands. It was small, compact, neatly styled, and usually reliable. A small SG-500 linear amplifier sat next to the 897D. He knew the amplifier was microprocessor controlled to help her activities, power needs, and antenna condition. The amplifier's main purpose was to provide a 500-watt boost to her radio power.

At the end of the table perched an antenna tuner. He leaned closer. The Nye Viking, a high quality, high-power antenna tuner, matched the rest of her equipment.

"Sure beats my rig in the truck. I only have my VHF radio hooked up at the present, but I do have an HF radio ready to install, if I ever find the time to do that. But that's another story." He straightened. "I'm curious about where you've put your antennas. I saw nothing when I drove up, and believe me, I always notice antennas."

"Oops, I forgot." She laughed. "No seriously, I've had to hide my antennas because the village restricts them, and besides, my dear sweet Ex didn't think much of the idea of me stringing up a large antenna farm. In order to get around that, George helped me rig a loop antenna, a long wire. He ran the wire around my house in the aluminum gutter. His specialty was antennas as you probably know, and he sure fixed me up. Any stealth antenna is bound to reduce one's signal, of course, but the amplifier and the antenna tuner offset that."

"I can understand that," Destin said. "I know some motorhomers who have linear amplifiers and antenna tuners to improve their output."

"Right." Karen snickered. "The neighbors have no clue about my hobby. It's really great. I'd expected to hear about it before now, but fortunately, the labs monitor commercial bands so they haven't discovered me here, right under their noses."

Destin turned and spotted another radio, blacker and smaller than the 897D. He finally made out the company logo and model: an Icom 2720H dual band VHF/UHF radio used with a repeater system for local communications, similar to his own FT 8800. He smiled but made no comment.

The walls were lined with world ham maps and a 24-hour clock, and below these he spotted Karen's station license. The certificate bore her call sign. "Your call sign is N7JJJ?"

"Yep." She nodded, her brown hair bouncing. "Juliet, Juliet, Juliet."

"I'll be darned!" Destin laughed. "I'm WR4RR. My friends call me Romeo."

"Well, don't get any ideas, fella'," she said, enjoying the joke, "because I've sworn off men in my life." The color faded from her eyes, turning them a flat gray.

Destin hesitated. "If it's all right to ask, what happened between you and your Ex?"

"He and I had some fundamental disagreements on how to raise our daughter, Tammy. That was the big issue. But we also disagreed about other issues."

"Such as?"

"Such as political and environmental issues. And we argued a lot about the research work and mission of Fontana Labs."

"Wait. You mentioned Tammy earlier."

"Yes, she lives here with me when she's not with my Ex. She's in school right now. That's her bedroom, next to mine."

"I see," Destin said. "You also said you disagreed with Fontana Labs. In what way?"

"Let's go back to the kitchen where we can talk." Karen led the way, and they reseated themselves in front of their Cokes and cookies. She inhaled. "Fontana Labs has been involved in the quark research for some time. Are you aware of that?"

"No. Had no idea at all. Not that I know much about that kind of research. One time I wrote a piece for the Orlando Sentinel about cyclotrons and how their research has led to new fields in medicine. My work with Lockheed Martin is more in the lines of conventional weaponry and equipment such as GPS units and the much more sophisticated azimuth alignment units. Not the same." He studied Karen. "I know George worked with magnetism, and you're in forensics. Tell me more about your work."

"Sure. Fontana has been investigating some really exotic diseases. Legionnaire's Disease is probably the best known one. Another is the Gulf War Syndrome. The list goes on and on.

"I spend most of my time examining bodies with those diseases. I work closely with the biology lab next door. In fact, one of my best friends, Norma Yates, runs the biology lab. She continues the research by taking cultures and researching possible ways to halt the different viruses."

"Important work, all right."

"Yes. That leads me to Earl, my Ex. He maintains Fontana's cyclotrons. It's top secret, and over time, he's told me far more than he should have.

"Fontana has developed a new form of tandem cyclotrons – for lack of a better term – and the cyclotrons have increased the speed of the particles so much that the contrived collisions of these particles have produced quarks and other sub-atomic particles easily and abundantly, unlike former cyclotrons, supercolliders, and what not."

"Heavy stuff." Destin shook his head.

"I know, but I figured you'd understand," Karen said. "Anyway, these tandem cyclotrons take far, far less area underground than conventional loop or straight-line colliders. It's opened a whole new area of research."

Destin listened closely and then sampled another cookie. "You said something about disagreeing with Earl over the mission of Fontana. In what way?"

"Earl let it slip that Fontana plans to harness the quarks they produce to make some sort of weapon. He never told me how it would work, but he mentioned something about a heat hotter than the surface of the sun. Think about that!" She pounded the table. "I can't possibly imagine why we need such a horrific weapon.

"Here I am, expending every bit of energy I have, and Norma doing the same, in our attempts to thwart deadly diseases. The irony is, some diseases were developed in the labs as biological weapons of war in the first place! Terrorists won't hesitate to use those same diseases as a weapon if we can't neutralize them. The same labs that work hard to *help*, also have no compunction whatever to try to *destroy*."

Destin shook his head. "Earl wasn't involved in the weapons research, was he?"

"Not directly. Nevertheless, he's similar to the guys who run the labs. He thinks only in terms of what will protect the U.S. militarily."

"But isn't that important to all of us?" Destin shifted in his chair.

"Yes," she said. "I'm not saying I'm opposed to the U.S. defending itself. Quite the opposite! I think 9-11 taught us that lesson. But Earl, you see, takes it to a different level. He and many of the brass at the labs are fanatical."

"There are those types in the field," Destin said. "I've seen a few through my work with LM."

"Yes, and at some point, the line between defensive and offensive seems to blur, and these guys, I believe, are ready to use such weapons offensively at the slightest provocation. They're terrorists. And scary."

She set her jaw. "There's also the bit about the 'black government' and 'black government funding.' The rumors say there is a world consortium of leaders secretly plotting the demise of all *national* political interests worldwide. It may not be true, but I do know Congress funds many agencies of government through a series of bills passed in the '40s. These bills prevent Congress from discovering the way money is spent due to the need for absolute secrecy. That's allowed many groups to tap unlimited amounts of money without any accountability whatever. Not now, not ever."

She pounded the table again. "That kind of power must be stopped. Even terrorism is no justification." She leaned back, balancing her glass.

Destin sighed and pushed the cookies away. "Not a good situation."

"Not long ago Earl happily told me that such funding has allowed the Department of Energy to build cyclotrons here and in other parts of the country and has funded a host of other projects designed to keep the U.S. as the world leader. What I see as a power run amok, Earl sees as a necessary power to maintain world order. For him the ends justify the means, and he's not disturbed at all by the lack of accountability. Don't you see my point? 'Power corrupts, and absolute power corrupts absolutely.'" She set her glass down, wiping a napkin across the moisture.

"That's only the beginning. From what I gleaned from Earl, the bosses at the labs support the whole idea of a one-world government. It seems that since 9-11, such issues scarcely get any mention. But a one-world government scares me almost as much as the terrorists. Why the leaders at Fontana – and Earl – would want that so badly still is a mystery to me, but it scares me. There are many wealthy businessmen and politicians all working toward the same end."

"Yes, it's scary." Destin slid his Coke from one red square to a white square on the red-and-white checkered tablecloth, as though playing chess. "Are you trying to tell me you think George found out some aspect of Earl's work or perhaps information about the weapon, and that's *why* he was killed?"

"Well, I'm not saying Earl was involved directly, but to answer your question, yes, I'd stake my life on it." Karen set her jaw. "I have no real proof though. Not a shred. Now you know why George told me to get in touch with you if anything bad happened."

Destin sat back in stunned silence. Then he told her how he met Ben Tirshaw in Stecoah, the firefighter who had found secret documents in the Foster home. A black, insidious thought had formed, and he did not know where the thought would take him. His headache returned with a vengeance but this time, he wasn't sure if he could blame the lump on his head. Karen saw his grimace.

"Is that where you got hit over the head?" She rose from her chair and walked behind his. She poked his scalp, and her touch was disconcerting. He shifted uncomfortably. "Wait a second." She walked out of the kitchen. A second later he heard the medicine cabinet slam. She returned with two aspirin. "Try that."

Destin swallowed the pills with the remainder of his Coke. "So we're back to square one. No proof." He sighed and tried to brush some of the cookie crumbs into a pile.

"Not necessarily." Stray hairs fell across Karen's forehead, and she pushed them back into the barrette. "George often talked about a friend of his named Mitch Bartow, a meteorologist, who works for NOAA, the National Oceanic Atmospheric Administration. Mitch works out of a regional office of NOAA at Morristown, Tennessee, although he previously worked as a meteorologist for Fontana Labs."

"Hmm, never heard of him. What makes you think he can help us?"

"Well," Karen said, "about three days before George left for Florida, we had lunch together. He was very upset about something, though he never told me what. He did say, however, that if anything ever happened to him, I should contact Mitch and talk with him. Needless to say, that line of talk scared me half to death, but George clammed up then."

"That is important. Maybe this Mitch can shed some light on his death. I should call Linda and bring her up to date right away." Destin glanced at his watch and winced.

"Yes, the day is almost gone," Karen said. "Tell you what – let me call Mitch first and get you an appointment to see him. You can call Linda then. There's no sense, though, in driving all the way back to Sylva for the night when Fontana is about half way to Morristown."

Destin knew that Karen might be stretching the truth and he dimly realized the implications. Before he could argue, though, she got up and used her kitchen wall phone. He could only hear one side of her conversation, but he overheard that Mitch had gone to a weather conference in Denver. She hung up, her shoulders slumping. "Did you follow that?"

He nodded. "He won't be back for three days."

She didn't answer.

"I guess this whole thing can wait a few more days," he said. "I wouldn't miss George's memorial service anyway."

"Me neither," Karen said. "Go ahead and call Linda. She'll want to know the latest."

"Right." He dialed her number. He was surprised to hear it ring repeatedly. A second glance at his watch confirmed that it was past five. Linda should have returned from making funeral arrangements some time before. He hung up and looked at Karen, puzzled.

"Maybe I got her telephone number mixed up."

"Let me try." Karen took the receiver. "I remember it from yesterday." She placed the call and Destin, standing almost shoulder-to-shoulder with her, could hear it ring. She was ready to hang up when he heard a sharp click on the line, and then a man answered. "Eisenhardt's."

The voice left Karen bewildered, but Destin recognized it as Detective Gilbretti's. "I was trying to call Linda," she said, "to offer her my condolences. Is she there?"

There was a lengthy pause. "She's not available at the moment," Gilbretti said. "Perhaps you can call tomorrow?"

"Sure," Karen said. "But where is she?"

"I said she's not available."

"I see." She was about to hang up when Gilbretti said, "Wait. I need to leave a message for her. What's your name and telephone number?"

"I'm Karen, an associate of George's at Fontana Labs."

"Last name?" Gilbretti's voice was icy.

"K-e-r-r." She then gave him her phone number. He answered, but Destin couldn't quite hear him. "Thanks," she added more civilly a moment later. "I'll call her tomorrow."

She hung up and swiveled to face Destin, her face one troubled question mark. "Something's up, but I have no idea what."

"Neither do I," he said. "That guy was Detective Gilbretti. Perhaps I need to drive back to Sylva and find out if Linda's okay."

"That's Gilbretti's job," Karen pointed out.

"Yes," Destin admitted.

"She knew you were out on errands, didn't she?"

"Yes."

"Then she shouldn't be worried about you. You're doing what she said, looking into George's death. Something simply detained her."

"Guess so," he said hesitantly. "

"Is it Gilbretti that's bothering you?"

Destin nodded. "I don't relish running into him again. He's very suspicious of my part in all this. He doesn't know or trust me. I was certain he was going to arrest me last night because I had not followed police orders to remain in Orlando, but Linda interceded and he didn't." He rubbed his aching head again, aware that a red mist had settled in front of his eyes. He blinked several times, groping for focus.

Karen was staring at him, concern etched on her face. "You don't look well at all."

"I'm fine, really." He fumbled to his feet, but the effort brought the mist back. He slumped back and shut his eyes.

"You are not," Karen insisted. "Stop trying to be so damn brave. Look, why not stick around here until tomorrow? When I call Linda, I'll find out what's been going on."

Destin hesitated. It had been a rough three days and he knew it. A drive to Sylva would be torture.

"I've got a pretty decent pot roast in the fridge from last night. At least stay for dinner and think about it. That way you'll have a chance to meet my daughter, Tammy, who'll be home from school in two hours. Meanwhile, you can rest until dinnertime."

"Okay," Destin said.

"There's a guest bedroom over my single car garage out back. It isn't very fancy, but you're welcome to it." Her smile was inscrutable.

"Earl left a bunch of his older belongings here. I put his shaving kit and pajamas out in the guest room. You can use anything you didn't bring."

"Actually, I have all my gear with me," Destin said. "I stayed overnight in an RV belonging to one of Linda's neighbors in Sylva last night. Anyway, I packed it all in the truck today because Linda and I never had a chance to talk about what I would do about tonight." The pot roast sounded great. Besides, Karen was one of the most unusual hams he'd met in a long time and hers was the best offer he'd had all day.

The afternoon and evening passed quickly. He took a nap in the guest bedroom over the garage. The knotty pine room reminded him of the main house. Two windows admitted light into the room from the west and east, and the curtains matched a hand-quilted bedspread.

Following a short nap that chased away his headache, Destin rejoined Karen in the main house and met Tammy. As dusk settled, Karen reheated the pot roast while Destin used the time to talk to Tammy.

She proved to be a precocious fifteen-year-old with Karen's small forehead. Tammy, a younger edition of her mom, had long brown hair and impish blue eyes. Throughout dinner, she dominated the conversation, and amused, Destin listened. She was a social gadfly at school and into everything, especially the cheerleading team for the Robbinsville Black Knights.

Following dinner, they all trooped into the living room and tried a round of "Up and Down the River," which Tammy won.

"The next time I play you," Destin said, "I'll not be fooled by your wild bids." He watched her put the cards away.

"Hate to admit defeat, don't you?" Tammy snickered. "You're not used to someone bidding aggressively like you, are you?"

"Watch it." Destin grinned.

"Yeah, right. I'm really worried." She laughed.

"Tammy, you're way past the line! I won't have any disrespect." Karen's eyes narrowed. "Don't you have some homework tonight?"

"Nope."

"I find that hard to believe. Nothing at all?"

"Well," Tammy admitted, "I do have an essay due next Monday, but there's plenty of time to finish it."

"No. Get it started now, Missy."

"Ah, Mom!"

"Now!"

Karen laughed as Tammy got up and closed the door behind her on the left rear bedroom. She turned, gazed at Destin, and lowered her voice to a whisper. "It's been tough on her." She motioned toward the closed door. "She was very attached to Earl, and though she sees him about every week, it's not the same. Seeing him only makes it worse. You see, he let her do about anything she wanted to do, and of course, she doesn't understand why I could possibly be opposed to that.

"On the other hand, she really understands my position about Fontana Labs, and my own serious philosophical differences with Earl. She agrees with me, even though she can't let go of the idea that she's Daddy's little girl. She's a mess and walking a barbed wire fence. Sometimes I don't know what to do with her."

Destin studied her. "Never having married, I don't have answers, but I did have a rough time when my dad died."

"Sorry to hear that. What age were you then?"

"About seventeen." His voice dropped to a whisper. "Dad was an alcoholic. Following Viet Nam, he couldn't keep a handle on things. Mom never left him, but it was agonizing for her at times. Before he died, he would alternate between abuse when he was drunk, and remorseful guilt when he was sober."

"That's sad." Her eyes glistened.

"I came to terms with it quite awhile ago. Actually, I owe him. His service career helped me get into the academy, and though I never finished, the academy helped me focus my goals and my determination to make a go out of my life."

"I see," she said thoughtfully. "Why didn't you finish at the academy?"

"I have a problem with my knee." Destin leaned forward and rubbed it.

"A football injury?"

"Not exactly, though that's what I tell everyone."

"Then what happened?" she asked.

"One day, right after my seventeenth birthday, Dad got drunk – and mean. He was about to hit Mom, and I tried to intervene. That's when he kicked me." Destin shifted on the couch.

"Oh, Lord." She shivered. "Can't believe your mom would put up with that and not leave him on the spot."

"She didn't have to. Even though Dad did what he did while he was drunk, he remembered, and the remorse drove him to more drink. He died three weeks later. He was so drunk he swallowed his own tongue."

Karen rose, stunned, and Destin instantly regretted his bluntness. "Forgive me. I shouldn't have told you."

"It's not your fault, silly. But I'm amazed that such an experience hasn't crippled you."

Destin straightened. "As I said before, it made me a better person, though I've never forgiven him. Through courses at the academy, I found I had a real interest in science, and I decided to make something of myself and someday become the family man my dad couldn't be."

Karen shook her head, amazed. "Whoever gets you is getting quite a catch."

Destin flushed. "I need some air. Do you mind if I go out for a short walk?"

"Good idea. I'll take care of the dishes." She rose and retreated into the kitchen as though she too, was embarrassed at the turn in their conversation.

Destin stepped out onto the porch and inhaled the crisp mountain air. The temperature had drifted down to sixty, and the clear night sky held no moon. Stars blanketed the sky. He imagined he stood on some threshold, able to reach out and grasp millions of glistening pinpoints of diamond-light.

Uplifted, he ambled along the avenue that intersected Karen's drive which paralleled a lower western ridge until it turned sharply downhill into a dark, wooded area. He shuddered, turned around, and retraced his steps to Karen's home. Tammy's bedroom, he saw, was dark, and only the kitchen light remained lit. When he entered her home, he found that she had finished the dishes. She looked up, welcoming him.

"Had a good walk?"

"Yes. The village is quaint, isn't it?"

"Sure is. But I like it. No commute to work either. Speaking of work, I have to be at the labs at eight, tomorrow morning. That won't be a problem will it? "

"No." Destin said. "The guest bedroom is great and I need the rest."

"Good." She stepped into the alcove between the bedrooms and opened a linen closet, pulling out an extra blanket. "I think this will do you."

"Thanks." He took the blanket from her. "I'll be fine."

"Help yourself to the bathroom next to Tammy's room." She pointed toward the small bath. "See you in the morning. Oh, Destin?"

"Yes?"

She hesitated and blushed. "I have to apologize to you, but I really don't know how. Being a friend of George's has meant a lot to me. He never seemed to tire of trying to help me through my divorce from Earl. Not that we...you know." She blushed even more deeply.

He took three quick steps toward her and pecked her lightly on the cheek. She inhaled sharply, and then pressed herself against him. Before he could protest, she had molded her hands about his neck and kissed him.

Destin, stiffened, embarrassed. "No," he said softly. "This is no good." He moved back.

It was Karen's turn to be embarrassed. "I know," she said, her breath still uneven. She wept silently, struggling to control a torrent of words. "I'm lonely. Trying to adjust. Not ready for a relationship either. Besides, any further shocks might destroy Tammy. I – I know better." A note of petulance and humiliation crept into her voice. "I know I'm not right for you."

He stepped back a fraction more and said nothing. She was desirable, but he didn't want her at an intimate level. A long silence passed between them.

"Don't belittle your ability to attract anyone. It's simply not the time for either of us."

Karen's eyes filled with gratitude. "Maybe later then?" She laughed.

"I'm trying to say that I want us to be close friends for now." When she stiffened, he hastily added, "But later could be a different story."

She smiled and the awkward moment passed. "Good night," she whispered, and before he could regret his decision, she stepped into her bedroom, and after the door closed, he could hear the lock turn.

CHAPTER 14

DAI YU wasted no time. She pushed past the security desk at the labs and strode to Petrowski's office. Though she tapped lightly on the door that stood ajar, she entered without waiting. "Why did you have someone wake me to tell me you wanted me here at the crack of dawn?"

Petrowski pushed his chair back and stood. "Got a matter I want you to supervise. It wouldn't wait. Want some coffee?"

"No, I've got a mug out in the car."

Petrowski stroked his chin and studied her. "Your skirt and blouse aren't the best. Wish you'd worn slacks."

Dai Yu frowned. She hated riddles. "I would have worn slacks if you had asked. What've you got in mind?"

"I want you to drive over to Almond, to this address." He pointed to a slip of paper. "It's not far off the main road. Should be easy to find."

Dai Yu scowled. "And what do I do when I get there?"

"I want you to be sure that the CIA operative does his job. He's messed up more than one time. I don't tolerate sloppy work."

She understood and straightened. "You're talking about that firefighter who has the documents, aren't you?"

Petrowski smiled faintly and nodded. "That's right. Gus Vayhinger. We'll have to eliminate his wife too. Can't risk the chance he's told her anything."

"What do you want me to do if your CIA guy botches the assignment?"

"Clean it up. Finish the job."

Though Dai Yu stood still, her heart was racing. A tingle coursed through her, right down to her fingertips. The day was looking up. She nodded. "Do I go along with your operative?"

Petrowski snorted. "He'd never go for that. No. I want you to go in after him. He should be out at the Vayhinger place right before eight, so if you get there by half past eight and stay hidden, you should have a pretty good show."

Dai Yu nodded. All right."

Petrowski stopped her at the door. "If you need a gun, don't use your own." He reached behind his belt and withdrew a gun. "Here's a throwaway."

"Hmm. A Baretta 32 semi-automatic. Good choice." She turned the gun over in her palm, examining it.

"Remember, I want to hear from you after it's over."

"Yes, sir." She smiled. "I won't let you down."

Since she had time to spare, Dai Yu went to her locker in the women's restroom and changed into some slacks and sneakers she kept there. Then she drove to Almond, an area south of Stecoah and near the far end of Lake Fontana. On a sleepy lane not far off the expressway, she spotted the Vayhinger home. It sat on a slight rise in the midst of a large expanse of lawn with few trees. She frowned. Not good cover.

She parked some distance away, near a large oak. She pulled out a pair of binoculars she kept in the glove compartment and used them to survey the home and grounds. Nothing seemed amiss. There was no sign of the CIA man. She sighed, impatient with the wait. Finally eight came and went. She studied her watch, becoming increasingly alarmed as the minutes marched on. Nothing happened, and no one moved. When it was half past eight, she decided to act.

She slid out of her car and sprinted for some bushes that followed the property line, working her way past them until she reached the back yard. There, she heard talk and laughter. Gus and his wife had an eat-in kitchen at the rear of the house, and though she used a tree on the adjoining property to hide behind, she had a front row seat.

"Tell me more about the fire, dear," the woman was saying.

Between bites of food, the Vayhinger man told her about it, especially how he and his partner had tried in vain to save the Foster garage.

"Well, at least you have the day off and can rest now," the woman observed.

"No. He shook his head. "Unfortunately, our crew is supposed to attend a briefing at eleven this morning, but I won't have to stay at the station all day. I'll be able to come home afterwards. What about you? Don't you have a beauty shop appointment today?"

"No, Gus," the woman laughed. "The appointment was yesterday, and it wasn't with the beauty shop. I saw Dr. Zachary yesterday about my anemia."

"How'd it go?"

"It wasn't anemia per se." The woman laughed. "I've got a worse problem."

"Rita, what's wrong?" Gus asked, alarmed.

Dai Yu heard the woman laugh. She tried without success to get a better look at Rita through the branches.

"My problem, dear, is that I'm pregnant."

Silence. Dai Yu struggled with the branches again. "I'm going to be a papa?"

"Yes."

"Wow!"

She saw them both near the glass, kissing. She crouched behind the tree. Several minutes passed, but they had left the kitchen.

Dai Yu ran back along the shrubbery and retraced her steps to the car. She had reached the street and gained cover on the far side in a cluster of trees when she heard the front door open and shut. She turned and watched Gus amble down the front sidewalk and slip into his Jeep Wrangler, parked outside the garage. Rita trailed behind, still in her pajamas. Out the open window, Gus yelled, "We'll have to trade this Wrangler in on something with more room for the baby."

If he had more to say, Dai Yu didn't hear it, because Gus turned the key. A blinding flash of light seared Dai Yu's eyes, and the light consumed the scream of the explosion. In an instant, the Wrangler disappeared, and the concussion threw Gus' wife to the ground. The reeking smell of burnt, twisted metal filled the air. Even from her distant vantage point, Dai Yu knew they had died. Good riddance, she thought. She couldn't have done better herself.

CHAPTER 15

ROCKY pulled his rig into the main gate at Edwards Air Force Base, California and handed a young airman his orders and manifest. A sergeant took them and strode over, squinting in the glare that reflected off the desert sand. "Pull your truck into the parking lot on your right," he ordered. He waved Rocky through.

After Rocky parked, the sergeant brought him the papers and his pass. "Put the pass on your dash," he ordered, "and keep those papers handy." He stepped onto the cab's running board. "Here's a map. I've marked your route to the warehouses. I'll call them from the guard shack and let them know you're coming. Any questions?"

Rocky glanced at the map. It looked simple to follow. He nodded. "One. Is there a place I can grab a bite of lunch? I've been pushing it since early morning."

"Where'd you drive in from?" the sergeant asked. He shaded his eyes with his hand against the boiler-hot sun.

Rocky let go of the steering wheel. "I left Las Vegas this morning, if that's what you mean."

A horn tooted from the line at the gate, and the sergeant sighed. "No, but never mind. I have to help out the kid if I don't want this gate to become a battle zone. Good luck."

Rocky nodded and looked at the map. The marked route took him through several turns and a few miles, but he found the warehouse in an area near several spurs of railroad tracks filled with boxcars. As he stepped out of the truck, the oppressive heat made him sweat.

A couple of airmen in fatigues took his documents and went right to work loading his truck. Another sergeant, this one a Master Sergeant named Bowers, supervised the loading. Rocky liked him immediately. The sergeant was a slender black man who reminded him of a young version of Morgan Freeman. His eyes held the same innate wisdom.

"Come into my office," the sergeant said. "It's too blamed hot to stand around outside."

"Thanks." Rocky took a seat near the window air conditioner. The room was similar to the dispatch office in Little Rock, except that the furniture was not scratched and dirty. "Any place around here where I can get a good lunch?"

"Not in this section of the base." Bowers chuckled. "The commissary, base exchange, and two restaurants are some distance from here. Tell you what. How about sharing a lunch with me? I keep all the fixings here."

"Oh, I can't eat half your lunch."

"Nonsense." Bowers stood up. "We have one of those pint-sized refrigerators in the next room. Keeps the crew from having to run all over creation for food. Follow me."

Rocky left the air conditioner and followed him into a small room defined by stacks of boxes. Two picnic tables were placed end to end in the center, and along one wall, near the bathroom, Rocky spotted the refrigerator. Next to it were two drink vending machines.

"Help yourself." Bowers pointed at the soda machines.

While the sergeant whipped two ham sandwiches together, Rocky bought himself a can of soda.

"I noticed you already had half a load," Bowers said. He set the sandwiches down on a brown paper towel and took a seat.

"Yeah? I picked that stuff up in Colorado. It makes no sense why they wanted me to stop on my way west, rather than on my return trip." Rocky took a large bite of sandwich.

Bowers laughed. "Because two of those crates were destined for us."

"Oh. No one told me." Rocky said. "You know, I thought the military had closed Cheyenne Mountain, but apparently, not the adjacent warehouse area."

Bowers nodded. "I understand. These base closures have everyone chasing their tail. It's hard to keep up with it." He paused. "Of course, Cheyenne Mountain may be closed, but it isn't as though the military doesn't have an equivalent or better research facility somewhere else, now." He set down his sandwich. "How long have you been out of the military?"

Rocky swallowed. "About five years now. How'd you know I was ex-military?"

Bowers grinned. "Your top secret clearance, your haircut, and the way you carry yourself. You can take the man out of the military, but you can't take the military out of the man." He chuckled at his own joke.

"I took a twenty year retirement."

Bowers whistled. "You don't look old enough."

"Which is why I decided to retire. I wanted to enjoy life a little before my age catches up with me. Heck, I've never been married either, but that's because I never had a girl I cared about. Then I met Arlene a few months ago."

"I see." Bowers chuckled. "You didn't rob the cradle, did you?"

"Nah. Arlene is thirty-five. Doesn't look it though."

"If you've retired, why do you drive truck?"

Rocky sipped his Sprite before answering. "I spent most of my military career stuck in remote desert areas outside the U.S. I took up trucking so I could become better acquainted with our country. Besides, I'd go crazy with nothing to do."

Bowers nodded between bites.

"I'm curious about my cargo. I was told it was parts for a new military weapon of some sort." Rocky said.

Bowers leaned forward conspiratorially, much as Shep the dispatcher had done in Little Rock. "You're right. It's for a weapon. Scuttlebutt says it's a humdinger. More destructive power than a nuclear bomb."

"Well, if that's so, why don't they have an armed escort following me?" Rocky shivered.

Bowers sat back. "You're not carrying the whole weapon, just some parts for it. Besides, they sometimes choose to hide their escorts so the truck looks like any other truck."

"No shit." Rocky hunched over the picnic table. "I can't imagine why the military feels they need a weapon that powerful."

"Weaponry must always be more powerful than your enemy's." Bowers' eyes gleamed in the dim light and he leaned closer. "And guess what. *They need it for the aliens. They're the threat.*"

Rocky choked on his Sprite. He gaped at Bowers who was not laughing. After a coughing fit, Rocky said, "You can't be serious."

"Oh, but I am," Bowers insisted. "Did it ever occur to you how close we are to the China Lake Naval Weapons Center? It's right up the road. We deal with those guys occasionally. China Lake is another Area 51. They even build UFO's at China Lake, based on retro engineering."

"Retro engineering?"

"Yeah. Don't you know anything? Look. Haven't you heard of the incident at Roswell, New Mexico?"

Rocky hesitated, sensing a trap. "Sure. A UFO reportedly crashed there."

"Right. Bowers leaned forward. "There have been many such crashes all over the world. When they occur, the military scoops up the wreckage and goes feverishly to work. They work backwards with the wreckage until they understand the use of the equipment on board and how the craft flies. That's retro engineering. And that's just the half of it. They –"

"Come on." Rocky hooted. "Bullshit. You're feeding me bullshit. You sound just like Shep, my dispatcher."

Bowers glowered. "Open your mind, idiot. I worked at China Lake long before I was reassigned to Edwards."

Rocky laughed harder. "China Lake is Navy. You're Air Force and — "

"And China Lake is joint military," Bowers said, still angry. "I'm telling you: all those stories you've heard about retro engineering and UFOs are true."

Rocky laughed so hard his stomach hurt. "Even if it's true, the aliens haven't attacked us, have they? So why do we need a weapon against them?"

Bowers stood. "Hey! *You* asked me about the weapon you're hauling and I told you. Don't say I didn't tell you." He headed toward the office. "Your load should be ready."

Rocky trailed behind him to the door. Outside, the heat was a triple digit menace. He slid on his sunglasses, signed the manifest, and climbed in behind the wheel. As he looked back at the warehouse through his rear view mirror, he saw Bowers standing in the doorway, a rigid military figure. He waved to him and put the Peterbilt into gear.

Outside the base gate, he eased onto Highway 15 and headed east toward I-40. As the miles ticked away, Bowers' ridiculous claims made him laugh, although his laughter sounded hollow in the cab.

The remainder of the trip was tedious. When he reached Little Rock two days later, he chatted with Shep and the warehouse crew as they loaded his truck with the parts from Minneapolis. He'd nearly forgotten Sgt. Bowers' words until, in the dim interior of his tractor trailer, he noticed that the sealed California crates were stamped "China Lake."

CHAPTER 16

DESTIN awakened to light poking through laceworks of leaves. He turned over, lay for a moment, and got up. It was a few minutes past seven, but no one had stirred in the main house.

After dressing, he went down the outside stairs, tiptoeing through the unlocked front door and into the kitchen. He found the coffee maker and put on a pot to perk. Afterwards, he helped himself to a towel in the bathroom and took a shower and shaved. He was dressing when he heard Karen and Tammy's voices. He finished and moved into the living room.

"Good morning, Destin," Karen called from the kitchen, where she was busy thawing some sweet rolls in the microwave. "Were you able to sleep in our garage?" She turned back to the microwave as Tammy shuffled out of her bedroom, half asleep. Tammy stumbled into the vacated bathroom and shut the door.

"Fine, though my head still hurts." He rubbed it. "But I'll live. By the way, I hope you didn't mind if I helped myself to a towel and the shower."

"No problem." She placed a plate of heated sweet rolls on the table and grabbed the orange juice from the refrigerator, pouring a small glass for each of them. She had already set out two cups of coffee.

Destin strolled into the kitchen with Tammy at his heels. He grabbed a sweet roll and smiled at them both.

"What are your plans for this morning?" Karen asked.

"If it's all right, think I'll try to get Linda again," Destin said between mouthfuls. "Even if I don't get her, I'd better drive back to Sylva and talk to some of the instructors at the WCU Science Center."

"Don't go," Tammy interrupted, pleading. "I could show you around the area after school."

Destin chuckled and glanced at Karen. "No, I really must get back to Sylva." He finished his pastry and stood. "There's a lot to do."

Karen glanced at Destin, and then turned to Tammy. "Tammy, the paper ought to be here by now. How about bringing it in?"

"Ah, Mom. Why must it always be me?" She turned and stomped out the front door.

Karen blushed as the door shut. "Kids!" She swiveled to face Destin. "Look, about last night." She blushed and left the sentence unfinished.

"It's forgotten, and if you're worried that I'll mention this to anyone, forget it. All right?"

"Thanks."

Tammy flung the door open. "Mom, Mom, look!" She thrust the paper into Karen's hands and bounced at her side, pointing. "The paper talks about Destin." She read aloud:

SUICIDE TRAGEDY AT BLUEBIRD COVE

SYLVA—October 13. Linda D. Eisenhardt of 733 Bluebird Lane was discovered dead in her home early this afternoon by Sylva Police Department officers, in response to a call from neighbors, who reported hearing a single gun shot. Detective Lewis Gilbretti, a spokesperson for the police department, reported that Linda, 39, wife of Dr. George Eisenhardt, may have committed suicide due to emotional stress and trauma, resulting from news she had received less than 24 hours prior concerning her husband's murder in Orlando.

The 9mm automatic found with the body was registered to Dr. Eisenhardt. Destin Campbell, a close friend of the family and believed to be a houseguest at the time of the suicide, is being sought as a material witness. Police are continuing to investigate.

"Oh, my!" Karen took the paper and sank into the nearest kitchen chair. "This is horrible." Tammy hovered over her as she reread the news item.

Destin rushed to her side and peered over her shoulder at the headlines that screamed of Linda's suicide. The last line in particular, troubled him. "So that's what happened to Linda." His voice sounded wooden to his ears. He sank into another chair.

"Mom, what's going on? Mr. Eisenhardt was killed, and now Mrs. Eisenhardt has committed suicide?" Tammy shook her head.

Destin rose and poured himself a glass of water from the sink. Back at the table, he pushed the glass around and around. "I had no idea," he said. "I knew nothing about this. Linda was already gone when I left the house. I had no idea she was so upset that she would take her own life." He cupped his hands over his face.

"I know," Karen's eyes glistened. "But I think it's time you face the fact that the police may be looking for you in order to question you. Especially that Detective Gilbretti."

"I think you're right."

"Mom," Tammy asked, "couldn't this have something to do with the weapon that Dad always talks about?"

Startled, Karen started to shake her head then stopped. She tried to pick her words carefully, as though sidestepping mines. "I don't know, Hon. Maybe that's a possibility. George may have been murdered because he knew too much. Maybe he was ready to blow the whistle on all those good old boys at the labs."

"Not only Mr. Eisenhardt," Tammy interjected. "I meant Mrs. Eisenhardt too. Couldn't she have been killed because she knew too much as well?"

Karen shuddered but offered no answer.

Destin could see that the idea had not occurred to her, nor had it crossed his mind either. "Yes," he said at last. "It' a possibility, I suppose."

Karen broke in. "I can't imagine anyone *wanting* to kill Linda. Can you?"

Destin studied her. "Let's try to analyze this. First, George is murdered. We don't know why for certain, but we know he may have known about the weapon at Fontana Labs. It's a better reason than some sort of random hit. "

"Go on."

"Then there's what Linda told me or may have implied. She thought I should question some of the professors at WCU. She may have been thinking one of them was involved, or maybe...maybe, it was about Fontana again. I don't know." He stopped when Karen cut him off again.

"Yes, Fontana is a top secret, government funded, research facility. So therefore, Linda may have been killed because someone feared she knew too much – probably about this secret weapon thing."

"It isn't much of a secret around here," Destin suggested, "if everyone knows about it."

"What do you mean?" Karen demanded. "Who knows about it?"

"Well, we do – even Tammy knows."

"Wait a minute," Tammy protested. "I wouldn't know if my folks – Mom – hadn't fought so much about that and other things."

Destin was silent for a moment. He stroked his chin. "Actually, even if that is the reason for George's death — "

"And Linda's death." Tammy added.

"Yes. Even if all that is true, we know nothing about the weapon. Nothing at all."

They all fell silent.

"Well, with two people dead already, I think it would be stupid of us not to be careful," Karen said.

"You're right. We could all be in danger."

"Shouldn't you turn yourself into the police then?" Karen suggested. "At least you'd be safe." She put an arm around Tammy protectively.

Destin abruptly froze. "Wait a minute! When I left Linda's home yesterday morning, there was no police guard out front. That's important because I distinctly remember Detective Gilbretti reassuring Linda the night before. He told her he'd keep a man at the house for her protection." He stood up.

"Couldn't he have been hiding somewhere or trying to keep a low profile?" Karen asked.

"Yeah, I suppose so," Destin said. "Still, the guard made no pretense of hiding the night before."

"Wait. Didn't you tell me a second ago that Linda left you yesterday morning to make funeral arrangements?"

"Yes, she did."

"So he probably left when she did," Karen said. "It wouldn't make much sense to hang around there if she was someplace else."

"True, but I can't help but wonder if the police are somehow involved in this. I didn't care for that Gilbretti, and he certainly didn't care for me. I'm not sure I can trust him or any of them at all."

Karen was silent and even Tammy, whose mouth was a bubble machine, had fallen silent.

Destin took advantage of her soberness. "Tammy, it's really, really important that you understand that no one, and I stress no one, must find out about this conversation. It could be dangerous for all of us. Understand?"

She nodded, and her glance took them both in. Karen turned to Tammy, moving closer. "Aren't you supposed to catch the school bus any moment? Or are you driving today?"

Tammy shook her head, laughing, and the danger seemed to pass. "Mom, if I were going to catch the school bus, I'd have missed it already. Nope, I'm getting a ride with Ryan Tackett. He should be here any second."

"And *who* is Ryan Tackett?" Karen stiffened.

"He's a guy who works at The Sub Shoppe in Robbinsville. A senior. Lives here in the village."

A horn honked outside at the curb. "That's him." She grinned. "See you after school, Mom." She turned to Destin. "Will I see you again?"

Destin stopped. "Don't know." He eyed Karen. "I may have to return to Florida, though at this point, I haven't had time to think it through."

Karen stepped over and gave Tammy a peck on the cheek. "Next time you tell me about your rides in advance. Oh, and listen to what Destin said and keep our conversation to yourself, okay?"

Tammy nodded. "I will. Promise." She ran down the stone pathway to the waiting Ford Mustang and hopped inside. They sped out of sight.

Karen shut the door. "What are you going to do?"

He flexed his jaw. "I must get to the bottom of this, not only for George's sake but now for Linda's. Right now, I don't think Florida is going to be any safer than North Carolina. If only I could find a place to hide out for a few days, at least until I get a chance to talk to Mitch."

"You could stay here."

"No, it may be too dangerous – not only for me, but it definitely might put you in danger."

"Wait, I have an idea." Karen brightened. "My forensics lab is one room beyond Norma Yates's biology lab. She's a friend.

"Norma's husband, Max, died about a year ago. She still has their houseboat but she tells me she never uses it any more. It's moored on Lake Fontana in the Tuskeegee area. Bet she wouldn't mind if you used it. Let me call her." Karen crossed the room to the wall phone.

Destin used the moment to retrieve his shaving kit from the bathroom. After he returned to the living room, Karen joined him.

"Norma says you can use the houseboat. It's fine with her. She has linens on the bed, though the fridge is empty."

"Then she has electricity out there?"

"No," Karen said. "You'll have to rough it."

"But you said she had a refrigerator."

Karen grinned. "She has propane, and that runs the refrigerator and the stove."

"What does she use for lights?" Destin asked. "Candles? Lanterns?"

"She has them, yes." She paused, thinking. "Come to think of it, she does have some power. Before Max died, he'd installed a set of solar panels on the houseboat. He'd hooked those to a series of batteries that feed an AC something or other – converter or inverter."

"Inverter, I'll bet," Destin said.

"Yeah. And it's all hooked up so the batteries run the refrigerator in conjunction with the propane, and the inverter then, provides the electricity for the lights on board."

"Wow," Destin said. "It might be enough power for my radios."

"Probably." Karen nodded. "Good thinking."

"What kind of batteries did Max put into the houseboat?"

Karen scratched her head. "If I remember correctly, Norma mentioned that he'd installed two or three golf cart batteries. They provide twelve volts."

"Ideal." Destin smiled. "How do I get there?"

Karen laughed. "Let me write it out for you. It's about fifteen minutes south of here, on the road to Stecoah."

He scooped up his belongings as she handed him the note. "Thanks," he said. "When I get situated, I'll set up the radios. Let's keep in touch."

"Good idea. You're going to be close enough to get me on simplex. I think that would be safer than trying to use the repeater on two meters."

"Yes. We could use 146.520, but sometimes that's monitored more often than .535. I think I'd prefer the latter."

"Smart choice," Karen said. "Can't remember any time I've heard anyone on 535. I'll monitor that simplex band, and since I have a good dual band radio, I'll monitor the local repeater at least until I know you can contact me without a problem."

"What's the local frequency?" Destin asked.

"It's 145.110, negative offset with a 151.4 tone. Okay?"

"Great, but let's go one step further, since we don't know what lengths these idiots will go to. I'm going to set up my long distance communications tomorrow, if possible. I prefer 20 meters."

Karen looked at him, puzzled. "You want to DX with me on twenty? Twenty meters would never work. We're too close to each other."

"I know that," Destin said. "I simply thought that a DX long distance frequency could be a back-up in case I have to travel somewhere and there's some urgent reason to contact you. Let's set up 7.230 on 40 meters for normal HF contacts. But let's keep a 20-meter frequency – 14.321 – for emergency long-distance situations."

"Okay," Karen laughed. "You actually brought your HF equipment along from Florida?"

Destin nodded. "I used to have my old HF radio rigged up in my truck, but about three months ago I decided I needed a much better radio, so I sold the old rig and bought an Icom 706 Mark IIG to replace it. I haven't yet gotten around to installing it in the truck, but it's on my to-do list. I think the Icom is going to be strong and portable — perfect for decent mobile HF communications. Anyway, it's been under the seat now for three months. Same with the antenna."

"Three months! I could never wait that long to use a new rig!" Karen's eyes flashed.

"Waiting wasn't what I wanted. This is the first time in months I haven't been buried in work."

"Okay, then you'll finally have enough time to hook it up."

"Yes," Destin said. "Come to think of it, I've been carrying a bunch of antenna wire and balun in the truck. I figure I have enough equipment to string a dipole for the houseboat. I can also use the time to install the radio in the truck. I want to rig it so I can pop the radio into the truck and take off, or pull it out as needed."

"Good," she said. "Take care and keep in touch."

"I hope to. I'll do my best." Destin started his truck and eased out of the yard. He wondered though, if keeping in touch would be possible, or if he'd even be alive to try.

CHAPTER 17

WHEN the doorbell rang the next day, Tammy frowned. She set aside her essay homework and trotted to the door. "Destin?" She flung the door open. Disappointed, she gaped at a red headed stranger. "Oh."

"Miss, is this the Kerr residence?"

"Yes." Tammy held the door tightly. "If you're looking for my mom, she's still at work."

"I'm looking for Karen, yes. We're long time acquaintants, actually, though I've never been here before. I brought some papers I think will interest her."

"Papers?" Tammy frowned. "What papers?"

The stranger's smile was enigmatic. He shifted his weight and leaned against the doorframe. "I'm Ben Tirshaw, a firefighter at the Stecoah Fire Department. Anyway, I met a fellow two days ago by the name of Destin Campbell and he told me he was coming to see Karen."

Tammy threw the door open. "You and Destin are friends?"

Ben smiled faintly. "I guess you could say that."

"Well, come on in. My mom will be home any minute." She led the way to the couch. "What's this about some papers?"

Ben sighed. "I really shouldn't go into that, but your mom — "

"She's home!" Tammy recognized the familiar crunch of gravel and the car door slamming. Karen opened the door a few moments later.

She stopped when she saw Ben in her living room. She scowled fleetingly at Tammy.

"Tammy, you know better than to let strangers in the house."

Ben rose and removed his ball cap. "Sorry to startle you, Karen."

"Ben? Oh, my gosh, it's been awhile! So sorry." Blushing, she came over to the couch and shook hands with him. "Destin told me he met you the other day. Told me about the Foster fire too."

"Yes. We had quite a talk. I know about George."

"Horrible business, all right. Did you hear that George's wife, Linda, is also dead?"

"Oh, no." Ben blinked and steadied himself against the couch.

"You haven't seen the paper then." Karen paused. "Come into the kitchen and I'll show it to you."

She led the way. Tammy took a seat at the table and Ben followed suit. He looked over the article and turned to Karen. "I have some bad news too. One of my fire crew at Stecoah, Gus Vayhinger, was killed yesterday. No accident. Killed by a car bomb, and worse, his wife died in the same blast."

"That's sick!" Karen shut her eyes. Tammy had rarely seen her mom that upset. She continued. "Yesterday, Destin told me about the Foster fire, and how you'd come into possession of some pretty important papers. He also mentioned how you two met." She paused. "Do you think there is any connection between their deaths and the papers you found?"

Ben nodded. "You've come to the same conclusion as I have. I think they were murdered because Gus was seen with the papers. I have them now."

Tammy stood. "Want something to drink, Mr. Tirshaw?"

"Iced tea if you have it, thanks."

She poured a glass of tea for everyone. "Not sure I understand about the papers."

Karen peered at her and then turned to Ben. "My daughter wasn't home at the time we discussed them, but you can speak freely in front of her. She's aware of the situation at Fontana Labs, though I wish she weren't."

"I see," Ben nodded in Tammy's direction. "Then it won't hurt to show you these." He reached into his jacket and removed the papers from his inner pocket and deliberately set them in front of Tammy.

"Wow!" Her eyes grateful, Tammy fingered the documents tentatively. She studied the heading that carried the Oak Ridge Laboratory logo along with the Fontana Lab subtitle and then handed them to her mom.

She watched as her mom read the two sheets. "Are these the only papers you managed to save?" Karen asked.

"Yes," Ben said. "Still, if I understand it, these sheets tell quite a lot. They speak about this weapon. Some sort of beam, I gather."

"That's my understanding too, and Fontana is in the thick of it."

"Yes. It appears they'll kill to keep it a secret." Ben scowled.

"So what do we do now?" Tammy began to pace the tiny kitchen.

Karen grabbed her arm. "You do what Destin said and keep quiet."

"I agree," Ben said. "Anyway, I promised to get these to Destin. By the way, where is he?"

"We have him hidden away nearby," Karen said. "I'll keep these papers in a safe spot for him."

"Good," Ben stood up. "I should be going now, but if you need any help, let me know. I'll do what I can."

"Thanks." Karen trailed behind him, walking out to his truck.

Though Tammy stayed in the house, she caught snatches of their private conversation about Karen's separation and divorce from Earl through the open door. Her mom, she knew, was speaking honestly about her problems, and yet the loss of her dad was something she could not analyze or rationalize. The loss only caused pain. She shut the door, and through her tears, she tore up her essay and went to her room.

CHAPTER 18

BONNIE'S buoyed spirits had deteriorated since the UT meeting and as her meeting in Morristown inched closer. She had spent the first of two days at the Center for Gorilla Research, the CGR, working with Ollie and Dollie and preparing for her father's memorial service in Maryville.

The second day was devoted to the actual service at the Chapel of Flowers, a sad affair that included only a few surviving relatives, followed by an Open House day at the farm, where friends had gathered to support her. Today she'd returned to work, even working through lunch, but by mid afternoon, she was spent and dejected. She decided to call it a day.

On the drive home, her mind reeled with memories of her dad, especially those last few minutes with him. Those memories haunted her, and it took a sheer force of will to stop the tears. As she pulled in her driveway, she could see Betsy in her back yard, trimming back one of two apple trees that formed a border between her lawn and the fields beyond.

Betsy hailed her, but the older woman's voice lacked its usual bounce, so Bonnie walked across the lawn and joined her. Betsy stood there, a lumpy figure, dressed in an old pink housedress and sporting a branch saw. She had pulled her grayish blonde hair back in an aged green scarf. Bonnie grinned. "Having trouble trimming the tree?"

"Nah, I'm about finished."

Bonnie watched her for a moment. "Isn't it a bit early to cut back the tree?"

Betsy shrugged. "I plan to visit my niece for a week, and besides, the weather service is predicting our second cold front of the season for this afternoon." She set her saw on the ground. "Haven't you noticed how the winds have been picking up?"

Bonnie shook her head. Not only had she not noticed the wind, she knew that she had been oblivious to a great deal. "When are you leaving?"

"Tomorrow. Harold, the old guy who lives across the street, is going to take me to the airport. Save me all those long-term parking fees." Betsy paused and picked up a basket. "What happened to you the other night?" She turned back to the tree again.

For a moment Bonnie stared at her uncomprehendingly. "What?"

"Don't you remember?"

"What?"

"You didn't come by for dessert, the strawberry shortcake, three nights ago."

A wave of remembrance rolled over Bonnie, and she could feel the heat flood her face. "Oh no, I forgot completely. I wish you'd mentioned it at the service." She groped for something else to say but was at a loss of words.

"You've had too much to worry about," Betsy said, but there was an edge in her tone. She shifted to another dead branch a little farther from Bonnie and picked up the saw again. Heaving from the effort, she sawed the crooked branch while Bonnie stood awkwardly, listening to the rasping, chewing sound. Finally, the branch gave way with a clean crack, and Betsy set it upon a pile of other branches near the fence.

Dejected, Bonnie stared at her. "You're right. The problems at work keep getting worse. They're all piling on top of my dad's death. And what I told you about the grant to the CGR being in jeopardy is true. It's worse than what I thought originally. At the board meeting the other day, I also learned that Doc, one of my best friends at UT, is having prostrate surgery. It could be cancerous."

Betsy turned back, studying Bonnie's face for a moment. Her features softened. "Yeah, I know you've had a tough time. The grant problem makes it tougher. It's a terrorist thing, isn't it?"

"What?" Bonnie asked, confused.

"Well, the stock market goes up and down – mostly down — and now the Bledsoe family wants to cut and run. That's terrorism."

"No, I actually think it's all about character," Bonnie insisted, still confused. "Jake Bledsoe was wealthy, but he was a nice person, a generous man. He originally got interested in helping me because he wanted to pay back some good to society."

"Okay, so Jake was wealthy and nice, but how'd he get interested in your gorillas?"

"He loved animals, and living nearby, he was one of UT's main benefactors. He also believed that certain animals had a capacity for language."

"I see," Betsy said.

"Jake was a friend, but I've never met Mark or Sam, though I've heard stories about both of them. Mark is purportedly more stable than Sam. That's why Jake groomed him for running the estate after his death." She sighed. "Now, Sam may have ruined Jake's plans."

"That sucks. Not good."

"It isn't. Sam feels he deserves more. It's a mess."

"What will you do?"

Bonnie didn't answer at first. She reached down into the small basket and grasped an apple, rolling it around her hand. The firm apple's skin glowed a blush pink serrated with green. She could see her reflection in it, and for a moment she wished she were a psychic who could see the future.

"I'm going to Tennessee to try and save the grant," she said. "It's my only hope."

"When are you going?" Betsy stopped and pulled her scarf off, which did much to improve her appearance.

"Tomorrow morning, actually."

"That soon?"

"Yes."

"Well, why not stop by tonight and have coffee with me," Betsy said. "I don't have any strawberry shortcake, but maybe I can dig up something for dessert."

86

"I would love to, but I have some packing to do." Bonnie kicked at some loose leaves on the grass. "Doc told me yesterday that the grant business may take more than one day, so I'm going to stay up in Morristown until it's finished." Betsy looked disappointed. Betsy, no doubt, had seen through her excuse. She bit her lip. *There I go again.*

"Tell you what," she said. "After we've both returned, how about I treat you to dinner? We could make it a nice night out. How about it?"

Betsy brightened visibly. "Okay. That would be fun." She whistled as Bonnie crossed the lawn to her home.

Bonnie, however, found nothing to whistle at. Later, after sorting through the last of her father's insurance papers and then packing for her trip, she made herself a quick dinner of leftovers. She ate silently in her dining alcove, even more discouraged. She could only wonder about her future.

Everyone near her – Doc, President Alcorn, and all her colleagues – had tried to reassure her that Jake's grant to the center would probably survive. Still, there was a gut-sense feeling that spoke otherwise. Long ago she had learned to listen to the insistent voice of dread. Now, her gut sense whispered its invisible message and she couldn't ignore it.

Her thoughts returned to Betsy. She had hurt her twice. There was a part of her that fought human contact when she needed it most, and she berated herself inwardly for her weaknesses and failures.

She poured a stiff drink of Jim Beam and water and sat at the table, nursing the drink. Her seat was rock-hard, and the backrest dug into her spine. She finished her drink and immediately poured a chaser. The liquor warmed her stomach while dulling the ache in her head. Setting the drink aside, she went upstairs, stripped to her underwear, and, in bed, settled against her reading bolster.

The endless reel in her mind remembered her father again. A restless soul, he had been an important influence in her life. She could still see him smiling, his crew cut making him boyish. He'd been an impractical dreamer, and yet, there were moments when his wisdom was unimpeachable. One time he'd told her that life often offers many lessons and challenges. The more difficult ones, he'd warned, could be devastating and sneaky. How true, she thought. Sleepy from the drink, she pulled the covers up.

Bonnie remembered what Abe had told her when they had still been dating. Those were the days, she thought, when it had seemed that nothing could ever come between them.

"You're intelligent, beautiful, ambitious. Loyal too," he had said. "But your best asset is your ability to win people to your cause through an unspoken capacity to be professional yet deserving of respect, even when these people are your adversaries."

Bonnie hoped he'd been right. Sometimes she was underestimated, but she had worked long, difficult hours with the gorillas, then even more hours compiling endless research notes and journals. Yet here she was, on the brink of one of the greatest linguistic breakthroughs in history, and it could be yanked from her. It reminded her of someone's grand entrance to a ball, marred by a humiliating stumble over a loose rug.

Was that the whole story though? Good question, she thought, for she was vulnerable in many areas known only to her. She turned the drink around in her hand, using her palm to wipe the glass and keep it from sweating. She felt a sense of defeat every time she examined her own ability to make and keep close friends or lovers. Invariably, her devotion to work drove them away.

Even Abe Kemp, her long time lover, had left her, accusing her of being married only to her work. Now, her dad's words stung her soul and her sense of aloneness had begun to rob her of sleep.

She finally moved the bolster and turned out the light. She allowed a drunken sleep to sweep her to oblivion.

"You don't care! You don't care about us!" Abe screamed. *"You're incurable, insensitive. I thought you were worth it, but you only care about your work!"*

"Why are you saying that?" Bonnie said. Nevertheless, guilt consumed her. *"I care...I care about things...You yourself said I was a loving person."* She sobbed.

The shadows of Abe faded then reformed to reveal Jake Bledsoe.

"You will be alone," Jake said flatly. *"And then you will learn."*

"What do you mean?" Bonnie pleaded.

"Sometimes one must be alone to find others," he answered cryptically.

Crying, Bonnie awoke from her nightmare. And though it was only midnight, sleep eluded her. It would be best to lie quietly and rest, she decided. She would need all her strength for what was to come.

CHAPTER 19

DESTIN carried the warmth of Karen's home and hospitality with him that day and the next. He drove to Robbinsville where he purchased a small stockpile of food, two paperback books, and provisions to last him several days.

He made his final stop in town at the hardware and bought two powerful flashlights, extra batteries, pliers, and rope. Satisfied with his purchases, he drove east to Tuskeegee.

Karen's directions were good, and he located the paved lane which soon gave way to dirt. He bounced through the potholes for a quarter mile until the road widened at a dead end. On the left, the road continued behind a locked pipe gate.

He parked the truck and walked around the gate, following the road which continued north over a slight rise. Less than fifty yards beyond, a fork to the right meandered down a gentle slope through trees and underbrush, ending at a shallow cove that hugged the wooded shoreline of Lake Fontana.

The forty foot blue and white aluminum-clad houseboat was tied to a short, floating dock anchored to some large trees on the shore. For most of the cove, two feet of banked red clay, mud, and rocks lay exposed to the air. In spite of the muddy shoreline, the water was a pristine emerald green.

Destin found the key to the houseboat hidden on the first pylon, where Norma said. He unlocked the door. Inside, he discovered that the front of the houseboat was the living area while the rear was devoted to one bedroom and bath.

Destin wandered back outside. He stepped off the bow and followed the dock around to its seaward side. At the rear end of the dock behind the houseboat, a winch and jet rail system held a jet-ski. He studied the watercraft, an almost-new Honda Aqua Trax R-12X, which was securely locked to the winch.

He had never seen the model except in pictures. Most of the hull was red, though the Honda logo was emblazoned in large, black letters below the black-buffered stripe that separated the hull from the top half of the machine. He knew the R-12X was turbocharged – the fastest personal watercraft of its kind – and it looked it. Near his feet, he discovered a tarp for the jet-ski in a rumpled heap. The wind had apparently blown it off, so he re-covered the machine.

Inside, the bedroom's double bed was made, and Destin found a fully stocked linen closet. The bedroom's built-in chest of drawers was mostly empty, though the top drawer contained several small shoeboxes filled with wires, needle-nosed pliers, electrical tape, and batteries.

He wasted no time unloading his supplies. With the advance of dusk, the smoke from Tuskeegee decreased. He lit one of the houseboat's gas lanterns and brought it out on the deck to serve as an outdoor light. The twilight dissolved into darkness the minute the sun slipped behind the steep hills surrounding the cove. He sat outside and basked in the silence for a while until the mosquitoes threatened to carry him off.

Although hungry, he put aside thoughts of food and strolled through the deepening shadows to his truck, and inside, he placed a call to Karen on the simplex local frequency of 535.

"N7JJJ, this is WR4RR."

"There you are," she answered a moment later. "Where have you been?"

"I bought some provisions. All is well, and I'm all settled in now."

"Good. I was worried. Are you calling from your truck?"

"Yes. When I have a chance tomorrow, I'm going to set everything up here, but I'll do it so I can move the radio from house to truck, as I told you earlier."

"Good. None too soon."

"Is anything wrong?" he asked, alarmed.

"Not exactly. Minutes ago, I was paid a visit by Gilbretti."

Destin straightened. "What happened?"

"He was anything but friendly. Told me he was simply looking into – matters – and he asked me several questions about Linda."

"What kind of questions?" Destin demanded.

"Wait. Is this a safe channel? I'm worried."

"Well, you know it only takes a scanner to find any frequency we could move to. Fortunately for us, this area seems to have few hams. The labs use higher frequency channels for their 'comm' stuff, so there's little chance they'll discover us here. If you're worried though, I'll come up with an alternate for you soon."

"No, it's okay," Karen said. "Anyway, he asked me how well I knew her – how close I was to her. He also asked if she had ever said anything indicating something was wrong or out of the ordinary. I told him no. I was totally mystified."

Destin's heart hammered. "Did he ask about me?"

There was momentary silence. "Yes, he asked me if I knew you. I told him no. And that ended the questions."

"Was Tammy there during his visit?"

"Fortunately, no. She had left only moments before and gone over to Ryan's home to study for an Algebra test."

"Good."

Karen shifted subjects. "Will you have enough to keep you busy there at the houseboat?"

"No problem there." He laughed. "Now, I'm hungry so I'll talk to you later, if you think you're okay."

"Wait. In the excitement, I almost forgot to tell you that Ben Tirshaw came by this afternoon. He left something here for you."

"QSL," Destin said. "Can't wait to see it."

"I know, she said softly. "73. N7JJJ."

"Wait, do me a favor and keep your eyes open. Be careful to watch that you're not followed."

"Okay. N7JJJ."

"73, Karen. WR4RR."

After he signed off, he walked back to the houseboat. The kitchen was well stocked with utensils, pans, and provisions, even coffee. He fixed a quick dinner of chicken patties, broccoli, and salad and ate at the small café table near the sliding doors.

After dinner, he found where Norma's husband had made a sealed compartment under the bow deck to hold the large golf cart batteries for the solar panels. He also spotted the two solar panels mounted on the roof. The day had drained him though, and the gentle rocking of the boat in concert with the lapping of the water, worked its hypnotic magic. He went to bed and soon drifted off to sleep.

The next day would have been an idyllic vacation day, Destin thought, had he not been in hiding. It was a crisp Indian summer morning, and the lake took his breath away. The narrow, liver-shaped cove with its gentle, heavily wooded hills rising on three sides provided him with lots of protection from visibility.

Following a light breakfast, Destin explored the houseboat and the cove. When he tried the houseboat key in the gate key lock, he found they were interchangeable. Pleased, he moved the truck through the gate and down to the edge of the dock, where it could not be seen from the gate.

He also found two green blankets stored in the houseboat, and he moved them out to the truck to use later as camouflage. That finished, he went to work and rigged a decent antenna for his Icom HF radio on the houseboat. He pulled out his portable Outbacker vertical antenna from the bed of his truck, along with a length of coax cable.

He managed to bolt the antenna to the corner of the right deck railing at the back of the houseboat, where it met the back bedroom wall. Then he attached the coax to the antenna and ran it through the rear bedroom window to the dresser in the room, a temporary home for his Icom.

Rigging his blue Ford proved to be more difficult. He moved the Icom back to his truck and attached a 12-volt cable to it for power. Next, after removing his old mag-mount, two-meter antenna from the truck, he fashioned a second holder for his antenna, which he bolted to his truck's rear bumper on the driver's side. He took a second length of coax stored in his truck and connected it to the antenna holder using a 259 connector.

That finished, he scooted under his truck, ran his coax from the rear bumper to the cab, wrapping it around the frame and chassis, fed it through one of the cab's drain holes, and connected it to the radio itself.

Before he powered up the radio, he attached the wire power cord directly to the battery. The battery would act as a filter for engine noise.

Satisfied, he placed the radio on the bench seat of the cab. The only thing he couldn't complete was the holder for the radio. For that he would need some sturdy aluminum bent into the shape of a "U" and bolted in place. He would then place his Yaesu FT 8800 on top of the Icom, piggyback style. A task for later. Until then, he attached the two together with Velcro and prayed they'd stay put.

He straightened and glanced at the truck floorboards, where the six-pack of beer from Florida still sat. He frowned. It had sat there since before the hamfest. Now, it was in the way.

He moved the beer onto the houseboat, though he didn't touch it. Perhaps, he thought, his secretary was right. She always fussed at him for taking the six-pack with him everywhere but never touching it. She'd told him he would never be a drunk, that his fears were groundless. Still, the thought of beer made his stomach knot, so he pushed his memories aside and went back to work.

Late afternoon shadows had enveloped the cove when he finished. As a precaution, he tried out the Icom and the Yaesu in the truck and then retested them on the houseboat. They worked fine in both locations, but best on the houseboat. He set the radios on his bed and worked some of the travel nets and west coast stations for an hour or two, until darkness crept across the cove. Following a hasty dinner, he rigged two fishing poles and tried some spinning. He worked the lure across the warm, liquid smoothness of the lake surface for almost an hour, but he had no bites. The pole felt odd to his touch. He missed his bamboo pole, back in Florida, and the memory overwhelmed him with grief.

The cane pole had originally belonged to George, who had given it up as a lark when Destin won a poker game against him. From that moment on, Destin had cherished the pole.

Sighing, he decided that the mosquitoes had done much better than he. It was time to try Karen on simplex, so he gave her a call.

"N7JJJ, this is WR4RR."

She answered almost immediately. "N7JJJ."

"How did work go for you today?"

"Oh, nothing much new there. Kind of dull, in fact. How was yours?"

"I got everything rigged," he said, with a touch of pride. "I can move either the Yaesu or the long distance Icom as needed from the house to the truck or back." He described his hook-up and his contacts. "Got in some fishing too."

"Catch anything?"

"No."

She was silent on the other end. Then: "I asked because I wonder how you're going to keep yourself busy until you can meet with Mitch. Aren't you bored?"

"No. I have several novels to read, and this place is perfect for fishing. But tell me, has there been anything further mentioned in the news about – well, you know what."

"Not a blessed word," Karen said. "Isn't that unbelievable?"

"Not if it happened as it was reported." Destin chose his words carefully. "Even in Sylva, such things get little press."

"Now you know better than that," Karen said, surprised.

"Of course I do," he said. "But I suspect the press believes what it was told."

"I suppose," Karen sounded unconvinced. "Look, maybe this won't wait after all. I spoke with Ben recently. He said his friend, a fellow firefighter, was killed in a car bombing. His wife too."

Destin's gripped the mike. "Thank heavens it wasn't Ben."

"Yes. Anyway, the radio is playing this bombing up. The newscaster said the guy had been one of the heroes who fought the garage fire at the Upper Sawyers Creek development. Otherwise, that fire might have become a serious forest fire."

Destin tensed. "Ben talked about that fire. He and his partner, Gus, are the ones who tried to save the garage."

"I know."

He swallowed. "This is simply too coincidental. I have a feeling the bombing must be connected to that fire."

"Me too, but we can't do much about it." She paused and switched subjects. "Destin, Tammy and I could be under surveillance, couldn't we?"

"Yes, though I think they haven't figured out that you're involved. Not unless, of course, they saw you and George together."

"No, I don't think so."

"Well, don't put it past them." He rubbed his whiskers, thinking. "Earlier, you said there was nothing we could do. Well, maybe there is something *I* could do."

"What?"

He ignored the question. "Will you be in tonight?"

"Sure. When can you come?"

He pondered her question. Darkness would be to his advantage. "About eight?"

"Fine. Tammy and I will be here, probably watching some TV. What is it?"

"I'll explain when I get to your place," Destin said. He could feel the adrenaline pumping. "See you then. WR4RR, clear."

"N7JJJ," Karen answered as she cleared the frequency also.

Destin arrived at eight, and as he parked, she turned on the porch light and stepped out to greet him, Tammy tagging behind her.

"Hi." Tammy giggled. Karen merely smiled, her hands clasped in front of her.

"Hi there, Bubbly," Destin answered. "How was school today?"

Tammy wrinkled her nose and made a face. "The usual," she said. "Boring. No excitement. The pits."

"What about Ryan?" he asked, grinning.

"Oh, he's okay," She tossed her head. "Are you teasing me?"

"Mwah?" he mimicked. She took a mock swing at him, and he ducked, laughing.

"Children!" Karen snorted. "Now, Tammy, you have dish duty tonight, so get in there and get busy." They both watched as Tammy disappeared inside, fussing as she went.

Karen laughed. "She can be lippy at times." When they could see her at the sink in the kitchen, they both moved down the front walk, into the shadows of the trees. Karen then turned to him. "By the way, Ben stopped here yesterday with the papers you two discussed. They're unbelievable. They talk about the development, at Fontana Labs, of the CCD – the computer controller interlink. It links their colliders to a beam weapon."

"I know." Destin shook his head. "That's why I can't let go of this. Especially when they kill innocent people to keep it secret."

"I'll keep the papers safe for you," Karen said. "Now, what is your plan? You said you had an idea."

"Yes, I do." He paused. "Don't know why I didn't think of it before. Linda and George had a home here in the village while George worked here."

"Yes. They had a place up this very road, about two blocks up. Why do you mention it?"

"I want to search their home. Whoever broke into George and Linda's home before her – suicide – may not have searched their Fontana residence. After all, Linda only left it the morning after George's murder."

"Fat chance of that," Karen said.

"Yeah, you're probably right, but it's worth a try. Besides, even if someone has gone through the house, there's a chance I might find something they missed."

"You're right," Karen pushed her hair into her barrette. "I never thought of that." Destin started to turn. "Wait," she said. "How do you propose to get in her house – break in or something?"

"Got any better ideas?" He grinned.

"No, but it could be dangerous."

He touched her arm, the touch of a friend. "I'll call you on the radio the moment I finish and bring you up to date. Promise."

"Okay. But be careful, please. Her address is 214 Mountain Lane. It's on the left side near the tennis courts."

He nodded. "I'll walk up there."

"You might need a knife,"

"I have one," Destin said. "I use my Leatherman as a tool a dozen times a day."

"Do you have a flashlight?"

Destin frowned. "Didn't bring one."

"Then take mine." She handed him a small one that could fit in his pocket.

"Thanks."

Destin walked up the street, keeping to the shadows. He found the home easily. Though similar in size to Karen's, it sat farther back on a heavily wooded, corner lot. The front yard did not meet the street directly, because a gurgling stream meandered through it a few feet from the pavement. The front walk was a free-form curve that began with a small, rustic wooden bridge which traversed the small brook.

He crossed the bridge and crept up to the front door, sticking to the dark shadows. The place looked deserted. Cautiously, he tried the knob, but it was locked. After a cursory look for a key under the front mat and along the porch posts, he crept around the side of the home and peered at the back yard. Darkened, gloom-filled shadows seemed to ebb and flow, and his heart hammered. A distant street light dispelled enough darkness so he could see an outline of the home. A kitchen door with its small porch roof was centered along the rear of the old cottage.

He slid onto the wooden porch. The back door was locked. He took his knife from his belt and tried to pry the lock open but it didn't open as doors always seemed to, in the movies. Defeated, he stepped back, peering right and left.

The kitchen window, to the right of the door, caught his eye. The old, screened casement style window was partly open. As he pressed his hand against the screen, he felt a waft of warmer air from the interior of the home. Smiling, he used the knife to cut the screen along both sides and the bottom.

He eased himself into the silent kitchen, coming down on the drain board near the sink. Inching himself to the floor, he peered through the semi-darkness. It was a small kitchen, only slightly larger than Karen's, though the back door entry opened into an alcove. A doorway opposite the kitchen led into a combined utility room and pantry. He tiptoed forward, an inch at a time, along the alcove until it opened into a living room.

He located the master bedroom and bath beyond the kitchen, and after a short exploration, he discovered a second bedroom and den combination on the front of the cottage. Searching was difficult in the gloom, but the place seemed neat and undisturbed. The mark of Linda's good housekeeping.

At the door to the den, he flicked on his flashlight because the room was pitch-black. Shielding the bulb with one hand, he played the light around the room. Heavy curtains covered the windows. Near a corner-shelving unit, he spotted a computer on a battered desk.

He stole across the den's shag carpeting and pulled out the molded vinyl chair in front of the aging computer. Reaching over, he flicked on a small desk light. Though light pooled over the desk, beyond the worn wood top, the blackness seemed to swallow everything. In the corners of the den, the charcoal shadows rustled sinuously. Destin shifted his weight. *Afraid of the boogey man?*

He eased himself into the desk chair. His movement, a cannon shot in the silence, died away, and in the echo of the silent shadows, he heard a rustle again. He froze, straining to hear each faint whisper, but he only heard the silence of dead air. He pulled the chair toward the desk, but the movement caused eddies in the shadows. Swallowing, he strained against the silence and then set aside his fears, trusting his ears.

Surreptitiously, he slid open the desk drawers of the maple desk. Within each of the upper drawers, he found office supplies, but nothing of any significance. In the bottom, deeper drawer, a partition separated a sheaf of copy paper from the rear of the drawer. Behind it, he found a collection of connectors, some leftover pieces of antenna line, and a filter. Destin grinned. Not a surprise. George had kept radio and computer equipment amongst his lesson plans and personal papers at the college.

Memories of George made his eyes mist. All of George's wonderful radio equipment would end up in someone's garbage heap. Even Linda wasn't alive to take care of it and preserve it.

He turned back to the lower desk drawer. Two plastic trays held pens, a three-hole punch, money wrappers, and an assortment of packages containing filing labels. He poked the material aside and spotted a plastic computer CD wallet, loaded with CDs.

Curious, he pulled the small box onto the desk, opened it, and flicked through blanks. He was about to set the CDs aside in disgust when he saw markings on the last CD. The letters, in George's handwriting, leapt out at him: "QGPB." He stared at the CD, unnerved. With shaking fingers, he slipped the CD into his inside jacket pocket, and returned the box to the drawer. Stunned at the implications, Destin sat there a moment before he pushed the chair back.

It was a soft sound, more a squeak than anything, followed by a thump. Startled, he tightened, but he had no time to react. In an instant, a shock-wave of light exploded before his eyes, and then the pain hit, buckling him. He never quite fell prone on the carpeting. Instead, he managed to catch his weight on his trick knee, and that pain was almost worse.

Through a sea of gray twilight, Destin saw a slight, dark figure move swiftly away, running now, and then he heard the front door slam. Darkness then moved in and enveloped him.

CHAPTER 20

"Dai Yu," Amy said over the intercom, "the Colonel wants to see you."

"Thanks." Dai Yu switched off the intercom and got up. She ran into him in the hall outside his office.

"You wanted to see me?"

"Yes. Grab a seat in my office."

She did so, and Petrowski came in a moment later. Harvey Spenser, head of security with the DOE, and Franz Stjernholm, his top engineer on the cyclotron project, scuttled in behind him, apprehensive. As usual, both men were rabbits running scared. She frowned. Spenser was the worse. He wore his pants supported with suspenders. As outdated as his personality. His dark eyes carried hidden pain, hard times. He shuffled about stoop-shouldered, whipped. Hardly the image of a top DOE official.

Petrowski interrupted her thoughts. "Harvey, you're the man I wanted to see. I haven't received your list on who's attending the test." Behind him, the bearded Franz Stjernholm looked at the floor.

Dai Yu studied Stjernholm, who was a different matter. Stjernholm had possibilities, but he misdirected his talent. A damn pacifist.

She turned her attention back to Spenser, an enigma. Why was his spirit broken? She didn't know but she detested it nonetheless.

"What are you talking about?" Spenser was saying. "I sent that list to Dai Yu yesterday." His voice was placid, but his face contorted. He was upset.

Dai Yu nodded. "He did."

Petrowski was angry. "You were to deliver it to me alone, Harvey."

Spenser cut him off. "Call me Harv or Spenser. You know I hate Harvey."

"Well, *Harvey*, then I suggest you pick it up from Dai Yu after this meeting and bring it to me. The way I word my presentation will depend on who attends."

Spenser turned to leave, as did Stjernholm, but Petrowski motioned them to stay. "DOE types are all alike, Dai Yu. Look at Harvey." He snorted. "So are the engineers. They feed on power and control but have the courage of jellyfish."

Spenser stiffened. "It's the bullies of the world who are usually the cowards."

Petrowski's eyes registered shock, and his face contorted with hatred. "Don't push it. Get me the list – now!"

Dai Yu giggled inwardly. *Score one for the opposition*. It didn't happen often.

He turned to Stjernholm. "Do you have the collider function and maintenance reports completed? I don't want any last minute hang-ups."

"I've already given them to Dai Yu," Franz said stiffly. "Anything else?"

"No, but make sure you're not late for the test."

When the men had retreated out the door, Petrowski readjusted his jacket. "Let's go to the bathroom, Dai Yu."

"Sir?" Dai Yu was shocked.

"I have to shave," Petrowski said. "I need you to take some notes. No time to wait."

"Yes sir," she said. She trailed behind as he strode into the sumptuously marbled executive bathroom and stopped, surprised. Though marble was cold, it was one of the most elegant natural materials of the earth. Streaks of subdued ochre, tans and browns decorated the walls. It had been modeled after the bathrooms at the dam, built by the TVA in the 1940s. In a fleeting glimpse, she wished she could have the Colonel to herself in a honeymoon suite made of marble.

Petrowski stepped up to the large, free-standing basin with its broad top, dropped a rubber stopper into the drain, and filled the sink half full of warm water. Whistling again, he stepped over to a recessed shelf along one wall containing cubbyholes. He pulled his shaving kit and towel from one nook and began his daily morning ritual of shaving the old-fashioned way – with a good hand razor and plenty of foam.

After finishing, he towel-dried his face and chin and inspected his handiwork in the mirror.

"Harvey's so naïve," he said. "But manageable. And whether Harvey admits it or not, he will do whatever is necessary to protect his career. I worry about Stjernholm, though. I don't trust him because he's an idealist."

"You called me in to tell me that, sir?"

"No." Petrowski studied her for a moment. "You did a fine job with the Vayhinger problem, so I thought you wouldn't mind keeping an eye on Stjernholm, especially during the test."

"Certainly. Anything else?" Dai Yu trailed him back to his office.

Before he could answer, his phone rang and he waved her to a seat. "Petrowski," he said. Even across the desk, Dai Yu could hear a series of clicks, and then a deep voice said, "It's me."

"Code name?" Petrowski said.

"Blue Skies," the voice answered.

"Good." Petrowski leaned back in his chair, smiling. "Been hoping you'd call. I heard you took care of my problem."

"Sure did. The firefighter won't talk."

"Fine." Petrowski put his feet on the desk. "No loose ends I hope?"

"Not exactly," Blue Skies said, hesitating. "We searched the home the night before we took care of Vayhinger, but our search turned up nothing. We'll go back through the home in a day or two, if you wish."

"That's a surprise," Petrowski said thoughtfully. "Vayhinger couldn't have had many chances to hide those papers. Odd, in fact. Have you any ideas about the whereabouts of the documents?"

"Yes and no," Blue Skies said. "Our search was thorough. It's my belief that Vayhinger didn't come home until late the night we searched his place. I'm doing some checking on that right now. If it's true, we searched his place too early. We'll have to go back."

"I see." Petrowski sat up. "Then search the home again and check into where he may have been before he returned home. And don't stop until you're satisfied with what happened to those papers."

"Done. Anything else you need?"

"As a matter of fact," Petrowski said, "there is. Since Thunder botched the job with George Eisenhardt—"

"That isn't true," Blue Skies said. "Eisenhardt was killed and the Orlando Police Department has no leads. Thunder carried out his assignment."

"He's a rookie by your own admission."

"New in my department doesn't necessarily mean 'inexperienced.' Get to your point."

"He left loose ends. I thought you understood that I wanted Eisenhardt's murder to be a robbery or a drug deal gone bad. I wanted no questions. But now we have Destin Campbell in the thick of this. He may even be able to identify Thunder, and since he's a PR man with newspaper connections, we have trouble. That's why I asked *you* to take care of Campbell. *You*, not Thunder, before it's too late. Got it?"

"But it doesn't look as if Eisenhardt told Campbell anything before he died," Blue Skies said. "Instead, your paranoia could be stirring up a hornet's nest."

"I can't take that chance. Their friendship goes way back, and Eisenhardt may have told him a great deal. I've had my own people looking into this, trying to find out what, if anything, he knows."

"Have you found out anything?"

"Not yet," Petrowski said. "But we now know that he's in North Carolina." He was not surprised when Blue Skies remained silent for a fraction of a second longer than normal. "You thought he was still in Orlando, didn't you?" Petrowski laughed and Dai Yu joined in.

When their laughter died, she could hear Blue Skies cursing. "Okay, so you know where he is. We'll get right on it and we'll take care of him, but save me some time and tell me where to find him."

This time it was Petrowski who was silent. "He's somewhere in the vicinity of our labs, though we're not quite sure exactly where. And as far as I'm concerned, that's too damn coincidental."

"How do you know that?"

"He left a note at the Eisenhardt home in Sylva and we intercepted it. Our operative spotted him there the night before but he wasn't in a position to take care of him at that time. Unfortunately, the note was rather vague. He said something about being called away to Fontana."

"You don't seem to be doing any better than us," Blue Skies said. "And shouldn't you be worried about Linda and what she knows?"

Petrowski didn't answer for several seconds. "Linda isn't a threat." His voice held a new note of malice. "Before you pass judgment, you'd better look at the papers from the other day. We did a fine job of putting a roadblock in Campbell's path. Now all we have to do is find and eliminate him. And I think you can do that job better than me. Take care of it personally this time, won't you? I don't want any more errors."

"All right." Blue Skies's voice was noncommittal. "I'll take care of this personally, but it's going to cost you."

CHAPTER 21

A STRANGE darkness enveloped Destin, leaving him conscious yet loath to move. The stranger, he was sure, had fled. He'd heard the front door open and close, and then he listened as the cat-like footfalls of the attacker receded down the front walk.

Painfully, he pulled himself up from the den carpeting and sat for some time at the desk, rubbing his knee. *Bad luck.*

The blow on the head had been light, and though his headache returned, he suffered no lasting damage. Same with his knee. The pain faded.

He moved to the front door, left ajar. The street was quiet and empty, and the vapor light at the corner cast a feeble light. He slipped out the front door, pulling it shut behind him. He crept across the porch and lowered himself into a bed of shrubs and bushes that stretched along the front of the cottage.

Sticking to the shadows, he sidled over to a large tulip tree at the upper edge of the property. In the shadows of the trunk, he again studied the quiet street. The crickets had resumed their evening chatter. The only other noise he heard was the babble of the small stream that paralleled the street. No one was about.

Using his good knee to take his weight, he jumped the small stream and then ducked down the street, sticking to the shadows.

When he limped into Karen's driveway, she came out.

"You didn't call me," she chided, but he ignored her.

"How did it go?" she persisted. "You all right?"

Destin winced and leaned against her door.

"You're hurt," she cried, reaching for him, but he shook his head.

"No, really, I'll be fine in a moment."

"Come in and let me look at you," she ordered, "and don't give me any lip." He didn't protest, and with her support, he limped into her kitchen. The bright kitchen lights made him blink.

"Is it your knee?"

"Yes," he answered. "No." He looked at her, red-faced.

She grinned. "I certainly can't look at your knee unless you drop your pants. So drop them." She had been one step ahead of him.

He unzipped his pants and let them fall to floor. "Where's Tammy?" he asked, looking about the kitchen.

"Oh, she left on a date with Ryan, but she shouldn't be too late." She examined the knee. "It's bruised. Let's put an ice pack on it." She grabbed up her kitchen hand towel, scooped some ice out of the freezer, and wrapped it up. "Here." She handed it to him.

He applied the ice until the knee became numb and then scooted the lightweight towel around so he could bear the cold. Karen seated herself opposite him at the table. "So what happened at the house?"

He told her how he had let himself in through a kitchen window and found the den, how he'd searched the desk and had located the computer disk.

"You found a disk?" She leaned forward, excited.

"Sure did." He reached into his inside jacket pocket and withdrew the CD. "See? And look at how it's marked: QGPB."

"What does that mean?"

Destin frowned. "I have no idea, but I'm convinced it has something to do with George's death." He told her then about his discovery of the slip of paper in George's hand at the hamfest. "There's more you ought to know," he added. "I was also attacked in my home the night I found George – later that night."

"Oh shit." Her eyes widened, forming round circles. "What happened?"

He then described the fight and how the attacker had fled after he broke the assailant's jaw. She sat in silence for a while and busied herself pouring him an iced tea. Finished, she began to pace the small kitchen.

"This is getting more serious every moment." She sank into her chair again. "We could all be in real danger. And that disk – if anything is on it – could be the evidence we need to find George's killer. Let's boot it and see what it says. You up to it?"

"Yes, of course." Destin rose stiffly. "My knee is feeling better too." He set the ice down and pulled on his pants. "Where's your computer?"

"Next to my radio gear. Come with me."

She led the way and Destin followed, applying the ice pack to his head. She seated herself at the computer, and then looked up.

"No. " She shook her head. "Don't tell me you got hit in the same spot again!"

Destin grinned sheepishly. "A glancing blow. I'm fine, really."

She frowned, eyeing him, and then slid the disk in. "Here it is," she said.

The monitor showed a lengthy document entitled "Quark Gluon Plasma Beam."

Destin gripped Karen's shoulders. "So that's what QGPB stands for."

"That makes sense." Karen straightened, smoothing her blue and white plaid shirt. "I'll bet the beam is a weapon – the one Earl talked about so much. A top secret weapon." She swiveled in her chair and eyed Destin.

"I'm sure you've hit it." Destin leaned closer to the screen and they both examined the document. It was more of a specs sheet than a narrative description, describing the beam as a weapon of war and how the power for it was developed from the use of three tandem accelerators. It also described how the final accelerator served as a collider for heavy ions, thus producing the plasma beam.

They read in awed silence. "No wonder they're willing to kill to keep this secret," Destin said.

"Such a weapon in the wrong hands could mean the end of life on Earth as we know it. Can you imagine what would happen if it ever got into the hands of terrorists? Those madmen wouldn't hesitate to use it!" Karen's shoulders sagged.

"Scary, isn't it?" Destin leaned over her. "As insurance, let's make a copy of this disk. I'll hide one and you can hide the other. But where?"

He thought about it while she made a copy of the CD for him. He straightened and set aside the ice pack. "Our hiding spots for these disks are going to have to be good."

"Don't we have enough proof already?" Karen asked, as she handed Destin one copy of the disk. "We take it to the police – perhaps that Gilbretti fellow – and tell them what we know. That ought to change his tune."

She stood up and turned off the computer.

"No, it isn't enough. Remember, the police in Florida never knew about the scrap of paper I found in George's hand. In fact, you're the only one who knows."

"Do you still have the paper?"

"No," Destin said. "It dissolved in all the blood when George was killed. The remnants got washed down the sink."

"Well, even so, I think the disk should be enough."

Destin shook his head. "Karen, look, it may not prove enough. It establishes motive for George's murder perhaps, but not a definite link."

Karen became rigid. "You're the damn link. You've been attacked three times now – *three times* – and any fool should be able to see that."

Destin shook his head again. "No, we need more. For example, if we could catch that guy in the white sneakers that attacked me, the police might get him to talk and then we'd have what we need."

Still upset, Karen met his gaze. "Destin, don't you see how this mess is bigger than George and Linda's murder? If we stop these maniacs and their weapon, we'll have avenged their deaths in our own way. Isn't that what George would have wanted?"

Unbidden, a picture replayed in Destin's head, and he could see his father, drunk, beating his mother. He sighed, but the memory persisted. He saw it again, how he had intervened, only to be beaten and kicked, over and over.

"Maybe," Destin said, "but you weren't the one who got attacked three times. Besides, George was my best friend – my closest friend. I owe it to him to bring his killer to justice. Whether you understand or not, I'm not giving up, not yet at least."

He picked up the disk and walked back into the living room with Karen trailing behind.

Still angry, she said, "All right. You win. Now let's find a hiding spot for my disk." She looked about the room and shrugged. "There aren't many good spots in this room. I suppose I could hide it in the couch cushions."

"That would be the first place they'd look," Destin countered. He sauntered into the kitchen. "Where do you keep your flour?"

Puzzled, Karen pointed. "In the cupboard directly above the sink."

Destin reached up and found a blue plastic set of two containers. The larger one contained flour, the smaller sugar. "This will do," he said, satisfied. "But I'll need a pint or quart-sized zip lock bag."

Karen found him one in the drawer next to the silverware, and he put the disk inside and buried the bag in the container of flour. He then returned the flour and sugar to their places in the cupboard.

Finished, Destin turned to her. "Where are Ben's papers?"

"I have them on the radio desk."

"Not good enough." Destin gazed at her thoughtfully. "Show them to me."

She led him to her desk and handed the sheets to him. He studied them, and then wandered out of the room and into Tammy's bedroom of pink ruffles and painted furniture. He ambled over to her desk. Over it, a shelf contained textbooks, a dictionary, and a notebook marked SAT. "What's this?" Destin asked, pointing to the notebook.

"Tammy's study guide for the SAT exam."

"Does she use it often?"

Karen pursed her lips. "As a matter of fact, no. That material is outdated now. She has the more recent material in her nightstand. Why?"

"Then it's a perfect hiding spot." Destin opened the binder's rings and slid the papers into the center of the SAT notes. He closed it and returned the notebook to the shelf.

Karen giggled. When they'd returned to the kitchen, she asked, "Where do you go from here?"

Destin set his jaw. "I'm going to see Mitch Bartow at NOAA tomorrow as we'd decided. Maybe he'll be able to help. God knows we need all the help we can get."

CHAPTER 22

BONNIE finished loading her luggage into the car the next morning on schedule. She was tired from a bad night's sleep, and a monotonous drizzle made it worse. The Nissan started roughly, then quit. "Lovely," she thought. "I may not even get there." She tried restarting it, but her efforts failed.

Betsy wandered out in her robe and scuffs, watching. "Can't start it?"

Bonnie got out of the car and kicked a tire. "No! No! Now what am I going to do?"

"That's simple, hon. Borrow mine."

"Yours?" Bonnie stared at Betsy. "But you need your Volkswagen to— "

"No, Harold is taking me to the airport. Remember? I told you yesterday."

"Of course." Bonnie sighed then grinned. "You wouldn't mind me borrowing the bug – really?"

"Not at all." Betsy turned. Let me pull it out of the garage for you. I'll be one minute."

Bonnie watched Betsy back the aged VW out of her garage. She had hand-painted it when the original paint job had faded. Now, the faded yellow only served as a background for a variety of large, kindergarten-style flowers painted over every open surface of the car. A vinyl luggage carrier rode atop a roof rack. Old fashioned but garishly cute. It fit Betsy.

After detailed directions about how to operate the VW's stick shift and the reserve tank, Bonnie waved goodbye, put the car in gear, and headed north. When she reached the open highway, her spirits lifted. Beyond Knoxville, the commercial buildings quickly gave way to small businesses and homes, and then farms bordered in white fencing.

Morristown straddled a ridge, one of several in the area. She passed several businesses and then more buildings congealed into a business district. Ducking into a downtown pharmacy, she asked the young clerk about a good place to stay.

"The Embassy Suites Hotel is nice," the woman drawled. "The hotel is a few miles north, near Cherokee Lake."

"Thanks for the tip," Bonnie said. She turned left onto 25E and headed down a steep hill. The remnants of the commercial district transformed into vacant lots, then open territory.

In spite of a persistent drizzle, she had no trouble locating the hotel on the outskirts of town. The entrance was fashioned out of large, sand-colored stucco arches reminiscent of the Southwest, and even from the outside, she could see that it formed a "U" around a swimming pool.

Bonnie parked the Volkswagen near the entrance portico and went inside to register. A huge stone fireplace dominated one side of the inn, and large, comfortable chairs were arranged near the fireplace. After checking in, Bonnie went straight to her room and took a short nap. Then she dressed for her meeting at five.

Somewhat refreshed, she sauntered out on the balcony overlooking the pool, and placed a call on her cell phone to Charles Edwards, the attorney representing Jake and Mark's interests. She got the receptionist at his office who told her that Mr. Edwards had left moments before. The woman gave her directions. The Bledsoe estate was nearby, located along the shores of Cherokee Lake.

She left the inn and headed for the meeting. The weather had gone from bleak to worse. Huge thunderheads bunched together on the western horizon, and the rain came in spurts, blitzing all landmarks from view for minutes at a time.

She located the shoreline road and followed it with great difficulty. After driving for some time, she wheeled the car around, angry. The numbers were too high. She retraced her path, checking the numbers along the road. Most of the homes were other large estates, set far off the road, hidden from view. Lovely brick or stone posts marked the entranceways, yet few, if any, had name plaques. She had nearly reached the main highway again before she found the number 312.

Disgruntled, she turned in the drive and followed it for some distance through mixed areas of woods and manicured lawns until she faced a large southern-style plantation house.

The estate was a duplicate of Scarlett O'Hara's Tara. It gleamed even in the downpour. Nevertheless, there was an aura about it that made her shudder. A foreboding, black and unbidden, crept in.

Parking under a large, three story portico next to a Porsche 911 Carrera, she got out, willing herself to be positive and to ignore her fears. She remembered Jake Bledsoe, the man who had owned the mansion and chided herself. He had been a consummate businessman, and yet, he always had a certain kindness. "Southerners are genteel," he'd often told her, "especially folks from Tennessee. And they'll give you the shirt off their backs if you need help." She hoped she'd find his kindness inside.

She rang the doorbell, answered by the fierce barking of a dog. She heard movement on the other side of the closed door, and a housekeeper opened it. She was a woman in her fifties, and she wore an apron over a gray dress. A large, very thin Dalmatian ran toward them, sliding the last foot or two across the tile. He snapped and Bonnie shrank back.

"Pinto!" the woman yelled. She reached down and grabbed the dog's collar, restraining the dog. "Stop it now!" She slapped the dog's rump, dragging him off. "Sam never did get him trained."

"Nice dog." Bonnie tiptoed forward.

"Come on in," the housekeeper said. "You must be Bonnie Rhodes."

Bonnie nodded.

"Then follow me." She led the way to the rear of the home, where a large library sat opposite a living room. Bonnie hesitated at the doorway, taking one last look at the elegant stairway that spiraled up two floors from the entrance hall. Overhead, at the peak of the house, two large skylights provided light on either side of the main supports, and from the apex of these supports, a large chandelier hung down, lighting the main floor entrance area.

She turned back and followed the woman into the library. It was the kind found only on estates in Europe. The ceiling of the room was very high along the inside wall, allowing for a built-in oak bookcase of unusual height. The windows at the rear and side provided a view of the backyard, the lake, and wooded areas flanking the estate. It was lovely, elegant even, and yet she could not shake her sense of ominous foreboding.

The room's lighting was soft, almost dim in the darkness of the storm, and it took Bonnie a few moments for her eyes to adjust. Two striped sofas and a Persian rug formed a grouping, and several men stood as she moved towards them.

A portly man with white hair shuffled forward, and Bonnie recognized him as her father's attorney, Charles Edwards.

"How are you, Bonnie?"

Before she could answer, he'd turned to make introductions.

"Bonnie, I want you to meet Lionel Brooks who is on your left, and next to him is Sam Bledsoe. On your right is Mark Bledsoe."

She nodded to each. Edwards drew up a wing back chair and placed it near the right sofa. "Have a seat," he said, and she did. The others seated themselves.

She studied Mark first. He was a slender man, dark haired, probably in his early thirties. Slightly stooped, he seemed pensive and preoccupied. Edwards had told her that Mark was married. His wife was not present though.

Sam, Jake Bledsoe's bachelor grandson, was slightly younger. An extremely tall, handsome man, his blonde hair contrasted with his deeply tanned face. Though his face had become lined from too much sun, it made him more virile. He could have been a male model. She remembered his reputation as a playboy then. No wonder he was a hot item with the girls. In spite of his virility, he had a cold, leering demeanor.

Lionel Brooks, the attorney representing Sam, was an older man whose bleary eyes bespoke of cataracts. He mopped his face frequently with his handkerchief and glanced at his watch. "You're quite late." He stared at Bonnie and his eyes, though bleary, were as cold as Sam's.

"I apologize," Bonnie said, "but the rain made it difficult for me to find your place." Edwards and Mark nodded sympathetically.

Brooks sighed. "Let's get right to business."

Bonnie turned toward Sam, but the only emotion she saw was his leer, and she blushed, immediately self-conscious that her rain-soaked white blouse had become transparent.

She cleared her throat and stepped back. "Yes, let's get to business."

"While we waited for you, we had a chance to go over the will and some of our options," Edwards said. "It's a complex issue. The will has several – ah – weaknesses all right. I doubt that it will be settled easily."

Brooks nodded soberly, and Sam openly smirked. "I want to go over those provisions if you don't mind," she said. "We need to know where my center stands in all this."

"I can understand your concern." Edwards said. "Unfortunately, your grant is the one aspect of the will that isn't muddy." He cleared his throat and looked uncomfortable. "The grant clearly provides that the inheritor of this estate, ostensibly Mark here, will be responsible for its maintenance and execution. Further, it is up to the inheritor to decide whether or not to abolish the grant.

"Now, the challenges to the will are formidable, as I said a moment ago. This case will go to court, and believe me, litigation will not be an overnight process. In the meantime, the will makes it clear that in such a case of litigation, the grant is suspended." He paused again.

"It's true that in the end your grant could be restored, but it may be a long time before that happens. Clearly, you're going to have to look to other sources for funding, at least for now." Edwards coughed, and it led to a series of coughing spasms that hung in the damp air. When he caught his breath he said, "I feel bad that you traveled all this distance in order to hear such depressing news."

Bonnie nodded bleakly and pushed wet tendrils of hair behind her ears. She noticed that Sam's eyes were undressing her. She reddened. "We have an attorney at the university — "

"You mean Doc Treadway?" Sam said.

"Yes."

"Brooks talked to him today before his surgery, and they discussed all the provisions, so Doc understands the situation. Brooks did so because he felt an attorney like Doc would understand the center's problems – better. Treadway knows that for now, the grant is on hold, as is the rest of this will. You're going to have to look elsewhere for your funding." Sam swaggered to his feet.

"My apologies, Ms. Rhodes. Maybe we can make some peace – some compromises. You see, I can think of a few ways you might be able to persuade me to help you. Let's start with dinner, shall we, and go from there?" His eyes held a lusty darkness.

Bonnie straightened. "No, thank you," Mr. Bledsoe," she said through clenched teeth. "I deal only with people I trust. Furthermore, I know a couple of nice gorillas I'd rather go to bed with, than you."

Sam's face flushed beet red. He stepped closer, menacing. "Why, you little whore!"

Brooks and Edwards both grabbed Sam's arms and restrained him. He shrugged them off but stepped back.

"Good day, Mr. Brooks." Still haughty, she spun toward Edwards.

Edwards looked at the floor, unable to meet her eyes. "I'll call you tonight at your hotel, if you don't mind," he managed at last. "Where are you staying?"

Bonnie hesitated, her mind in wild turmoil. She glanced at Sam, who had moved near the set of windows. Although his back was toward her now, he had a cocky set to his shoulders. She cringed, wishing she had never come. "I'm staying at the Embassy Suites Hotel," she said. "Thanks."

He nodded and she retreated outside to her car. The Volkswagen wheezed to life in a puff of blue smoke. She put it in gear, and as she passed the parked red Carerra, she noticed that the name *Sam* had been detailed on the driver's door. It figures, she thought.

Back at her room, she threw herself on the bed and sobbed. She pounded the quilt and pillow, her punching bag, but her torrent of tears gave her little comfort. Later, exhausted, she pulled herself together. Her first instinct had been to run, to get in the car and drive home, then and there. But she didn't relish a trip home in the storm and darkness.

She went into the bathroom and showered, scrubbing herself until her skin turned pink. She wanted to get rid of the disgusting scent of Sam. Feeling better, she chose a black sequined dress from her luggage and piled her hair atop her head. Stray curls lined the sides of her face, but they looked nice in the mirror.

She wiggled her tongue at her reflection in the mirror. *Take that, Sam. What goes around, comes around.* She nodded, heartened. Perhaps it was time to send resumes to some of her colleagues. UT wasn't the only game in town. Ready at last, she rode the elevator down to the lobby and went into the restaurant.

The restaurant was a mixture of textured wallpaper and dark wood. At one end, an inside bar provided smaller tables and dimmer lights. She entered and ordered dinner. The dimness felt good, and she ate with more gusto than she expected. Many hours had gone by without a real meal.

After she had eaten, a white-shirted bartender came and asked her if she wanted anything to drink. She ordered a bourbon and soda, and as she waited, her eyes drifted around the plush bar. A man sat at another table, and his eyes met hers. He was, she thought, very familiar.

Then she placed him. He was the man she had met at the Orlando Police Department only a week before. Surprised, she stared at him. Then it became admiration. He was muscular, with broad shoulders, a wide forehead, and blue eyes that lit his face. He smiled and rose. She liked the black knit golfing shirt he wore, and his gray slacks looked expensive.

"Would you care for some company?"

Bonnie felt the heat rise in her face. "Sure. Destin, right?"

He nodded and took a seat next to her.

"This is such a surprise. What on earth brings you to Morristown?"

"I came here today for an appointment which didn't pan out, and I'm here unexpectedly for the night," Destin said.

"I, too, had an appointment that didn't pan out." A hint of a smile tugged at the corners of her mouth, and she set aside her drink. "What didn't work out for you?"

"I was to meet a man at the weather station south of town, but he hasn't returned from some trip. He's supposed to be back at work tomorrow, so I hope to see him in the morning," Destin said.

"Is this part of your work with Lockheed Martin or with the Orlando Sentinel? I remember you mentioning that."

"No, not that." Destin's face became drawn and thoughtful. "Remember that friend of mine who died recently?"

Bonnie nodded. "Yes."

"Well, like me, the man I am to meet tomorrow, Mitch Bartow, was a friend of his." He twisted the cocktail napkin that had been placed under his iced tea, and Bonnie knew that the subject was painful for him.

"I'm so sorry," she said. She gazed into Destin's eyes and the blue of them, honest and clear, held the pain. It touched her heart.

"So tell me, what do you do for a living at UT? I don't think you ever mentioned that," Destin said.

Bonnie smiled. "I'm an anthropologist, a linguistics anthropologist. I specialize in the research of primates – gorillas – and their ability to communicate."

Astonished, Destin sipped his tea. Then, "How on earth did you get involved in that line of work?"

"It's a really long story." Bonnie looked down, twisting her hands in her lap. Her heart raced. The hunk seated opposite her was one of the most exciting men she'd ever met.

She fumbled for words, a quick way to tell Destin. "I worked a long time in college and graduate programs, and I even studied overseas for a while. Then I went to work in San Francisco at a primate center, where a rich man from here in Morristown met me. Have you ever heard of Jake Bledsoe?"

"Who hasn't heard of the king of chicken?" he said. "Didn't he die recently?"

"Yes." Bonnie's face contorted. "He was a fine man, a great man. He helped me a great deal. In fact, his death is why I'm here. He'd given the University of Tennessee a grant, which paid the bulk of the university's expenses to run and maintain my baby, the Center of Gorilla Research."

"I see."

"His death means an end to the grant, it would seem, so I'm faced with finding a new job." She sighed. "It hasn't been the best day of my life, and the storm this afternoon didn't help either."

"Amazing," Destin remarked, and he gathered up her two hands and squeezed them in sympathy.

"We've both lost more than one person recently."

Bonnie nodded, but she wondered who, besides his friend, George, had died. He looked too sad to question, though, so she kept silent.

"They were people who helped us, meant a great deal to us. Without them, we're both stumbling around. We're in the same fix, you and me. We don't know what the future holds for us." He retreated into the silence of sadness.

Destin had not fully withdrawn his hands, and Bonnie became aware how one of his fingers still touched her own. She felt his warmth, his masculine virility, and loved the way her stomach twisted at his touch. She withdrew her hand and downed her drink. "I...I really must go to bed. It's getting late, and I need to get back to UT first thing in the morning." She rose.

Destin had risen as well. "Let me get your drink." He moved toward the waiter.

"No, really, that's all right," she said, but he ignored her and paid for their drinks. She stood awkwardly, waiting for him to return, wishing he would return, and yet afraid to stay longer. But before she could decide, he was at her side again.

He gently propelled her toward the lobby in silence. Near the elevators, he stopped and faced her. "It was a pleasure meeting you tonight. You gave meaning to my day and brightened it."

"Me too." Bonnie stepped into the elevator.

"Wait," he said. "I would love to call you sometime."

Bonnie smiled, and she realized that she had ached to hear those words. "I'd like that." She fished a business card from her purse. " I gave you one in Florida, but here's another."

"Yes, I remember," he said.

She left him then, and back in her room, she slipped into her pajamas. As she lay down to sleep, she stretched. The weight of a bad day melted away, and the sheets felt delicious. Maybe the world had not ended, she decided at last. In fact, it might just be a beginning.

CHAPTER 23

DAI YU poked her head into Petrowski's office. "Anything else I need to take care of before the test? Most of the visitors have arrived."

Petrowski looked up from his paperwork. "Yes. Stick with Stjernholm today. I don't trust him. Which reminds me, did Franz complete a full inspection of the particle accelerator this morning?"

"Yes sir," Dai Yu said. "I went along with him. When will you be coming to the test area?"

"Right now." Petrowski stood up. "Do I look all right?"

Dai Yu studied his uniform. It was neatly pressed and his medals were precisely lined up over his pocket. "You're fine."

"Then let's go in together."

"Yes sir." Dai Yu felt a thrill ripple down her spine. He was formidable in his uniform.

They took the elevator to the lower floor, and then walked the long halls to the viewing area. Spenser joined them at the entrance, but Stjernholm was already there, seated in the front row, a few seats away from Congresswoman Valerie Blake. Dressed in a gray suit, she was a polished woman with gray hair in a French twist. Two government officials sat on either side of her.

Everyone fell silent as Dai Yu, Petrowski and Spenser moved to the front of the room near a bank of computers and monitors. As she seated herself behind one computer console, Petrowski and Spenser moved to the podium at the front of the room.

Petrowski spoke first. "As you know, I'm assigned to Fontana Labs as a military liaison, working on civilian top secret defense contracts. It's my honor to have you here today to witness the first official test of our Relativistic Heavy Ion Collider, the RHIC." He paused. "I first want to introduce you to Franz Stjernholm, a physicist here at the labs. He was the man who developed the RHIC."

Stjernholm nodded from his seat in the front row.

"And at my side is Harvey Spenser, our security man with the DOE. Mr. Spenser is going to brief you today about the RHIC and what the test will consist of."

He stepped back, and all eyes turned to Spenser. Though stooped, Dai Yu saw that Spenser spoke in calm, measured words.

"Gentlemen – and Madame – as you may know, this facility is under contract to the Department of Energy. The DOE has been involved in the Star Wars project since Reagan was president." He paused so the audience could digest his statement.

From her console, Dai Yu listened to his words. Star Wars was a program for the defense of the U.S., providing an early warning system and a network of defensive weapons in space, originally designed to protect the U.S. from Russia, though the war on terrorism had broadened the playing field.

At its conception, the Star Wars program was the brainchild of the Reagan administration, and it depended on accelerator research for the technology it would provide. That was why the Supercollider, the SSC, and other kinds of accelerator projects gained approval at a time when the funding these projects worried everyone. She looked up as Spenser continued.

"Fontana Labs has now developed the Relativistic Heavy Ion Collider, the RHIC, which is the most advanced, most powerful accelerator and collider in the world today. In fact, we've developed two of them, one on either side of the dam, and they're below your feet at a depth of several hundred feet. Each one can achieve velocities that make other accelerators, such as the SSC, seem slow in comparison. And, our RHICs were each built in a very small circle, 3.8 kilometers in circumference, unlike the SSC.

"Your handout will give you the stats, but take the SSC at the Texas Energy Research Institute, TERI, for example. They use two, fifty-four mile superconducting synchrotrons in order to smash atoms. Or, as in the case of some lineacs, about the same distance in a straight line." He paused again.

"The RHIC uses several accelerators and boosters in tandem: a Random Van de Graaf, the Booster, then an AGS, and finally, the RHIC itself.

"The DOE has spent over ten billion dollars on accelerators to date. Take the SSC, for example. It hasn't produced the results it should have for the cost." Spenser cleared his throat. "Now that the RHIC is a reality, the DOE plans to close most linear accelerators as well as some SSC's."

The scientists who crowded the room groaned. They, and Dai Yu, understood that the unemployment rolls were about to grow.

Dr. McLean from the Texas Energy Research Institute stood up. "I object to your statement about results," he said. "Our work is making simple X-ray technology passé. And look at what TERI has accomplished when it comes to cutting steel."

Petrowski interceded. "TERI has made gains, but nothing compared to our operation. At first, our work focused mostly on the AGS, as well as an off-shoot of the old Klystron. But we realized that unless we could make greater advances, the DOE would lose interest, and then our program would be cut." He paused.

"Then we began experimenting with electrostatic accelerators, which we used in tandem with some of our other accelerators. Each one is a staircase and accelerates the particles at less cost than one or two working together. Because of these changes, we've advanced our understanding of particle asymmetry interactions. Our research, literally, is reinventing quantum physics and our understanding of the universe. This is only the beginning." Spenser stopped, pointing at Petrowski. "Colonel?"

Petrowski stepped forward. "Although the RHIC can be put to many uses – and will – we have to think of our world situation right now. Three double agents have been caught within the past eight to ten years, and we now know that they passed along our accelerator technology to Russia. That's left the U.S. vulnerable and compromised. Even though our relations with Russia are better, we shouldn't be foolish and assume that our technology won't be passed on to the Middle East and elsewhere."

Bleakness settled on those assembled. "The RHIC, however, puts us in the lead again," Petrowski said.

"Congresswoman Valerie Blake here," the woman said, who was seated near Stjernholm. "Exactly how does the RHIC work?"

Colonel Petrowski pointed to Franz. "Let Dr. Stjernholm answer that." He stepped back as Franz stood up and turned around, facing the group.

"The RHIC sends out two beams of heavy ions, atoms stripped of their electrons. In other words, all that remains in the beams are bare nuclei," Franz said, his voice filling the hushed room. "One beam is sent out in one direction, and the other is sent in the opposite direction. Both travel at the speed of light or nearly so. And when they collide, they explode, producing an enormous amount of plasma energy.

"The Booster is more powerful than the Van de Graaf and the AGS. That means the particles are already speeded up by the time they reach the RHIC. At that point we extract the ions in bunches and then we transfer them to one of two collider rings in the RHIC. The explosion that results in the rings produces plasma and is being used to further science and industry, and — "

Petrowski put a hand on Franz's shoulder and gently propelled him back a step or two.

"A slight correction, Dr. Stjernholm," he said. "We've modified the accelerator this past week so we could conduct a weapons test."

"Last week? I – was on vacation except for yesterday, spent on reports." Dazed, Franz licked his lips. "You can't be serious. Fontana Labs was withdrawn from the Star Wars program a few years back. We're devoting our work to science and industry."

"Correction again, Dr. Stjernholm," Petrowski said. "That was what you heard and believed, but we've always been a part of Star Wars. Where do you think the money has come from, and why has it always come so readily? Huh?"

The room became deathly still, and Franz looked ashen. Spenser's voice filled the void. "We modified the RHIC so at six different points, the ions collide. With that many points in the ring, there are literally tens of thousands of collisions each second.

"The best part is how we devised a way that these collisions could occur *outside* the accelerator. In order to get that to happen, we had to cross the beams in six alternate conduits that reach right up to the surface."

Congresswoman Blake spoke up. "Are you trying to tell us that you have developed a laser weapon?" A stir swept the room but quickly died.

"No, there's a big difference between a laser beam and our quark gluon plasma beam," Spenser said. "Though we use a laser to cut a path for the plasma."

Dai Yu watched Franz step forward defiantly. "Even if you are able to focus the plasma into a beam, it would only last for an infinitesimal part of a second. Therefore, there's no way you could direct it at a target."

"Wrong again," Petrowski said. "We've rebuilt the control center behind us, where our scientist, Dai Yu Chin, is sitting." Petrowski pushed Franz aside.

Dai Yu turned to Petrowski and waited expectantly, shivering with anticipation.

Petrowski continued. "A CCD provides the interface, and we're using a grid diversion and an alternate accelerator path module, and of course we have a satellite overhead in stationary orbit at the moment to provide telemetry and alignment."

Aghast, Franz stepped back. "The beam is extremely dangerous," he warned. He looked at the gathered group for support. "That kind of a beam is hotter than the surface of the sun. It could vaporize us instantly. It might start a chain reaction that no one could stop. It might even cause a tear in the space-time continuum. More frightening is what can happen to the accelerator and the ground below us." He closed his eyes against his own terror.

Spenser tucked his hands under his suspenders and he rocked on the balls of his feet. "Not a chance."

Petrowski scowled at Spenser, a withering look. Spenser shrunk on the spot. "When we first tested the atom bomb, many scientists were concerned that a chain reaction would occur during the explosion, which might even destroy the planet. However, scientists argued that such a chain reaction would not occur, because the farther the particles travel away from the reaction, the more they become spaced apart, and at a certain point, the reaction stops." Petrowski paused.

"It's the same with the plasma reaction. Nothing, and I repeat nothing, is going to go amiss, so let's get on with the test."

A general spoke up. "Why did the labs choose to settle in this remote area? It must take, for example, enormous amounts of money to truck in equipment through these mountains on back roads."

"You're right," Petrowski said, "but it's a secure location, and Fontana's research work calls for incredible amounts of electrical power. The dam gives us that."

A murmur of hushed voices reverberated in the closed space, but Petrowski said, "Enough!" The visitors became instantly quiet. "Why you pompous, posturing fool," Stjernholm said under his breath.

"What did you say?" Petrowski turned beet red.

"He said nothing," Spenser said, pushing Stjernholm into his seat.

Amused, Dai Yu beckoned to Spenser, and between the two of them, they initiated the program that allowed the labs to control particle acceleration. A loud magnetic hum filled the room and everything began to vibrate.

"The magnets are now pulsing," Spenser said. "Look at the monitors. We have a special, heavily shielded camera, and it is trained on the spot of the collision." Everyone waited and watched.

"All right, see the clock on the monitor? When it reaches 2:00 p.m., we should be generating the beam."

As if in slow motion, they watched the digital clock tick. 1:59:56, 1:59:57, 1:59:58, 1:59:59....

A dazzling flash lit the monitor. Dai Yu reached up and tried to wipe away the effect, but she saw a halo on the periphery of her vision. Then all went black in the room. Complete blackness. Blacker than night. Only the halo remained with her. Emergency generator lights then lit the room in a soft orange, and she heard several alarms echo from chasms below her feet.

Congresswoman Blake rose unsteadily to her feet. "What on earth happened?"

"Damn!" Spenser spat.

Petrowski turned to him, furious. "What *is* the problem?"

"The heat alarms." Spenser gazed at Congresswoman Blake, hesitating. "We've had a bit of a problem – but nothing to worry about, ma'am."

Stjernholm leaned over Dai Yu's shoulder for a look and answered Blake. "Not much of a problem, really, if about thirteen hundred feet of molten dirt and rock isn't a problem. It looks as though part of the accelerator is gone, along with some other equipment. We're lucky to be in one piece."

Petrowski glared at him and then looked at the visitors. "The problem is minor. I want you to bear in mind that the reaction apparently lasted a few milliseconds too long, but that will be easy to adjust for future tests. The important thing to remember is that the beam works. It works! It's more advanced than anything on this earth. Think of it – a beam that no enemy could defend against, a beam so deadly it will achieve peace for the earth at last. Think of it!"

Applause hesitantly filled the room, buoyed by some of the military brass who clapped enthusiastically. Everyone stood, and their chatter of voices filled the room with congratulations and good wishes. Then the assembled group left the room one by one.

Dai Yu got up hesitantly, stretching her knotted and painful muscles. Petrowski and Spenser moved closer and studied the console screen.

Petrowski spoke first. "My God, get the heat dampers on and get some coolant pumped into the areas near that mess."

Dai Yu nodded, reseated herself, and feverishly typed at the computer, entering the activation codes.

Spenser rested his hand on Stjernholm's shoulder. "Calm down. It's minor, really. The rock will solidify and be fine in no time." He paused. "Franz, you could never understand why we decided to put the accelerator two hundred feet down. Remember that?"

Franz faced him. "Oh, I understand *now*, all right. Any more glitches and none of us will be around to argue the point." He shook his head. "I'm getting out of this hell hole."

CHAPTER 24

DESTIN awakened before seven. He stumbled into the shower at the hotel and enjoyed the way the hot water stung his skin in a thousand pinpricks. His thoughts turned to Bonnie. How lovely she had looked the night before. The thought was bittersweet because it was so hopeless. She was a professional deeply involved in her work. Not exactly conducive for a romance. He tried to put her out of his mind as he dried himself with the stiff, white towel. Not now. He had crucial work to do.

He dressed quickly, packed, and headed for the lobby. Because it was early, he found the foyer quiet. The hotel staff had placed a circular table near the entrance, and it was loaded with donuts, juice and coffee. After he turned in his key, he poured himself some juice and headed out to his truck.

When he reached the main highway, he punched the accelerator and headed southwest for the National Oceanographic Atmospheric Association's weather facility (NOAA), which was located a few miles beyond the town limits. Perhaps today, he thought, Mitch would be there, waiting for him.

NOAA was a modern facility on the east side of the road. Hard to miss. The compact brown brick building sat in the center of a large expanse of pasture. In the field on the station's right, its white radar dome gleamed in the morning sun. In the distance to the northeast, Destin could see the end of a small airport runway.

He pulled into the parking lot and strode to the front door, which was on the side of a small lobby. The door was locked for security purposes, but a microphone system allowed visitors to identify themselves and ask for someone to let them in.

Mitch Bartow himself opened the door. A nice looking man with a dark complexion, Mitch was solidly built, though his chin was losing its firmness.

"Come on in." His tone was reassuring. "Are you Destin Campbell?"

"Yes."

"Been expecting you," Mitch said. "Karen left me a pretty detailed message."

"Yes. I understand George was a close friend of yours."

"That's true. I worked for Fontana Labs for some time before I took a job as meteorologist here at NOAA. I met George at Fontana early this year, and we became good friends. I've seen less of him since I took this job in July, but we've called each other quite often."

"He's been a long time friend of mine too," Destin said.

"We seem to have mutual friends then."

They walked from the glassed-in portico through a second set of doors into the main lobby. Mitch led him to a counter, dividing the lobby from the reception area.

"Would you sign in here?" He shoved a sign-in pad across the counter. "A necessary formality."

Destin filled in the log and followed Mitch into a rectangular conference room beyond the lobby. An enormous table filled the room. Opposite him, the back wall held windows that looked onto the main floor of the weather station, with its computers, video screens, desks, and equipment. In one corner Destin glimpsed a complete radio system.

Mitch caught his glimpse and grinned. "Yep, that's the broadcasting studio we use for weather broadcasts. The broadcasts cover a large area of Tennessee and adjoining states.

"I'll give you a tour of the station after we talk. You might find our Doppler Radar system interesting." He waved Destin toward one of the cushioned executive chairs at the table and chose one across from Destin. "So what brings you here to Morristown?"

Destin leaned forward in his chair. "Haven't you heard about George yet?"

Mitch's brown eyes narrowed. "No. What about George?"

Destin's stomach tightened. "This isn't easy for me, Mitch. You see, George – is dead."

Mitch's dark complexion paled, and his eyes dropped to the table. "No."

Destin then told him about Linda. When he'd finished, Mitch arose and paced the small room. He went over to a small coffee stand placed near the entrance, poured a mug of coffee for himself and Destin, and returned to the conference table.

"How do you fit into this and why me?" He sat down.

"Because George apparently knew his life was in danger before he died. He went to Karen, and specifically told her that if anything happened to him, that she should come and talk to you. I only came here in Karen's place because I'm involved in this mess."

"How are you involved?" Mitch voice became measured again.

Destin studied Mitch. A stoical man by nature, he worked logically and methodically at what he did. Destin liked him.

"I'm involved because I found him moments before he died." Destin described his long friendship with George, how they shared a mutual interest in ham radio, and George's attack at the hamfest. He also described the subsequent events leading him to Morristown.

He drank some coffee and continued. "I feel I owe it to George – and Linda – to find their killer or killers. I may have enough information now to stop the weapon, but my problem is that I don't think there is enough of a strong link to George's killers to bring them to justice."

Mitch leaned back and studied Destin, mulling over his story. "So you feel that George was silenced because he knew something about the weapon."

"Both George and Linda, yes. The disk George wrote exposes the weapon and is probably specific enough to stop its development. When George worked at the labs, he was researching something new in magnetics. At this point I don't know how George found out about the weapon, but he did."

Mitch studied him. "Perhaps it isn't so strange. Even Karen, for example, knew about the weapon. She told me more than twice about her ex, Earl, and how he used to brag that Fontana had developed some sort of powerful weapon."

"Yeah, she told me that too."

"Right. Which proves Fontana Labs hasn't kept strict security. The weapon story fits; heck, it all fits. As far as I know, George's work in magnetics hasn't produced any earth shattering top secret. However, I can well imagine what George might do if he accidentally learned about their weapon of mass destruction. George is the kind of person who'd refuse to be quiet about it, especially if he thought such a weapon was capable of destroying the world."

"I think the existence of the disk proves that," Destin said. "Besides, the George I knew had a healthy distrust of the government."

Mitch nodded. "Yes, distrustful. He was particularly upset at the way both the military and the DOE struggled to have the upper hand at the labs. I saw that myself, which is why I was glad to find this niche here at NOAA."

"Can you tell me anything more that will shed light on George and Linda's deaths?" Destin persisted. "I really want to bring their killers to justice."

Mitch rubbed his broad, dimpled chin, which already had a five o'clock shadow. He looked grim. "Maybe I can," he said at last, "though I fear it isn't the kind of proof you're going to need."

"What do you know?" Destin rose and clenched his fists. His knuckles whitened.

"George gave me most of the story as you've told it," Mitch said. "He stressed that this weapon generated heat hotter than the surface of the sun. He also said the weapon was capable of emitting a narrowly focused beam of energy, or it could be diffused to wreak wider destruction. It would make nuclear bombs passé – think of it."

"Then it's exactly as Karen and I suspected," Destin said. He walked over to the windows that looked into the weather room and stood there, silent for a moment. He swung back to Mitch.

"Your testimony would help stop the weapon," Destin said. "But not the murders."

"I know. Maybe this will help. When George talked to me, he knew that some of the lab officials had discovered his involvement, his knowledge." Mitch paused. "More than that, he named the man involved – the man who'd try to silence him. But as I said earlier, knowing it is one thing, but proving it is another."

"True. Who did George name?"

"Colonel Jared Petrowski, who heads the lab as its military liaison," Mitch said. "Apparently, Karen's ex told him about the weapon. He – and others. George also said Petrowski had threatened his life. If that's not enough, George named Petrowski, Spenser, and Chin, who all work at the labs, as misleading several scientists working on the project, especially their chief scientist, Franz Stjernholm. When he talked to me, George thought Petrowski would do his level best to make good on his threat to kill George."

Destin set his coffee cup on the table. "It would seem that George was right – dead right."

CHAPTER 25

THE insistent rings of the motel phone awoke Bonnie. Her wake-up call. She arose and stumbled into the bathroom, eyes half-shut, still basking in the euphoria of sleeping long and well. After a shower, no longer groggy, she leaned toward her image in the mirror. *Damn.* She wiggled her nose and stuck out her tongue. *I'm a silly teenager with stars in my eyes. All due to Destin.* She'd probably never see him again.

She sobered and studied her reflection for some time. It was a real fiasco yesterday: Bonnie the washout, not Bonnie the success. Then, in an instant of clarity, she knew she wasn't to blame for the loss of the grant. Some things were beyond her control.

She rewashed her face and towel-dried it until her cheeks flushed and the towel didn't smell of commercial soap. When she felt better, she set it aside and applied scented face lotion. Her life resembled her face. Life was a bumpy road and needed lotion to smooth out the bumps.

She sniffed the ginger concoction and smiled. Nice. A new direction for her life was the spice she needed. There were other universities or groups who might be delighted to add her to their faculty. She paused, wondering what would become of Ollie and Dollie. Perhaps she could move them with her. Washington State University had a language research program, only their specialty was chimpanzees. *A bunch of monkey business.* She laughed at her own joke. Perhaps WSU would make her an offer. Then she remembered the farm, and the thought caused heartburn. "Maybe I will have to sell it," she told herself, determined to be brave.

Afterwards, she dressed in a pair of navy blue slacks and a white silk blouse, and packed. She took the elevator down and hauled her heavy Samsonite into the lobby, placing her key on the registration counter. The manager took her key eyeing her with sympathy. "That bag looks heavy," he said. "Let me to help you load it in your car."

"Thanks." Bonnie looked at the poker-faced man with his cauliflower ears but kindly, dark eyes. She giggled. "If you don't mind, please wait a second."

She scuttled toward the table that held the coffee in the lobby and picked one up, tagging behind him as he headed outside. "My car is down three slots. The VW."

She ran to keep up, but the coffee in her cup sloshed, a mini-tidal wave of the dark liquid spilling on her blue slacks. "Damn," she muttered, grabbing a tissue from her purse. She dabbed at the wet stain, catching up with the manager at her car, where she set the Styrofoam cup on the hood.

"No rush, lady." The man watched coffee dribble from her wrist.

Embarrassed, she opened the car then unzipped the luggage carrier on top. He slid the bag into it with difficulty. "That suitcase barely fits." He laughed.

Bonnie flushed. "Well, I do appreciate the help, Mr. — "

"Therman, ma'am," he said, "though most people call me Thad. The manager here."

"Well, thanks so much, Thad." She handed him a nice tip. He trudged toward the entrance as she turned the key in the ignition, but then he stopped and headed back. Bonnie saw him and rolled her window down. "What's the matter?"

"Don't you want to move your coffee off the hood?"

Bonnie flushed again and swung open the door. "Thanks."

She waved as she pulled out, heading south past fields of grass that flowed out to the horizon. In spite of wisps of clouds, the sun was a mellow ball that gave the October day a golden luster.

She rolled the window down, allowing the wind to lift her heavy hair and blow the curls into ringlets. It felt good on her neck.

Without warning, she heard a ripping sound from the vinyl luggage carrier overhead and then a muted crash. Horrified, she swiveled around and watched her old suitcase sail through the air and hit the highway, exploding into a million pieces of brittle, hard plastic.

She careened onto the shoulder of the road, braking hard to a fast stop. It sent the remnants of her coffee across her lap. Wryly, she thought her life couldn't get worse. She was only half right.

CHAPTER 26

THE next day, Dai Yu parked at the lab's lower entrance parking lot, preoccupied with her workload. As she swung out of her car, Franz Stjernholm pulled in. He looked preoccupied too, and she smirked. They were both near the entrance when Petrowski blocked their paths. "Glad you're here," he said to Franz. "Was wondering if you'd show up."

Dai Yu slid by Petrowski but stopped beyond, fascinated.

"Of course I would. It's a workday. There's much to do – reports and follow-up testing with the particle accelerator after the rock has cooled."

"I know that," Petrowski 's eyes were veiled. "I thought you might still be upset about yesterday's test."

"Of course I am." Franz scowled. "You deliberately used me. And you knew that I wouldn't approve of the RHIC being used in that manner."

"You're right." Petrowski's eyes narrowed. "But the question now is what you're going to do about it."

Franz's ears turned red. "I haven't thought about it."

Petrowski stepped closer until his face almost touched him. "This is no time for foolish, idealistic courage, Stjernholm. The DOE, the military, and the government, right up to the President, expect our work here to be kept secret. That's true now, more than ever, because the beam's involved."

Franz straightened. "So that's it – you're afraid I'm going to talk."

Petrowski's face became a scowl. "If you do, you'll die conveniently. A car accident, an overdose of pills, a heart attack — "

"Don't you threaten me!"

"I don't threaten." Petrowski walked over to the door. "The rock is still too soft for tests, so take the day off. You're pale, Stjernholm. Get some rest." He laughed as he walked into the lobby beyond, and Dai Yu fell in behind him, trying to keep up.

CHAPTER 27

"Mom," Tammy said. "This is totally uncool. I don't see why I have to come with you to the labs."

"I already told you. I have to pick up some notes, so I can finish some reports before work tomorrow morning."

"But it's a Sunday, Mom."

"Stay put. I'll be but a few seconds." Karen got out of the car and strode toward the lab's river entrance.

Tammy sighed. She had rewritten her essay and was free to see Ryan after he got off work. That would be soon, if her mom didn't ruin it. She looked through the windshield. No sign of her mom yet.

She climbed out and strolled across the clipped lawn to the river bank. Piles of huge, jagged boulders lined the steep slope below the dam, preventing erosion. She stood looking at the nearby wall of concrete that rose hundreds of feet into the air. It made her feel claustrophobic. Below her, the water danced and foamed. The current looked deadly as it assaulted the jagged boulders that littered the riverbed. She was ready to turn back when she heard a moan. Curious, she walked to the edge of the grass and peered at the riverbank rocks.

A man sat, perched on one of the nearest boulders, his back to her. He was bent over, and his head, a thatch of frizzy hair, was buried in his hands.

"Tammy?" Karen tapped her shoulder. "What are you doing out here?"

"Mom, look." Tammy pointed to the man.

"It's Dr. Stjernholm. Wonder what's bothering him?" Karen turned to go, but Franz heard them. He stood up and picked his way across the rocks until he reached them.

"Nothing to concern yourselves about," he said. He managed a thin smile. "I was outside for some fresh air. How's everything in forensics, Karen?"

"Not a dull moment. Not half as exciting as your work, though. What's this I hear about a weapons test going bad?"

"Where'd you hear that?" Franz stiffened.

Karen chuckled. "Actually, I heard of it from Tammy, here, who heard it from Earl. You know he has visitation rights. Terms of our divorce."

Franz nodded. "I know." He stepped closer to Karen. "Seems the colliders have a new purpose. That's what I discovered yesterday. The DOE is now using the RHIC and the other colliders to produce quarks, which are focused to form a deadly beam."

"Then you didn't know about the beam?" Tammy asked.

"Right. I didn't know about it until the test. It was Petrowski's doing. Spenser helped him too, though Spenser is scared shitless of the good Colonel and only does what he's told." He shifted his weight. "It's a deadly weapon, the beam."

Karen nodded. I've heard bits and pieces about this weapon for some time. Earl was in on it."

"I'm not surprised. Sorry." Franz shifted his weight.

"I'm dealing with it," she said.

"Worse, the beam, the QGPB, melted some bedrock beneath the labs yesterday." He laughed bitterly. "Perfect, isn't it? All of these government agencies make a fine set of bedfellows."

"Have they hooked up the colliders on the far side of the river to handle the weapon?" Karen asked.

He blinked. "I hadn't thought of that possibility, but yes, it wouldn't surprise me. Not that I can do anything about it."

When Karen did not answer immediately, Tammy interrupted her. "You can, too. Stand up to them! Don't let those slime balls get away with it!"

He looked at her, surprised.

"Tammy, I won't have you talking that way!"

"It's all right." Franz's voice became calm, controlled. "If you buck them, they won't hesitate to kill you. No one bucks them and wins."

Tammy balled her fists. "There must be a way."

Franz shook his head. "No way. Petrowski threatened me only minutes ago."

Karen laid her hand on his shoulder. "I know they're capable of murder, but Tammy's right."

She told him about George and Linda's murder, and about Destin. They stood silent for a moment, staring at the roiling, foaming torrent below the bank, before she summed up. "We want to expose the weapon to the world and nail Petrowski and the others for their crimes."

"See? You can't buck them." Franz said

"I'm not disagreeing with you," Karen answered. "But I think there's a point and time when people have to expose what's wrong. Look at what happened in Nazi Germany during World War II. Most German citizens were simply average people that got duped at first and then were too afraid to buck the system."

She released his shoulder and slid her arm about Tammy. "We need your help in exposing this, Franz. Please think about it."

He nodded. "I'll do that."

CHAPTER 28

DESTIN pulled out from NOAA, anxious to return to Fontana and tell Karen about his meeting with Mitch. As he mulled over all that Mitch had said, he despaired. The computer disk, he hoped, held enough evidence to go public with the information, and yet, until it was thoroughly checked, he could not be certain. Still, he could not tie the weapon to George and Linda's murders, at least, not without more than circumstantial evidence.

He sighed and drove, lost in thought. The October sun peeped through dark clouds and warmed him. It made him anxious to return to the houseboat on Lake Fontana.

He barely noticed the small, older Volkswagen ahead of him, until, horrified, he watched a suitcase bounce out of a luggage carrier atop the car.

The suitcase hit the highway and blew into smithereens. Destin swung left and braked hard, trying to avoid the carnage, and to his amazement, panties and bras, hosiery and dresses fluttered skyward in the breeze of the Volkswagen. The lightest of the garments blew up eight feet or higher. Abruptly, one bra hit his windshield. He lost his vision and careened right then left, braking to a stop in the median grass.

As he opened his door and retrieved the lacy black bra from the glass, he laughed. Across the empty highway, the Volkswagen skidded to a stop, and as he watched, a beautiful girl with curly hair and a shapely figure slid out from behind the wheel. She darted onto the empty highway and scooped up clothing, which now littered the roadway for several yards.

She stared at him, askance, as he held up the bra between fits of laughter. "Lose this ma'am?" Then he recognized Bonnie.

"Destin?" She froze by the side of the road. A car swooped past between them, crushing her makeup kit on the pavement and sending several other garments floating on the breeze. "Oh...Oh!" she screamed. She ran down the road, trying to retrieve more clothing.

Destin walked around to his passenger door and lounged against it, still holding the black bra aloft. He laughed until his sides hurt, and the more he laughed, the funnier it all seemed.

Bonnie retrieved a lacy nightgown and scooted to the median near him, barely missing an approaching car. She held a handful of clothing in one hand and her nightgown in the other. When she saw him laughing, she stopped and her eyes narrowed.

"What do you think is so damn funny?" She placed both hands on her hips.

The first car slowed down as it approached the clothing carnage while two other cars braked to a crawl. The drivers laughed when they saw Destin. Bewildered, Bonnie turned and ran across the highway, carrying the clothing back to the Volkswagen.

Another knot of cars approached as she stepped out onto the highway, and Destin shouted a warning: "Bonnie, look out! You could get hit!"

"Well, you might have the decency to help me pick up my stuff." With rigid shoulders, she stomped out into the middle of the highway.

"I'll be glad to help. Really." Destin sobered instantly. "I shouldn't have laughed either. Sorry."

"Sorry doesn't cut it," Bonnie said angrily. "It's not funny at all, you know – not at all. It so happens that I worked hard for all of this, and *look* at it now! Most of it is ruined." She held up a pair of shredded hosiery. "And to think I had a drink with you!"

"Ah, come on." Destin said. "Please, I'm sorry." He rushed out on the highway and began picking up the clothing.

"Oh!" Bonnie's finger stabbed the air and she pointed to the roadway. "That's my good blue jacket in the middle of the lane." She stepped back into the highway, but another car appeared in the distance, moving at a high rate of speed.

"Careful, silly," Destin warned. He grabbed her arm.

"Silly?" She burst into tears. "Why you egotistical, self-centered, male....thing! I am not silly."

"I didn't mean it literally."

"Well, I'd appreciate it if you'd—"

An approaching police cruiser slowed to a crawl. The officer flipped on his blue lights and brought the patrol car to a stop behind the Volkswagen. He got out and through narrowed eyes, surveyed the highway. "What happened here?" He took off his cap and turned to Destin who still held the black bra.

Destin looked at his hand and tried to stuff the bra in one pants pocket, but the cup and strap from one side of the silky nylon piece hung out.

"The zipper on the luggage carrier let go," Bonnie told the uniformed officer. Still crying, she turned toward several pieces of clothing still littering the highway. "Could you slow down traffic so I can pick up the rest of my stuff?"

"I'll help you pick it up, ma'am." He glanced back at Destin, his blue eyes full of humor. Then he pulled a pair of dark sunglasses out of his shirt pocket, put them on, and walked up the highway.

"I'll help too," Destin said, and between the two of them, they picked up the remaining clothing. Destin realized that most of the drivers and passengers were getting their money's worth rubber-necking.

"What am I going to do?" Bonnie wailed. She stared at her disheveled clothes, now stuffed into the back seat of the Volkswagen.

"You'll need a new suitcase," Destin said.

"This is the last straw." Bonnie's tears formed rivulets on her cheeks.

"Perhaps I could make this up to you," Destin suggested. "Let's have lunch together, and maybe afterwards, I can help you find a new suitcase."

The officer smiled and tipped his cap at Destin. He climbed into his cruiser and pulled away.

"No, I really couldn't. I need to — "

"To what – go back to UT?" Destin asked.

"Now, wait a moment!" Bonnie stiffened again. "You — "

"I'm sorry. I wasn't laughing at you, really I wasn't. And it would be a real honor... seriously...if you'd join me for lunch."

Bonnie became silent, her brown eyes softening. She then noticed the bra hanging from his pocket, and she laughed. "I might go to lunch if you dress appropriately."

Destin laughed too, pulled the bra out, and handed it to her. He looked at her dark eyes, and warmth flooded his heart. Bonnie took the bra. She blushed, turned back to the Volkswagen then added the bra to the heap on the back seat. She shut the door and nodded at him.

"I *am* hungry. That would be nice."

"That's *your* car? Somehow it doesn't fit you."

"It's a long story." She sighed. "How about I tell you over lunch?"

They found a nondescript café down the road. The number of cars in the parking lot attested to its popularity. Inside, the pine walls and booths of the small, L-shaped building showed wear and tear, but it was clean, and the food was both wholesome and home-cooked.

Over heaping plates of club sandwiches and coffee, Bonnie told Destin how her car had broken down, and how she had borrowed the Volkswagen. When she finished, they ate for a while in silence, both enjoying the homespun cuisine. Between sips of coffee, Bonnie said, "You told me last night that you were going to visit a man at the weather station, a friend of George's. If you don't mind me asking, how did your meeting turn out?"

Destin hesitated. "It went very well. Mitch Bartow is a nice guy and was very close to George. In fact, they used to work together."

Bonnie mulled over the information. "Have you ever found out who killed George?"

Destin hesitated again. "It's best I don't answer you. George's murder, if you'll excuse the cliché, was merely the tip of the iceberg."

Bonnie leaned forward. "Surely it can't be that serious."

"You have no idea." Destin shut his eyes. "Have you seen a newspaper in the last couple of days or watched television?"

"No. Why?"

"Because I'm a wanted man. At any moment, this restaurant could be stormed by the police."

Bonnie reached across the table and touched his hand. "I'm a big girl, Destin. I want to hear what has happened to you. Every bit of it. And who knows? Maybe I can help." She sat back.

"I don't know where to start."

"Please trust me." She brushed her hair back, and for a moment her beauty took his breath. He also knew she was trustworthy and honest, and he could stake his life on that.

"Well, do you know who murdered George?" she asked again.

He sighed. "Not yet, but I now know who ordered the murder."

"Really?" Bonnie looked up, shocked.

Destin then told her about George and how George had died. He told her about the clue on the scrap of paper, and the way George's killer had attacked him at the hamfest. He also described the parts she didn't know about his trip to the hospital and his interrogation at the jail.

He told her about the second assault in his home, his trip to North Carolina, Linda's suspicious suicide, and his acquaintance with Karen and Tammy Kerr. He explained how he had been using a houseboat on Lake Fontana, and how he'd searched Linda's village home, only to be attacked again.

"Whoever attacked me at Linda's cottage never realized I'd found George's computer disk about the secret weapon," he concluded. "I get chills when I think I may have beat George and Linda's killer to that disk by only a few minutes."

Bonnie nodded. "Thank heavens your attacker ran." She set aside the remnants of her sandwich. "But tell me about Mitch Bartow and how he fits into this."

Destin then described Karen and George's connection to Mitch, and how Colonel Petrowski had threatened George's life.

He sipped his drink and continued. He told her what he knew about particle accelerators and colliders, and how research around the country had led to many new tools to benefit people.

"Nevertheless, I wonder if we haven't opened a Pandora's Box. Right now, much of the world is holding its breath, waiting for some crazy terrorist to use a nuclear bomb or a dirty bomb – or even use bio-terrorism. It's as though we are on a downhill slide to hell, and there is nothing, not one thing, any of us can do to stop it. With the quark beam, someone could do worse and destroy our planet."

The sandwich on his plate lost its appeal, and he pushed it away. Instead, he focused on Bonnie. Her lovely, black hair hung down her back in untamed curls, and her brown eyes held a depth of sweetness that took his breath. Her softness and beauty excited him, energized him, and the warmth he'd experienced earlier swept him again.

Her eyes met his, and in an instant he realized that there was passion and longing in hers. He was not alone. "What are you going to do now?" Her voice was concerned.

He finished his coffee. "Don't know for sure. I can't stay away from work much longer, maybe four or five days, but I can't return to Florida either. I think the answer is to work with two of my LM clients in this area while continuing to hide out near the labs." He paused. "I need to investigate the key people at Fontana Labs and see if I can uncover more information."

Bonnie looked curious. "Two clients?"

"Yes, one is Diotech and the other is Ten-Tec."

She leaned forward. "Diotech? I think I've heard of them."

"Yes. That firm is in Maryville, a few miles south of Knoxville."

"Really!" Bonnie said. My dad and I – I mean I – have a farm south of Maryville."

"Oh." Destin digested the information. "Diotech is near the airport."

"What does Diotech do?"

"They build azimuth alignment units for rockets," he said. "They're a big client of LM."

"So you're going to return to Fontana for the next few days, until you run out of leave time?"

"Yes, and I hope I can gather enough evidence by then," Destin said. "I think I'll begin by taking the disk to a library somewhere – probably in Knoxville – and looking closer at it. Karen and I only skimmed through it the night I found it. Maybe it will take some guesswork out of this mess."

Bonnie reached out, and for a fleeting instant, her hand touched his, and he felt an electric shock spread with lightning speed to every corner of his body.

"It sounds to me as though you are putting yourself in a lot of danger," she said. "These people are very committed, and if they represent our government, it's going to be tough. Please be careful."

Destin covered her hand with his. "I promise."

She looked about the restaurant and withdrew her hand. "Would you mind if I went with you to the library? I could show you where it is. Besides, that disk sounds fascinating."

"I'd love it if you tagged along."

She rose from her seat as he stood, and a smile lit her face.

"What is it?"

"Nothing really; it's funny, actually," she said. "I remembered a nightmare I'd had the other night."

Concerned, he looked at her, but he saw that she was radiantly happy. He studied her a moment longer. "Okay, let's visit that library." He touched her again, this time resting his hand upon her shoulder. He guided her toward the register, and again, a thrill stirred him.

CHAPTER 29

BONNIE led the way to the library in Knoxville. They entered the old concrete building with its Roman-style portico. Inside, a librarian seated Bonnie at a computer. Destin hovered over her as Bonnie accessed the disk.

"Look at this." Destin pointed to the screen. Together they studied the specifications George had meticulously detailed for them about the functions of the Random Van de Graaf, the Booster, the AGS, and the RHIC. The document also described how the labs developed the Quark Gluon Plasma Beam, a product of the collisions, and how the beam used conduits to reach the surface and beyond, into space. "I don't know whether the Quark beam is a defensive or offensive weapon," George had written, "but I fear the worst. Even in the right hands, this is information that I really don't think we're prepared for."

They read on in silence.

"Look!" Bonnie stabbed at the screen. "I can't believe this. See all these footnotes on the pages? And see this one?" She pointed at the tiny print.

"He says here that Petrowski, with the help of the CIA, has killed one – maybe two – scientists who wouldn't go along with the project, but admits he lacks sufficient proof."

Destin's voice dropped to a husky whisper. "Karen and I missed that footnote. We only skimmed the disk. It was late that night and I wasn't in the best of shape."

"Oh, don't blame yourself." Bonnie pointed at the monitor. "Look, it's hidden among a bunch of footnotes. You know, I think George put it there deliberately so the casual observer wouldn't see it."

"You're right." He rubbed his forehead. "Well, you can bet that George and Linda met the same fate at the hands of Petrowski."

They finished studying the disk and, together, they left the library. Outside, he propelled her to his truck. "Come sit in my truck for a second. There's something you should know."

Destin got in, and puzzled, Bonnie slid into the passenger seat. Destin touched her sleeve. "I want you to know about where I'm hiding this disk – in case they kill me."

Stunned, she could only gape. He took out his Leatherman knife and leaned across to her side. He pulled down the sun visor and made a small, neat slice in the fabric. With satisfaction, he slid the CD into the slit and flipped up the visor. "I hope that will do it. Now, a copy of this disk is in Karen's possession, and I'm telling you this as a precaution."

Bonnie's eyes widened. "Now I *am* going to worry about you." She shivered. "Maybe this whole affair is too big for us to deal with."

"Try not to worry. Look, I'm armed now." Destin leaned over her again and opened his glove compartment. Inside was a pistol in a leather case. Bonnie shrank into the corner of the seat. "Don't get that thing near me!"

"Sorry. I only wanted to reassure you. It's properly licensed, and I carry a concealed weapons permit."

"All right." Bonnie reached for the door handle. "I'd better head for home."

Destin reached out and touched her arm. "It's only two, the day is young, and frankly, I'm not ready to lose you yet."

Bonnie smiled, enjoying again the way his touch twisted her stomach. "What have you got in mind?"

Destin thought for a moment. "Let's visit Ten-Tec."

"Ten-Tec?"

"Yes, we could go there now. Ten-Tec is a radio manufacturer that deals mostly in defense contracts, and Lockheed Martin has been doing business with them for some time. In fact, LM planned to send me to see them about a new radio they've developed for our use. I called them a few days ago about a possible meeting, and they said any time would be fine."

Bonnie smiled at his enthusiasm. He continued. "This is perfect. We could drive there, I could take care of our business, and we could have some fun while we're there."

"Fun?" Bonnie grinned. Work was fun for him. A good thing.

"Yes, fun. You see, the company makes ham radios for civilian use, and I've always wanted to see more of their rigs. Wouldn't you enjoy visiting them too?"

Bonnie laughed. Radios might not be her forte, but Destin was. "Sure, I'd love it. Where are they located?"

"I don't have my appointment book with me, but I know how to get their address." Destin reached behind the seat and found a QST magazine perched on his overnight bag. "Give me a second," he said, thumbing through the pages. Finally he pointed to an advertisement. "Sevierville is a few miles east of Knoxville, on Dolly Partin Boulevard."

"Ah, that was Dolly's original home town."

Destin nodded. "Why not leave the VW here and come with me? We can pick it up on our way back."

"Sure." Bonnie fastened her seat belt.

Destin headed out into the early afternoon traffic, and in less than a half hour, they were at Ten-Tec in Sevierville. The firm was housed in a rectangular building that had been faced with brick across the front. A portion of the structure near the center was two stories high, with a large HF Yagi antenna in front.

Gary, a bearded engineer, met them inside the glassed-in portico at the main entrance, and while she waited, he and Destin took care of business in an adjacent office.

Later, Gary showed them around the plant, which included a thorough look at their repair section, tool and die room, and transformer and coil manufacturing section. He paused by the coils.

"Ten-Tec is the only amateur radio manufacturer that hand winds its own transformers and coils. Not the case with our competitors."

"That's one reason why the defense industry likes their products," Destin said. Bonnie nodded.

Beyond the transformers, Gary showed them the parts and shipping room, and finally the production and assembly area, the heart of the building.

"Are those all ham sets?" Bonnie asked.

"Not all," Gary said. "Right now we're building a special radio with some unusual features for the FBI."

Following their tour, they thanked Gary and strolled out to Destin's truck. "Were you able to finish your business with Ten-Tec?" Bonnie asked him.

"Yes. Speaking of radios, I need to call Karen." He flicked on the radio and tried 145.110, the VHF frequency, but was not surprised that Sevierville was too great a distance for the repeater. He switched to his HF radio and tried the DX frequency that he and Karen had agreed upon, 7.230 on 40 meters.

"N7JJJ, N7JJJ, November 7 Juliet Juliet Juliet, this is WR4RR, WR4RR, Whiskey Romeo Four Romeo Romeo, do you copy?" He repeated the transmission without success. As he reached for the power button, he heard Karen's voice.

"WR4RR, this is N7JJJ. Where've you been? I've been worried sick."

"Nothing to worry about," Destin assured her. "Mitch didn't return until this morning, but I did see him, and it was an important meeting. Anyway, I've been busy taking care of loose ends. I should be returning soon."

Bonnie smirked and he reddened.

"Look, I have lots to tell you, but it will have to wait until I return."

"When will that be?"

His flush spread to his neck. "I have one stop to make. Right now, I'm in Sevierville on business. I'll get hold of you first thing tomorrow."

"All right." Karen's voice softened. "I'll put on the coffee pot for you tomorrow."

"Sounds good. 73, and we'll see you soon. WR4RR."

"73. N7JJJ."

He left the receiver on, but cranked down the volume until the chatter became background murmur. Then he turned to Bonnie. Amused, her eyes still twinkled. Before she could speak, he chuckled. "Yeah, I know. I have *a lot* to tell her."

Destin drove back into Knoxville and she rode in companionable silence, but it turned to sadness before Destin pulled into the library parking lot. He too, seemed downcast. He squeezed her arm and stood there, unwilling to leave her.

"Bonnie, I could stay awhile longer. For one thing, that VW seems to be leaking some oil. It could break down soon."

"Don't worry about it," Bonnie said. "I'm going to stop by a grocery and head home, but I'll check the oil before leaving the grocery store."

Destin brightened. "Wait. Let's eat out. Do you know of any good restaurants in Knoxville?"

Bonnie grinned. "Plenty. The Clam Shack is my favorite, but I'm not in the mood for seafood tonight."

Destin thought for a moment. "Well, I know of one. I saw it while driving over here. Follow me."

Still smiling, Bonnie shrugged and started the VW. She followed Destin across town. Back on Highway 129, they passed the airport and near the Foothills Mall, Destin pulled into the parking lot of a restaurant specializing in chicken wings, a red brick building with striped awnings.

She parked and climbed out of the car, grinning. "Hooters? Of all the restaurants in the world, you chose Hooters?"

Flustered, Destin said, "They have great chicken wings."

She snickered. "I love wings. Let's go."

They walked inside. He propelled her past the high tables that lined the edges of the room, and he seated her at a table for four placed on the diagonal. From both their viewpoints, they could see several televisions at the corners of the room, all of them televising a stock car race.

A woman with blonde hair, fastened back, took their order. A lovely femme with flawless legs, she wore orange shorts and a white top with orange trim. For an instant, Bonnie felt jealous at the way the blonde eyed Destin. But as she studied him, she knew he only had eyes for her. She'd truly discovered a man who cared about her, maybe even more than Abe had.

Over dinner, they talked about the weather, about their lives, about their likes and dislikes, their interests, their hobbies, their favorite music, their childhoods, their parents, and even their favorite colors. Destin told her about his injured knee, and how his father had kicked him. She reached out to him then and squeezed his hand, and the touch made her tingle. She told him about Abe, and finally, she talked about the grant and what she might do in the future.

She discovered with a thrill, how much they shared in common, such as their love and passion for travel and the desire for a family.

At some point in the evening of chatter, she realized she had a friend – not the kind of friend that promises to write and never does – but one who would always be a part of her life. Also, she understood that she wanted him, and the sensation was delicious. It warmed her, moving her in ways that Abe never had.

As they finished their meal of wings, she sensed he desired her too, and she knew then that they would spend the night together. They left the restaurant hand in hand, enjoying the moist night air, cooled by a brief shower. Neither wanted the evening to end. Tendrils of fog moved in, and for a moment Bonnie shivered, but Destin slid his arm protectively across her shoulders. Again, his touch thrilled her.

"Are you driving all the way back to Fontana tonight? It's awfully late."

"I know." He sighed heavily. "I am tired."

She cocked her head. He looked anything but tired. "Why not come home with me then? I have a small place right on your way to Fontana. You could get some rest and return there tomorrow."

Destin smiled, swept her into his arms, and kissed her. "Nothing would make me happier."

This time Bonnie led the way to the farm, Destin following in his truck. After they'd parked she took him inside and gave him a grand tour, which ended in her bedroom. The room was pleasant and warm with swirls of pastels in the quilted bedspread, set against a background of slate blue.

Bonnie slid out of her sweater. She felt his hands upon her shoulders, and as she turned to him, they kissed. For an instant, their tongues met. Then, as if by mutual unspoken agreement, Destin stepped back to search her eyes. "Perhaps," he said, "we're moving too fast."

He paused and she touched his arm. His thick brown hair had become tousled, and one lock of it had fallen forward across his forehead. He was muscular, and she saw the outlines of his well-developed chest and shoulders beneath his blue polo shirt. As her gaze swept down his frame, she could see his compact thighs and legs, and the leanness of his buttocks filled her with pleasure. She looked into his blue eyes, and she could see his desire, his longing, reach out to her.

She thought of Abe again, and in a moment of revelation, she realized she'd never loved him, only admired him. *That's why I let him go.*

She studied the man before her. *This is love.* The thought awed her.

CHAPTER 30

DESTIN gazed at Bonnie, amazed. For a moment she appeared as a goddess, rising out from the shadows of her Maple four-poster bed, and he happily reached for her, his hands touching her shoulders. This time his hands slid down the soft silk, tracing the outlines of her breasts, and with both hands in unison, he found her nipples, which hardened to his touch. Her ragged breathing, filled with longing, encouraged him, but he moved slowly, gently, exploring her.

His hands slid along her back. He traced a path along the knots of her spine until his fingers reached her narrow waist. He caressed her sides and explored the curve of her hips and the flatness of her lean, taut, stomach. Slowly, gently, he crouched before her, his hands moving down her sides, along her slacks, until he found her legs and ankles.

She moaned in pleasure and then gasped, begging him to move faster. When she placed her hands on his head, caressing his hair, her touch aroused him as well. He stood again and reached for her breasts, squeezing them tenderly.

Ever so gently, he unbuttoned her blouse for her. Still fondling her, he reached behind her and unsnapped her bra. He reveled at the firm breasts and hard nipples. He leaned forward, kissing her hair, her eyelids, her nose, ears. His lips slid down her neck to her breasts, where he flexed and massaged them with his hands while his tongue explored her flesh.

She groaned with pleasure, and leaned forward, grasping him between his legs, and he rose, hard to her touch. She unzipped his slacks and smiled as they fell at his feet. And then it was his turn, but as her slacks slipped away, he ran his hands under her panties, exploring her. She moved closer, inviting him. They slid out of their underwear and this time, it was his turn to groan with excitement. He lifted her onto the bed. Finally, consummately, he entered her, gently exploring her nooks and crannies. He wondered if he had ever known the kind of pleasure and love he had found. Again and again, he moved, and in unison, their love built and crested, subsided, only to build again. Much later, exhausted, they parted, satiated and complete.

As he lay there in the darkness, hours later, he knew his world had changed forever and his love would never die. But even more curious was the desire to stay alive. Before, he'd had little fear for his life, but now his will to survive was overpowering.

CHAPTER 31

ROCKY turned his Peterbilt rig off I-40 at the western outskirts of Knoxville and headed south on back roads bound for the Carolina border. A late afternoon shower reformed in tendrils of fog that clung to ditches, creeks, and hollows.

Some distance south of Maryville, Tennessee the Smoky Mountains rose as a jagged barrier, though the fog made it impossible for Rocky to see them. Night descended, and he was forced to a crawl. The fog made him question his decision to take Highway 129, a narrow two-lane road, rather than I-40.

Beyond Lake Chilhowee, the road became a series of three hundred eighteen switchbacks in eleven miles as the highway rose and dropped over three thousand feet. Known as the Dragon's Tail, many of the switchbacks were so sharp that a large rig needed both lanes to inch through them. But time was critical and he knew it.

The weapon. During his entire trip to North Carolina, Rocky hadn't stopped wondering about Sergeant Bowers' incredulous assertions four days before, at Edwards AFB. *Bunk,* he decided for the hundredth time.

He turned his attention back to the highway. At a pull-off about one third of the way across the spine of jagged peaks, he turned on his ham radio and went to the prearranged frequency of 7.241.

"CQ, CQ, CQ. This is N4OZZ, November Four Oscar Zulu Zulu. CQ seventy-two forty-one." The purr of static filled the cab so he tried again. "CQ, CQ, CQ. November Four Oscar Zulu, Zulu. Anyone copy?"

Silence.

He dialed down to 7.230, another prearranged frequency. He hoped to talk to his friend Jacob Wells, another trucker.

"K2PTQ, K2PTQ, this is N4OZZ. Do you copy?"

The hiss of static cleared and he heard Jacob's southern drawl.

"N4OZZ, I copy you. Got you 5-9 tonight, 'Ooze.'"

Rocky grimaced. "Keep it O-Z-Z if you don't mind."

Jacob laughed. "Not much happening here on I-30. I'm heading home now. Been on a turnaround to Texarkana. Where are you? Still on I-40?"

"No. I'm taking 129 into North Carolina."

"You crazy?" Jacob snorted. "Why would you ever drive across all those twisties?"

"No choice," Rocky said. "My load is going to Fontana Labs and they're only seven miles from the end of this kinky mess. I-40 would be an extra fifty miles."

Jacob clucked in sympathy. "Hauling anything back to Little Rock?"

"A load of furniture. The mill is in Robbinsville, only a few miles from Fontana." Rocky paused. "Sure miss my Arlene. She's so fine, a playboy centerfold."

"So when is Arlene going to wake up to the fact that she's too good for you?"

"Hey, watch it there," Rocky said. We make sweet music together. And when I get back, I'll take Arlene to Maxine's."

"Maxine's?"

"Yeah, it's a new lounge with a live band on weekends. You'd love the Hydraulic Bananas, the band."

"Bananas?" Jacob laughed.

"Laugh if you will, but they have the beat. Hey, got an idea. Why don't you and your YL join us at Maxine's?"

Jacob sobered. "I'm a married man. My YL isn't exactly a 'young lady' anymore, nor am I young either. No, I prefer a quieter life, thank you very much. Someday you ought to try settling down. You might enjoy it."

Rocky considered his words. "If I ever marry, it will be to Arlene."

The voices of his two other friends, Loco and Milt, broke through the static.

"N4OZZ, this is W4DGI," Loco said.

"KG4PIR here too," Milt said. "PIR – parts in rust."

"Knock it off, Milt," Jacob said. "You're not that old. Anyway, keep it clean. You know FCC rules."

Loco interrupted. "Did you get time to see Arlene and celebrate her birthday yet?"

Rocky ground his teeth. "No. No time until this run is finished." He gunned the rig through a sharp curve.

"Well, she's one beautiful chick," Loco said. "Those types are hard to keep. Be careful."

"I plan to. Which is why I got her a nice gift, a camcorder." He glanced at the passenger seat where it sat.

A high pitched whine began, pulsing through the radio. It rose into a screech that reverberated from some point beyond the cab. Stunned, Rocky hit the brakes. As quickly as the whine began, it ended. In its wake, a dazzling light filled the cab and blinded Rocky. Then it too, blinked off, along with the engine and headlights of his rig. Shaken, Rocky sat in the darkness.

He restarted the truck and the headlights blinked on, but the fog made visibility impossible. He picked up the mike.

"K2PTQ, N4OZZ. Do you copy?" Silence.

"Kilo Two Papa Tango Quebec, this is November Four Oscar Zulu Zulu."

"Gotcha man," Jacob answered. "Had me worried there. What was that horrible noise?"

"I dunno. Strangest bit of QRM, manmade noise, I ever heard. And that was only the half of it. My engine died, headlights too, as a blinding light filled my cab. Then the light simply blinked off."

Loco heehawed. "You're seeing UFOs? Little green men? Or maybe you've been drinking? W4DGI."

"W4DGI, you know I never drink and — " He stopped as he remembered Sergeant Bowers' words and his own response. "Forget I mentioned anything, you nimwits. But right now, I can't talk and get through these curves, so I'll talk to you tomorrow evening if propagation is good. N4OZZ clear."

He listened to his buddies laugh until he shut off the radio. Now he was the butt of their jokes. Damn. If he'd only captured the incident on the camcorder.

Silence filled the cab and his thoughts careened down wild paths. He wondered if the light and the noise were somehow connected to the weapon Bowers had told him about. The possibility gave him the shivers. He also wondered if he was the only person who'd ever undergone a life change in such a short time.

CHAPTER 32

WRAITHS of fog blanketed the cold water below the dam. The temperature had dropped. Dai Yu frowned and tightened her jacket. She left the lab entrance behind and strolled along the entrance road. Jagged cliffs rose on one side of the road, while a grassy strip lined the other. Farther down the road, the cliffs became a boulder-strewn hill that flanked a large, oval field of grass near the gates and the main highway. Tonight, though, the inky fog blotted it out and the air was raw.

She turned and plodded back toward the entrance to the labs, exhausted. Yesterday's test problems had meant lots of extra work for her. Time to call it a night.

She picked her way past the freight docks, and skirted an eighteen-wheeler when she heard voices. Curious, she eavesdropped from the shadows of the rig. One speaker, the freight supervisor, was talking to Dwight, one of their workmen. The supervisor sounded angry, so she inched closer, sticking to the foggy shadows. She caught his words, "...get him unloaded as quickly as possible, and say nothing to him." Then the supervisor disappeared inside.

She watched as Dwight shrugged and moved over to the trucker who stood near his rig. "Don't pay no attention to him, Rocky," Dwight said. "How was your trip from Little Rock?"

Rocky snorted. "Terrible. Since I was late, I tried a shortcut, the Dragons Tail. I've heard tales about that road, but I had no idea it was so awful."

Dwight was sympathetic. "Bad move, man. That road has three hundred eighteen switchbacks. The bikers love it though." He paused and changed subjects. "Where you headed now?"

"Back to Little Rock tomorrow."

"You still involved with ham radio?"

"Sure am. I was on the radio earlier, in fact. Remember me telling you last time how I have two other trucker friends, Milt and Loco? Well, I was on with them tonight."

"Yeah, that's good." Dwight scratched his head. "Got any more stops this trip?"

"Yes, some furniture to haul back from Robbinsville," Rocky said. "I'll have to stay here tonight because I'm not scheduled to pick up the furniture until late tomorrow." Rocky changed the subject. "What was that all about, Dwight?"

Dwight looked around. "Don't pay them no mind. The bosses think none of us know what goes on here. But I know, because word gets around, you know, even to the loading docks."

His voice dropped to a whisper, and impatient, Dai Yu crept closer.

"...What? Melted rock beneath our feet?" Rocky bellowed. He looked around and shivered. "It figures. Now I know this place is tied to what I saw and heard on the Dragon's Tail."

"Dragon's Tail? What happened?"

Rocky threw up his hands and they glowed in the effervescence of flood lights in the fog. "No way, man. I've had enough for one night. This place gives me the creeps. Next time."

When he moved toward the cab, Dai Yu crept back into deeper shadows. After the truck rolled away, she returned to the labs. She decided to have a heart-to-heart talk with Petrowski about Dwight. It would be a real pleasure to fire him herself.

CHAPTER 33

DESTIN awoke to the beauty of Bonnie, asleep next to him. Morning sunlight filtered through the shades, forming a narrow pattern of light on the carpeting. Her hair spread into endless series of natural waves that framed her bare shoulders on the pillow. He leaned toward her and brushed her ears and hair with his lips. She groaned, awakening. He kissed her and she moved to him. He felt her warmth near his chest. He kissed her again, his lips forming a pathway as they slid from her neck to her breasts.

"Oh, I love the way— "

He kissed her again, and she pressed against him. Then she caressed him, her soft lips exploring his arms, chest, thighs, and her every movement caused him ecstasy.

She slid out of her sheer nightgown, and together they united as one until they were fulfilled. Spent but happy, Destin kissed her again, this time a satisfied peck on the cheek, and got out of bed.

"You happy?"

"Never happier." She got up. "You've got a cute rear."

"Watch it, honey." He reached around and tickled her, sending her shrieking out of bed. She flung a pillow at him, but he tossed it back until giggling, they rolled across the bed.

"I have an idea," she said, tweaking his nose. "Let's have breakfast out on the back patio and enjoy the sun, even if it's cool."

"Good idea." He swatted her rear.

After a light breakfast, they relaxed on the patio sipping coffee while Bonnie told him again of her fear for the future of the CGR. "Now I may have to sell this place. Dad wanted me to do that, anyway." She paused, eyeing him critically. "You don't drink, do you?"

Destin sat back. "What makes you ask?"

"The night we met and then later, you stuck to iced tea or cola."

"You're right," he said. "I don't drink."

"Why not?"

He straightened. "Because my father drank. I don't want to be another Gavin." He described his father's drinking, abuse, and death in more detail, and recounted the incident when his father had injured his knee. "I intervened in that fight in order to save my mother from being next," he added.

She reached out and touched his arm. "Are you then saying you're against someone drinking?"

"No. I simply vowed I'd never become a drunk."

Bonnie refilled his cup from the carafe. "It's true some people have serious drinking problems. On the other hand, an occasional drink doesn't hurt most people unless they can't control their drinking. Do you have such a problem?"

Destin flushed. "I don't know. I mean, I've had a drink or two before, but..."

"Did you have a problem controlling it?"

Destin looked down. "No, but I abhor the temptation."

"Oh," Bonnie said, cocking her head. "So you don't have a drinking problem, but you're afraid that you *could*. Right?"

Destin reddened. "Look, I can take or leave most drinks, but there's something about beer..."

Bonnie put her cup aside. "You're especially scared of it because you enjoy it. You want to hate it but you don't. Right?"

Destin stood. "Yes. I've kept a six-pack of my dad's brand near me for a long time. It reminds me of the danger."

Bonnie stood also and gathered up the dishes. "I'm not telling you to drink. But your father's abuse has left you with a lot of scars. Maybe it's time to be yourself and let go of him."

She left the dishes in the sink and went upstairs to change. When she returned, he was reading one of his QST magazines.

"You really enjoy ham radio, don't you?" Bonnie said.

"Yes, I do."

"My father was a ham for years, but he gave it up after Mom died."

"No kidding? Then do you know much about the hobby?"

"Yes and no...it was hard not learning some, since Dad was involved in it."

"Did you ever think about getting into it yourself?"

"Yes, and Dad would have loved that, but my work has been time consuming and I never got around to it."

Destin was silent for a moment. "I suspect that's why the hobby has always had more senior citizens involved in it than young folks."

"I'm sure you're right." She paused also. "I did notice the radio you used in your truck yesterday, by the way. It's a Yaesu FT 8800 mobile radio – dual bander – right?"

Destin glanced at her, surprised. "Right on the money. Very good. Now, did you see the other rig it was mounted on?"

She nodded. "I saw it, but didn't catch what it was."

"It's an Icom 706 Mark IIG."

"Does it work well?"

"Well enough. I enjoy it."

She nodded again. "I think my dad had an Icom also. Isn't the 706 a radio that has VHF and UHF on it already?"

"Yes."

"Well, why do you have a second VHF/UHF radio?"

Destin smiled. "I prefer keeping my UHF and VHF in a separate unit. I don't use the UHF and VHF on the Icom 706. Besides, my old Outbacker antenna doesn't have VHF and UHF capabilities. Unless I update later on, I think my setup works pretty well."

"Guess so." She fell silent. "I noticed that you didn't have the radios fastened down. Won't they scoot around?"

He laughed. "You're putting me to task, aren't you? You're right. I did fasten the 8800 to the Icom by using Velcro, but I haven't had a chance to make up a bracket to fasten them both. I only set up the Icom 706 a few days ago. For a long time it rode around in my truck, still in the box. I'm too busy to get all the things done that I intend. Work accounts for most of that. We're alike on that score."

She nodded in understanding and squeezed him. He cleared his throat. "Let me take a look at the Nissan," he said. They walked outside together and following his directions, she unlatched the hood. After a moment of checking the engine, he looked up. "Give it a try," he said.

She slid behind the wheel and turned the ignition. The Nissan started smoothly. She jumped out, radiant. "How'd you do that?"

"It was only a loose coil wire," he said. He loved the way her nipples rose hard and defined beneath her sweater. She giggled self-consciously. "Are you able to stay awhile longer or must you head back to Fontana?"

He hesitated. He knew Karen needed an update, but he was loath to leave Bonnie a minute before necessary. He looked at her, and his eyes traced every inch of her toned skin. He sighed. "I really need to get back to Karen. We have to decide what we should do next about George and Linda's death."

Bonnie nodded, sobering. "Of course." She trailed him into the house, and watched as he quickly gathered up his belongings. After he had loaded up the truck, he gave her a parting kiss. She responded with intensity, reluctant to let him go.

"I don't have Karen's number if I need to reach you," Bonnie reminded him, and her voice was ragged.

"You're right." He got a slip and pen out of the glove compartment and wrote it out for her. "I'll call you soon," he promised. He tried not to look at her face as he pulled out of her driveway. She was too tempting. Later, as he approached Lake Chilhowee, he knew his world had changed. First, he realized he loved her, and his love would never die. But even more curious, he thought, was the desire to stay alive. Before, he'd had little fear for his life, but now, his yearning to live was overpowering.

As he maneuvered through the Dragon's Tail, he felt alone in spite of the sunshine and the occasional motorcycles that roared past him. His sense of aloneness became an acute ache he couldn't relieve. Then he thought of George and Linda, and the hurt receded, replaced by determination – what he must do, right or wrong. The determination assuaged his loneliness until a new something, yet unnamed, threatened to replace it. Before he could analyze it, he understood. It was a sense of foreboding, and as it grew, it filled him with a dread for what lay ahead.

CHAPTER 34

WHEN Tammy entered the Sub Shoppe the next afternoon, Ryan, who was wiping tables, looked up, surprised. "What're you doing here?"

She pouted. "I brought my car in for a tune up but the mechanic now says it won't be ready until tomorrow. Could I get a ride home with you?"

Ryan set down his cloth. "Tammy, I wouldn't mind, except we won't be closing until almost eight. That's going to be a long wait."

"I know," Tammy said. "But Mom is working swings tonight and she's going to see it as really uncool if I call her and ask her to give me a ride home."

"Who's that?" Sean leaned around the partition. "Hey, good to see you, Tammy." He disappeared into the back room again, amid the clanging of pots and pans.

"I have plenty of homework to keep me busy until eight," Tammy said. "By the way, our cheerleading squad has decided to sponsor a Thanksgiving dance at the old hall in the village. We may have a band lined up. Want to go?"

"If I'm not working." Ryan picked up the washrag again. "When are you going to hold it?"

"The Saturday before Thanksgiving," Tammy said.

"I'll put it on the calendar."

"What's Sean doing?" she asked, looking around.

"He's out back, cleaning pots, and if I were you, I'd leave him alone," Ryan said. He's in a foul mood. Seems he broke up with Janet." He went back to wiping tables.

Tammy looked up as the bell tinkled and watched a large man enter. In awe, she studied him. Even though he wore a lined jeans jacket against the cold, she could see he was muscular. A stranger. Definitely not from around Robbinsville. With the exception of Ryan, the town was a virtual wasteland when it came to exciting men.

"Care to order, Mister?" Ryan wiped his hands on his apron.

"Tuna salad sub with the works," the trucker said, "and a Sprite."

"Coming right up." Ryan began fixing his sub.

"By the way, are there any perfume shops in town?"

Ryan's brown eyes twinkled, and he shook his head. "No way, man, not in this small town. The drug stores sell cologne, if that'll do."

The trucker grimaced. "Maybe. I might look later. My girl, Arlene, is having a birthday. I got her a camcorder, see?" He held up the camera box. "But I was hoping to get her some perfume too. She loves the stuff."

Outside, Tammy could see his blue Peterbilt truck gleaming in the sun. Ryan reached down, put the finishing touches on the sub, wrapped it up, and handed it to the man.

"Thanks." The trucker moved over to a table by the front window and dove into his sandwich. He was on his second bite when Ryan came over.

"Here, Mister," he said, handing him a small order of fries.

"I didn't order those."

"I know." Ryan grinned. "It's because you looked kind of down, and I thought these might pick up your day. They're on the house."

The trucker smiled broadly. "Thanks so much. I'll enjoy them. By the way, the name's Rocky."

Tammy asked for a Coke and Ryan got her one, and as she drank it, she watched the trucker study the camcorder manual until he'd mastered it. Ryan disappeared into the back to help Sean, so when Rocky wanted another drink refill, she got it for him. "Anything else you need?"

"No, I have to pick up a load of furniture and head for home."

He got up and she watched him step outside into the cold of the late afternoon. After he had disappeared, she moved back to the counter until Ryan reappeared from the back. "This town is so boring," she said abruptly. "Nothing ever happens here. Nothing! I wish we could have more — "

Ryan stopped. "Did you hear those bangs?"

Tammy became silent. "No. I didn't hear anything. Do you still hear it?"

"I don't know. Now I hear the roar of water." Ryan moved to the door. "Oh my gosh, look!"

Tammy crowded near his shoulder. A car had lost control on the highway and hit a fire hydrant, which sat at the edge of the Sub Shoppe parking lot. Water was shooting up over thirty feet.

The fire department crews responded quickly, followed by the water department workers. As they worked feverishly to control the water, Ryan shook his head and laughed. "You get what you wish for," he said to Tammy. "My only question is this. Did you put a limit on your wish?"

CHAPTER 35

BEN TIRSHAW pulled into the parking lot at the Stecoah Fire Department, ready for the night shift. He hustled up the stairs and into the dispatch room in time to hear the phone ring. The dispatcher took the call. As the alarm sounded the dispatcher yelled, "Car fire! Out at Reverend Michael Statler's home."

"All right." Coates, the fire chief, pointed to Ben. "Glad you're here. You and your crew get going. There's a broken fire hydrant in Robbinsville, so Sal and I will stay here in case they need us as backup."

Ben climbed on the pumper with his crew and left the station, running at top speed to the north end of Fontana Village.

Two minutes past the village, they located the Statler home near the highway. The car fire was hard to miss. Flames had already enveloped the sedan, which sat in the Statler's front driveway. They went to work to contain the flames so the home would not be the next casualty.

Reverend Statler, a frail figure with thinning white hair, shuffled out on the porch moments after Ben and his crew began hosing down the car. Statler's wife joined him, still clad in pajamas. In stupefied amazement, they watched Ben work.

A police car pulled in moments later, its lights blinking. For several minutes, Ben was only aware of the noise of mayhem in Michael's small front yard and the putrid smell of burnt rubber, gasoline, and metal. Statler watched them from his porch, his arm around his wife.

Ben kept his attention on the car until the last of the flames died. The Mercury was totaled. Statler then skirted the smoking carnage, walking stiffly toward the uniformed officer in the yard. "Can you recommend a tow service?"

Ben watched them, standing by the porch. The officer, Sheriff Eric Freitag, was a small man with dark hair, oily tanned skin, and an oily reputation to match.

"You're Statler?" Freitag asked, ignoring his question.

"I am."

"How'd the car catch on fire?"

Michael shook his head. "I've no idea. Alice, my wife, was asleep though I wasn't. I'd worked later than usual on a sermon for Sunday. When I finished it, I entered the front bedroom and sat on the bed. That's when a blinding light lit our house, our clock radio and our bedside lamps started turning on and off, and so did the car engine. I looked out the window and saw puffs of smoke, then flames, pouring from the car."

Freitag cut him off. "Are you trying to tell me something *weird* was going on here?"

Michael shook his head again. "I didn't say that. I was — "

"Yeah, right," Freitag's voice became sarcastic. "Who was the driver?"

"No one," Michael said.

"How do you know that?"

"I told you, I looked out my bedroom window. It was hard to miss."

Freitag turned to the deputy behind him. "Oh my God, we *do* have a certified nut case here." He grabbed Michael's thin shoulder and propelled him toward his front door.

"Don't hurt him," Ben warned from behind, and Freitag released his grip long enough to look back. Ben scowled at Freitag while Statler took a seat on the porch next to his wife.

"Let's start from the top and go through this story again," Freitag said, and Ben noticed that his voice had a sharp edge. It reminded him of a fillet knife ready to gut a trout.

Michael told him again of the blinking lights, car radio, and how his car had erupted in flames, but Freitag's face became molten fury.

Alice, scared into silence, clung to him. Ben wished he could comfort her, but Statler beat him to it. He abruptly stood. "Let's go, dear." He helped her up, but Freitag grasped his shoulder and spun him around. The sheriff's face was an inch or two from the preacher's.

"If you think I'm going to stand here and listen to all this nonsense about little green men coming down and setting your car on fire," Freitag said, "you've a lot to learn about me. I'm not going to waste my time with you, standing here in the middle of the night, discussing dribble."

"I told you the truth," Michael protested. Faint, he sank into one of the porch chairs. Freitag's eyes narrowed. "You're on medication, aren't you?"

Michael didn't answer. At that moment, one of the sheriff's deputies framed the door. "Johnson," Freitag said to him, "this man's a real basket case. We've got a live one here."

He swiveled back to Michael, and this time, pinned the old man's shoulders against the chair. "I want an answer," he threatened.

Alice, who had stood stock-still, now whimpered, and Michael looked at the sheriff as though he were seeing him for the first time.

"Yes, I take medication for my diabetes," he said. "But what I saw was real enough."

Freitag cut him off. "I knew it!" He turned to Johnson. "Take him to the clinic at Tallulah. He's not in his right mind."

Bewildered, Johnson climbed the three porch stairs. Ben turned to the sheriff when Freitag's radio crackled. "What? A stabbing?" Freitag turned away, and though Ben tried to catch the words, he couldn't.

"All right, I'm on my way."

Scowling, Freitag stepped off the porch and strode toward his cruiser. "Johnson, get him to the clinic," he said. "When you get what you need, join me out at the Jordan place on Franks Creek."

"But Sheriff— "

"Do what I say. Make sure the good Reverend finds out what happens when he messes with the law."

When Ben returned to the fire station, he went to see his boss, Jonathan Coates. Ben brought him up to date on the Statler car fire, and he wasn't surprised at the fire chief's reluctance to believe what Statler said caused the fire. After he finished, Ben asked, "What's the situation on the broken fire hydrant in Robbinsville?"

Coates looked chagrined. "They have their hands full. Seems that the electronic solenoid shut-off valve failed in the water transfer plant."

Ben shook his head. "Well, what about the manual shut-off, the back up?"

"It's frozen. Can't be shut. Moreover, the plant's night man was called away – family emergency. The only men left are two rookies on the job, and they can't get the valve unfrozen."

"What about the Robbinsville Fire Department crew?" Ben asked. "Can't they help?"

"The RFD is busy with another house fire at the moment." Coates turned to him. "How about you run over to the water transfer plant and help them out?"

"Fine," Ben said.

He left the station in the early evening darkness and sped into Robbinsville. He arrived at the transfer plant and found Zack working with another man, trying to turn the manual valve by hand.

"Let me help," he said. He found a one-inch pipe, a cheater bar, amongst some equipment stored near the valve. "Watch how it's done," he told them. He slid the pipe into the valve. "Okay? Now we have leverage. Zack, grab the pipe and push – hard."

At first the pipe refused to budge. But when it broke free, the sudden release sent them backwards. Zack staggered, lost his balance, and crashed into an adjoining valve. He fell to the floor, groaning.

"You all right?" Ben bent over Zack. Zack placed his hand on the back of his scalp. Ben kneeled for a better look. "You're bleeding, Zack. Where's a first aid kit?"

"On the desk," Zack said.

Ben got the kit and brought it back, cleaning the scalp wound and applying a dressing. "Hold that on there," he told Zack. "Keep pressure on it."

The other worker finished the job of shutting the stubborn valve. "That ought to do it," he said. "Will you be repairing the hydrant now?"

"No," Ben answered. "Robbinsville will do that when they get back. Right now, Zack should be taken to the emergency clinic at Tallulah."

"That's not necessary," Zack said. "It's a minor cut."

"It probably is, but it might need stitches."

Zack raised a hand in protest. "There's no way I'm going to climb into an ambulance for a ride of about three blocks. No way."

Ben sighed. "Head wounds are nothing to fool with. Tell you what. I'll drop you off there myself. I could be fired for this, but if that's what it takes to get you fixed up, I'll do it."

"Fine."

He led Zack out to the SFD utility truck and helped him into the passenger seat. They drove the three blocks in silence until he'd parked by the front door under the portico lights. "Let me help you out," Ben said, and together they entered the clinic.

The recently opened wing for emergencies was overflowing. Zack was led to a cubicle almost immediately, and as Ben left, he spotted Michael Statler in the adjoining cubicle. Statler was alone, sitting on the exam table, and he was shivering violently.

Ben looked around and then stepped in. "Reverend, you okay?"

"I'm cold." Michael looked at him with glazed eyes. "The deputy, though, said he was going to get my pajamas."

Ben looked around the cubicle, startled. "Your clothes aren't in here? That seems a bit odd." He leaned over the preacher. "You must've been here awhile. What has the doctor said about your condition?"

Michael laughed bitterly. "What doctor? I've only seen an orderly. All I need is my insulin shot, but that Deputy, Johnson, won't listen to me. He left me here in this gown. Wouldn't even get me a blanket."

Ben straightened, angry. "I'll get a doctor right away."

"No need," Michael said. "About ten minutes ago, after the tenth time I'd told Johnson I needed a shot, he said, 'Tell you what. We'll get you that insulin, but first you need to sign a statement I've drawn up.'"

"What kind of statement?" Ben asked.

"I asked him that too," Michael said. "But when I read it, I understood."

"Understood what?"

"The statement said my car caught fire due to some faulty wiring. That isn't what happened. Then the deputy became condescending. He said, 'Look at it this way, Statler. After you sign that form, your insurance company will replace your car without a problem. Not only that, but you'll get your insulin.'"

"Did you sign it?" Ben asked.

"Yes, and the orderly brought me an insulin shot right away. After the orderly left, the deputy said the doctors would get reprimanded for ignoring me so long. You know that's a crock. This clinic has nothing but fine doctors. I'm sure they were intimidated somehow. Anyway, he finally left the room and I haven't seen him since."

"I see." Ben sighed. "I'll be right back. I'm going to try and find your clothes." He stepped out and entered the cubicle across the hall, where he found Michael's pajamas in a plastic bag. "That was easy," he said, handing the bag to Michael.

The preacher dressed quickly and turned to Ben, distressed. "I don't know how I'll get home," he said.

"I'll take you as far as the Stecoah fire station. My boss can probably find you a ride home from there, all right?"

"Thanks," Michael said.

As they pulled into the fire station twenty minutes later, Michael rested his hand on Ben's arm. "You know, when my car caught on fire, I had been trying to write a sermon on forgiveness, but I couldn't find the right words. Now I know I needed to revamp the speech."

"Go on," Ben said.

"I'm going to tell my flock that forgiveness is good but should never be confused with passive acceptance of evil. They need to understand the nature of insidious evil and how to resist it. And when I'm done," he said, "I'm going to tell them I'm retiring." He smiled in the dark cab. "Alice will be happy."

CHAPTER 36

DAI YU raced toward the second RHIC console room, a replica for the one across the river. She shivered with excitement. *It was happening.*

She found the room a beehive of activity. Spenser, Stjernholm, and Petrowski had all arrived ahead of her, and only Franz stood frozen in amazement. "My God, what in the *hell* is going on here?" he asked. His eyes remained locked on her as she took her place at the console.

She looked at the screen, which had been pulled down. On it she could see the clear night sky, resplendent in a million pinpoints of light from the stars. But as she watched, several images emerged from the stars.

She felt her heart hammering. From behind her, Franz muttered in disbelief. Four objects became clearer on the monitor. Three of them were not much larger than private jets, though they were triangular, with smoothed and rounded edges.

The fourth craft, slightly more globe shaped and much larger, glowed with a luminescent light that lit the night sky brighter than the moon. It led the other three craft, and they all formed a V formation.

"Oh shit," Franz said.

The group watched the shapes, spellbound, and time seemed to stand still. The only movement seemed to come from the skies. As Dai Yu studied the screen, she could make out the faint shapes of a band of Comanche helicopters way to the rear. They moved in the same direction as the craft, north by northeast, and they kept a respectable distance behind the four UFOs.

Dai Yu looked at Petrowski. "I'll punch up the accelerator path module for the weapon and activate all the grid diversion equipment."

"Activate it," he ordered. His phone beeped then and he took the call.

"Yes, General," he said. "Of course we're on it. They won't get away." He hung up and turned back to the monitor.

Harvey Spenser stepped toward Dai Yu. "Give me the satellite uplink."

Dai Yu nodded and typed feverishly. "I've linked with the satellite so you should have it now."

The picture of the night sky dissolved and the screen showed an outline of the east coast of the United States, and as Dai Yu watched, their eye in the sky zoomed into western North Carolina.

She could see the dam, flanked on both sides by the lab buildings, and beyond it, to the south and west, was Fontana Park. The dark, smooth stain of the lake stretched beyond, branching into myriads of forks along the deep valleys south of the dam. In a moment, she could discern four small specks of light arranged around a larger, more luminescent globe of light, moving fast. "My God, they're at Mach 8 or 9."

"Be quiet!" Petrowski barked. He stepped closer. "Have to stop them. We have very little time." He leaned over her, his body tense. "Wait. They're slowing down."

"Yes." Spenser nodded. "We now have a better chance. Don't miss, Dai Yu. We'll only have a couple of minutes."

Dai Yu remained cool. "We'll only get two shots." She went back to the instrument panel and feverishly punched more controls.

"What's that?" Spenser pointed at the satellite view on the screen, and Dai Yu could see the edge of the park. A few yards beyond the grass, she made out the intersection where the highway met the marina road and the road to the top of the dam, which skirted the edge of the park.

Pulled off the road at the junction, Dai Yu spotted an eighteen-wheel truck, a smaller truck, and a car. A group of onlookers had stopped, and the eye in the sky revealed two men, adults, as well as three teens, all staring and pointing.

"Unwanted visitors. Damn!" Petrowski frowned and turned to a sergeant at the edge of the room. "Kiley, this is going to cause a huge fire. Get a Seal team over there as fast as possible, and for God's sake, get those roads blocked *now*. Also, get a military fire and rescue team out there. P.D. too."

"Yes sir!"

An alarm sounded at that moment from somewhere in the bowels of the building, and the lights flickered.

"Colonel!" Dai Yu warned. "The dam – the power grid – they aren't giving us enough power. If I don't have power fast, the beam won't work."

"I can fix that." Petrowski grabbed the cell phone and dialed. "Do it by the book, the way we've practiced," he barked into the phone. "Hit the switches and give us all the power you can." He paused, listening. "No, I don't care if the whole region goes dark. We need the power now, all of it!" Dai Yu heard someone answering him on the phone.

"Right," Petrowski said, "the activation code is 'big bang.'" He hung up and turned back to Dai Yu.

She punched one last control and sat back. The lights brightened and then, beneath her, she felt the supercollider vibrate.

"Got full power now." She turned her attention to the screen. In an instant, the plasma beam of light shot skyward, producing an enormous flash on the globe-shaped mother ship. The big ship hovered for an instant more, and then pulverized in a great explosion of light.

Several people in the room grunted from the searing brilliance.

"Yes!" Dai Yu exulted. She hunched over the controls, rapidly typing in the next firing sequence.

Petrowski leaned near her. "Get those other bastards!"

The other three ships darted about in confusion. Two of the three glowed briefly and shot straight up into the stratosphere and out of sight. Only one remained a second too long.

Petrowski gripped Dai Yu's shoulder so tightly that she yelped. "Get that one!" His voice was icier than the dead of winter.

"Sir, he's moving away, so he's not a threat," she said, but her voice trailed away as his fingers dug into her shoulder. "Ai-yai...."

"No," Petrowski said. "Set the power lower for that ship. I want to capture a few of them alive. And we need another one of their ships. Canada got the last one; it's our turn now."

Dai Yu looked at the Colonel, wide eyed. "Do I shoot it now?"

Petrowski grabbed her hair. "Do it!"

"Give me twenty percent power," she said into a speaker. "Yes, locked on."

A second beam of light lit the night sky, flashing against the surface of the one remaining triangular sphere. Its glow, a dying light bulb, lasted ten seconds. The sphere wobbled, slipped sideways like a kite, then turned on end and crashed to the ground near the center of the park. When it hit the ground, a fluid stream of flame billowed high into the heavens and the ground shook as from an earthquake.

"Good God," Franz screamed. "Are you crazy? How do you know they're hostile?"

Petrowski shut his eyes. "We told them what they needed to know. We told them to leave us alone and never come back, but they wouldn't listen." He turned back to the console as his phone rang.

"Yes?" He listened. "Yes, we caught the sorry asses flat-footed. We pulverized the mother ship and shot down one of the smaller escorts." He paused again. "Yes, we hope to salvage some of the smaller ship. The fire crews are on their way. By the way, we could use those Cobras at the park." He was silent, listening.

"Good. I'll be in touch." Petrowski turned to the assembled group, recognizing Franz as though for the first time. "What the hell are you staring at?" he demanded.

Franz shrugged, and the Colonel grabbed him by his lab coat, almost lifting him off the floor. He muttered expletives under his breath. "Then get this. Not a word, unless you want it to be your last." He shoved Franz aside and turned to Dai Yu and the others. "That goes for you too."

CHAPTER 37

THE DINNER crowd had waned at the Sub Shoppe. Tammy watched Ryan's every move as he finished cleaning the empty tables. Sean was across the restaurant, cleaning the floor.

"We're about done," Ryan said. "Let's hope no one else comes in."

"Isn't the water shut off now?" Tammy was staring at the mop water.

"Sean was smart enough to fill several tubs and the bucket. Can't do too much cleaning though."

Sean spoke up. "We can't stay open with the water off. Would you call the boss and see what he wants us to do? I'll finish with the garbage."

Ryan nodded and disappeared into the shop's tiny office. Tammy helped Sean bundle all the plastic bags and put them in the dumpster. As they came through the rear door, Ryan met them. "Hey, the boss said we should simply close up for the night. And since Tammy's mom won't be home until late, we can go out and make it a date, or at least have fun and ride around awhile."

Sean's shoulders slumped. "Don't even mention the words 'women' or 'date' to me. Not now, not ever."

"What do you mean?"

"Janet broke up with me, that's what. And frankly, I've sworn off women."

Ryan laughed. "Oh Sean, come on. Two days ago Janet was but one of ten women you liked. Now she's your one and only heartthrob? I don't buy that."

Sean stalked to the door. "Oh, yeah? Well, you obviously didn't know how much we cared about each other. Besides, if I want to feel miserable, it's my right."

"Wait a minute, bro," Ryan said. "Everything else picked up? All burners off?"

"Yeah," Sean said. "Let's go."

Ryan slipped his arm around Tammy's shoulder and she liked the way it warmed her. They walked out to Ryan's Mustang and hopped in. Sean sat in the back. As he left the parking lot, Ryan whistled along to a rock song on the radio, its hot beat reverberating through the car.

"Give me a break," Sean said. "I can't stand that tonight. It's too – well – happy." Sean reached over the seat and switched off the radio.

Ryan shook his head. "Come on. You'll feel better soon." He turned the radio back on but lowered the volume.

They rolled past the grade of Stecoah Gap, turning toward Fontana Village. After a long silence, Ryan turned back to Sean. "Is your mom at home?"

"Nah. Only my older sister."

"Then that means you'll get out of some homework, doesn't it?" He winked at Tammy.

Sean laughed. "Not hardly. My sister is worse than Mom. It's going to be one really boring night."

"Too bad." Ryan was approaching the intersection at the park, and he slowed down for possible traffic.

"Hey. Hey!" Sean swiveled in his seat and pointed toward the rear seat window. An eerie, bright light lit the car. Tammy turned to look. Out of the corner of her eye, she saw an eighteen-wheeler pull off the road ahead of them. The driver climbed out of the cab. Across the road, an older Ford pickup also pulled off and the driver scrambled from his truck.

Ryan braked to a crawl. "It's the man who was in the Sub Shoppe this afternoon," Tammy said, pointing to the big rig. Ryan, though, had leaned out the window, craning to get a glimpse of the light's source. She looked up too.

"What the....?" Ryan said.

"Pull off, pull off!" Sean's excitement was contagious, so Ryan yanked the wheel and pulled the Mustang onto the shoulder, jerking to a stop. They almost rear-ended the big rig. As they all piled out of the car, Tammy peered up again.

"Look, look!" The truck driver pointed skyward. He jumped up and down. "God, this is the greatest, the *best*." He pulled out a camcorder from under his driver's seat. "This will astound my sweet Arlene!"

Mesmerized, Tammy stared at the clear night sky. Four pinpoints of light had appeared, and she knew they were unlike any craft she had ever seen.

The mother ship, the largest, was a huge luminescent globe, and the craft hummed softly as it glided overhead, forming the forward point in a V-shaped formation of four ships. The other three craft, small rounded triangles, moved soundlessly behind.

"Holy shit!" Ryan breathed. "Too much." He shoved his dark hair back from his face and turned toward the highway.

The owner of the pickup ran over to the driver of the commercial rig, and they whispered excitedly.

Tammy grabbed Ryan's wrist and pointed at the sky. "Unreal!" Seconds later, she giggled and ran up the highway. Ryan followed her, with Sean behind.

"Do you see them? Four UFOs!" She stopped short. "Destin!" The two hugged. Ryan stepped back, watching.

They all looked back to the UFOs. The large globe emitted an iridescent, electric blue beam that bathed the park in its eerie light. Several helicopters followed the UFOs at a respectable distance. She had seen many military choppers before, but these were new to her.

"Does anyone know what kind of helicopters those are?"

Destin nodded. "I do. They're Boeing Sikorsky RAH-66 Comanche helicopters and they can evade detection by radar. They were first flown in the spring of 1999 not too far from where I work in Florida. Aren't they something?"

Tammy ignored him and turned back to the UFOs as they passed overhead, low and slow. Their hum, more felt than heard, made the hairs on Tammy's arms rise. A prickly sensation swept her as the hum intensified. Destin's truck engine turned on, then off, then on again, its lights flickering.

"Hey, hey!" Destin said.

An HF radio inside the commercial rig sprang to life and a loud male voice filled the night air: "N4OZZ, N4OZZ, November Four, Oscar Zulu Zulu. This is K2PTQ, Kilo Two Papa Tango Quebec. Do you copy?"

Tammy watched as Destin laughed. "Hey man," he addressed the trucker, "I'm a ham too."

The trucker grinned. "Way to go! Hang on a sec." He hopped into his cab and grabbed the mike. "Dang it, Jacob, this ain't a good time for me 'cause I'm out eyeballing a pretty bunch of real live UFOs. And before you jive me, let me tell you right now that I got it all on film. So do me a favor – dig? Call my sweet Arlene and tell her I've got some photos that will knock her socks off!"

"Yeah, right! You're smoking again!"

"Nada. Gotta go. Call you later." The trucker swung out of the cab.

Ryan moved closer to Tammy, Destin, and the trucker. "I'm Ryan," he said. "And this is Sean Garver."

Sean nodded at the group, as the trucker extended his hand.

"I'm Rocky. Out of Little Rock." Everyone shook hands.

"And everyone, this is Destin," Tammy said. "Destin is a friend of our family." He nodded.

Rocky studied the group. "If anyone has a camera, you'd better grab it and get some shots before it gets too far away." Frustrated, they shook their heads.

Without warning, the amber lights at the intersection began to flicker. They went out, one by one.

"Did the UFOs do that?" Sean asked.

"Don't think so," Destin said. "I could be wrong, but I think that somebody is drawing lots of electricity from the power lines."

At that instant, a beam of light from a point about two miles to the north hit the mother ship. The onlookers shielded their eyes from its blinding intensity.

"Whaat?" Sean shrunk back, ready to flee.

"Holy shit, that light's from Fontana Labs!" Tammy stared at the mother ship, now aflame. As they all watched, the ship exploded. The fireball lit the night sky. Three of the smaller ships immediately shot straight up for the stratosphere, disappearing.

The remaining scout ship wobbled as a second beam of light hit it. The triangular craft slipped sideways and careened to earth on a forty-five degree angle, crashing into the center of the park several hundred yards beyond the group. The ground trembled and flames engulfed a stand of trees.

Rocky's voice trembled. "My God, I got it. All on the camcorder." He turned to the others. "What in the heck was that beam of light? A weapon maybe?" He stared at the inferno to the north.

"Exactly," Destin said. "It's a particle beam. The Quark Gluon Plasma Beam."

Awed, everyone turned to him except Tammy, who grinned, nodding. "Believe him. He knows."

"Yeah, it's true." Rocky said, "I'd heard rumors about some sort of deadly weapon at the labs." He looked toward the devastation. The UFO had sheared the tops off the trees at the crash site, allowing them a better look at the flames.

Tammy turned to Destin. "Come on! Let's go into the park and see if we can get to the wreckage."

Destin shook his head. "You don't want to do that. For one, the fire might be toxic. After all, we don't understand what propels those UFOs. Second, since those craft were deliberately shot down, I'd be willing to bet that the military will be here faster than you can count. If we're smart, we'll get the heck out of here as fast as possible." Everyone nodded.

Rocky gripped Destin's shoulder. "Let's not run off before we get each other's call signs. I'm N4OZZ. What's yours?"

"WR4RR."

"That'll be easy to remember. A good call sign. By the way, do you monitor HF?"

"Yep. And I got the truck rigged for it."

"Good! I listen to 20 meters mostly," Rocky said. "14.235, when I'm on the road. My friends hang out on that frequency. Let's keep in touch."

"You got it. Whenever you're closer in, let's use 7.230. Here's one of my QSL cards." Destin handed one to Rocky.

Rocky smiled and pulled one of his own QSL cards out of his wallet. "And mine."

Everyone turned as they heard sirens approaching.

Destin nodded knowingly. "Here they come."

Rocky said nothing, but he slid his camcorder out of sight under his seat in the cab. The Comanche helicopters passed overhead and hovered over the crash site.

Two police cars sped into sight, marked with the county sheriff's logo. They careened to a stop and blocked the highway. Two officers got out. The driver approached them while the other officer, a deputy, watched the fire in the park.

"Enough is enough. The party's over," Sheriff Freitag said, when he'd reached the group.

No one spoke for a moment and Tammy stared at him, also mute. "That was an aircraft out of the Army Air Reserve Station in Maryville." Freitag pointed to the crash site. "Nothing special to see."

"Wait a minute," Rocky spat on the ground. "That isn't what *we* saw."

Freitag shoved Rocky against his cab and frisked him. Then he slammed his head into the hood. "You truckers think you know everything?" He spun Rocky around but the deputy, Johnson, restrained him.

"You're right," Destin forced a laugh. "None of us saw anything but that aircraft crash into the woods. Right Rocky?"

Rocky straightened, wiping blood from his lip. "Sure man. Just one of your everyday, run-of-the-mill crashes. Nothing to get excited about."

Infuriated, Freitag grabbed Rocky again, but everyone screamed. He stepped back, shrugging. "All right, kids." He whirled around and faced them. "I have no beef with you, so now you have one or two options. I can check your cars now for license, registration, inspection sticker, good tires, alcohol, drugs, whatever – *or* – you can go home and forget tonight. Which is it going to be?"

Sean spoke up. "We only saw a plane crash, *officer*." He turned towards Ryan in disgust. "Come on Ryan, let's go home."

"Wait." Ryan eyed Tammy. "Anyone want to go to Tootie's?" Tammy and Sean shook their heads in unison. "Nah, we pass," Tammy said.

Ryan shrugged and slid into his car. Sean and Tammy followed suit without comment. He slipped out onto the highway and idled up to the roadblock. "I live at the village," he said to Freitag. "Let me by."

"Then go straight home."

Ryan eased past the roadblock, and in his rearview mirror he could see the others leaving.

"Wait. We could park up one of the side roads and sneak back to the crash site," Ryan said, squeezing Tammy's hand.

"Not a good idea," Sean said from the back seat. "Besides, I'm no longer sure what I saw. Are you?"

Ryan offered no answer and they rode back to the village in silence. As Tammy sat there in the darkness next to Ryan, she shivered. It was one thing, she decided, to oppose the labs, but with the police on the side of the labs, they were far more powerful than she had originally assumed. She wondered how long they would allow her to live. She wasn't happy with the odds.

CHAPTER 38

BACK at the fire station, Ben had little time to think about the strange events surrounding Reverend Statler's car fire and the preacher's subsequent mistreatment. After his return, the fire chief found the preacher a ride home. A few minutes later, the alarm sounded again.

Coates assembled them quickly. "This is a bad one. Got ourselves an aircraft crash in the park by the dam. Fire crews from the labs are already on the scene."

"Mother of Jesus!" Ben said.

Coates peered at Ben. "Since you're the only crew member with nuclear radiation and biohazard training, you'll be in charge at the crash site."

An icy claw gnawed at Ben's gut. "Nuclear?"

Coates nodded. "Get going, now. Rudy, you'll drive."

They ran for their equipment and climbed aboard the pumper. Meanwhile, Ben darted over to his own truck, returning in less than a minute. He grabbed his gear and swung into the front passenger seat. When they pulled out of the station, Coates, the fire chief, followed them in the utility truck.

Rudy drove in silence for several minutes. Finally he turned to Ben. "Earlier, when we put out that car fire, I noticed something odd was going down between that preacher and the sheriff. Do you know what that was all about?"

Ben shook his head. "I don't, but it was weird, all right. The preacher was being harassed. I think he was telling the truth about his car fire."

Rudy nodded. "It's similar to one of those UFO stories. Makes me think UFO's might be real after all."

"You know," Ben said, "the way that Sheriff Freitag acted, he must be in tight with the labs."

"I know." Rudy was silent for a moment. "Freitag's related to my wife, Sarah's, family, so we see them occasionally. Not long ago at a picnic, Freitag mentioned that he did a lot of work for the labs on the side."

Rudy looked over at Ben, and though Ben couldn't see his face in the darkness, he seemed thoughtful. "Where did you disappear to, back at the station?"

"When?"

"Right before we left."

Ben grinned. "I got something out of my truck."

When they reached the park, a barricade blockaded the highway, and behind it sat two empty patrol cars. Deputy Johnson directed traffic. A knot of cars had formed behind the police cars, and Johnson was turning the vehicles around. They pulled past the barricade and parked on the shoulder of the highway, waiting for clearance. As they sat there, Ben heard the police car radio blare. "Car 47, do you copy?"

Johnson leaned into the car and grabbed the mike. "Whatcha' got?"

The woman dispatcher's voice blared to life. "The labs ask that you detain a blue, 1979 Ford truck, Florida license number R-5-2-3-7-9. Copy that? The driver is wanted for questioning in connection with the murder of George Eisenhart and his wife, Linda Eisenhart of Sylva."

Johnson's face contorted in rage. "Freitag isn't going to be happy," he said. "The suspect left this location about twenty minutes ago. We have our hands full, so send two deputies and see if they can locate him. He was southbound on Highway 28." He pounded the roof.

"Roger that, Car 47."

Rudy shook his head. "Hey, we haven't come to a picnic, so let us through, unless you want this fire on your head!"

Johnson waved them by, and the fire truck sped across the wide expanse of grass to the edge of the woods.

Everyone craned to see the fire, which had hungrily spread across several acres of trees. A bitter electrical smell hung in the smoke. Flames were everywhere, and in the center of the park, Ben saw an iridescent yellow glow surrounding the flames. It was an exceptionally hot fire. Eerie.

After they had parked, Coates pulled in next to them and got them together. "Ben, I want you at the crash site. Since the fire is spreading to the east, the rest of you spread out along that fire line. But before you go, I have something to read to you."

He pulled out a badly wrinkled paper and began. "Standard Operating Procedure for Handling a UFO crash." Ignoring the crew's murmurs, he read the provisions for handling it.

"But gentlemen," he concluded, "this UFO does NOT exist. It's essential that each and every one of you understand that. And you are absolutely, and I stress that – absolutely – not allowed to discuss this incident with reporters or the media. Understood?" He waited until they nodded. Ben felt for the camcorder, which bulged slightly under his jacket.

Rudy, who was at his side, poked him. "So that is what you went and got out of your truck," he whispered. "You do realize, don't you, that this crash is classified? And if you break their rules, you could be in big trouble? Ben, think! Don't throw your life away."

Ben looked at Rudy's eyes. They reflected friendship and concern. For a moment he wavered. Then the specter of Gus and his pregnant wife, lying in a coffin, floated before him. "I'll be careful, Rudy. Don't plan on them catching me. Now, come with me. I'll direct you."

Rudy nodded, moving towards the flames, and Ben followed. They entered the crash site, and around its perimeter, Special Forces troops took up positions. The helicopters created a huge draft, which only heated the fire until the choppers moved away.

Without warning, Ben spotted a large metallic UFO in the center of the clearing. Still aflame, the triangular craft had broken into several pieces. An other-worldly cloud clung to the crashed ship. Stunned, he gaped at two bodies wrapped in shiny Mylar, lying on the ground. He slid his hand under his jacket and turned on his camcorder.

When Coates gripped his arm, Ben jumped. "Don't stand there gawking! Start hosing the perimeter trees right now." Coates scowled. He swiveled toward Rudy. "What are *you* doing here? You're supposed to be with the crew on the east perimeter."

"Ben asked me to help."

Coates sighed. "All right, since you're here already, you can stay. But for goodness sakes, be careful."

Coates disappeared into the cluster of Special Forces at one end of the clearing. Rudy poked Ben and pointed. "What in heaven's name is *that*?"

"Not human!" Ben said. On the ground, near one piece of the wrecked craft, the creature sat, slumped to one side. It watched everyone in the clearing.

"I'll bet it's one of your garden-variety aliens," Rudy said.

From between the folds of his fire jacket, Ben panned the scene with his camcorder.

"You bet it is," Coates said, thumping Rudy on the back. Ben slid the camcorder out of sight.

"He's the only one that survived the crash. Probably one of the pilots." Coates moved closer to the fire.

Ben gaped at the figure on the ground, who studied him intently as well. He slid his camcorder out as far as he dared, panning the alien.

"He's definitely not human," Rudy said.

"What would you expect? And this is no ordinary fire either. Look at that milky cloud." Ben turned off the camera and he and Rudy fought the blaze for some time until Coates reappeared with a lab official in tow.

"This is one of my top men." Coates pointed at Ben. "The men think a lot of him. They'll listen to him." He paused. "Ben, the folks at the labs say it's very important that you convince the rest of the crew that, never again, is this crash to be talked about or discussed, especially with their wives or families. Never. And again, this is a standard Air Force military jet crash. Got it?" He leaned closer. "We can't go off scaring the whole world. Don't need to see alien bodies in the headlines of every paper either. You must give me your solemn oath to keep this secret, and as I said, Ben, you need to convince the men of that too."

Ben nodded.

"And you Rudy?"

Rudy nodded and Coates left, headed for the roadblock.

Rudy whistled, punching at the bulge under Ben's jacket. "What are you going to tell them if they catch you with that?"

"I'll tell them I had it along for a seminar – oh, I don't know!"

Coates returned a moment later leading the rest of Ben's crew from the woods.

"A new fire crew showed up and insisted we leave," one firefighter said. "They were a mite unfriendly about it." He stopped dead in his tracks when he saw the alien. "Oh, God." He studied the alien. "He acts as if he knows what we're saying."

"I know," Rudy said. "He's definitely intelligent."

Ben nodded. "What an understatement. They build spaceships, cross the galaxies, and we observe that they are intelligent."

The others of their crew crowded in, and they laughed. One pointed at the creature. "Did you see him? He moved his head so fast, my eyes couldn't follow it. Weird. Some sort of reptilian thing. And look at his eyes."

They all turned back and stared. The alien was small, maybe 4'10" or so, with a grayish green skin and an upside down, pear-shaped head. He had no hair. His eyes were huge black almonds, and he looked similar to the aliens in countless drawings.

A group of Special Forces men surrounded the injured alien while two others sidled up, carrying a stretcher. Everyone, including Ben, hung back, as though afraid to get too close. Then in the blink of the eye, the alien was no longer propped against the wreckage, but instead, was lying on the stretcher.

"Did you see *that*?" Rudy asked.

"Yes, definitely intelligent," Ben said.

A lab official appeared. He wore a large nametag, which identified him as Spenser. He strode to the center of the clearing, carrying a bullhorn. "All you men leave the area. We've secured the crash site. Only the 'Rad' crew will stay. We'll handle it from here."

Ben, who had turned the camera back on, merely shrugged. He wondered if his camera was getting the audio, even if it was out of sight under the jacket.

"Sir," Rudy said, "shouldn't we clear a fire break before we go? That fire is a heck of a lot hotter than most, and the surrounding trees keep exploding into crown fires."

Spenser shook his head. "I said we'd take care of it. And stay away from the ship. It's radioactive. Only those with suits are going to stay."

Coates approached them, nodding. "Let's go, men," he said. "We've done all we can do here."

The ride back to the firehouse passed mostly in silence. Ben rode in back, and in the blackness he clung tightly to his jacket. Before they pulled into the station, he knew what he must do next, provided he had Karen and Destin's help. He would get the film copied, write up his testimony, and go public with it. The thought, though, petrified him.

CHAPTER 39

DEVASTATED, Bonnie had watched Destin drive off toward Fontana Village before noon the prior day. She felt tears sting her eyes, but she dabbed them away. Because the uncertainty of her future haunted her, she kept busy, first cleaning and afterwards, mowing the grass until well after dusk.

The next morning, she packed her father's clothing into empty cartons. She had finished when Doc called. "Bonnie, so glad I caught you," he said. "You weren't at the CGR."

Bonnie cradled the phone against her ear, using her hands to push her hair back. "What's wrong? Did you hear from the Bledsoes?"

"No." He paused. "Look, I have some unusual news."

"What?"

"It's crazy really, but President Alcorn received a call moments ago from a private research firm in North Carolina, and apparently, they asked him numerous questions about you and your language research with gorillas. As I said, their call goes beyond – *odd* – because they told President Alcorn they wanted to hire you. They need you for a temporary period that might range from a few weeks to several months." Doc paused.

"Apparently, they're into some sort of top-secret government project that requires your services *immediately*. They wouldn't tell Alcorn why they were in such a hurry or anything about the work."

"And what did Alcorn tell them?"

"He was upset at first," Doc said. "Declined their offer. He told them about the loss of Bledsoe's grant. Said there were far too many details for you to attend to."

"Of course. We all have a huge job ahead of us." She paused. "What firm asked about me?"

"Fontana Labs."

She froze. "Fontana?" She could feel her pulse pounding through the earpiece.

"Yes, ever hear of them?"

"Yes, but that's a long story." Bonnie gripped the phone. "Who called President Alcorn?"

"A DOE man, Harvey Spenser. Said he was calling on behalf of Colonel Petrowski, and Alcorn gathered that both men lead missions at the labs."

"I've heard of the one man," Bonnie said.

"Well, there's more." Doc's voice rose. "Bonnie, when Alcorn told that Spenser fellow that you weren't available, he then made an offer the university couldn't refuse."

"What kind of offer?" Her hands began to sweat.

"Spenser said that the Department of Energy would guarantee to pick up the grant and continue funding our center if you'd take their offer. Needless to say, Alcorn didn't refuse."

Bonnie's mouth was dry. "You said Fontana Labs wanted me to start immediately. How 'immediately'?"

"As I said," Doc repeated, "the whole deal is odd. They asked that you drive over today, if possible. Do you know where the labs are located?"

"Yes," Bonnie said, "I do. But I can't imagine why they need me. Must be a new project with animals and language." Her mind raced. "But how can I begin work without my computer program and my notes, or at least the cards I use?"

"Oh, that's no problem," Doc said. "Alcorn already mentioned that you would need some of your equipment. That Spenser guy said he wanted the university to ship any required materials by overnight express, and Alcorn said he'd do it."

"But Ollie and Dollie — "

Doc interrupted. "The grad students will continue working with them. Perhaps on weekends, you can come back to oversee their work."

"Then I guess that leaves only me. Did they mention where I would be staying?"

"Yes," Doc said. "They have a lodge in their village and a room for you if you want to stay there, rather than driving back and forth."

"All right." Bonnie shrugged. "I'll pack a few things and go. You know, this is very bizarre."

"But we can't pass it up, can we?"

Bonnie sighed. "No, we can't. But until my work at the labs is finished, will you make sure my assistants have free access to me in case of any problems?"

"Consider it done," Doc said.

"Then I'll call when I have a better idea about this work."

"Okay," Doc said, and hung up.

As Bonnie replaced the receiver, she wondered what type of animals she would be trying to communicate with.

The drive to Fontana Labs, late that night, was harrowing. The trees along the Dragon's Tail formed a primeval canopy and the blackness beneath chilled her to the marrow. She crossed the sharp flanks of mountains until she dropped down through Deals Gap and followed the shoreline of Lake Cheoah. For a distance of several miles, the road straightened and she watched the moon reflect across the placid waters on her right. When she left the lake behind, she climbed a long ridge near the dam and entered the village.

She followed the signs to the lodge. It sat astride a knoll and massive stone pillars supported the lodge entrance. She parked and trudged into the deserted lobby. It was elegantly decorated in a blend of mountain and western furnishings. A faint scent of furniture polish followed her.

The only person in the lobby was a lone clerk at the registration desk, an overweight man who was out of breath. He looked up. "Dr. Rhodes?"

"Yes."

"Good. Been expecting you. Your trip here was no problem?"

"Rushed," Bonnie said.

"Sorry. Let me get you a key." He fished it out from below the counter and handed it to her.

"What's next?" Bonnie shifted feet. "When will I be briefed about my job?"

He smiled. "I'm glad you reminded me. You're to meet with Mr. Harvey Spenser tomorrow morning at eight. His office is located in the labs across the main highway. Use the main entrance. You can't miss it." She nodded.

"Let me show you your room then."

He picked up her bag, one of her father's suitcases, and led the way down the hall to the last room by the exit sign. The clerk set down her suitcase, took the key, and opened the door for her, stepping aside so she could enter.

Bonnie looked over the room. It was clean and could have passed for any typical, somewhat pricey lodge room.

"Fine," she said, and he left. She lugged in several cartons of clothes and supplies from the car, and settled in. After changing, she fumbled through her purse and found Karen's telephone number written on a business card Destin had left her.

She glanced at her alarm clock. It was nearly one. *Shit.* She paced the room for a moment, reached for the room phone but replaced the receiver. It might be monitored. She remembered the pay phone across the hall from her room. *Safer.* She snuck out into the deserted hallway and used the phone.

"Who's calling at this ungodly hour?" a sleepy voice said.

"Sorry, Karen. I'm Bonnie Rhodes, an acquaintance of Destin's. Has he told you about me?" She kept her voice low and cupped her free hand over the mouthpiece.

Karen didn't answer for a moment. "Why, yes he did, about three hours ago. We talked on the ham radio. I'm a ham too."

"Yes, I know." Bonnie smiled faintly. "He mentioned — "

"Why are you calling?"

"Because I'm right here in Fontana Village, at the lodge."

Karen was silent for a moment. "Bonnie, this isn't a good time to contact Destin and renew your friendship. A lot happened last night – bad things, exciting things."

"If you're thinking I followed Destin here, you're all wrong, Karen. I simply want to tell Destin that I've been temporarily assigned to work here at the labs. Look, it's a long, incredible story, but I wanted Destin to know." She waited.

Karen's voice was both surprised and cautious. "Destin is in hiding. I can make radio contact with him, but I don't know whether or not he'll still be listening this late. Look, if I can't get him tonight, I'm sure I'll have no trouble tomorrow, and I'll let him know." She paused. "I'm sorry I said what I did about your being here. That wasn't called for."

Bonnie laughed. "No offense taken."

"Aren't you an anthropologist?"

"Yes. I specialize in linguistics – animal communication."

Karen whistled. "What kind of work will you be doing here?"

"I've been wondering the same thing. I didn't know the labs were researching Simian linguistics."

"That's because they don't. But I have a pretty good idea what they want you to do."

"What?" Bonnie asked.

"They want you to communicate with an E.T. – an alien."

Bonnie's left hand trembled. "Oh, come on! Get real! What makes you think that?"

Karen then told her about the events of the evening: the use of the quark gluon plasma beam weapon against four UFOs, how the mother ship had exploded, and how the second beam had caused a smaller scout ship to crash. "A large chunk of the woods in the park is still smoldering," she said. "In fact, you may still catch a glimpse of the fire from your window if you look southeast. Of course, you can't get anywhere near that park now. It's been sealed off." She paused.

"I didn't know what had caused the explosion, but my daughter, Tammy, witnessed it first hand and so did Destin, quite coincidentally. They told me what happened."

Bonnie leaned against the wall for support. "Incredible. And you – you believe that they may have captured one or more extraterrestrials?"

"I admit it's way out," Karen said, "but it would explain their sudden, urgent need for your services. Right?"

Bonnie laughed. "I'm going to have a lot of fun tomorrow after I find out what *really* happened. But don't worry, because you'll be the first to know. I'll call you on a break or at lunch, if I can find a phone or use mine."

Karen sounded slightly wounded. "Truth can be stranger than fiction, so don't be surprised." She lowered her voice. "And Bonnie, use a secure phone."

Bonnie then thought of George and Linda's murders, of the computer disk, and of Destin's danger. She sobered. "I'll be careful," she promised.

CHAPTER 40

TAMMY awoke and lifted her bedroom blinds. It was a pleasant fall day. Five squirrels darted back and forth, scurrying up trees, storing acorns for winter. Nevertheless, she felt that the world was on hold, watching. She could sense it, and it scared her. She closed the blinds.

After the UFO crash, sleep had been impossible. Her bed was a battleground. She straightened it with more care than usual, and when finished, she joined her mom in the kitchen. Karen poured herself some coffee as Tammy slid into her spot at the table.

"Did you get any rest last night?"

"Not really," Tammy said. Karen frowned. "But I'll be all right. A bad night is no big deal." Tammy picked up her juice and drank it, turning then to her cereal and toast.

Karen sat down and slid her arm across Tammy's shoulders. "Look honey, any kind of horrible accident has that effect on people. I can still remember the first fatal car crash I ever saw. I couldn't sleep after it either. It's normal to be shocked and sad."

Tammy looked down at her plate. "I know, I know. I feel bad though. At first I was so excited to see real UFO's, but now all I feel is guilt."

"Don't blame yourself," Karen said.

"I can't get it out of my mind that there were beings on those UFO's who died," Tammy said. "And on top of everything else, that bozo of a sheriff gave us all such a bad time. The only good thing about any of it is that the truck driver, Rocky, had a camcorder and filmed the whole thing. If the sheriff had found his camera, I bet he would have confiscated it."

She looked at her mom, who gave her a second squeeze. "Mom, who called us late last night? I heard the phone ring."

Karen sipped her coffee. "Bonnie Rhodes, a friend of Destin's. She's been hired by the labs." She then explained how Bonnie and Destin had met, and how Bonnie had come to work at Fontana. She paused, set the cup down.

"Bonnie thought she was here to teach language to animals, but I know of no such program here at the labs, and in light of last night, I have a more interesting theory. I think Bonnie is here to establish communications with one or more captured E.T."

Startled, Tammy turned to her mother. "Oh wow, that's so cool," she said. The morning showed promise.

Karen paused. "Don't forget that I'm working the graveyard shift tonight. I may have Mrs. Cummings look in on you a couple of times."

"Ah Mom, I'm not a baby."

"Well, we'll see." Her mom was silent for a moment. She sighed. "I may have to leave you some dishes to wash, because I'm going to be really busy this morning. I want to contact Destin, and I think I'll call Franz Stjernholm, that nice engineer on the RHIC project, about the crash in the park."

"Why him?" Tammy said.

"George liked and trusted Franz. Besides, I think it's time we all share what we know, and put our heads together to figure out how to bring this out to the public." Karen moved the cup to the sink. "Which reminds me. You and Destin also said the truck driver, Rocky, who was at the crash site last night, was a ham. I'm hoping he can join us as well, if he's still in the area."

"Where will you all meet?"

"Tootie's Café in Stecoah is a good spot," Karen said.

"Cool. Why not let Ryan, Sean, and me come as well? After all, we saw the crash too."

Karen shook her head. "No, you have school."

"Mom!"

Before they could argue further, Ryan's Mustang pulled into the driveway and Tammy scrambled up. "Gotta' go, Mom." She gave her a perfunctory peck. At the door she stopped and turned. "Do you mind if I tell Ryan what you said a moment ago about Bonnie? After all, he saw the crash."

Karen hesitated, and then nodded. "Go ahead, but remember to tell him this is to be kept confidential. I'm serious now. Destin's life could depend on it."

Tammy flashed a grin at her through the open door, "Thanks, Mom."

She crossed the driveway and slid in next to Ryan. Ryan's face lit up at the sight of her. "How's my girl?" he asked, pulling out onto the road. She didn't answer him until they were out of sight of her mom. Then she scooted closer, touching his arm. "Ryan, did you have any problems sleeping last night?"

He peered at her, though his dark eyes did not register surprise. "No. Unless it was because you weren't there." He laughed.

She punched him lightly. "No, I'm talking about the crash. Don't you realize that last night's sighting and crash may be one of those defining moments in our lives?"

Ryan's face sobered. "Yeah. I never really believed in UFO's and little green men until last night. I wish I could have met the crew aboard that craft."

Tammy yanked at his sleeve. "Pull over! Pull off the road. I want to tell you what happened last night after I got home."

Ryan shrugged and pulled off. Tammy told him all about Destin and how he was involved in George and Linda's murder, about the quark gluon beam, and then about Bonnie's arrival at the village, and her mother's theory about Bonnie's new job.

"Unreal," Ryan said, running his fingers through his dark hair. "I think your mother must be right. It makes sense."

"Yep. Mom said she's going to get Destin, Stjernholm, and all who know about the crash together, in order to share information. Since she's working tonight, she thought she'd try to make this a meeting for lunch today at Tootie's Café."

Ryan paused. "You know, we should go to that meeting too. And Sean." He didn't wait for a reply, but instead, he wheeled his car around and drove toward Sean's cottage in the village.

"Mom told me no." Tammy pouted. "She said I had to go to school."

"Well, let's cut school and go anyway," Ryan said. He pulled into Sean's driveway and after several toots, Sean came out, carrying his backpack. Tammy opened her door, so Sean could slide into the back seat.

"Hey, thought I was riding the bus today," Sean said.

Tammy turned to face him, grinning. "Are you up to skipping school today?"

Tammy brought Sean up to date as Ryan drove. The route to school took them by the park and the crash site, and they looked in awe at the cordoned-off park. The crash site was too far back in the woods to be seen from the road, though the tops of many trees were still-smoldering black toothpicks. Some had been snapped off. Muddy wheel ruts crisscrossed the chewed up grass.

Several National Guardsmen were stationed along the perimeter. The teens stared at them until they passed the park and began their descent into Stecoah Valley.

"Why are we headed this way?" Tammy asked. "Surely you don't want to sit around Tootie's Café for a couple of hours, waiting for the meeting."

"Got any better ideas?" Ryan asked.

"Yeah, I do," Sean said. "Remember how we saw those two fire trucks go past us into the crash site last night? Well, they had the SFD logos – Stecoah Fire Department. So I say, let's see if we can get more information about the UFO crash from them. After all, they were right in there."

"Not bad," Ryan said, pounding the steering wheel. "Not bad at all."

Minutes later, they left Highway 28 and followed a narrow paved road across a small portion of the valley to the fire department.

The large bay doors were open, and inside, two large fire trucks gleamed red in the shadows of the open bays. A few firefighters were cleaning the larger of the two trucks, so Tammy sauntered toward them. She stopped by a pile of equipment near the open bay doors. The boys followed.

"Hi there." She grinned at the first man, whose burly frame and crew cut hair made him look powerful. "I'm Tammy, and these are my friends, Ryan and Sean. We thought we'd stop by because we saw the crash and the fire at the park last night, and we wanted to find out what you saw." Behind the burly man, a firefighter had stopped work, and he stood, fascinated.

The burly man spat in the dirt, eyeing her coldly.

"Aren't you all supposed to be in school?"

"We're on a field trip," Ryan said. "School project and all."

Tammy knew the man wasn't that easily fooled. "What did you see at the fire?"

"There wasn't any crash in the park last night, nor was there any fire for that matter."

The teens stared at him and looked at each other, stunned into silence.

"How could you not know about the fire?" Sean said.

"Look, kid. I'm Chief Coates and I'd know if there was a fire anywhere in this county." He spat again on the ground.

The firefighter behind him, a man with a shock of red hair, picked up a slip of paper and wrote something. Tammy thought he was familiar, but she couldn't place him.

Angry, she took a step forward, clenching her fists. "My mom works at the labs and we all know better," she said. "And— "

"And you, young lady, shouldn't poke your nose where it isn't wanted," Coates said. "The only fire last night was a car fire. Belonged to a preacher."

Coates turned back to the fire truck. Tammy stood her ground a moment more, while the red haired man ambled toward the pile of equipment at her side. He reached down and picked up a Council rake, but it slid out of his hands and landed near her feet.

"Oops. Excuse me, ma'am." As he reached for the rake again, he shoved the small slip of paper into her hand. "Sorry." He carried the rake toward the rear of the bay.

Tammy remembered him then. Ben had delivered the documents so Karen could pass them on to Destin. She turned and wiggled her eyebrows at the boys. "Let's get out of here." She looked back to the two firefighters. "They're a bunch of schleps, if you ask me."

"I agree," Ryan said. "Bad air here." They moved back to the Mustang and hopped in.

"Get out of here!" Tammy hissed. "We'll talk in a minute."

Ryan started the engine and pulled out onto the road. "I saw that guy slip you a note. What does it say?"

Tammy opened the paper and read, "Meet me at the Stecoah Arts Center in an hour."

Sean sighed. "The folk center isn't open yet. What are we going to do for an hour?"

Tammy looked back and grinned. "Let's explore the upper end of Tuskeegee. I've never seen the falls up there. That isn't far away."

Ryan pursed his lips. "I haven't heard of any falls in that area, have you, Sean?"

"Nope."

Tammy shrugged. "Got a better idea?"

"No," Ryan answered. He drove past Stecoah Gap until he reached the Tuskeegee cutoff.

They drove in silence up the meandering road through rectangular fields and quaint farmhouses. They followed Yellow Creek, which paralleled the road, though they never found the falls. The drive, though, did not pique Tammy's interest. Instead, she kept looking at her watch until Ryan wheeled the car around and they'd reached the art center in Stecoah.

They spotted Ben in a Chevrolet pickup. He rolled down his passenger window, and they did the same.

"Hi, Tammy. Glad you could meet me." He turned to the boys. "Name's Ben. I'm sorry about the way Chief Coates treated you. He's actually a nice guy, but he acted that way because he's worried about your safety, and so am I." He paused. "You're right, of course. There was a crash there last night, and it was a UFO. I was there. I saw it. What's more, there were three aliens in that craft. Two are dead, but the third survived."

"Wow!" Tammy said. "Do you know where they took the live one?"

"I'm not sure," Ben said, "but I think someone mentioned they were moving him to Fontana Labs."

"See?" Tammy turned to Ryan and Sean. "My mom is right then." She turned back to Ben. "This is Ryan and Sean." She pointed to each. "Ben, my mom is holding a meeting today. She's invited several people who witnessed the crash or who know about it. I think you should go. Can you?"

"Where and when?" Ben shut off his truck engine and stepped out, strolling over to Ryan's open window.

"Mom didn't tell me the time," Tammy said, "but I think it's going to be at Tootie's Café at noon, if that time works for everyone."

"That'll be fine. I can take off for lunch then." Ben grinned, hopped into his Chevy, and pulled out in a cloud of dust.

Ryan rolled up the window and turned to Tammy. "We've got another hour or so. Got any more waterfalls we should explore?"

CHAPTER 41

BONNIE'S first day with Fontana Labs was nightmarish ecstasy. The crisp, china-blue sky sent a message of tranquility, but the moment she met Colonel Petrowski the next morning, she received an entirely different message. After meeting Spenser and clearing security, she had been ushered to Petrowski's office. Normally, the richly paneled office would have impressed her, but the man was another matter.

Petrowski waved her to the armchair across from him, and for a moment, regarded her. Bonnie sat down, and though she met his eyes, she had to look away. They were as rigid and calculating as his military bearing, and she felt as though she were a bug under a microscope. She sensed an emptiness in him that made her want to flee. "Ms. Rhodes, you're here to fulfill a very unusual mission for Fontana Labs," he said.

She nodded, waiting. "We've had quite an unusual guest drop in on us." He smiled, though there was no friendliness in it. She nodded again.

"Ms. Rhodes, what I'm about to say must *not* leave this room. Before I go further, I want you to understand the importance of what I've said. I'm talking about a matter of top security to the United States."

"I understand, Colonel." She shifted, avoiding his eyes.

"You'll be expected to sign a security agreement today."

"All right."

He leaned back in his swivel chair and studied her a moment longer. "All right, Ms. Rhodes," he said, rising. "But I warn you. I expect your loyalty. If we go further, I need to know that I can rely on you."

Nausea rose in her throat, but she thought of Destin and of his friends, George and Linda, and how they had died because they could not be loyal to this man before her, or to the mission of the labs. A sudden flame of revulsion, then anger, surged through her. Cleansed, she found it easy to meet his eyes with equal coldness. "That should not be difficult, Colonel," she said evenly. "Now what *is* this all about?"

"There was a crash of an alien craft near here. We have an alien from that craft in custody. We want you, Ms. Rhodes, to communicate with him. He – it – has been silent since his capture, and he hasn't responded to any stimulus yet. We thought you might be able to communicate with him, much in the same way the gorillas communicate with you."

"Unbelievable!" Bonnie breathed. Her heart hammered in her chest. In spite of her hatred for the Colonel, she was so excited and intrigued by the possibility of an encounter, she would have climbed in bed with the devil himself for the opportunity.

She dug her fingernails into her other palm. "When do I start?"

Petrowski moved past her. "Now," he answered. "I'll take you there. We've already placed some supplies that you might need in an office next to where the alien is being held. Until the rest of your materials arrive, we hope they'll suffice. We've made some cards of the sun, moon, solar system, and a sketch of the alien's ship. We've also included pictures of other galaxies." Bonnie stood, clutching her briefcase.

"We hope to find where he comes from and why his people have visited Earth," Petrowski said. "We're especially curious about his particular mission at the time of his crash. Any questions?"

Bonnie followed Petrowski to the lobby alcove. "None, at least for the moment."

He punched the elevator buttons, and they descended several levels. "Ms. Rhodes, this alien and his people pose a threat to the U.S. Therefore, it's important that we keep him detained and under guard. He could be dangerous, so be careful when you're with him. All right?"

"Okay. She thought her voice sounded calm, though she felt otherwise. They left the elevator and walked a short distance down a long tunnel until it turned left, where it opened into a broad alcove. A lounge and canteen with glass windows and an oak door separated it from the alcove. Beyond, a long hallway ended in a second wide alcove, and the hall was lined with offices.

Opposite the canteen, a pair of narrow stairs led down to a dark hall below, and Petrowski led the way. In the hall beyond, he stopped at a metal door with a small window in the top, reinforced with an imbedded metal screen.

"Here you are." Petrowski reached into his pocket and extracted a key. "One more thing," he added as he bent over the lock. "If you make any headway with the creature, let our security man, Mr. Ingram, know right away. Ingram will only stay for part of the day, so if he's gone, you can still reach me by using the phone in the lounge. Speaking of the lounge and the canteen, feel free to take lunch breaks."

Ingram appeared from the adjoining room as Petrowski unlocked the door. Ingram, a chubby man, ambled forward. He stared at them both while munching a candy bar.

Petrowski swung the door open. Breathless, Bonnie strained to see inside. The room was bare, save for a single cell bunk fastened by chains to the far wall. A steel sink and toilet fastened in a similar fashion to the right wall. A wooden desk and chair had been placed near the center of the room. A small figure lay on the bunk, and at first, Bonnie thought she was staring at a wax figure until it moved its head. The movement was a blur.

"Oh my," Bonnie whispered. The four-foot figure, she noted, was devoid of hair, its skin a grayish-green cast. His eyes were huge, which made his button nose and nearly non-existent ears disappear into his pear-shaped head. His mouth was small and lipless. Unusual, Bonnie thought, but not at all monstrous. He had a serious gash on one leg, and the area surrounding the wound was black. She stepped into the room while Petrowski held the door for her.

"I'll need those cards," she said, "and a notepad on a clipboard, a pencil, and some white drawing paper."

Ingram nodded and shuffled away. Hesitantly, Bonnie took the wooden chair and swung it around so it faced the creature. The alien, she thought, watched her with inscrutable eyes. Still, curiosity won, and she studied him also.

Petrowski left.

The hours melted together, blurring day into evening. She noticed little movement in the alien at first, except that his eyes followed her, and even that assessment, she concluded, was more a feeling than anything. His sex, she decided, was also based on intuition rather than anything she could observe, for he lacked genitalia or other evidence of sexual organs. Nevertheless, she *knew* he was a male.

When considerable time passed without any hostile moves on his part, she moved her chair near his bunk and began using her cards.

Over and over, she pointed to herself and said, "Bonnie." Then she would point to him and wait, but every attempt was met with silence.

She moved closer, showing the alien each card. "Sun," she said, pointing to the sun card. No response.

"Solar system," she said next, referring to the sketch of the solar system. "Sun," she repeated, pointing to the large yellow circle at the center of the sketch. "Earth," she said, pointing to the earth. No response.

She finally stood up, sweeping her arm around the room. "Earth," she said, waiting. "Home," she said lovingly. "Earth, home." No response.

Next she held up a photo of the Milky Way. "Milky Way." She carefully enunciated the two words again. No response.

Bonnie told herself to be patient. She wondered if it would take months to make a break-through, and then she shook her head, remembering that the alien next to her might be the size of a child, but he probably had a mental capacity that was beyond her ability to understand.

Her final attempt was to take the paper and draw the alien and herself. She pointed to the picture and said, "Alien," as she pointed to the alien, and then "human" as she pointed to the sketch of herself. "Bonnie," she repeated, setting the picture aside. "Bonnie," she said again, pointing to herself. He did not move.

Hungry and thirsty, she finally glanced at her watch. It was already past seven. Time to take a break. She looked at the inert figure before her on the cot and stood up. "I know you don't understand me, but please don't be afraid. I would never hurt you." She paused, searching for more words. "I'm leaving you for a while," she said. "I need something to eat."

She turned to go, but in an instant, her legs became cement. She could not move. Even as the first wave of terror gripped her, she felt warmth. A glow of indescribable peace swept her. It was a sense of love, so profound and so bottomless, that tears welled in her eyes and she thought her heart would break.

She swiveled toward the alien, realizing then that her legs could move. In awe she studied him, and though his face remained impassive, she literally heard words, all in English, accompanied by pictures. She was watching a movie, but this movie, she discovered, was inside her. And it was beautiful, touching, and filled with love. She wept.

When she recognized a picture of the Milky Way before her, she nodded. A mere speck of a planet in the cosmos of spiraling light blinked in neon-billboard fashion. "Home," he said in her head, clearly, lovingly, in the same way she had named Earth. "Home."

Faster than her eye could follow, he moved in his reptilian fashion. He sat up, and this time the voice in her head was urgent. "Home!"

It took her a minute to grasp his plea.

"When?" She waited, taut with excitement, but he did not answer. She eyed the surveillance cameras. Perhaps she, too, could mentally speak with him.

After some deep thought, Bonnie used the paper and sketched the earth at different points around the sun, representing the four seasons. The earth at its nearest point to the sun would have to represent the present.

She next drew a picture of a house with a sun near its side. Next to it, she drew the house again, but used her pencil to shade the sky as though at night and added the stars of the heaven next to a crescent moon. It looked ridiculous, a child's attempt at drawing, but it was the best she could do.

Finished, Bonnie pointed to the pictures. "When? Now?"

He did not answer.

"Earth now," she licked her lips and pointed to the picture of the earth near the sun. "When?"

His answer was instantaneous and his words reverberated in her head. "Now."

Her thoughts became frenzied questions. Did "now" mean today, this week, or this month? Bonnie turned back and flipped to the picture of the house. She erased the sun, and placed it lower on the horizon, and then she showed it to the childlike being.

"Now." She thought the words, showing the picture she had corrected. Then she pointed to the picture of the home at night. "Night."

The alien answered her immediately, "Home," he said, and again the thought was sent with a love that she could feel, a truly physical sensation of indescribable emotional warmth. She cried unabashedly.

"Home, night, night," he said inside her head. "Night, night."

Bonnie sat back in the chair and studied the figure. What did he mean by "night, night"? She pondered his words, and at the height of her confusion, she understood. "Night, night." Two nights!

She grabbed a sheet of paper and drew a disk, hoping that it would be recognized as a typical UFO. "Ship?" she asked in her head. "Ship coming night, night?"

The alien nodded and the words in her head confirmed it. "Ship coming night, night."

"And you want me to help you, don't you?"

He nodded. "Help alien, night, night." Another wave of love swept her. She looked at him and she said, "Love. Bonnie feels love. Love, love, love."

"Yes," he said again. "Alien love. Bonnie help."

Bonnie gasped. He already understood the word *help*. She wondered how many words he knew, but before she'd finished the thought, he'd answered her.

"Many."

"Do you understand time? Earth time?" No answer.

She thought a moment and then drew two watch faces on the paper, filling in the numbers. "Day," she said finally, pointing to the first watch. She started at 6 a.m. and counted out loud, until she reached 6 p.m. Then she pointed at the second watch, and said "Night," and counted out the same numbers a second time. The alien nodded, and then the words were there. "Watch, watch, watch, watch. Home, home, 2 a.m. Ship. Earth. Alien home."

"Good," Bonnie thought. "We call that tomorrow night." She repeated the phrase, *tomorrow night*. She stood again. "Bonnie help alien at 2 a.m., tomorrow night. Bonnie love." She hesitated but continued. "Bonnie has human friends. Human friends help Bonnie." Feeling silly, she decided to speak normally.

"I have to go now, but I will be back one watch, in day...time." She pointed to the picture of the watch. "Tomorrow, daytime."

The alien nodded and lay back on the bunk.

She stepped out of the room into the empty hall and locked the door. Ingram was not in the adjoining room. Bonnie raced to the canteen. She would make a phone call to Petrowski's office and tell him that she had made no breakthroughs. After that, she would find a pay phone and call Karen because she wanted Karen and Destin to know that she was going to try and smuggle the alien out to freedom.

CHAPTER 42

DESTIN watched as high clouds scudded across the sky, mere wisps of cotton. The disintegrating cold front held a hint of change. The temperate, fluttering breeze refreshed the air. As he seated himself on the patio of Tootie's Café, Karen arrived. He quickly rose to help her into a chair next to him.

She looked at him and laughed. "I almost didn't recognize you," she said. "Planning on doing some fishing?"

Destin looked down at his outfit and chuckled. He'd come dressed in a fishing outfit, complete with fishing hat, lures attached. He also wore sunglasses. "I came disguised. It's Norma's husband's stuff," he said. "I disguised my truck too. I would've loved to have changed vehicles, but that wasn't possible."

"How'd you disguise it?"

"I painted my blue truck black. It won't win any awards, but it does look different. Then I muddied up the plates. It's parked out behind the restaurant."

Karen laughed. "Did you paint it with a brush, or what?"

"No. Used twelve cans of Krylon spray on it. I could've done a better job if I'd had fourteen cans, but beggars can't be choosers. Norma's husband had them stashed in his storage locker at the houseboat."

Karen belly-laughed. "Can't wait to see that truck!"

When Tammy, Ryan, and Sean ambled across the patio, Karen frowned in surprise. "What are you doing here?" she demanded, hands on her hips.

Tammy spoke first. "Ah, Mom, we couldn't stay away. After all, we saw that crash last night, so we're a part of this."

"Young lady, your first responsibility is school. I won't — "

"Mrs. Kerr," Ryan interrupted, "Please don't get mad. What we witnessed last night was the single, most important event of our lives. None of us will ever be the same again."

Tammy nodded. "Please let us stay, and then, if you want, we'll promise to go on to school."

Karen turned toward Destin, her eyebrows arching.

"He's got a point." Destin shrugged.

She turned back to the teens. "All right. This time."

Tammy came over and gave Destin a hug. "Glad you could make it. Mom must've raised you on the radio."

"She sure did." Destin eyed the square tables that dotted the side patio. "Come on kids. Let's push some of these tables together."

As they worked, he asked Karen, "Have you heard from Bonnie today? Since you called me on the radio this morning, it's been all I've been thinking about. It's amazing, unbelievable, that she has gone to work for Fontana Labs."

"Not a word." Karen straightened the tablecloths. "We'll have to wait, I'm afraid. She must be having an unbelievable day."

"What kind of work?" Sean asked.

Destin rubbed his hands together. "It's a long story. Let's wait to go into that after everyone is here. He turned to Karen. "Who's coming today?"

"Franz Stjernholm, an engineer scientist I know. A friend. He's the Project Engineer on the RHIC collider."

"Aren't you concerned about an engineer?"

Karen shrugged. "I've known him through work, and he's a friend of mine. George's too."

Destin chewed his lip. "All right. After you called me this morning, I got on the HF and gave Rocky a call. He's the truck driver who parked on the highway last night. And guess what?" Before Karen could answer, he continued. "With all the roads closed after the crash, Rocky had to turn back to Robbinsville. He contacted his dispatcher who gave him a hard time but finally agreed to a layover until today. Fortunately, I caught him on the ham radio as he was leaving town. He said he'd join us for lunch today, considering what it's about."

"Fantastic! Mom, he was the one who filmed the whole crash with his camcorder." Tammy grinned. "By the way, Ryan, Sean and I have a surprise for you too. We've invited a firefighter to join us today."

"Firefighter?" Destin said, and Karen echoed his word. When the implications hit him, he looked at Tammy with new respect. He turned to Karen. "She's talking about Ben. Bet he fought that fire last night. Your daughter is one smart cookie. So that's what you've been up to this morning!"

Tammy blushed. "It didn't happen that way. Actually, it was Sean's idea."

"Yeah, but it was Tammy who had the courage to walk up to the fire fighters and ask them if they'd fought the fire at the crash," Sean said.

Tammy broke in. "Look, here he comes."

Destin looked up as several men walked across the patio and joined them. Ben led. Behind him strode a shorter man with thick, kinky hair and brows. And at the rear, Destin recognized Rocky, the truck driver.

Destin rose to greet them, as did the others. A waitress arrived a minute later, took their orders and left, returning with their drinks. After she disappeared, Karen took charge of the meeting and briefed everyone.

She told them about Destin's work, and described George's murder and Linda's subsequent "suicide." She then related how Destin recovered George's computer disk. "We now possess a great deal of information about the quark gluon plasma beam weapon. But the story isn't finished yet." She grinned. "Hear what Ben and the others have to say."

They all took turns, explaining their involvement. Rocky, who spoke first, described how he had filmed the UFOs, and how he, Destin, and the teens had seen the firing of the quark beam, which caused the subsequent obliteration of the mother ship and the crash of the smaller scout ship.

Franz then spoke. He described how Fontana Labs had conducted a test the day before the UFO incident, and of Colonel Petrowski's role in the use of the weapon. "He's a man who has been corrupted by power."

Next, Ben told everyone about his work as a firefighter and how he and Gus had fought to save the garage of the Vince Foster residence. He described how they discovered the documents from Oak Ridge and Fontana Labs, naming the quark gluon plasma beam weapon. He also described Gus's murder. "I'm sure that's why Gus was killed," he said. "Mr. Foster saw him with those papers. What he didn't know was that I kept the papers, not Gus. I have since given them to Karen."

"Yes," Karen said. "I brought them today, and Destin has them now."

During the profound silence that followed, the waitress trotted out with their food, disappearing inside again. It was quiet while everyone ate. Afterwards, Tammy spoke. "I really don't understand what you've said about this weapon. Subatomic particles must be really small, but it's Greek to me."

"Perhaps I can help," Franz said. "Think of our world first. Everything in it, everything physical, is made up of atoms. In fact, everything in creation is made of atoms."

Tammy nodded. "Right."

"Now think of a solar system. It's quite similar to the atom. Within the atom we would find electrons, protons, and neutrons. Heard of them?"

"Well, duh!" Tammy said.

"Okay. These electrons, protons, and neutrons behave in certain ways, depending on the atom, but each of those particles move along paths similar to the way planets move in our solar system.

"I know." Tammy rolled her eyes.

"Good. Now they ride along with what you might call "space" between them, but it isn't exactly air or 'nothing,'" Franz said.

For a moment Tammy looked bewildered. "Then what is it?"

"It's a force. An energy. It's in everything and it's everywhere."

"But not in outer space," Tammy said.

"Quite the contrary," Franz said. "When I said everywhere, I meant everywhere, even space."

"Oh."

"Look," Franz said. "This force, this energy, is composed of polarities, some negative and some positive. The polarities resemble electricity. Now let me stretch this analogy to help you understand. It's almost as though this energy has a mission, which is to balance its components of positive and negative. Many scientists who are religious point to this mind and mission of the force as proof of the existence of God."

"What do scientists call that force?" Ryan asked.

"They call the force the quarks of the atom," Franz answered. "These quarks are subatomic particles whose effects as energy can be measured, but the particle or force itself cannot."

"Go on," Tammy urged.

"The supercolliders are used to smash atoms together. The collisions allow the energy to be released. Fontana Labs has taken that energy and focused it through a tight beam, and that beam has a destructive heat greater than the sun. The release of that much energy is difficult to even imagine. When it was directed toward the UFOs, it literally atomized the mother ship and crippled the smaller one. Not even the aliens on that ship, with their advanced technology, could withstand such an attack." He leaned back and Tammy nodded.

Karen turned to Ben. "Please tell me about the crash site."

"Okay. He shifted in his seat. "You might find this hard to believe, but the remnants of the ship were there, all right, along with two dead aliens and one live one." He went on to describe the entire crash. "We were told never to say a word about what we saw if we wanted to live," he finished. The group sat spellbound, and they barely touched their food.

Destin sat back. He thought of Karen's words on the radio earlier that morning, and how Bonnie must be working with the alien at that very moment. Daydreaming, he visualized Bonnie before him, her long hair cascading around her.

He cleared his throat. "Look, we have lots of proof now. We have the computer disk that George left for us, and thanks to Rocky, we have the video of the weapon being fired and of the UFOs in flight. Ben gave us crucial papers about the weapon. My only failure is that I can't nail anyone to George's and Linda's murder — "

"And I'll bet, the same ones were responsible for Gus's death," Ben said grimly.

"Right," Destin said. "But I question whether we have enough evidence to tie it to Petrowski. Obviously, he didn't kill these people directly. That leaves me out in the cold." He sighed again.

"Don't forget our testimony," Franz said. "We're all committed to bringing this out in the open, discrediting Petrowski, and halting the use of this weapon unless it's with the consent of the people."

"You're right. I'll have to settle for exposing this deadly weapon and discrediting Petrowski, even if I can't nail him for murder. I wish we had some video footage of those aliens," Destin said. "Then our case would be even stronger."

"We do," Ben said quietly. The group turned and stared at him. "I was getting around to that. I secretly filmed the crash site and what happened there, and it's all on my camcorder. In fact, I spent the entire night, trying to decide if we should go public with the film, and then these teens here, showed me the way." He chuckled. "But I do have another question."

"Yes?" Karen said.

"Where did they take the live alien?"

Destin looked at Karen and said, "They took him to the labs. Karen found that out last night when she got a call from Bonnie Rhodes. You see, Bonnie is a friend I met recently. She's an anthropologist at UT specializing in language development in animals. She said she's been assigned to Fontana Labs temporarily. Karen figured out that since the labs have no projects involving animals, it must be for the alien they've captured. Makes sense."

Again the group digested the news, and the silence hung in the air.

Franz peered at Destin. "There's one thing you said that doesn't make sense. Remember when you told us how you went to Linda's home in the village?"

Destin nodded.

"Well, you told us you were hit over the head, and whoever did it ran off."

Destin nodded. "Yes."

"Did you get a good look at your assailant?"

Destin sighed. "No. I only caught a glimpse of a slight figure running off. It was really dark, and he was in the shadows."

"Do you think it was the guy who assaulted you in Florida?"

"Not at all," Destin said. "I broke that guy's jaw. Besides, I'd say this man was smaller. Perhaps more agile."

"That makes it stranger." Franz stroked his chin. "You see, I can't figure out why he didn't finish the job. After all, he had you down."

Destin wadded his napkin. "I agree. It's strange. He must've panicked."

Karen spoke. "Look, everyone. It's not safe for us to hang around here longer than necessary. After all, these killers would think nothing of killing again. Our lives are in danger, so it's important that we plan carefully what we do next. If we all agree to go public, then I think we should figure out who we trust to put this out to the media."

Ben spoke. "If Franz agrees, he could handle that part well, because he knows all about the labs and the collider."

Some of the group nodded, but Karen interrupted. "No offense to your skills, Franz, but I believe Destin is a better choice since he works as Lockheed Martin's PR guy and he writes for the *Orlando Sentinel*. Besides, he's not working for the labs, which could give him the advantage right now."

After a quick discussion, it was clear that everyone agreed with Karen. Destin felt self conscious, but he nodded. "Yes, I think I can get the job done, though I already know that Petrowski and his goons are looking for me. I can write up our testimony and assemble the documentation tonight, and then I could leave for Orlando with the film first thing tomorrow."

He turned to Ben and Rocky. "Would both of you be willing to entrust the film to me?"

Ben hesitated only a second. "Here," he said. "Take the whole camera. It might prevent questions about the film being genuine. And you have the documents, right?"

Karen interrupted. "I brought them today – in case."

Destin hesitated. "Okay, I'll take them now." He then shook Ben's hand. "Thanks, man."

Destin turned to Rocky. "How about you?"

Embarrassed, Rocky looked down at the tablecloth. "I know everything you're saying is true. I know my film is important, but I'm not happy about giving up the original. I don't think all our proof should be in the hands of one person." He thought a minute. "Tell you what, let me take my camcorder with me, and I'll have the material copied in Nashville. I have a friend who has a camera store there. I know he'll keep my stuff safe. He'll make a copy for me, and send you a copy. Okay?"

The group nodded, although the teens, especially, were disappointed.

Destin looked at Rocky. "Let's stay in touch by radio for a couple of days," he said. "In case of trouble. I'm sure that Petrowski would go to any limits to stop us."

"Good." Rocky nodded. "If you don't mind, let's use 14.235."

"Yes, I remember you mentioning that frequency at the crash site," Destin said. "And let's use 7.230 or simplex while you're in the area."

Rocky nodded. "Gotta go. I'm almost three hours late. We'll keep in touch." He stood, humming as he left. "Got to get home to my sweet Arlene!"

Everyone chuckled. Franz then stood. "I'd better go too. My wife, Marcia, needs me for yard work."

Karen hesitated. "Then you're staying with the labs?"

Franz looked miserable. "What else can I do?" He reached inside his jacket pocket. Here's my card. Contact me if I can help – behind their backs.

Ben looked at Destin. "I've gotta' go too. If Coates or anyone else finds out about this, I'll be toast." He reached across the table and shook Destin's hand. "If you need me, this is my address and home phone." He handed Destin a slip of paper and left.

Destin picked up his own bill and grabbed Karen's. "I'm going back to the houseboat to pack. If you hear from Bonnie, will you call me right away?"

She nodded, and he guided her toward the cashier. As they stepped out into the parking lot, she shivered. "I don't know, but for some reason, I'm getting really scared. We're sitting on a volcano that's ready to erupt. You, me, Tammy, all of us."

Destin reached over and gave her a reassuring squeeze, but he couldn't find words of assurance.

CHAPTER 43

TAMMY followed Ryan and Sean out to the parking lot and into the mellowness of the Indian summer day. She shaded her eyes and watched Rocky's rig kick up dust as it rolled out. "He's heading over the Dragon's Tail. Must be in a hurry."

Ryan kicked the parking lot's gravel with his toe for a moment until he'd managed to coat his old sneakers with a new layer of reddish dust. "Rocky said he was late and was anxious to get back home."

Tammy watched as Franz left, followed by Ben. Then she turned to the others. "There's a real live alien a few miles from us, and here we sit, doing nothing. Nothing!" She pounded her fist against the top of the Mustang. "It's the greatest moment in history. If we could get inside Fontana Labs and see him, we might know a lot more."

"Such as?" Sean asked.

"Such as whether or not he's friendly. Or whether or not he can talk. And if he can, I want to know why he and his people came here."

Sean shook his head. "The labs might as well be Fort Knox."

"Yeah, but they're not. And I might know a way to get inside."

"What about your mom?" Ryan asked. "She'll never stand for this."

Tammy tossed her head. "Mom is working a double shift tonight. She won't have a clue."

"Idiot!" Sean muttered under his breath and walked around the car.

Ryan glanced at Sean, amused, and then he hugged her. "This is going to be good. What have you got in mind?"

CHAPTER 44

DESTIN was the last to leave Tootie's. He watched as Karen swung her car onto the pavement and headed north toward the village. Worried, he eased around the café to his truck. He had been all bravado inside, but he'd been entrusted with a great responsibility. He wondered if he could succeed against such madmen and the power of the government. Worse, he was one step away from being a sitting duck in his truck, and he knew it.

After starting the Ford, he stowed Ben's document and camera under his seat. He headed north, the way Karen had gone, though she had already disappeared over the long, straight incline toward Stecoah Gap.

He drove with the window down, allowing the scent of hay and harvest to fill his cab. If it weren't for his job and the labs, he might not ever leave. He thought of Bonnie. Leaving North Carolina also meant leaving her behind for the second time, and yet he knew everything depended on him.

He pushed back his hair, trying not to think of George and Linda. As so many of his friends had already reminded him, he should be content to expose the weapon. Nevertheless, the question pestered him.

Back at the houseboat, he drove through the gate and locked it. As he pulled the truck to a stop, he spotted a small helicopter. It flew slowly over him, veered away, and disappeared beyond the trees. Uneasy, Destin swung out of the truck. As he shut the cab door, the helicopter flew over again, this time much lower.

"Shit!" Destin got back in the truck, turned on the VHF/UHF radio, and grabbed the mike.

"N7JJJ, this is WR4RR, 535 Simplex."

"N7JJJ. You're breaking up a bit."

"Can't be helped," Destin said. "Bad news. I've been spotted."

"Oh no!" Karen said, alarmed. "What do you want me to do?"

"Not much, except stay glued to the radio. I may need you."

"All right. Shouldn't I call the police?"

"Don't trust them. I'll get back to you later. WR4RR clear." He flipped off the switch. Reaching into the glove compartment, he withdrew his Glock 9mm model 17 semi-automatic. Crouching, he bolted for the houseboat.

Behind him he heard a squeal and then a crash, as a black Buick sedan burst through the closed gate. Destin smiled grimly. The gate, set in cement and heavily chained, must have caused some damage. Clouds of dust billowed up as the car side-slipped to a stop in the loose dust along the shore.

He ran as two shots whined by his head, chewing up wood on the gangplank. Behind him, he could hear cursing and shouts, but he didn't look back.

He slid inside, but a rapid-fire search of the closets revealed no stashed weapons. He grabbed an extra clip from his luggage containing seventeen rounds and jammed it in his pocket. He returned to the sliding doors and was met by a hail of bullets from the shoreline.

Destin heard the whine and plunk of more bullets burying into the sides of the boat, and he watched as a man on foot worked his way northward along the shore. The helicopter had disappeared.

Destin slipped outside and around the corner of the houseboat. A barrage of shots followed his retreat, but when he was safely on the far side of the boat, he fired back toward the shore, pinning the man down. He heard the man swear.

He took his time to aim and shot again, but the wooded shoreline made it difficult to hit his assailant. Likewise, he thought, the man wouldn't have an easy time rushing him, for the gangplank was narrow and exposed. He looked about for a way out, and behind him, he saw the Honda R-12X, tethered on the jet rail system.

A volley of shots rang out. "Damn!" he said. Bits of wood flew at him from the railing. Destin peeked around the corner. His assailant had already crawled onto the gangplank, where a large wooden box with netting on the top, built to hold live crickets, sat in its own homemade wooden holder near the shore. While Destin watched, the man scooped it up. Using it as makeshift cover, he advanced along the boat ramp.

Destin swiftly winched the R-12X into the water and unhooked the craft. The R-12X rocked gently, ready for him. With the rope still holding the boat, he slid back to the corner and fired at the figure behind the bait box. The man, whom he glimpsed fleetingly, was dressed in dark slacks, black shoes, and a light tan pullover. No broken jaw.

Resolute now, Destin took a deep breath, steadied the gun, and fired. His bullet found one of the man's legs.

The man cried out and fired several wild shots as he scrambled for better cover on the shoreline. He did not fire again. Destin smiled, hopped onto the Honda, and started the engine. The jet ski sputtered, then the engine caught, smoothing out.

Casting an anxious glance toward the dock, Destin released the tie-down and scrambled back on the seat. A shot rang out, shattering some black fiberglass and plastic above the jet pump of the watercraft.

The attacker's next shot missed because Destin hit the throttle, and the rocket-styled R-12X leaped forward beneath him, scooting across the glassy lake. Never, Destin thought, had he seen a jet ski move from zero to a plane as fast.

The wind blew his hair back. He leaned forward, shoving the Glock deep into his pocket. He focused on the shoreline, but his only thought was to put lots of distance between him and the shooter. As Fontana Dam loomed into view ahead, the cement monolith appeared as a dead-end trap. In despair, he looked about. Where could he run? He began to pray then, for he needed all the help he could get to stay alive.

CHAPTER 45

WHEN Dai Yu entered Petrowski's doorway after lunch, she passed Spenser who lurched out, ignoring her. Petrowsky looked upset, so she seated herself quietly and waited until he composed himself. Smugness replaced his chagrin, only to be replaced a second later by focused energy. He should have looked tired, but instead, the events of the recent days had energized him. An electric current of desire coursed through her.

The phone rang and he answered it. She frowned.

"This is Baylor," the raspy voice on the other end of the line said. Dai Yu knew Baylor. He was a beefy man, crew cut and all. Tough.

"Thunder was out in the chopper as you asked, looking for that man, Destin Campbell. Not long ago, he spotted him south of the park. I was only a mile away, so I chased him onto a houseboat on Lake Fontana. I'm there now."

Petrowski sat up. "Shoot him."

"Believe me, I've tried, but he's put a bullet in me and I can barely walk. Besides, he took off on a jet ski and he's out on the lake now."

"Wonderful!" Petrowski said. "A newspaper man can outshoot and outfight two CIA men and get away? Great track record. Can you at least tell me which way he went?"

"North," Baylor said. "When he took off, he was following the shoreline. It would be my guess that he's headed for the marina."

"So that's what the great Baylor Trapp guesses, huh?" Petrowski said.

"Got a better guess?"

Petrowski's voice developed a cutting edge. "Use my code name."

Dai Yu leaned forward. Petrowski's conversation was getting interesting.

"You used my name first," Trapp reminded him.

Petrowski's fury was barely contained. "I'll have Thunder get a bead on him. Broken jaw or not, he should be able to shoot him out of the water. Oh, and in case that doesn't work, I'll send one of the security guards over to the marina to cut him off. He won't get away. Meanwhile, take your car up to the marina— "

Trapp's voice smoldered. "First I have to get my leg bandaged up. I'll be lucky if I can get back to the car. I'll call from there if I make it."

"No," Petrowski snapped. "Stay on the line a minute— " He got no further, for the line had gone dead.

CHAPTER 46

DESTIN skimmed across the quiet water, barely cutting its surface. Sunshine lit the spray, and he drew energy from the moist wind. He had to run farther out into the lake than he wanted because of the rugged shoreline, which bent into cove after cove.

The Honda, a bright red and black slash in the sunlight, was clocking nearly sixty miles per hour. The marina came into view, and Destin saw several boats out. A few bass boats had anchored in nearby coves. Beyond and to his right, Fontana Dam stretched its concrete band of gray across the fluid, dark surface.

He powered back, moving toward the rows of boats at the marina. A man in a blue security uniform unexpectedly ran out on the main pier, shouting at another who stood framed in the doorway of the small store nearby.

Destin frowned. He could not hear them above the noise of the Aqua Trax engine, but he could smell trouble.

He eased off the throttle and started to swing the R-12X around. The security man ran along the pier and jumped onto another jet ski tied to two pylons.

"Damn!" Destin gunned the engine and steered his craft into open water. He looked back. The jet ski, a Sea Doo, powered by a three-cylinder Kawasaki engine, was gaining on him. A fine machine, but the Honda was more powerful.

The open water near the dam was choppy and the Honda began to buck. Destin hung on, trying to find a speed that would reduce the pounding. He looked again. The jet ski was closing on him. Bullets spattered the choppy surface.

He pulled out his Glock and fired to his rear, but his shots went wild. No good. He replaced the gun in his pocket and turned up the throttle.

He heard a dull, resonant thudding overhead. He glanced up at the underside of a helicopter, a Bell 206B Jet Ranger III. Destin could clearly see the props on the lightweight, commercial chopper. Two men were in the helicopter, and the passenger was gesturing wildly at the pilot.

Destin tried to cut to the right, away from the helicopter, but the chop was too heavy to maintain his speed. Reluctantly, he swung back to his original course and headed directly toward the dam.

Bullets again knifed across the water and one barely missed his head. He ducked, molding himself into the seat. He glanced up again, and found that the green Jet Ranger was still overhead. No surprise. The Honda was no match for the chopper's airspeed.

Destin watched as the passenger in the Jet Ranger opened his door, pulled himself out on the struts, and began firing a small pistol. One shot barely missed Destin's leg, chewing at the plastic coating that reinforced the Honda's hull.

"Damn!" Destin repeated. Though he had accelerated, the dam loomed ahead, blotting out the sky. Since it was fall, the TVA had already begun lowering the water level of the lake for the winter, and the wall of concrete was formidable.

He glanced up again. This time, the helicopter was dangerously close and he saw that the man on the struts wore a jaw brace. George's killer. He withdrew the Glock and aimed at a spot above the man's white sneakers.

When he fired, his shot hit the skids. Gesticulating wildly, the assailant slid into the open cabin door as the helicopter veered off to the left and dropped back.

Determined, Destin held his course. He would turn away from the dam at the last possible second. He turned on his seat and sent a wild shot toward the Kawasaki chasing him. Anxiously, he peered overhead, but the helicopter had fallen behind. He swiveled to the left in time to see Broken Jaw at the open door, lifting a shoulder mount SA-18 rocket into position.

His heart lurched, and he swung left instead of right, directly toward the shore a few yards away. Broken Jaw fired the rocket, and the trail of smoke rolled forth in a heartbeat in time. Destin turned back and could see nothing but the shore. He swung the R-12X around in a half circle, barely missing the lake's exposed bank. The water dragged at the craft, nearly stopping it.

While he watched, the tail of smoke and flame rocketed right at the rear of the Kawasaki, which had not made the turn. The earsplitting explosion and fireball deafened him, and he held tight to the handlebars as the concussion rolled over. Horrified, he watched as the security man's body was thrown against the wall in bloody bits, along with the wreckage.

Destin's heart hammered and for a second, he shut his eyes to the carnage. He looked up at the silhouette of the man in black still framed by the open door, but the chopper angled away from the dam at the last second. Broken Jaw almost lost his footing, and for a moment Destin heard him screaming oaths at the pilot as he clung to the door frame, half in and half out. For the first time, Destin grinned. He had managed to teach the man the meaning of fear. He turned back for the houseboat.

The helicopter followed him, but it stayed well to the rear, and no more shots creased the water. Unexpectedly, the chopper veered away and headed north. Puzzled, he watched it go.

He continued moving south along the shoreline until he spotted the familiar blue houseboat, nestled in its cove of greenery. He throttled back and eased the Honda in, wondering if he would meet a hail of bullets.

Instead, the houseboat was deserted. It rocked, riding the swells of his wake. He pulled the craft up, rolling it onto the rails easily, but left it there in the water so he could make a hasty retreat if necessary.

One step at a time, he inched his way around the front of the houseboat, but the place was deserted. He went inside, noting a trail of blood. The man he'd shot. In the bathroom, he discovered the contents of the houseboat's first aid kit strewn about. Crouching, he ran down the gangplank to the shore. No shots rang out, but he kept his Glock ready.

His truck stood where he had left it, undisturbed. He shook his head. Apparently, he'd seriously hurt the beefy man and won himself a few, precious minutes. Racing back into the houseboat, he grabbed his large, carry-all bag and madly scooped all of his belongings into it. Before he reached the sliding doors, he turned and ran back for his jacket and shaving kit. When he reached the truck, he dumped his gear on the passenger floorboards and climbed in.

He quickly checked his HF and VHF reception. Satisfied, he started up the truck, and as he pulled out he called Karen.

"N7JJJ, WR4RR, 535 simplex." Nothing. The only sound was the hum of empty airwaves. Then Karen's voice boomed through the radio.

"N7JJJ. I've been worried sick! What's going on?"

"I've been shot at, chased across Lake Fontana, and attacked from a helicopter."

"Whaat?" Karen's voice screeched.

"No time for that now. I'm back in my truck, headed out toward the highway. I'll go to Sylva if the road is clear."

"Oh, my God," Karen said, shocked into near silence. "Destin, if the labs are smart enough to build the beam, I doubt if they're going to leave that route wide open for you. What if they...?"

Destin bit his lip. He reached up and wiped his mouth, leaving a trace of wet blood across his knuckles. "Wait. I've got a plan."

"What?"

"My plan is to see what happens."

"That's no plan," Karen snorted.

"That's a line from some movie," Destin said. "Hold on a minute. I've reached the highway." He set the mike down, and peered north. The highway seemed empty. He crept forward, but as he glanced south, he saw the black sedan sitting broadside in the southbound lane. He'd been spotted. The sedan squealed around, kicking burning rubber smoke high into the air.

Destin picked up the mike as he mashed the accelerator. The old truck groaned and leaped forward. "Karen, you were right. They'd blocked the southbound lane and when they spotted me, I had no choice but to turn north. I'm headed your way. Unfortunately, their car is faster than my truck. Any suggestions?"

"Destin, I — "

Karen broke off but her mike was open. Destin heard voices but too distant to make out the words. "Karen, you okay?"

"Fine. Ryan and Tammy have arrived, and they heard most of this. Look, Ryan's trying to tell me something. Hold on."

For a moment no one spoke. She returned then. "Destin, Ryan has an idea. If you could make it to Deals Gap, he feels you might have a chance. He has a friend who keeps his motorcycle at the small resort there. Ryan can call him and arrange for you to use it. Cycles can negotiate those three hundred eighteen curves of the Dragon's Tail better than any truck or car. What do you think?"

Destin hesitated. "If they send their helicopter back out after me, I might be a sitting duck."

"I doubt that," Karen said. "Those mountains are rugged, so they won't be able to get in very close."

"Well, it's a plan."

Destin glanced back. The sedan came up close behind the truck and pulled around to pass. Destin shoved the steering wheel hard to the left, scraping the sedan. The car wobbled and swung sharply away, but it recovered, dropped back a half a car length, and rode along in the opposite lane.

"Wait, I have an idea." Karen sounded excited. "Rocky's had the radio on since he left Tootie's. He's on the Dragon's Tail right now. Let me give him a call."

Before Destin could protest, the sedan pulled alongside again, and this time, the beefy man had the passenger window down. He whipped out his semi-automatic and shot through the window. The bullet whined through the splintered side window, barely missing Destin. The slug tore the old headliner, and the ripped fabric flapped in the breeze.

Destin shoved the wheel to the left, smacking the car's rear passenger door. A shower of sparks flew between them and the road. The sedan veered left. When the driver gained control, he fell back several car lengths.

Destin tightened his hold on the wheel until he became aware of the pain in his hands and arms. He forced himself to relax his vise-like grip, but he remained vigilant.

He swept past Fontana Park and climbed the short steep hill into Fontana Village. When he cleared the crest, he saw a roadblock dead ahead, formed by two sedans.

His opponents had chosen their location carefully. Brushy hillocks rose on both sides of the paved, two-lane road, and beyond, thick woods stretched in both directions. The Chevrolets were older models, and each bore the Fontana Labs insignia. Desperately, Destin looked around for an alternate route but there was none. He peered through his rear view mirror. The Buick had slowed.

"Thank you!" Destin said, and pushed the pedal to the floor.

The truck leapt forward and he braced as best he could. He hit the cars head on, and the shock of the impact shoved Destin against the seatbelt, bruising him from his shoulder to his waist.

The truck shuddered and almost in slow motion, Destin watched the cars spin around and away, and then back again. By that time he was beyond them, so when one of the two exploded, only a few fiery remnants threatened the truck. His speed carried him to safety. Portions of his truck's hood were smashed, but his reinforced front bumper had kept his radiator and engine intact.

He peered through his rear view mirror. The explosion had sealed the road. "Yes!" he shouted. Without warning, shots rang out. One broke the rear window of the cab, and he ducked again.

He sped past the village, and below the dam, he heard the whine of the chopper behind him. It swooped in well below the tree line and nearly touched the truck's roof. Destin swerved then gained control of the wheel. Ahead, the road entered dense forest. Trees closed in overhead, a green tunnel of safety, and he ducked under them. The chopper climbed away. Then the canopy disappeared.

He swept across the bridge at Cheoah Lake and followed the northern shore, heading toward Deals Gap and the Dragon's Tail.

On his left, the chopper flew very low over the shoreline, near the highway. He saw Broken Jaw as the man leered at him from the open door of the Jet Ranger. Broken Jaw slipped the SA-18 into place.

Desperate, Destin pulled up his Glock from between his legs and fired several rounds into the chopper. One of his first shots caught Broken Jaw squarely in the chest, and he fell forward out of the chopper, hitting the water. Confused, the chopper pilot held his course a moment too long. Destin continued firing, and this time he hit the Ranger's fuel tank.

The explosion seared his eyes. He reacted at once and braked along the empty highway. Breathless, he watched the disintegrating helicopter hit the water and turn on its side. Fiery chunks slipped below the surface. Then it was gone.

A Subaru appeared from the opposite direction, and its startled driver braked hard, her careening car crossing the line. Destin hit his accelerator again, grazing the corner of her bumper. Then he was past her, and he did not slow down until he reached the intersection at Deals Gap.

He pulled behind the motel office. His truck was less noticeable there. He slumped in his seat, catching his breath and trying to think. Finally, he picked up the radio.

"N7JJJ, you there?"

"Yes," Karen said. "Thank heavens you're alive. Where are you?"

"Deals Gap."

"Good," she exclaimed. "Is anyone on your tail?"

"Not yet, but I don't think it will be much longer before someone catches up."

"Well, I talked to Rocky a moment ago," Karen said, "and he was madder than hell when he heard. Says to call him if you can on the HF, all right? Said you'd know what channel."

"Okay. WR4RR clear."

He didn't wait for Karen to sign before turning on the HF band to 7.230.

"N4OZZ, N4OZZ, this is WR4RR." The band was static-free.

"WR4RR, this is N4OZZ. I hear you're in a spot of trouble."

"That's an understatement." Destin ruefully rubbed his bruised arms and ribs. "Look, I'm at Deals Gap now, and I think I'll be riding a bike from here on, if all goes well. Do you think you could help me out if they follow me across the mountains? See, if they do, I'm pretty much a sitting duck on a motorcycle after I leave the mountains behind."

"You're right," Rocky said. "There's a long, straight, open stretch along the shore of a lake beyond the twisties. Not much cover there." He paused, thinking. "By the way, when Karen called me, I turned around right away. In another fifteen minutes or so, I'll be back along that lake."

"Thanks. Destin said. That's Lake Chilhowee. I'll look for you there."

"Right." Rocky paused. "Look, I have an idea. Before you reach the lakeshore, you'll come to a small bridge, and on the west side, the far side, there's a small road. That's where I'll be, if you make it across the Gap. If you see me, don't slow down. Just keep going. I'll try to take care of the rest."

"Thanks, man," Destin said. "WR4RR, clear."

He shut off the radio and quickly walked around the corner of the small Deals Gap Motel. Inside the registration office, a teen manned the tiny counter. Destin hadn't ever seen a skinnier kid.

When the teen glimpsed Destin, he stepped forward. "Been expecting you." The boy's smile lit his bony face. "I'm Josh, a friend of Ryan's. Come with me."

He led the way out the front door and down the row of motel rooms until they came to a covered walkway that allowed access to the rear of the motel. The kid stopped and pointed. There, parked in the alcove, was a red motorcycle. Destin smiled, but saw the boy's grin fade. The teen had noticed the Glock protruding from Destin's waistband. "Oh man." Fear flitted across Josh's face.

Destin put his arm out and patted the boy's bony shoulders. "Don't worry. I've ridden bikes before, and I'll take care of yours. What kind is it?"

"Dukati 999S," the boy said. "A V-twin, six gears, with lots of carbon fiber in its construction. Here," he said, pointing at a slogan on the helmet he handed Destin. It had the words "Testa Stretta" emblazoned on it. "I think it means *Head of the Street*."

Destin nodded. "It's a great bike. But I don't have time for talk. They can't be far behind." He swung his leg across the bike, getting a feel for the seat as the teen handed him the key.

"Wait a minute, Mister," the kid said. "If anything should happen to the bike— "

"I've got plenty of insurance." Destin slid the helmet on, and it was tight, but it would have to do. He kicked the starter, and took confidence in the smooth throatiness of the engine.

A sedan squealed to a stop at the intersection. The black Buick. Horrified, Destin rolled the Dukati forward. The driver, the beefy man, spotted Destin's truck. He careened into the parking lot, kicking up dust and gravel.

"Gotta' go!" Destin kicked the gearshift. He cracked the throttle and the Dukati leaped ahead. Destin had no choice but to steer the bike right past the sedan.

The driver, Beefy Face, looked stunned and the surprise worked. By the time he got off several shots, Destin had passed him and entered the highway. Beefy Face gunned the sedan, swung it around in a second cloud of dust, and chased Destin.

The Dukati, Destin discovered, was every bit as good as advertised. He leaned over and it was a union of body, mind, spirit, and technology. The world was no longer beyond his senses, but rather, the world of the Dragon's Tail was a part of him. It was as though the mountain had claimed him and the bike, and he had claimed the road.

The asphalt, an undulating ribbon, swept under the Dukati, under him. He would lean left, straighten the bike, lean right, straighten, lean again – and again. He found he could lean so low that his ankles and shins almost touched the pavement. It was also a lesson in control, for he had to slow on every sharp turn, and then speed up on the short straight stretches.

Each movement was intoxicating in its own way. Destin loved and hated it. He loved the sensation and he wondered if riding the Dragon was a gift from God. But he hated it too, because the car chasing him could never quite close the gap, and yet neither could he rid himself of the danger. He shivered.

Unbidden, he remembered seeing the movie "Never Cry Wolf" for the first time, and how he could never shake the thought that when nature is its most beautiful, it is usually most deadly. He wondered if the mountains were his enemy now.

Time became suspended, reduced to the motion of the curves. The sedan remained some distance behind, but when he passed an open summit, the road straightened long enough for the sedan to gain. Beefy Face used it to fire several shots at the Dukati. There was no way he could return fire. He had no choice but to lean further over the machine and pray that the bullets would not find their mark. The only other car he passed during the eleven-mile ride was before the summit, and for that, he was thankful.

After the summit, the road descended a steep slope in several shallow switchbacks, and then the mountains were behind him. Destin accelerated as the road straightened. Beefy Face continued to shoot, but none of the bullets came close. By some miracle, Destin widened the distance between them. The road then leveled out, the screen of trees on his left fell away, and before him was the long mountain lake. On the far side, steep mountainsides dropped into the water.

He looked back. The sedan had gained. He glanced back at the road as he raced onto a narrow cement bridge that spanned an inlet. Beyond the bridge, a dirt road used by fishermen cut down along the brushy shoreline of the inlet. When he passed the road, he saw Rocky's eighteen-wheeler but he ignored his friend, and only when he was a quarter mile beyond, did he brake and finally bring the bike around.

He swiveled around in his seat in time to see the sedan reach the bridge at ninety miles per hour. At the last possible moment, Rocky gunned his rig across the highway. Then he braked, sending blue smoke billowing upward. The truck cut off Destin's view of the sedan in that instant.

A ball of fire burst skyward, followed by a thunderous rumble. Intermingled in the melee of sound was the long, wailing screech of metal ripped apart. Destin could only wonder at the scene, and it took him several long heartbeats to realize that the sedan had not hit Rocky's truck at all. Slowly, very slowly, Rocky inched his truck forward onto the parking area near the lakeshore. When he'd cleared the highway and had brought the truck to a stop, Destin finally understood what had happened.

Beefy Face had panicked when he saw the commercial rig pull across the highway, and he instinctively pulled to the right, hitting the cement railing, disintegrating his car. Pieces of mangled steel remained on the bridge, but the fire left no doubt about survivors.

Destin drove the Dukati over to the truck, pulling alongside the cab. He put down the kickstand and walked over as Rocky stepped out. They stood there, looking at the inferno for a moment, and Rocky grinned. "Good day for a wienie roast, isn't it?"

"If you enjoy your wieners well cooked."

"Is that all of them?" Rocky asked.

"I doubt it," Destin said. "But at least for now, I think I've slowed them down."

Rocky looked over the motorcycle critically. "Nice machine."

"Yeah, but I noticed that it had one flaw."

"What?"

"It didn't have a ham set installed on it."

"I see your point." Rocky chuckled. "Where are you headed now?"

"I'm heading back to the labs."

191

Rocky gaped at him. "Are you crazy man? You've got the police after you for murder, not to mention half of the government and probably every bad dude in a thousand miles. I've known some people with rocks for brains, but you— "

"You don't understand," Destin said. "It's personal now. I have to nail Petrowski. Everything points to him."

"You're still crazy, man," Rocky insisted. "Petrowski may have been the one to get George and Linda and Gus killed, but— "

"You're forgetting his pregnant wife."

"And almost you." Rocky chided. "But you know he had orders from higher up. There are some fights in life you can't win. Now me—my family crest is a chicken." He chuckled at his own joke.

Destin smiled. "I'll watch my back side. But remember, Bonnie is in their clutches."

"That was her choice," Rocky reminded him.

"Perhaps, but who can blame her! She may be part of the most memorable event in the history of the earth. Rocky, this is no sci-fi story – this is *real*. I can't leave Bonnie and I couldn't leave now, anyway, because this whole mess isn't over yet."

Rocky shrugged, conceding. "It's your funeral." He beamed and shook Destin's hand. "She must be one good looking broad." He climbed back into his cab. "I'm getting out of here before the police come. You should too."

Destin smiled. "Take care of your film and stay on the radio. I'll stay on twenty meters – 14.235 – when I get back to my truck. That's where I'm headed now."

Rocky started the engine and over the noise shouted, "Where are you going to hide out now – assuming, of course, some bad ass doesn't get you between here and the labs?"

Destin raised his brows and smiled. "I'm not sure but I'll work that out. Take care of yourself."

"You bet." Rocky waved as he left.

Destin hesitated only a moment. He then turned the bike around and pointed it toward the mountains. "Maybe they won't expect me to crawl right into the dragon's mouth," he said to himself.

CHAPTER 47

THE moment Ryan and Sean pulled into the yard at midnight, Tammy ran outside. She slid across the car seat and cuddled near Ryan.

He leaned over and kissed her. "Hi there, gorgeous," he said. She giggled, grabbed his ears and tweaked them.

"Hey! That hurts. Wouldn't you rather kiss?" He reached for her again.

Tammy poked him, laughing. Her own kiss, however, was merely a peck on the cheek. "If we're going to break into the labs tonight, we need to get out there now."

Sean snorted from the back seat. "You've said a lot about breaking into the labs, but you haven't given many details."

"I have a plan," Tammy said, hedging.

"What kind of plan? Get to the point."

She straightened. "I know all the guards out there, and the best one, Larry Ingram, is working tonight."

"You're hair brained," Sean said. "First of all, breaking in is a felony, and second, the last thing you want is their best security guard on duty."

"How can you twist everything I say around? Larry isn't the best; he's the worst, which is why he *is* the best for our purposes."

"Women!" Sean sighed. "Go on."

"So anyway, he thinks I'm kind of cute, and he does most anything I say. He probably wouldn't get me into real trouble if he caught me."

"It's still a big risk," Sean argued, "especially with us along."

"Who said anything about you going along?"

"Wait!"

Tammy laughed. "Gotcha! See? You *do* want to go."

Sean reddened. "I still say we can't get past lab security."

Ryan caressed her hand. "Sean's right. We can't."

"Yes, we can," Tammy insisted. "Larry Ingram is a tub of lard, and he never stays awake when he pulls the graveyard shift. I figure that if we wait until he falls asleep, we could probably creep right past him."

"How do you know that?" Sean said.

"Because I've snuck in there before," Tammy said. "It's easy."

"All right, Smarty, and how do you propose we get back out of the labs, assuming we get inside without waking him?"

"I'm willing to bet that he'll still be asleep. But if you're that worried, I'll drop a sleeping tablet in his coffee. He drinks the stuff all the time. In fact, that might make it a lot easier for us to get in there earlier."

Ryan had been quiet but she knew him. He liked her plan. She opened the car door. "I'll be right back. Mom has some sleeping tablets."

She paused at the door. "By the way, how did you spring Sean tonight? His folks keep him on such a short leash."

"I fixed that." Ryan grinned. "My folks are out of town but Sean's parents don't know that, so I invited him to stay the night with me."

They drove out to Fontana Labs, where they parked along the entrance road far enough away from the lights to escape notice. The night was calm and silent. Tammy shivered with delicious excitement. "I've got to take care of Larry alone," she reminded the boys. "Otherwise, he'll be immediately suspicious."

"Be careful," Ryan cautioned. "Don't do anything stupid."

Sean stirred in the back seat. "This whole plan is stupid."

Ryan straightened. "We've been through that already, Sean. If you don't want to go, you can bail out any time now. But after we go inside those labs, we're in this together. Got it?"

Sean sighed. "I hope I get a good cell when this is all over."

Tammy swung out of the car. "I'll be fine, y'all. I can handle Larry. Trust me."

She jogged along the road, crossed the parking lot, and turned into the floodlit entrance.

Inside, Larry was leaning back in a chair that barely held his bulk. In front, a desk console almost filled the narrow entranceway. Behind him, a corridor led into the heart of the bedrock. Tammy looked back at Larry, who had set aside his boating magazine.

"What brings you here, Miss Tammy?" His eyes, she saw, were his usual bedroom eyes.

She straightened her knit blouse, which clung to her breasts. "My mom left her pager at home." She pulled it from her purse. "She doesn't want to be without it, so I thought I'd drop it off for her."

Larry hitched up his pants. "No problem, Missy. I'll have the next person who comes by deliver it to her."

Tammy slipped around the console and rested her hand on his shoulder. "Larry, sometimes no one comes by here for hours. You know her office isn't that far away. Can't you run it to her now? I could watch your booth for you."

Larry shook his head. "Can't do that, Missy. You know the rules. But I tell you what: I'll leave it for her in her locker and I'll call her to come get it. All right?"

"Okay. Thanks." Tammy sauntered toward the entrance and watched until Larry disappeared into the adjoining locker room, and then she tiptoed back to the console and dropped the pill into his coffee. There was no spoon nearby so she used her finger to stir it into the tepid liquid. When she heard the locker slam, she darted to the entrance.

"You're still here?" Larry said.

Tammy smiled, imitating his bedroom eyes. "I remembered that Mom is having a get-together with some of her friends next week. Want to come?"

Larry's grin became a leer. "I'd love to come. When?"

"We haven't set the date yet, but we'll let you know." Tammy pushed through the glass doors. "Bye, Larry."

"Come visit anytime, Missy."

Back at the car, Tammy slid into the front seat. After a long minute of silence, she said, "Now we wait."

A few minutes before one, the trio tiptoed past Larry, who was inert and snoring raucously. With Tammy leading, they crept along the main hall and turned the first corner. The left corridor led to her mom's work area, though it branched at several spots. At an intersecting hall, Sean, who had been moving along the wall, collided into a metal trashcan. The noise echoed the length of the corridor.

"Butt head!" Ryan swore under his breath. "In a totally empty hall, you have to run into the only obstacle. Lame brain!"

"Knock it off," Tammy said. "Whisper, for heaven's sake, both of you."

Aghast, they heard footsteps. Larry Ingram had awakened.

Ryan gathered himself for a sprint to the right, but Tammy grabbed his arm. "No!" she hissed. "Follow me!"

She ran up the dead end hall and turned into the first office beyond. The boys piled in behind her and they shut the door before Larry strode down the corridor.

"Tammy?" Norma Yates was seated on a stool, bent over cultures. She stared at them, amazed. "How'd you get in here?"

"I was looking for Mom's office." Tammy wrung her hands. "Look, Larry, the security guy, is hot on our tails. Do you have a place we can hide?"

"Hmm." Norma pushed back her gray hair, hesitating only a moment. "I can hide you in the culture room." She led them to a door at the far end of the room, past the shelves that held brain, heart, and spleen tissues, all arrayed in petri dishes. "Get in! And not a word," she hissed. They piled into the small room and shut the door.

At that moment, Larry threw open the door to the Biology lab. Tammy could almost picture his livid face.

"Where are they?" he demanded.

Norma's voice remained cool. "Where are who?"

Larry became confused. "The teens. Tammy and her friends."

"You mean Tammy Kerr? She isn't here, or any of her friends, as you can see." Tammy heard Norma step aside. "Besides, this isn't Karen's office. Hers is next door."

His voice hardened. "I know you're pulling a fast one." For a moment, there was silence. Then his voice came from a closer spot. "Aha!" he said, as though he'd sprung a trap on a mouse. "I know where they're hiding." Tammy heard him turn the knob. Desperate, she clung to Ryan.

"Wait!" Norma said. "I don't think you want to go into my chiller."

"Why not?"

"Our work with AIDS," Norma said softly. "We've got some nasty cultures in there and if you go inside, I can't guarantee what might happen to you."

Larry had opened the door a crack, and through it, Tammy watched as his hand froze on the door. He dropped it, rubbing it on his uniformed trousers, and stepped back.

Norma continued. "We believe AIDS was secretly developed as a deadly weapon. Our most recent cultures have mutated, and we now find ourselves dealing with a serious problem. If you — "

Larry's florid face turned ashen. He backed across the lab toward the hall. "That's all right. But if you see those kids, tell me right away."

"How do you know it was Tammy and her friends? Did you see them?"

"No, but I heard them." Larry stepped out and shut the door. A second later, Tammy could hear him next door, arguing with Karen. Finally, their shouts ended and Tammy heard his footsteps receding down the adjoining hallway.

The teens piled out of the culture room. Ryan was shaking. "AIDS? You deliberately exposed us to AIDS?"

Norma laughed. "No. We've never dealt with AIDS."

The outer door opened again. This time, Karen entered. When she saw the three teens, she stiffened. "What in the *hell* do you think you're doing, sneaking around here?"

Norma put her hand on Karen's arm, restraining her. "It *is* kind of humorous. You should have seen Larry's face."

"I most certainly don't see it that way!" Karen's eyes narrowed to slits, and Tammy's giggles died away. "Sorry, Mom."

"Why did you sneak in here?" Karen demanded.

Tammy then recounted their plan to find the alien in the labs.

"It's far too dangerous," Karen said. "You'll have to leave before Ingram comes back this way. Besides, we don't know where the alien is. Only the Colonel, his friends, and Bonnie know that."

Norma listened in awe. "Did you say an alien was captured and brought to the labs *yesterday*?"

"That's right," Karen said. "Last night."

"Oh, my God," Norma said, and her hand shook as she pushed back wisps of gray from her broad forehead. "That's why they told me to go home and take three days off."

"They did?" Karen looked at her, puzzled.

"Yes. They said I'd worked hard and deserved a break. They broke right into my shift and sent me home last night. I wasn't supposed to be here tonight, but I stopped in because I needed to observe growth on a few tissue samples." She paused, and then continued.

"It's funny, really, because I found out that somebody used my lab while I was gone last night. Lots of my papers and things had been moved." She stepped around a shelving unit. "Didn't you say that two aliens died in that crash?"

"Yes," Karen said. "But — "

"They might have taken some tissue samples of the dead ones. That would explain why they wanted my lab and most of all, wanted me out of the way."

"You're right," Karen said. "Now, if only we had some proof of that."

Tammy, who had been wandering down the rows of Petri dishes, abruptly stopped before a specimen near the culture room. "Mom, we may have." She pointed to one of the dishes. "Look at this dish. It's labeled 'E.T.'"

CHAPTER 48

THE next day ripened nectarine-sweet. The morning sky deepened to a robin's egg blue, while soft yellows and greens carpeted the mountains. All life clung to the warmth of the fading summer. But Bonnie, oblivious to it, spent most of the day trying to talk to the alien.

She began the session by pointing to herself. "Bonnie," she said. She pointed to him.

He did not respond at first, but the second time she tried, he said, "Dayju."

"Dayju?" He nodded.

"Nice name."

Bonnie tried new words, but the alien, reluctant to say more, merely repeated what he had said the day before. Before leaving at the end of the day, she tried a new tack. She left him for a short time, returning to his cell with several magazines from the lounge. She brought her chair near his bed and opened one after another, selecting various ads that depicted Earth. "Earth," she said, pointing to the pictures, one after another. "Earth is beautiful. Beautiful Earth."

Immediately his reply came inside her brain. "Yes, beautiful Earth."

She then pointed to a lovely woman who was holding hands with a handsome man. "Beautiful woman," she said. "Beautiful man. Love. They love each other."

He again answered. "Yes, beautiful. Love." He reached out and touched her hand, and for a moment she saw a world, its golden sky ablaze in a diffused glow, and among fields of grain, she saw several aliens, but each stood slightly apart. Then he let go of her hand and the picture faded.

"No man, no woman," he said. "Alien man, woman. Dayju man, woman."

Bonnie nodded. She felt certain he was bisexual, or nearly so. She had suspected that since he carried no obvious signs of reproductive organs.

As she rose to go, he said, "Tonight, ship."

She nodded, touching his hand lightly, and said, "Yes, tonight, home."

Bonnie returned to the labs past midnight. Larry, the guard, set aside one of his magazines and checked her in.

"Why are you working at this hour?" He stifled a yawn.

"The Colonel needs results," she said. She picked up her pass and pushed through. It worked, for he picked up the magazine and reached for his coffee.

She walked to the lounge and waited there for almost two hours. Then she eased down the stairs. As she crept along the deserted lower hall, she pondered her call to Karen earlier.

Karen had been excited. She'd explained how several assassins tried to gun down Destin, and how he'd returned to her home that morning after a deadly chase across the mountains and a night hiding out in his truck.

Bonnie recalled her immediate reaction. "Is he all right?"

"He's fine," Karen assured her.

Karen explained how Tammy, Sean, and Ryan broke into the labs, and how Tammy discovered the tissue sample of the dead alien. "It will be difficult, I imagine, for the labs to deny their use of the Quark beam on an alien ship when we produce that sample," she said. "Considering all the evidence, we now have plenty to go public."

Bonnie told her of her remarkable breakthrough with Dayju, and how she planned to sneak him out of the labs. "I thought that you, Destin, Franz, and Ben might want to watch him when his people pick him up."

"We wouldn't miss it for a million dollars," Karen said.

Now, as Bonnie opened his door, she prayed that they were outside already, for she did not want to be the only one in the world to watch the alien leave.

Inside, she found Dayju was already on his feet. Without speaking, she gently grasped his arm, and together, they made their way down the hall and up the stairs to the canteen. Near the top, she gently pushed him against the wall, motioning him to stay. She inched up the final stair, searching the corridor, but the upper hallway was deserted, as was the canteen and lounge.

She returned to the staircase, and guided him up. They crept along the upper hallway as she led the way through the maze of corridors and into the narrow foyer of the lower entrance. From the rear, they could see the broad frame of Larry, whose head hung forward over his console desk. He was snoring and Bonnie grinned. Her luck was holding.

She motioned to Dayju to be quiet, and together, they tiptoed past the console. The door was more difficult. She spent over a minute inching it open. Together, they slid outside and she closed it with the same care.

They crept across the parking lot. Then Dayju took over, leading Bonnie along the river to a place where the lawns formed a wider expanse. Beyond the lawn and the huge boulders, the river churned, its noise blanketing all other sounds.

Bonnie glanced about, but the broad expanse of lawn lay deserted. Something, though, did not feel right, and the sense of wrongness scared her. Then she sensed, more than heard, a deep hum, and the hairs on her body stood on end. She froze. More swiftly than she could grasp, the alien moved away from her, and she now saw that he stood alone. Without warning, dazzling lights flipped on. The light enveloped him, and he spread his long, hairless arms out to embrace the light. The hum increased, and Bonnie watched, mesmerized.

A shout arose from the river's edge, and a cadre of twenty soldiers rose from among the boulders and began firing their M-16s and AR-15s at Dayju. As he stood in his cone of light, bullets riddled his fragile, hairless body. Bonnie shrieked again and again.

She fell to the ground as bullets screamed nearby, spitting into grass. Chunks of grass pelted her face and exposed arms, and she sobbed.

Nevertheless, she could not hide from the carnage, and as she watched, the lifeless body of Dayju rose in the beam of light, and he disappeared into the hovering UFO.

The light made it difficult to see much of the craft, but it was a huge, saucer-shaped ship. Lights in whites and greens ringed the bottom edges. The hum increased, and she gasped for air. Then the light blinked off, the hum ceased, and the craft vaulted upward at light speed.

She pulled herself into a sitting position and sobbed desperately. The troops moved toward her, and leading the group of soldiers was Petrowski. "Grab her," he said. "Put her in one of the detention rooms."

She could have resisted, but she no longer cared. Nothing mattered. Her feet couldn't be attached to her body. They wouldn't move.

"Bonnie!" Destin's voice receded into oblivion. Her world turned black.

CHAPTER 49

HIDDEN among the trees and shrubs of the steep slope above the lawns, Destin, Karen, Franz, Ben, and the three teens huddled together, watching the drama unfold. But when Bonnie collapsed and was dragged off by the soldiers, Destin screamed. Almost instantly, the troops swung searchlights and guns onto the group of seven. Trapped, Destin froze.

Unbelieving, he watched a petite woman move out of the shadows and join the group on the lawn. She put her arm around Petrowski's waist, hugging him, and he, in turn, pulled her tightly against his side. Amazed, Destin studied the familiar figure. And then he recognized Linda, George's wife.

In a blinding moment of insight, rage, and shock, he understood. It had been Linda who had hit him in their village home. Only because she wasn't very strong, and possibly surprised and frightened by his presence, had he lived to tell about it.

Sick inside, he raged with hate for Petrowski, for Linda, and for the massacre. Nonetheless, he also felt a sense of regret and guilt. His friends crouched nearby and he'd acted stupidly. He'd put them at risk. Worse, his fear for Bonnie's safety threatened to destroy his sanity. He turned to Karen as hot tears dampened his cheeks. Surprised at himself, he brushed them away.

"I haven't – no, not since my father..." He left the statement unfinished. Helplessly, he fingered George's freshly charged capacitor, his good luck charm, in his pocket. Maybe good luck had died with George though. He faced his friends. "We have to give up."

He stood up first and raised his arms. Ben reached out and touched him before he too, raised his arms, and then Karen and the teens followed suit. Franz, however, stepped away and hid behind a scrub tree. Destin turned, too late. Franz was holding a Smith and Wesson 9 mm.

"No!" Destin screamed and dived for cover.

Franz opened fire on the crowd below while Karen and the others scrambled for protection behind bushes and scrub. The soldiers below scattered for cover while Petrowski screamed, "Get that son of a bitch!"

Before Franz could empty his clip, a soldier's bullet found its mark, and Franz tumbled forward, rolling and sliding down the steep slope, the searchlights following him. He slid into a crumpled heap near the bottom. The shooting stopped. Karen screamed repeatedly until Destin raised his hands again and in the glare of the searchlight, he stepped to her side, comforting her.

"Move down slowly," Petrowski shouted at them from below. They obeyed. They scrambled down the steep slope. After they reached the field below, the soldiers surrounded them, weapons held at the ready.

Angry, Petrowski grabbed Destin's windbreaker and shook him.

"You fool! Idiot!" He shook him again. He glanced at the soldiers who ringed the group. "Take him to detention. Take them all to detention," he ordered. As the soldiers moved in and prodded the group with their guns, Petrowski held up his hand. "No, put Destin in solitary. I'll deal with him myself."

The soldiers shoved them across the parking lot and through the lab doors, where they were led the length of two corridors and down some stairs. Ben, Karen, and the teens were placed into one room, and Destin watched as the door to their cell slammed shut. He was led to the adjoining room and shoved through the door into the darkness beyond. Destin stumbled. His knee throbbed from scrambling down the steep slope.

He paused, leaning against a wall for support until his eyes adjusted to the darkness. The only light filtered through a small glass in the door. He limped over to a bunk and sat down. He wondered about the fate of Bonnie, and when they would all die. He sighed. A great deal of good he'd accomplished.

He rested on the bunk, but sleep eluded him. Later he heard a squeal of his metal door swinging inward, and he sat up, blinking from the sudden bright light. It was Petrowski, and he was alone.

"Come with me," Petrowski ordered. He stood aside and allowed Destin to slide past him and into the hall. He shaded his eyes as the Colonel led him up the stairs and through several corridors, until they reached a service elevator. Inside, the elevator took them up swiftly, and when the doors opened, Destin was in the tiled main entrance of the labs. It was gray outside, barely the first light of dawn. The security guard at the front security checkpoint ignored them. Petrowski led him down the hall to the right, and when they reached another alcove that contained the restrooms, he held the door open for him.

Destin blinked again. The men's room was unlike any he had ever seen before. The room was entirely made of tan marble, polished to a rich luster. Oval steel sinks graced the length of one wall, and towel rods, complete with towels and washcloths, hung between the sinks. Cubbyhole shelves had been built into the wall beneath the rods. Two oak chairs sat near the sinks, and Petrowski pointed to one. "Have a seat," he ordered.

Worn and disheveled, Destin hobbled to the nearest chair. Petrowski, meanwhile, pulled out a bag from a shelf near one sink and began to shave the old fashioned way. He applied a foaming soap with a round brush after steaming his beard with a hot washcloth, and then, using an old Gillette razor, he began shaving the stubble off. He worked carefully, and Destin rubbed his own stubble.

"Want some breakfast?" Petrowski asked.

Destin frowned, suspicious. "I'm not hungry."

The Colonel shrugged and kept shaving. "Have it your way." His voice was amused. "We have to settle some business, you and me."

"You and I," Destin said.

Petrowski's face darkened, but he laughed. "You hate me, don't you? You see me as some kind of evil creature you despise. Right?" He cocked his head.

"Yes," Destin said. "You killed my friend, George. You had Ben's friend, Gus, and his wife killed, and tonight you murdered Franz. Oh, and let's not forget the alien." He shut his eyes. "What did it take to turn Linda into a whore? Was it easy?"

Petrowski's eyes became slits, and he waved the razor. "Your life, Destin, depends on my patience. Don't ever talk to me that way. Ever. You hear me?"

Destin sat still, not breathing.

Petrowski turned back, taking a stroke with the razor, but he cut himself. Swearing under his breath, he applied the washcloth to the cut. He studied Destin through the mirror. "You understand so little."

"Oh, I understand quite well." Destin stood up. "You developed the Quark Gluon Plasma Beam secretly as a weapon, after your scientist, Franz, who built the RHIC, was told the research into quarks would have only peaceful applications. You duped him, and many, many others. Worse, you used that weapon on a UFO without provocation. Your senseless act may have destroyed our first contact with an alien race, and it may lead to war with them. You're disgusting."

Petrowski laughed. "As I thought, Destin. You *don't* understand. So let's start with our use of the beam against the alien ship. That ship, for your information, was on a direct heading for the White House in Washington, D.C. Such a heading within our restricted air space is cause for war."

"No, it only — "

Petrowski cut him off. "If it had been a bomber from an enemy country, wouldn't you have ordered it shot down?"

Destin hesitated.

"It wasn't our first contact with that race of aliens either. Our contacts with them go back to the 1940s. We made a peace agreement with them and in exchange, they agreed to help us with some technological advances. But they wanted something from us in return. They wanted to mine for minerals under our oceans and they wanted to conduct some biological experiments on certain humans so they could preserve their own species." He paused.

"They warned us too. Said we must move as quickly as possible toward a one-world government because we're headed on a path to nuclear and biological annihilation. We agreed to most of their terms. Actually, we had little choice. There's a problem, though. They haven't kept their part of the bargain, and at a certain point we realized we needed to gain the upper hand.

"Our solution was to develop a weapon that could destroy their ships. Franz's energy research paved the way. And everything Franz worked for is still usable. Even the QGPB will have peaceful applications. So you see, Destin? I am not your evil maniac but quite the opposite. I'm saving us all."

Destin sat, stunned and sickened. He shoved his hands in his pocket, toying with George's capacitor.

Petrowski was apparently correct. He had understood little. He pulled his hands out of his pocket. "You should have gone public with this a long time ago," he said weakly. "People shouldn't be kept in the dark."

"If our government had gone public with this, it would kick off a panic that would kill millions," Petrowski insisted, stabbing the air with his razor. "Is it worth that kind of panic?"

"I think people aren't that childish," Destin said. "You see people as inferior and stupid, but I think people are essentially logical beings. All people deserve to know the truth and be a part of these decisions. Besides, our enemies will develop the beam, sooner or later."

"You've answered your own second question," Petrowski said bitterly. "With or without us, others will get the weapon. Therefore, it might as well be us. At least, we're not the terrorists. We're responsible."

"That brings us right back to the first issue," Destin said. "You see 'others' as incapable of properly managing their own affairs. You believe that 'you' are different, wiser. Your attitude is as flawed as the terrorists' because you both operate from the *same premise*."

"There's a big difference," Petrowski said, "between benevolence and evil."

"Perhaps. But arrogant people inevitably become corrupt."

Petrowski shrugged. "Maybe we can agree to disagree." He took another stroke with his razor and shook it in his water-filled sink.

Destin nodded and stepped to the sink next to Petrowski. He looked in the mirror at the Colonel, who put the finishing touches on his chin. "You still had no right to kill George, Gus, his wife, and Franz because they knew about the weapon."

"Sometimes the ends *do* justify the means," Petrowski said. "And that means we're at an impasse. You see, it boils down to this. Either you agree to never tell another human being of this incident and of the weapon, or you die. It's as simple as that. Your death could happen now, next week, or next month. You can't fight the whole government, you know. If you're as damn logical as you've insisted, then you should see that you have no choice.

"Your friends, incidentally, have already seen the light. They've signed their copies of the agreement to keep silent, and they've already been released. Yours, my friend, is in my office right around the corner, and since I'm about finished here, you have about a minute to make up your mind." Petrowski dipped the razor into the water, and for a moment his hand remained there as he waited for Destin to answer.

Destin didn't answer. Instead, he opened his hand, which held the high voltage capacitor given to him by George. He dropped it into the sink of water. Petrowski's eyes flared in surprise, but he never had a chance to move his hand. The electric shock was immediate.

He jerked in his death throes, and though he tried to scream, no sound escaped his lips. The spasms were merciless, and he crashed against the marbled floor, dying from the electrical current that killed his heart even before his skull split on the marble.

"Between a rock and a hard place, huh." Destin gazed at the inert figure. "You were wrong, by the way."

He continued. "The only system of government that can ever survive *must* view its citizens as worthwhile, dignified beings. That is as necessary as liberty, morality, and representative government."

Grabbing a towel, he pushed open the sink stopper, allowing the water to drain out. Then he picked up the spent capacitor, dried it off, and replaced it in his pocket. He refilled the sink and left Petrowski's shaving brush and razor sitting in the water.

Satisfied, he strolled out of the restroom and right into Petrowski's office. He found the agreement on the top of his desk and signed it before he walked right past the guard and out of Fontana's main entrance.

CHAPTER 50

One Year Later

ONE of the best-kept secrets in Tennessee is Knoxville's magical autumns. Florescent yellows, reds, and browns herald the approaching deep sleep of winter in the best carnival fashion. Happy, Destin sniffed the currents of crisp air that blew across the Tennessee River as he slid his arm around Bonnie. Together, they walked into the Clam Shack.

Inside, the reunion party had already begun. Several large tables had been pushed together near the long expanse of view windows. There, awaiting them, sat Karen, Tammy, and Ben who all stood up as they entered.

"You made it!" Tammy ran around the long table and gave Destin a hug. Everyone laughed and spoke at once. Later, as they munched seafood, their talk became less desultory.

Destin turned to Karen. "What have you been up to?"

"Tammy and I have moved to Washington, D.C. The government recommended me for a job in the new Homeland Security headquarters. I know that allows them to keep close eye on me, but under the circumstances, I'm well paid and enjoying it."

Destin nodded. "What do you do, exactly?"

Karen laughed. "Forensics. The same. I get full health benefits and insurance for Tammy and me." She paused.

"Tammy is happy too, though she misses Ryan from time to time. As for me, I'm dating a certain bachelor senator from Illinois."

"I'm glad to hear that." Bonnie reached across the table to squeeze Karen's hand.

Karen smiled. "Destin, I've been wondering about Linda for a whole year."

"Yes, tell us every juicy detail." Tammy leaned forward. The group became still.

He threw his hands up in surrender. "All right, though I don't think it's juicy. From what I've gathered, Linda met the Colonel through various social engagements at the labs. Apparently, George became too engrossed in his research, and he ignored her. Being bright and full of life, she couldn't take being a social fixture any longer. So, when the dashing Colonel came along with all his DOE and Washington connections, she was enchanted with him." Destin reached for a fry and continued.

"Apparently, she believed in America's need for the quark weapon and the need to keep it secret, so when George opposed Petrowski, she was forced to take sides.

"I think George had a pretty good idea about Linda's duplicity. When he left for Florida, he only told her that he was going to attend the hamfest. Of course, the Colonel had already decided George had to go, not only because he opposed the use of the beam and was prepared to go public, but also because he wanted Linda for his own." Destin paused, looking at his friends around the table.

"I'm sure it was Linda who hit me over the head during my search of her Fontana home. I think she wanted to search it too, only I beat her to it."

Karen nodded. "Do you think Detective Gilbretti was in on her faked suicide?"

"Yes," Destin said. "Too bad. He probably thought he was helping the government. He still faces charges for his involvement. So does Linda."

Ben looked up. "What about the other detective involved in your case?"

"You mean Detective Howell of the OPD?"

"Yes. Did he ever talk to you after Gilbretti's involvement became known?"

"He sure did. He told me he never seriously considered me to be George's killer."

"Really?" Tammy raised her brows. "Why?"

"Because he said George's murder had all the earmarks of a professional hit."

"No joke?"

"No joke. He told me the hit man shot George in the head, not the chest and that was the mark of a professional hit man. Next, they determined that George was killed with a 22 long rifle, a Walther PP Auto Pistol, equipped with a silencer. That is not something an amateur uses. Also, they found no shell casing in the restroom. That means the killer picked it up. He may even have used a gadget made for such weapons that captures the spent shell casing."

Destin leaned closer. "If that isn't enough, the volunteer guards then told Howell they remembered a man who pushed out of the restroom minutes before they found me – and the body. He left out the north entrance, wearing a dark gray or black wind suit and white sneakers and carried a packet of some sort. That fit my description. No one had more than a general description of him, however.

"Then there was the matter of me. Howell told me I had a fine reputation in Orlando and no record of any kind. Most compelling of all, he reminded me I was caught in that restroom near the stall, yet I had no weapon, no way to dispose of it, and it was clearly not there. They ran a nitrate test on my hands at the hospital, and I had passed on that score too. No traces of gunpowder, and that's not a substance that I could have washed off in the sink. I could have worn gloves – rubber or something, but I had no gloves on me when I was discovered." He continued.

"It's true that rubber gloves could've been flushed down the toilet, and for a while they thought that's exactly what I did. But the volunteer guards at the hamfest remembered no noises of weapons being discharged, so a silencer was used. They had only remembered a crashing noise. Which fit my story of the swinging stall door. No matter which way Howell spun the story, he couldn't explain how I got rid of the gun. They concluded then that my assailant must've packed it out. Which brings us back full circle to the mystery of the missing gun. Your assailant must've packed it out."

Ben looked up. "Destin, what did you say—or do—to Petrowski that made him have a fatal heart attack? I know you did something. It was too coincidental."

Destin's hand touched Bonnie. "Let's simply say that his heart lacked a certain capacity for good."

When he finished, Karen turned to Ben. "What are you doing now, Ben? And what's this about possibly moving to Colorado?"

Ben nodded. "I have an offer to become a fire chief in Buena Vista, but I'm going to let my fiancé, Missy, make the final decision."

"You're engaged?" Tammy bubbled. He beamed at her and she returned his smile. "It's a long story, but yes."

"Why didn't you bring her with you tonight?" Bonnie asked. "We would have loved to meet her."

"Unfortunately, she's in Atlanta," Ben said. "At an insurance seminar. But she said hi. She's anxious to meet you all."

"Way to go," Tammy said, and a hubbub of best wishes filled the room.

Bonnie looked up from her meal. "It's been a mystery to me about Franz and why he felt he had to fight. We all knew he was a peaceful person, and he wanted his work to stand for something good."

"I think you answered yourself," Karen said. "Franz wanted his work to stand for good, and when it was deliberately misused, he decided to fight."

"But it was a hopeless gesture," Bonnie said.

Karen looked at her plate. "I know. He knew it too. Hopeless or not, he was courageous and not the coward Petrowski thought."

"Here, here." Ben hoisted his beer. "To Franz." They all raised their drinks and toasted him. "By the way, gang, the rumors say Vince Foster and Dai Yu have disappeared. Isn't that wild? Even the lab records on them have vanished."

"Where'd you hear that?" Destin asked.

"From one of the labs' crewmembers." Ben pursed his lips. "Speaking of disappearances, where's Rocky? Wasn't he invited to come today?"

Destin set aside his fork and stared at the table. "You haven't heard?" he asked.

"What?" Ben wiped his hands.

"Well, do you remember how he wouldn't give us his film?"

"Yes," Ben nodded. "After Petrowski's heart attack, I remember you told us how Rocky saved your life on the Dragon's Tail."

"Right. After saving me at the bridge, he drove straight on to Nashville, and as he said, he left his film with his friend. But when his friend realized the value of the film, he contacted the labs, demanding compensation. They compensated the man all right, and Rocky too, I'm afraid. Rocky's friend was found murdered in his shop. The authorities say it was a robbery. When I heard about it, I had one of my friends inside the Orlando Police Department check on the details of the murder with NPD. And guess what? Apparently, no video tape was recovered by the police." Destin cleared his throat.

"I see. But what about Rocky?" Ben leaned forward.

"That's the strangest part of all. No one has seen Rocky. He simply failed to show up for work three days after his return to Little Rock. It's as though he simply vanished into thin air. His family and his girlfriend, Arlene, mounted a nationwide search for him, but without success. I'm surprised you missed the alerts on TV."

"I don't watch much TV."

Destin nodded. "Then there's even more you need to know. The police discovered that Rocky's apartment had been ransacked. They think he was robbed and abducted, even though it appears that Rocky's clothing and personal effects were not stolen. The apartment yielded no further clues, so it's quite a mystery."

"No." Ben slumped in his chair, and silence hung around the table for a long minute.

Destin spoke. "Let's face it. We're never, ever alone. They follow us everywhere. They're here now. Look at those men at the rear of the restaurant."

Tammy stifled a sob. Then she stood up, waving her napkin at the two men in dark suits and glasses who sat across the room, studying them. "Hi there," she shouted. "Can you hear me now?"

Karen grabbed her arm. "That's enough!" Surprised, Tammy retreated into silence.

Destin reached across the table and gave her shoulder a squeeze. "It's okay, Tammy. I love your spirit."

He spoke to Ben. "Have you heard that Bonnie and I got married in June?"

"Wow!" Ben said.

Destin held up his hand. "There's more, everyone." He turned to the group. "Now, Bonnie is expecting!"

As the uproar of congratulations finally died, Ben asked him, "Do you still work with Lockheed Martin in Florida, or is Bonnie no longer with UT?"

Bonnie spoke. "Lockheed Martin wasn't the only defense contractor who recognized Destin's talents. Diotech, a manufacturer of azimuth units and satellite equipment here in Knoxville, offered him a management position, and he took it. And last month he became a board member with Ten-Tec, his second love."

"Do you still write?" Karen asked Destin a moment later.

"Occasionally." He sat back. "For science magazines."

Ben looked at Bonnie. "And what about your work?"

"I'm still with UT. The government kept their promise and funded the CGR."

Karen interrupted. "Bonnie, tell everyone what you told me on the phone last week about Dayju."

"You mean the alien that was killed?" Ben asked.

"Yes." Tammy answered him.

"All right," Bonnie said, "though it's hard to explain. You see, right after the UFO took him away and I'd regained consciousness, he told me he was okay."

"Huh?" Ben said. "I don't understand."

Bonnie then explained how the alien had spoken with her mentally before his escape. She also described the sensation of love he was able to send her.

"But his body was riddled with bullets!" Tammy said.

"Yes, but don't forget, he's reptilian." Bonnie smiled. "Lizards, for example, are able to grow new tails and heal in ways that are hard for us to understand."

"Awesome," Tammy breathed. The others nodded.

Tammy cleared her throat. "Whatever happened to your film, Ben?"

"The labs still don't know about it," he whispered. "Destin thought it best to wait with its release for a year or so, because of the agreement we had to sign. However, he hasn't been idle. He sent that film, the E.T. sample, and the documents through a maze of hands, and some Canadians will be releasing everything this week. Kind of fitting, isn't it? According to the exposé, Petrowski himself took the film! It will be hard for the government to turn on a dead man."

"I love it," Karen said.

Everyone toasted Ben and Destin. Destin joined in and raised his own beer while Bonnie giggled. She poked Karen. "He wouldn't drink before, but now he'll have an occasional brew."

Karen turned to Destin after the toast. "You weren't very specific about Petrowski's death," she pointed out. "So tell me, how *did* Petrowski die?"

"He had a heart-stopping experience," Destin said, grinning. "Electrifying."

"Ah, come on," she said, exasperated.

"I mean it," Destin said. "Look at it this way if you'd prefer. It was a matter of destiny."

Follow the further adventures of Destin Campbell in the *Agenda 21 Conspiracy*, a work in progress.

Printed in the United Kingdom
by Lightning Source UK Ltd.
119378UK00004B/238-243